Sweet Beulah Land

Marilyn Denny Thomas

Sweet Beulah Land
by Marilyn Denny Thomas

Printed in the United States of America

Library of Congress Cataloging-in-publication date
ISBN 978-1-60791-049-7

Unless otherwise indicated, Bible quotations are taken from The
King James Authorized Version.

Edited by Edie Veach
www.furrowpress.com

Front cover art is entitled, "Beulah Land." Copyright © 2008 by
Hope G. Smith (Art of Hope).
www.hopeg.smith.com

Cover art inspired by the photograph collections of Miss Ermie
Sanderson and Mrs. Roma Dare Horne.

This book is a work of fiction. Names, characters, places and
incidents are the products of the author's imagination or are used
fictitiously.

www.xulonpress.com

Also by Marilyn Denny Thomas

The Gentile and the Jew

Going Home

Acknowledgments

I am eternally grateful to my great grandmother, Anna Gresham Waller, for the love, the prayers and the memories she shared with me before her death at eighty-four in November of 1969. How I wish I had asked her more. She is, herself, a precious memory indeed.

As always, I want to thank my husband, Ricky Thomas, and my daughters, Joelle Thomas and Jodi Fucili, for the continuing encouragement they give me. I thank them particularly for their support in my writing *Sweet Beulah Land*, which is, of course, a significant segment of their story as well as mine.

Very special thanks go to Evelyn (Shorty) Horne Thomas, my husband's mother, who passed away at eighty-seven during the writing of *Sweet Beulah Land*. Much appreciation also goes to her sisters, Verdia Thomas and Myrtle Thomas. The three of them faithfully tromped with me through many a graveyard hidden back in the woods on a long-lost path somewhere in Duplin or Onslow County, North Carolina. Their conversation and companionship were priceless as well as the love and support of their two younger sisters, Mary Lynn Edwards and Betty Jo Frazelle.

There were many present-day Beulahlanders who shared their precious memories with me. Some were used in the book and some were not, but all were invaluable to the story as a whole. My great aunt, Genette Williams, granddaughter of Dr. Daniel Williams, lovingly shared her memories just before her passing at ninety-three. Sarah Bolin, widow of the doctor who delivered me, took time to answer my questions and tell me her stories. Grace Brown, a Thomas descendant, not only gave me information and escorted me to cemeteries, but shared old photographs of Thomas ancestors and others as well.

Roma Dare Horne, a Gresham descendant, shared her collection of Gresham data and photographs along with her own knowledge of Beulaville's history. Her pictures of the town are among the very earliest and are extremely valuable to our history. Mrs. Horne's interest in conserving the history of our area is very admirable.

I also would like to thank Mrs. Grace Pate who graciously shared the history of the Presbyterian Church with me as well as photocopies of Mrs. Phoebe Pate's paintings of Beulaville's Main Street in the early 1920's.

Mrs. Josephine Lanier, a Gresham descendent, shared the history of the Hallsville Baptist Church as well as glimpses into the lives of many Gresham ancestors.

Thanks go to Mary Jane Gresham Rhodes, a former Beulah school librarian who has spent many years doing research on the Gresham family.

I so enjoyed the visit I had with Jean Sanderson whose husband, the late Russell Sanderson, was a descendant of two of the oldest families in the area. A picture is truly worth a thousand words, and the old photographs Jean shared from the late Miss Ermie Sanderson's treasured album were delightful windows into the past which helped bring the story together in my mind. Thank you for guarding the pictures, Miss Ermie, and for saving them for future generations.

I would like to thank Stanley Bratcher who took time to share his memories and stories with me at the Fish Market. The heady odor of spots and croakers and shrimp has now been transformed into a sweet fragrance that will forever trigger fond memories.

I wish to thank my dear lifetime friends, Jeff and Marci Lanier and Kay and Virgil Williams, who expressed great interest in a book about our common hometown and encouraged me all along the way.

Special thanks go to my faithful friends: Della Futrell, Judy Smith, Peggy Guthrie, Beverlie Brewer, Rudene Kennedy and Julie Greene. Just call out my name and I'll come running!

And once again, thanks go to Peggy Rhodes, our office manager and human guinea pig who read what I thought was the final manuscript and exclaimed, "You're not finished, are you?"

Hope G. Smith not only painted a wonderful scene for the front cover art, she did it at my last minute invitation and in the midst of the grand opening of her new studio and retail store. Hope's heart is as lovely as the pictures she creates.

Additionally, I thank Leon (Sonny) Sikes who graciously shared his research on early Duplin County communities. His book *Duplin Places* was a wonderful resource as well.

Long before the idea came to incorporate a portion of Beulah's history into novel form, I spent many evenings and Saturday mornings with Dr. Dallas Herring in his extensive historical and genealogical library in Rose Hill, North Carolina. Throughout his lifetime—he died in 2007 at ninety—Dr. Herring collected a large and amazing assortment of historical and genealogical material that covers not only Duplin County but is invaluable to the history of the state of North Carolina and that of our nation as well. Dr. Herring's library is now overseen by the Duplin County Historical Foundation, Inc.

Lastly, I want to thank my excellent editor who is now my friend, Edie Mourey. Not only is Edie an extremely talented editor, she also offers a wealth of knowledge and pertinent information. Her humor and delightful personality create a pleasant and enjoyable atmosphere for the tedious editing process. Edie is truly a jewel to work with.

Dedication

This book is lovingly dedicated
to my six precious grandchildren:
Anna Lynne Brown, Blair Nichole Taylor,
Matthew Edward Taylor, Nicholas Thomas Taylor,
Lucas Allan Fucili and Abigail Grace Fucili—
descendants of the families of
Sweet Beulah Land.

In Loving Memory

Ivonne Montealegre Grady

Preface

Although the story you are about to read is fictional, the cast of characters is filled with persons who may have lived in and around the small farming community of Beulaville, North Carolina, from 1900 to 1905. A few of the characters are based on certain of my ancestors or those of my husband's. Others are composite characters, formed through an amalgamation of friends or acquaintances of those who were related. And then there are quite a few who never existed at all in any way, shape or form. They just make the story more interesting!

Considering the relative void of written history concerning our little corner of the world, I have taken great liberty in embellishing oral stories I have collected from friends and family through the years. The most prominent family in this story, the Greshams (sometimes spelled Grisham or Grissom), immigrated into eastern North Carolina from somewhere north of the Mason-Dixon Line circa 1750, or possibly much earlier. The first patriarch on record, Thomas Gresham, Sr., came from a long line of "Thomas" Gresham fathers, uncles, brothers and cousins. The incredible number of Thomas Greshams in U.S. census records and the scarcity of personal written accounts make it extremely difficult to narrow down his specific ancestry prior to 1750. There are now Thomas Greshams scattered from New York to Florida, Alabama and Mississippi and from North Carolina westward to Missouri and on across the United States.

We do know, from census records, land deeds and oral history that our first known Thomas Gresham, born in North Carolina in 1770, was living alternately in Duplin and Jones Counties in southeastern North Carolina in 1790. He married the former Anne Weeks from Onslow County, a neighbor of Duplin, in 1801. Thomas and Anne had five children: Thomas Gresham, Jr., William Washington Gresham, Willis Peale Gresham, Lewis Cullen Gresham and Celia Gresham.

The most familiar tale in the Gresham family is the treasured love story of Thomas Gresham, Jr., and his beloved wife, Barbary Bishop. Thomas Junior was born in Duplin County, North Carolina, in 1808 on land from which the village of Beulah developed into the town of Beulaville 106 years later. According to family histories, census records, land deeds and wills, the Greshams were often linked with the Bishops and Halls, other land owners and farmers in Duplin, Jones and Onslow counties.

Now, I must interject here to say that owning large tracts of land in southeastern North Carolina in those days certainly did not mean a family was wealthy in any context of today's definition of the word. Other than the mention of possibly hundreds of acres of land, the majority of "Last Wills and Testaments" in Duplin County consisted mainly of farming tools, a feather bed or two, kitchen implements such as iron pots and iron frying pans, possibly a great coat and sometimes a horse and buggy. Often, a cow or two was added in.

Of course, if a farmer owned enough land to call for a will, a few slaves were usually included. Compared to antebellum-themed movies and even recorded histories of plantations in South Carolina and states further into the Deep South, Duplin County farmers had few slaves, varying between one and three in most wills, if any at all. More than that was an extreme exception…but there were exceptions, particularly before 1800 when the definition of a planter was one who owned one thousand acres of land and at least twenty-five slaves.

We would hope the comparatively small numbers of slaves meant the good citizens of Duplin were against slavery, but in most cases, it more than likely indicated they were just too poor to afford more. History does prove, however, that North Carolinians in general were of the anti-slavery persuasion. The Old North State continued to stand with the Union until Lincoln called for a total blockade of southern ports, which not only cut off trade with the northern states but stopped the flow of much-needed importing and exporting with England and the islands. Free trade was a much larger issue in the Civil War than most people realize. We Tar Heels were a people torn between two worlds. Perhaps that's one of the reasons we came to be called the Rip Van Winkle State. But that's another tale to be told. Back to the love story.

Sometime between 1830 and 1837, Thomas and Anne Weeks Gresham decided to move their family further south to Limestone County, Alabama, where other Gresham families had settled earlier. There is no evidence to confirm how long this arduous journey lasted or how many stops were made along the way, but the Gresham family arrived in Limestone County, Alabama sometime in the mid 1830's while the area was still Indian Territory.

Now it seems that young Thomas Junior regretfully left his sweetheart, Barbary Bishop, behind in eastern Duplin County, North Carolina. One can just imagine the pressure that must have been placed on the young man to travel south with his family, especially since he was his father's namesake. As to why the lovely Barbary didn't go ahead and marry Thomas and accompany the Greshams to Alabama, the saga is silent. Perhaps Barbary's father and mother, Willis and Margaret Bishop, would not allow their daughter to be taken hundreds of miles from her home and family. Or, heaven forbid, she just wasn't as crazy about Thomas as he was about her!

Whatever the reasons, like Sweet William in the old English ballad of Barbary Allen ("Sweet William on his deathbed lay, for the love of Barbary Allen"), young Thomas found himself unable to tolerate life in Alabama without his own true love. And so he endured the long trek on foot back to eastern North Carolina to woo and wed Barbary Bishop. They were married in 1839 and eventually produced eight children, a clan of their own. My great-great-grand-father, Caleb Frank Gresham, was their youngest son.

Although each and every tale in this book is fictitious, a few contain a hint of truth! The families mentioned in the story are familiar eastern Duplin County families who settled the area along with the Greshams, Halls and Bishops. As the names indicate, the earliest pioneers were English, Welsh or Scots-Irish, but mainly Welsh.

My goal in writing *Sweet Beulah Land* was to create something of lasting historical and personal value for my own children and for the people of Beulaville, North Carolina. Daily life in eastern Duplin County, as described in *Sweet Beulah Land*, is pretty much a culture of the past. My own generation was more than likely the last to experience "barning tobacco" as did the Greshams in 1900. For many years now, farmers have used gigantic harvesters, leaving the old barns lonely and forlorn and filled with lost stories of days gone by. The cotton fields of Duplin disappeared for many years, but with the decrease of tobacco, King Cotton is now making a comeback. My childhood generation is the last as well to have experienced the pleasure of walking "downtown," with its two grocery stores, one fish market, I. J. Sandlin's General Merchandise, two gas stations and a bank plus a few beauty shops, to the picture show on a Saturday evening through the deep ruts of dirt roads and mud holes. There was a sense of childhood freedom in those days that will never be felt again.

Well, dear reader, I'll stop rambling and let you read the story yourself. To take up for myself and all the other boring grandmothers who have tales to tell, I must say I believe it is very important that our stories be passed down to our children and grandchildren. Were it not for the storytellers, how would succeeding generations know who they are and from whence they came? And if we don't know where we have been and who we are, how can we possibly know where we are going?

Marilyn Denny Thomas
Beulaville, North Carolina
July 22, 2008

Chapter One

*F*all, 1900—The Gresham home stood back off the narrow dirt road that ran alongside the Northeast Cape Fear River, near the small community of Hallsville (previously called Limestone). It was built before the Civil War by old Solomon Hall, Sarah Jane Gresham's father himself. Sarah Jane had grown up there in Duplin County on what was called a plantation in antebellum days, though worlds apart from the plantations in South Carolina and further into the Deep South. Most men who were called "planters" in south-eastern North Carolina held large tracts of land but were very seldom prosperous enough to build impressive houses with giant oaks leading up to the front portico. This was particularly the case in Duplin County, North Carolina. A small, one-story farmhouse was the custom, usually clapboard and nearly always left unpainted. Even so, planters and plantations were rare, especially toward the end of the century. Sherman took care of that.

By 1900, men farmed the land with their wives and children by their sides in the fields they had cleared with their own hands. It was back-breaking work, chopping down pine and sweet gum trees with hand axes and pulling up the giant stumps. It often took a year or more to clear new land for farming.

Cotton and corn were the mainstays in the early years, but King Cotton slowly yet gracefully yielded his white-capped fields to the golden-leafed Ruler of eastern North Carolina's economy—Tobacco. And then, around 1919, King Cotton finally gave up his reign completely when the government started handing out tobacco allotments.

Only one animal was raised in anticipation of real income, and that was the pig. After frigid hog-killing days in the winter months when cash was scarce, it wasn't unusual for a farmer to haul a few sides of bacon to Kinston, a bustling market town just thirty miles north of Beulah. And although the vast pine forests were steadily dwindling by 1900, the ancient turpentine and naval stores commerce continued on into the new century. Many men continued to tap the giant pine trees for the precious sap that was later transformed into pitch and tar. Sadly to say, the old turpentine stills also continued to prosper through those who used them for a less prosperous but highly addictive product sometimes referred to as moonshine.

Back at the Gresham home, Jeb and Sarah Jane Gresham's five daughters were moving about the kitchen engrossed in their morning chores. The large kitchen was attached to the rest of the house by a covered porch that ran the entire length of the front.

"Maaaama!" Liza whined. "Nell won't let me wear her blue shawl to town."

"I'm sure she has a reason, Liza. Nell has never been selfish. Have you considered she might want to wear it herself?"

"No, she dudn't, Mama. She's not even goin'!" Fourteen-year-old Liza stood with both hands on her hips, glaring at her oldest sister who fed her anger by seeming to ignore her completely.

"Not goin'?" Surprise was obvious in Sarah Jane's question. "Why aren't you going to town with your Pa, Nell?"

Liza had finally gained her mother's attention, though not for the reason she had intended. Angrier than ever, she pushed the screened door open and stomped out, letting the door bang loudly behind her.

"I thought I'd stay home to work on my quilt and have supper ready by the time y'all get back, that's all." The quietest of the five sisters could almost feel her mother's eyes boring through her back as she poured the last of the coffee into her papa's cup. She began to collect the breakfast dishes from the table, hoping Sarah Jane would let the issue drop.

Hannah, the second-oldest at sixteen, had already been out to the pump by the porch to fill the bucket and was heating the water on the wood stove, appearing not to be interested in the strained conversa-

tion. She poured the hot water into the big white enamel dis
while Nell filled it with the tin plates and dirty forks and spoons.
The two sisters were careful not to look at one another, highly aware
that their mother, who oftentimes seemed clairvoyant to the girls,
was studying them, determined to figure out what was going on.
From past experience, they were sure she would know all in the end,
but for now, Nell quickly finished her morning chores and quietly
slipped out the kitchen door and on down the porch through the
doorway that led into the sitting room, the poor person's parlor.
Within minutes, she was rocking by the low burning fire with the
darning basket in her lap, trying to decide where to start—worn out
stockings or papa's button less shirt.

Sarah Jane paused in her work. Placing a ragged cloth in a
large pan, she carefully took the kettle off the burner and poured
the steaming hot water into the pan. She'd have to let it cool a few
minutes before wrapping the cloth around her painful arthritic fingers.
They had been swollen for days this time, and she was longing for
even a small measure of relief.

Holding her hands over the steaming cloth, she casually asked,
"Hannah, why doesn't Nell want to go to town on votin' day?
Everybody'll be there."

"I don't know, Mama," replied Hannah who saw all and revealed
nothing. Throughout her life she would excel in honoring the privacy
of others, even if it often meant pretending she was either ridicu-
lously naïve or downright ignorant. She probably had never heard of
the three monkeys, "Hear no evil, See no evil, and Speak no evil,"
but everybody in and around Beulah knew the three axioms consti-
tuted Hannah Gresham's unspoken philosophy of life. She may not
have been pretty like many of the young women in the Gresham
clan, but she possessed a beauty that radiated from deep within.

"I'll stay home with her if you want, Mama. I don't mind."

"No, child, you go on and visit with your cousins. I'd planned to
stay home anyway if these old swollen joints didn't swage. I truly
don't feel like bouncin' around in that cart agoin' and acomin'. I
might be able to handle a ride in the buggy, but Jeb has too much to
haul. He'll need the wagon, what with Kate and you girls plus all the
supplies we need."

Hannah dried her hands on her white apron and looked with concern at her mother. "I'm sorry your joints hurt so bad, Mama."

"I'll be fine, child. Now, go get ready and help Liza find somethin' to wear before she has a pure conniption."

Hannah laughed with her mother, easily picturing the dreaded scene.

"Whoa, Nellie! I said *whoa*, not *go*, you dumb ol' mule! Don't you look at me like that. You'll be glue by winter, I swear!" Jeb Gresham jumped off the wagon as if he were twenty years younger than he looked; his shoulders bent and skin the color and texture of leather dried too long in the sun. He may have lost what good looks he was born with during his fifty-five years on this earth, but not his vigor. He was tough, that one, like most all the men who were reared between Turkey Branch and Limestone in the days when the land was still covered in dense pine forests. The gigantic evergreens reached so high into the sky you'd have thought they touched the stars.

"Come on now, Kate. I'll help you climb up."

Jeb was speaking to the young woman waiting patiently on a big oak stump by the side of the muddy road, her face nearly hidden by the sage green bonnet she wore tied neatly in a bow under her chin. She didn't look as if she paid him any mind. Back straight, eyes gazing far off into the colorful autumn countryside, she seemed to be looking for something or someone others couldn't see.

Liza and Frannie were giggling and playing, their legs dangling off the tail of the old wagon. They were sorely tempted to splash their feet in the mud holes, but they didn't dare for fear of their mother's wrath at the sight of their ruined shoes. "Good shoes are hard to come by," she'd be sure to say.

Hannah held eight-year-old Susie in her lap as she waited silently on the wagon's second seat, her face expressing deep concern for the cousin and friend just two years her senior.

"Kate Grissom! Can't you hear, girl? Or is it you're just as stubborn as ol' Nellie?"

"Now, Uncle Jeb, whether I'm deaf or just plain stubborn is neither here nor there. Anyway, I'm not a Grissom anymore. I'm a Kennedy now…I reckon." The young woman slowly rose and turned toward the side of the cart, holding her hand out to Jeb. "Alright," she said with a sigh. "I reckon I'm ready as I'm ever going to be."

As she stood to take Jeb's hand and climb up into the wagon, the cool November breeze blew Kate's bonnet back from her oval face. She was a pretty young woman with hair the color of a strawberry roan mare, her long tresses pulled back at the nape of her neck and rolled into a tight bun. Her eyes were the clear green of her British ancestors.

All summed up, she was a fairly pretty young woman. But when Jeb looked up at her, he didn't see a woman, only a terribly disheartened young girl. She wore sadness like a dark cloak that she seemed to draw tighter about herself as the days of her youth faded into the distance to become only sweet memories of another lifetime.

She's too young to look like that, Jeb thought.

Kate grabbed her uncle's calloused hand and held it tightly. Placing one foot on the running board, she nimbly heaved her slender body up into the wagon. One glance into Hannah's compassionate eyes brought quick tears to her own, so she turned quickly and settled herself on the hard wooden seat beside her uncle.

"That girl never seems to be where she is. You know what I mean?" Jeb had questioned Sarah Jane before he left home that morning. He was chewing the last bite of the ham biscuit he had dipped in the sweet, milky coffee.

"I know what you mean. She's been like that ever since she came back from the Grissom Cave. It's a terrible shame she can't just get on with livin'. Even if her ma and pa were wrong insistin' she marry Doc Kennedy, it's the way things are now, and that girl will have to accept her life as it is or be miserable and make everybody 'round her miserable the rest of her days. Lord knows, we all have our troubles."

Sarah Jane opened the door to let some of the heat escape the kitchen. It was still too warm in eastern North Carolina to need much of a fire on an early November day.

"How come she's not in Beulah with the doctor, Jeb?"

"Heard she's visitin' her cousin down the road a spell, one of her Hines kin. She wanted to stay another day or so, but I heard Mack Hall say Doc Kennedy sent for her. Said she was to go back to town on votin' day. Said if she was a'goin' to be a doctor's wife, she had to act like one and show up at public functions and the like. Heard she weren't too thrilled about that."

"Poor girl. I do feel sorry for her." Sarah Jane sighed as she stood looking out the door toward the Hall Field, gently rubbing the swollen joints in her left hand.

"Now don't let it get you down, woman. You got five females of your own to worry about."

"She's your kin, Jeb. Don't you feel for her?"

"Sure, I do. But like you said to begin with, this is her lot and she's got to gird up her loins like the Bible says and get on with her life. Whatever's goin' to be is goin' to be."

"Jeb! You're not Hard-shell Baptist!"

"No, I ain't. But you never know who's exactly right about all this stuff. Presbyterians ain't much different in the long run, prewhatever and all."

"Predestination?"

"Yep. Whatever's goin' to be is goin' to be."

"Oh, Jeb, you don't believe that. We've raised five girls, preparing them to marry and give us a yard-full of grand young'uns, and we put our only boys in the grave, trusting in the goodness of God. He didn't make our twin boys die wee babes, and He didn't cause the war that set us back a hundred years."

"Well, woman, who's to say? I'm just a mere mortal a'wanderin' through this world and so are you." While the last words were coming out of his mouth, Jeb got up and patted his stomach. "Time to load up the girls to fetch Kate and get on to town. I'll stop by Nate's store and trade a ham for the sugar and other stuff on your list. Be back afore sundown."

❈

About that time, the wagon's left front wheel hit a sudden pothole in the muddy dirt road and jolted Jeb's thoughts back to driving the wagon and the mountain of tasks he was hoping to accomplish by the end of the day. Liza and Frannie were still sitting on the back of the wagon, singing and laughing, happily enjoying the rare weekday holiday. Hannah was perched carefully on the seat behind the close friend she would always call Cousin Kate as was the manner of the day. Like Jeb said, the somber young woman was definitely in another realm as the wagon bumped and slid along the narrow road that wound from the remote Hall farm to the old riverside settlement of Hallsville, then on four more miles to the slowly growing village of Beulah.

The place was nothing but a turpentine camp in the early days when adventurous pioneers migrated down from New Bern and over from Onslow. Others followed the Northeast Cape Fear River up from Wilmington and settled about half way in between. Now, the tiny conglomerate of no more than ten or so homes ten years ago was fast becoming an actual little village. Way back in '73, Beulah had boasted a post office, but now a couple of dry goods stores, a bank, a school house with two teachers and a barber shop were interspersed between the ancient stills that oft times produced more moonshine than turpentine. Unfortunately, it was those old stills that had earned the small community the prior infamous name of Snatchet. First time visitors traveling through the settlement on most any Saturday night understood the meaning all too well. If they escaped before their valuables were snatched away, they considered themselves very lucky, usually vowing to avoid the area in the future if at all possible. That is, unless the visitor enjoyed drinking and fighting. If so, he might feel right at home.

But, times were changing. Even before Miss Ida Wash Sandlin became the postmistress, she loudly declared that something had to be done about the name of the small but growing village. (By the way, Wash was short for Washington, her deceased husband's name.) She often said the community would never amount to anything if it was forever called such a horrible name as Snatchet. So Miss Ida made a public proclamation which had a more profound effect upon the area than anyone could have dreamed at the time. She took a name straight from the Bible, the sixty-second chapter of Isaiah, verse four, declaring that Snatchet would now and forever more be called "Beulah" so that if a soul was in Hell's Swamp (three miles west) or in Purgatory (three miles east), he could lift up his eyes and see Beulah, the land married to the Good Lord.

Yes, sir, from that time on, things began to change.

For the good, they say, thought Kate, as she spied the dust from the corn mill rising up ahead. Her mama and papa insisted the change was good, anyway. She wasn't so sure. The thick pine forests that had covered eastern North Carolina since time immemorial were gradually diminishing as settlers wandered into the backwoods with their axes and bush hogs, slowly clearing new land to farm with their wives and children alongside. But Kate didn't like living so close to everyone else in the open land. She remembered the good days when the closest neighbors to her father's farm were her grandparents, Thomas and Barbary Gresham, at their home place on Turkey Branch, about a mile north, and Barbary's Bishop kin to the southeast. Now, though nearly surrounded by a dried cornfield, her childhood home was situated on the western end of the little settlement that was to become her family's greatest accomplishment fifteen years later—an incorporated town, the youngest in Duplin County.

The Greshams were a proud people. *Too proud*, thought Kate, peering around her Uncle Jeb, anxious to spot her mother or one of her sisters through the long rows of dry cornstalks. But there was no sight of anyone in the field or out in the yard as the wagon bumped and squeaked and rattled on by.

"Want to stop and visit a spell?" Jeb could almost feel the desperate longing in the young woman's aching heart.

She sighed deeply and shrugged. "No. Looks like nobody's home. But, it's just as well. They're all still mad at me anyway. Might as well have stayed in exile at the Cave. It was warmer than the cold shoulders turned to me since I got back."

A cool autumn breeze whipped down the dirt road the proud citizens of the little village now called the Main Road. Actually, it was the only street there was, just about a half-mile strip of black dirt mixed with river sand. The Main Road connected the road to Hallsville and Kenansville with the road to Kinston and New Bern, running catty-cornered through what was once Thomas and Barbary Gresham's farmland. Most of it now belonged to their eldest son, Willis T., Kate's father.

Kate turned away, gazing down the wide rutted road towards her Cousin Nate's store, her green eyes searching. But she quickly turned back, knowing Jeb would think she was dying to see one of her parents or her brothers and sisters. She told herself they loved her; of course they did, and like all loving parents, they wanted the best of everything for their oft times rebellious daughter. The problem was she thought they had aimed their sights a bit too high more than once.

We're not Wilmington socialites, she fumed. *We're just back-woods, country farmers who happened to have inherited a few hundred acres of land nobody else probably even wanted.*

Oh, but she did love this land—the massive pine forests, sprinkled with huge sweet gums, sycamores, maples and the dainty dogwoods that whitened the landscape in spring and speckled it bright red in the peak of autumn. She loved the fragrance of honeysuckle and magnolia in the spring and pine straw and morning glories in autumn; it was all hers as sure as the air she breathed. Since she was a sprightly little girl, consumed with curiosity and a natural wanderlust inherited from her pioneer great grandfather, Thomas Gresham, Sr., Kate had reveled in long treks through the woods behind her house. Her mother often was forced to send one of her older brothers to retrieve her, interrupting many happy hours of exploration and imaginative play. More often than not, they finally found her sprawled out on a bed of sweet-smelling pine straw in the warmth of the late afternoon sun, gazing up at the bright blue sky and imagining all sorts of animals and objects and people in the puffy white clouds.

And now, she sighed, *I have to wear bonnets and corsets and long dresses that trip me when I run.* She blinked back the tears welling up in her eyes and pulled the brimmed bonnet a little lower, thinking to hide her unhappiness from her perceptive uncle.

But Jeb had already seen her tears. Trying not to embarrass her, he turned his eyes away, quickly scanning the half-acre section of land roped off for Election Day 1900. Two long tables had been taken out of the small school house and set up in the yard so there would be plenty of room for everyone in Limestone Township to get in line and register to mark a ballot for the candidate of choice.

The winding line was fairly long by the time Kate climbed down from the cart with Jeb's unappreciated assistance. She settled her bonnet back on her head, straightened her new sage green dress to match and took a deep breath. He could hear her angry mumbling as she marched off toward the voting tables. Holding Susie's hand, pausing often to speak to acquaintances along the way, Hannah calmly followed her fuming cousin.

Jeb grinned, happy to see that Kate had regained control of her emotions and was back to her normal ornery self. Straining to hear her last words, he caught sight of the large crowd lined up in front of the tables and the even larger group hanging around to argue politics until the election results came in later in the week.

"I'd not be havin' to come to town on voting day if Mama and Papa had let me marry the man I wanted. I'd be sitting on a log some-where in the woods watching my young'uns play. I'd be having me a good old time, listening for the train just a'whistlin' down the track, bringing my railroad man back to me. Voting! Before you know it, women will have to vote! Who cares who gets to be President of the United States?"

"They care," Jeb said aloud to no one in particular. His eyes rested on a small group of men who were downright glaring at one another. They didn't just care; they cared enough to fight about it, and he was certain there would be one—a fight, that is. If the town's history was doomed to repeat itself, the old stills would be doing a booming business well before sundown. By the time the Potter's Hill Republicans and the Snatchet Democrats got their fill, what were called minor political discussions earlier in the day would become all-out battles long before midnight.

Not everyone drank, of course. Actually, most of the upstanding citizens didn't, but those who did made up for those who didn't, substantiating the reputation Beulah's non-drinkers had long struggled to live down. No one had ever heard of a middle ground. You were either a teetotaler or a drunk. Of course, most everyone made a little homemade wine from the fruit of the scuppernong vines in the backyard, but that little bit didn't count. Anybody could have told you it was only to soak the fruitcake in at Christmas.

"Papa! Papa!" Liza and Frannie squealed for Jeb to come and help them down from the cart. They would have jumped, but they knew their mama would hear about it somehow and chastise them for their unladylike behavior.

"Go on and have a good time, girls, but keep your eyes on me every now and then so I can gather you up when it's time to go."

"Yes, Papa, we will!"

"Got the picnic your Mama packed for you?"

"Yes, Papa," replied Liza, smiling proudly. "And don't you worry. I'll take good care of Fran and Susie." Liza drew back her shoulders and set her mouth as maturely as she could.

That's what worries me, thought Jeb, handing each girl a penny for lemonade and another for a big stick of hard candy that should last them most of the day.

"Hey, Jeb!" yelled Nate Gresham. The English surname was sometimes spelled and pronounced "Grissom" or "Grisham" in the rural South in 1900.

"Well, I'll be darned, Nate. Good to see you! Who's mindin' the store?" Grinning to beat the band, Jeb pushed his perpetual wide-brimmed hat that looked something like a frayed gray fedora back on his head and reached out to shake his nephew's hand.

"Laney's taking care of business. She only has about a week to go before the baby comes, so I can't depend on her much these days. But she says she's feeling fine and needs to be moving around some. You know Laney. She's got to talk to somebody about every five minutes or she's lonely as all get out, especially if she knows something's going on in town."

"Yeah, that's Laney." Jeb chuckled. "Tell her I'll be stopping by the store after I vote. Got to get Sarah Jane's list filled and load up the wagon. Then I got to go by the post office, and then get me a haircut. I'll come back after that to fetch Hannah and the young'uns so I can get home afore dark." Jeb was counting the list of tasks on his fingers, wondering how he was going to get it all done and still have time to chew the fat with folks he met along the way.

"Saw you brought Kate back to town." Nate's eyes followed Kate as she spoke soberly with Doc Kennedy near the curtained-off voting booth. Neither one of them could have passed for a happy newlywed. "How is she?"

"Miserable at best. It's heartbreakin' even to a tough old gopher like me to see the change in that girl. She's like a wild filly that somebody captured and harnessed and then went and tied her up with one of those fancy English bridles."

"I know." Nate sighed. "But it's too late now, I reckon. She agreed to leave the Cave and come back home to marry Doc Kennedy. She's not little Kate Gresham anymore. She's Mrs. Kathleen Kennedy, and she's going to have to accept her fate."

"Hm. That's about what Sarah Jane said just this morning," answered Jeb. He stared at Kate thoughtfully and then said, "But acceptance is a big word, Nate, particularly for a young person whose dreams have been buried." Suddenly, his wrinkled face lit up in a mischievous grin. "But come to think of it, I don't know which one I feel sorrier for at this point, Kate or the Doc."

Nate laughed. "Yeah, I know what you mean. Hey! There's old man Quinn with a face as red as a beet. Let's find out what's got his goat."

"I'm bettin' we already know," replied Jeb, dryly.

Nate moved toward the tallest man in the crowd, the only one wearing a suit jacket instead of overalls and shirt sleeves.

"You'd vote against McKinley if a dog was runnin' on the Democrat ticket," Lem Weston was saying—more like spitting—as the two Gresham men strode up to the group of five, each one storing a wad of tobacco in his bulging cheek.

"Jeb, cain't you talk some sense into these crazy Democrats? Bryan ain't nothin' but a smooth-talking politician, and if he gets in the White House, we ain't gon' get nothin' but religion crammed down our throats."

"I ain't gettin' into it, Lem. I always say it's a great privilege to vote. Every man has a right to vote his own conscience, whichever way he thinks is right." Jeb stood back, each hand gripping a strap of his best overalls.

"But that don't mean you can't try to get others to see your way, does it?"

"Nope. But, it don't mean you ought to fight about it, either."

"Well, some things are worth fightin' for!" Lem stomped off toward his mule and cart, looking as if he was going to explode long before he got there.

"You sure set him straight, Jeb!" McConnell Quinn—Mack for short—grinned proudly and spat a stream of tobacco juice in the direction Lem went.

"I meant what I said for ever'body, Mack. This is 1900. It's the beginning of a new millennium, and we ain't living in the Wild West. We ought to be able to discuss politics without it ending in a brawl. Why can't we have just *one* year when we do our votin' fair and square and then accept the results like civilized human bein's?"

"Because of the Republicans, that's why!" Mack huffed and strutted off like an angry rooster, turning to call to Jeb as he went, "Who are you votin' for, Grissom?"

"Ain't telling nobody who I vote for." Jeb pushed his old fedora back on his head and grinned, sort of like the cat that ate the canary.

Mack's face turned a brighter shade of red as he looked around for someone else to argue with. The gangly old man looked like a boxer itching for a fight even if he was one of Beulah's most outstanding citizens and one of the first at that.

Nate had squatted down and was lighting up a cigar. "That man thinks he's right about everything, not just politics, mind you. And he's got the money to prove it according to the way his mind works."

"Yeah, he's done real good, that's for sure. He's got a prosperous farm and a store, plus a mighty fine house for these parts. But all that don't make a person better 'n everybody else."

"Or smarter, either," Nate added, snickering as he puffed on the cigar.

"Yeah...." Jeb paused in thought a moment or two. "But when it comes down to it, that old man comes through every time. Remember that winter Theophilus Brinson stayed drunk so long Emmy and the children didn't have anything to eat?"

"Yeah, but I seem to remember it was more than one winter," Nate replied, nodding his head. He took a puff off the cigar.

"It was old Mack who took her enough supplies from his store to keep her and the young'uns from starvin'. I heard he didn't want it told, either, but 'course Emmy did. She said the Bible says give honor to who honor is due or somethin' like that."

Jeb looked down at Nate. "Well, come on, boy. Let's see if we can get to the votin' booth without gettin' shot."

Nate stood up and threw the cigar stub on the ground, grinding it with his foot. His uncle was probably joking, but what he said was too close to the truth to be funny.

A few horses and buggies but mostly mules hitched to wagons were pulling into the voting area as Jeb entered the curtained booth. Kate wandered about, visiting with friends and relatives she hadn't seen since she was sent off to the mysterious Gresham Cave that everyone talked about in whispers but didn't seem to know where or what it was. She didn't see her mama and papa when they descended from their buggy and merged into the mounting drove of potential voters. But her younger sister, Jessie, had already spied Kate in the crowd and quickly climbed down from the buggy almost before her papa pulled the old mule to a sudden halt.

"Kate! Kate!" Jessie yelled, running into the mob, waving her hand high to get her sister's attention. "Kate, wait!"

Hearing her name called, Kate glanced back over her shoulder. She was overjoyed to see her little sister fluttering through the crowd. "Jess, what are you doing here? Women can't vote yet, thank the Good Lord."

"I'm not here to vote, you silly girl. I'm here to socialize!"

Kate laughed, throwing her arm around her sister's thin shoulders as they happily strolled through the bustling assembly of Limestone Township.

"Okay, Kate," Jessie giggled, pulling her off to the side. "Now that we're away from big ears, you have to tell me. How's married life?"

"Don't ask, my dear sister. Just know you'll be next."

"Me? Never!"

"Oh, yes, you will. You being the romantic soul that you are, some handsome man will come along and sweep you right off your feet one of these days. So don't let my experience cloud your expectations, you hear?"

"I hear. But, are you happy, Kate? I can't bear for you not to be happy."

Kate took a deep breath and frowned. "I don't know yet, I guess. Some things just take time."

She hugged her sister once again and kissed her forehead, hoping with all her heart and soul that little Jessie would have the life she dreamed of—that she wouldn't be disappointed as Kate had been. Jessie smiled up at her sister, but Kate glanced away just in time to witness the admiring look Big Rufus Bostic was giving Jessie. She wondered if her little sister's day was closer than she had previously thought. Thankfully, Jessie didn't see him…not that day.

By that time, Jeb had placed his vote and was deciding what to do next when all of a sudden he felt a hard whack on his back. He turned around and looked into the slushy red eyes of Uz Brinson and his brother in crime, Theophilus. Although the sun was lowering itself in the November sky, causing Jeb to worry that he wouldn't get all his tasks finished so as to be home before sundown, it was still much too early for most of the town's men to take a nip, even on Election Day. However, it was certainly the norm for the Brinson boys, the whole bunch of them. They usually worked as hard as anybody in the county all week long, but come Friday night, you'd find them at either of the three local stills or hanging out at the crossroads near Nate's store, sloppy drunk.

We're a weird bunch, thought Jeb, trying to shake Uz's trembling hand and figure out what he was saying in his loud, slurred speech. Of course, he should have guessed.

Theophilus finally got out a few clear words before his brother could get his tongue in order. "G…got any money on y…you, J…Jeb?"

"Nope. Don't have any money, boys. And even if I did, I sure wouldn't have it on me today."

"Aw, J…Jeb," Uz slurred, "you mus' haf a nickel or two?"

"Nope. Now, go on, boys. Go find yourself a place to sleep it off. You started too early today."

The two wasted young fellows wobbled off toward another group of men, trying to walk a little straighter, hoping they might fool someone into believing they were sober.

"The only good thing about the Brinson boys' drinkin' is that instead of fightin', they'll fall in some ditch before too long and sleep for a few hours," said Jeb as he walked with Nate back to his mule and cart.

"Yeah, they're harmless enough. It's a shame, though," replied Nate. "Those boys could have made something of themselves if the drink hadn't gotten them first."

"Yep." Jeb climbed up to the wagon seat. "Well, Nate, I need to get going. Stayed too long as it is, I reckon. Will I see you at the store?"

"Oh, yeah. If you see Laney before I do, tell her I'll be there shortly."

"Sure will."

Jeb looked around for Liza and Frannie and then scanned the crowd for Hannah. He spotted her leaning against a giant oak, listening intently to Jessie who was chattering away like a happy little Blue Jay. Kate was smiling at her younger sister, reveling in her innocence and freedom. It took her mind off her own troubles for a few precious moments.

Jeb tried to get Hannah's attention to signal her that he was leaving and she would be responsible for the younger girls for the remainder of the day, but he caught Kate's eye instead. He waved good-bye and smiled as she threw one hand in the air, keeping the other around her sister's shoulders.

She may be ornery and a bit rebellious, he thought, *but she's got a good heart underneath all that. She surely does.*

Jeb smiled and climbed up onto the wagon seat.

"Hup, Nellie," he said, clicking his tongue to the dutiful old mule.

Chapter Two

Doctor Samuel Williams and his son, Cloudy, were discussing the good turnout for Election Day with Corbett Thomas and his two boys. Corbett was descended from a long line of Duplin Thomases who had migrated from Wales via Pennsylvania in the early 1700's. He had served as the community's first postmaster when the post office opened in 1873. Doc Samuel, as most folks called him, also came from one of the oldest families in eastern Duplin and Onslow Counties. And considering that both immigrant ancestors had sailed to America from Glamorganshire, Wales, in the mid 1600's, he and Corbett often speculated through the years whether or not their forefathers might have come to America on the same ship, both incredibly ending up in the same obscure little settlement in the Carolinas.

"Of course, it may not have been as coincidental as it seems," one would say to the other as they relaxed in the rockers beside the wood-burning stove in Nate's little store on cold winter days, discussing current events and the early days in Duplin. William Thomas and Whomever Williams could have been cousins or close friends, sharing their dreams together in the old country and then setting out to fulfill their destinies in the new. But whatever had conspired to bring the two aging friends together was considered by both to be a great blessing.

They didn't get together very often. Corbett and his large family lived on the road to Gander's Fork, and Samuel's home place was on Wagon Ford Road, a few miles east of Beulah. Samuel's time-consuming occupation preempted most any social life he might have desired. A doctor's life was round-the-clock ministering to the critically sick or injured. Most people knew enough natural medicine to take care of their own until some terribly dangerous ailment attacked or someone got kicked by a mule or broke a bone or two. Then, they sent for Doc Samuel no matter what time of day or night, and he would heed the call, sending one of his sons out to ready the horse and buggy while his wife, Delia, stirred the coals in the wood stove to prepare a basket of food for Samuel to eat on the way. No matter how long he was gone, she never worried about how he would fare. She knew the patient's family would take good care of her husband while he cared for their loved one. More often than not, after as long as two weeks away, he would ride back up to the home place in the old black buggy, his pockets empty, but the back of the buggy loaded with anything from a live rooster to a smokehouse ham.

However, even though finances certainly figured into the problem, the greatest concern Samuel had at sixty-one years was not a financial one. No, it wasn't that. The fact was, a few of the beloved doctor's sons were fighters, and like most of the area's rambunctious young men, the Williams boys' entanglements were usually instigated by a visit to the turpentine still closest by.

"Why don't they grow up and settle down?" Samuel had asked Corbett too many times to count over the past five years. "It breaks their mama's heart and causes her more grief and worry than if they were off to war. At least she'd know what they were doing if they were in the army. Every Saturday, she starts wringing her hands and looking out the window to see if somebody's coming up the path to tell her one of them is hurt...or dead. I don't know how much longer she can take it, Corbett. I'm concerned about her health."

Samuel would shake his head, his compassionate blue eyes sometimes filling with tears as his friend patted his back and sighed, shaking his head, too, not knowing what to do or say. He didn't understand it any more than his disheartened friend. Corbett's two boys were doing fairly well for themselves. Evan had married one of Brythal Thigpen's girls three years ago and had made his father very happy by presenting his first grandson a year later. The other son, Ned, didn't seem interested in marrying anytime soon. He was a hardworking young man of twenty, closely tied to the land. Yes,

Corbett was proud of his boys. They had grown into respectful, responsible young men.

Now, Corbett Thomas was one of six brothers, all of whom had served the Confederacy well. Miraculously, all six brothers had barely survived the carnage forever after known in the South as the "War between the States." Since that time, each of them had built homes of some sort up and down Gander's Fork Road, just outside Beulah.

They didn't breeze through the war, mind you. All but Corbett came trudging home with either a body part missing or skin so sewed up they couldn't remember where they got which wound. But like thousands of other sons and fathers, each of them had somehow managed to put their living nightmares in the past and go on to build a new life—alas, a much poorer one than before the War. Actually, like everybody else in the area, most just managed to survive.

During the thirty-five years since the devastating war's end, the Thomas brothers had managed to eke out a living from their inherited land for themselves and their families. If not particularly prosperous in the eyes of the world outside rural North Carolina, their lives were nonetheless fulfilling. It could certainly be said that each of them had added something significant to the community in which they worked and lived.

All but Pete Thomas, that is. He had lost a leg at Shiloh. But whether it was the loss of the limb or the horror he went through to lose it, Pete Thomas had become a mean man. Not even fairly easy-going Corbett or his brother, Will, just down the road, could handle Pete when he lost his temper. Not that he was particularly kind and decent before his traumatic experience. Nope. He had always been mean, and he had always had a temper. But after the war, when he got mad he was like a maniac.

You wouldn't think a man like that would be given more children than his own unlucky brood to raise; however, it was the custom in those days for a family too poor to feed all their children to loan one or two of the older ones out to a neighbor—sort of like indentured labor. The child worked for his room and board (usually a bed of hay in the barn) until his own parents could afford to take him back or until he was old enough to move out on his own. Unfortunately, the latter was usually the case.

Pete was getting old now. He had run his exhausted, nervous wreck of a wife to her grave a few years back. His children, who had only stayed nearby because of their mama, had hauled buggy soon after, migrating down the river to Wilmington where it was said jobs were plentiful. Nevertheless, though the farm had dwindled down to just a few acres in the years since his boys left—Pete had sold most of it off bit by bit to pay the taxes—there was still a small farm to run and he couldn't do it by himself. Actually, he could do very little. A man with one leg could hardly work a farm at twenty-five, much less at seventy.

And so that was the reason, when Ike Hatcher came by about a half hour after sunrise and said he had a boy who needed work, Pete Thomas ended up with somebody new to pick on. And pick on the child, he did. But first of all, he was mad as fire at that miserable-looking Hatcher man from Cypress Creek. Pete had eyed the small boy hiding fearfully in the shadow of Ike's frame, but he never dreamed the boy Ike was offering for hard labor and the little blonde fellow with the sad blue eyes were one and the same. Pete had been gypped and he knew it. And now, Ike was suddenly nowhere to be seen, and there stood a little boy only five years old who seemed just as scared of mean old Pete as he was of his ominous daddy.

He had no idea what to do with the boy. There would be no way to get the kind of work he needed out of the no more than fifty pounds of skin and bones standing in the doorway. Pete glared at his new workforce while the boy stared at his feet, fumbling his frayed, hole-ridden hat in his small calloused hands.

"Don't just stand there!" Pete finally yelled. "Might as well come on in 'til I figure out what to do with you. Come on, now!" He started to turn. "Shut the screen door behind you, boy! Flies are bad enough without askin' 'em in!"

"Y…yes, sir," replied Johnny, quickly plopping the old hat on his little head so he could pull the door to behind him.

"Take your hat off in the house, boy! Don't you know nothin'?"

Johnny jerked the hand-me-down hat off his head and stuffed it under his thin arm. He didn't look at the old man. Again, he stared at his feet, standing first on one foot and then the other.

"You hungry, boy?"

"A…a little." The words were almost a whisper. Actually, the boy was almost starving.

"What'd you say, boy? Speak up! Cain't you see I'm old?"

"Y…yes, sir. Yes…yes, I am hungry, sir."

"Well, come sit at the table then. There's a biscuit around here somewhere." The white haired old man who looked a little like God but was meaner than the devil finally turned his fiery eyes away. Leaning heavily on a whittled crutch, he limped over to the wood stove.

The little fellow stepped hesitantly over to the table. It was made of long wooden planks that had never been painted or stained, so it was now a dreary gray, weathered by years of use. Slowly, Johnny took a seat on the bench and scrunched his hat under his bottom, confused as to what was the correct thing to do.

Old Pete took the last two biscuits from the tin pan lying on top of the stove and tossed them across the table to the boy. He wasn't expecting it, and even if he had been, the little fellow couldn't have caught two biscuits at a time, so one dropped to the floor and instantly broke into more pieces than Johnny could count. Horrified, the boy scrambled down and frantically began to pick up the pieces, all the while stuttering, "I…I'm sorry! I'll…I'll get it! Don't worry, I'll get it."

"You better be sure you pick up ever' crumb, boy!"

"I…I will."

"That's all you'll get 'til supper!"

"Tha…thank you, sir. I won't leave a mite. I'll clean it all up."

"You'd better, boy."

Pete watched from the doorway as the boy picked at the floor boards with his thin dirty fingers, pushing the bigger pieces into his mouth as he worked feverishly. Something about the boy pulled at his heart—the heart he was shocked to discover he still had. If he had known Johnny Hatcher's story, the hardened old man might have even shed a tear.

Neither Pete Thomas nor the boy realized it as yet, but Ike Hatcher was not just loaning his five-year-old child out to work, he was giving him away, and not for the first time. The day before had turned out to be the worst since little Johnny's mama died. Trembling violently, the little five-year-old boy had hidden behind the trunk of the largest pine tree he could get to fast enough in the dense forest, thick with underbrush and prickly thorn vines. Early that morning, only he and his sister, Maggie, had been ordered to follow their pa into the forest to mark the gigantic pines to be tapped for turpentine in early spring when the sap started running. The remainder of the nine children born to Sallie Sue and Ike Hatcher before her sudden death last August had been allowed the unheard of opportunity to spend the day with an aunt who lived near the beginning of the path leading into the deep woods.

It seemed they had been walking among the tall trees for hours. Filtered sunlight was splashing on the brilliant red dogwoods and golden maples made even more spectacular in contrast to the giant evergreens and holly trees that even now boasted huge clusters of bright red berries. Johnny knew the abundant berries were a sign of a cold winter just ahead. His pa had taught the children these things in the happy days before his mama died. He taught them lots of things then, patiently showing each of the eight children, no matter how young, how to tell exactly when the earth had warmed enough for new life to be released, causing the sap to course through the tall pine trees and seep through the protective bark in thick little golden bubbles. But those days were like a dream now—a dream that would never come true again.

Only a few months earlier, young Johnny and his brothers and sisters had been dealt a nightmarish double blow. One unbearably hot afternoon deep in the dog days of August, Johnny's mother had spread a colorful quilt out on the grass under the gigantic oak tree in front of their small cabin so the children could rest from the heat of the day. They would have baked inside, even with the doors and windows wide open. She told Martha, the oldest girl, to watch the newborn who was sleeping peacefully in a basket.

Sallie Sue had experienced an unusually hard time with the birth of this last baby, her ninth. It might have been her age, considering she was over forty by then, but no one really knew what caused the dreaded childbed fever she had suffered from since the baby's birth. But that particular morning, worried that the chores were mounting up and the little girls had too much to do, she had forced herself off the bed to do the wash early. While the children rested, though dizzy and weak as water, she struggled to take the sun-dried clothing off the line. Martha would sprinkle what needed ironing to save for the next morning when the day was new and the air was fresh and cool. But Johnny's mama had only taken two white sheets off the line when a sudden stabbing pain shot through her temples. Reeling from the pain and shock, she threw the warm sheets over her shoulder and stumbled back towards the children, holding her head with both hands. Just before she reached the children's quilt, Sallie Sue Hatcher fell to the ground amidst a puddle of white sheets. She died instantly.

Oddly enough, just three weeks before her death, Sallie Sue had said, "Children, three weeks from now you won't be happy as you are today." Her premonition proved to be prophetic. They were not happy again for a long, long time.

The dark days that followed were surreal for Johnny and his siblings. Had they known of aliens in those days, the children would have agreed that the term described their predicament perfectly. They belonged nowhere and to nobody. The papa they had known and loved had disappeared just as suddenly as their kind and gentle mother. Had they been older and wiser, the children might have understood to some extent how the shock of his wife's death had affected Ike, but the eight little ones didn't understand, and no one bothered to explain. It seems to be the corporate crime of the ages that children are left in the dark when family tragedies occur. The Hatcher brood was no different. They only knew their precious mama had gone from them in an instant and the man who was left to raise them was not their papa.

For some time following her death, Ike wondered around in a daze, nodding his head up or down if asked a yes or no question. But if the query required a more complicated reply, he only stared into the distance as if he couldn't quite grasp the situation. He ambled around in that state for weeks it seemed, gradually drinking a little more moonshine each evening as the sun went down on Sallie Sue's grave where he sat until it was dark and he was too drunk to find his way home. Back at the cabin, the children fell asleep watching out the window, waiting anxiously for their papa to come home and take care of them, wondering what happened to the man who used to tuck them in at night and dance with their mama in the light of the moon when he thought the children were fast asleep.

August, September, October and now November, the months had rolled agonizingly by, both father and children suffering more than they could possibly endure but none knowing how to reach out for help or comfort, particularly the father. He only knew to reach for the jar full of the clear liquid that burned his insides like a cleansing fire, somewhat dulling the unbearable pain in his heart.

Neighbors and kinfolk helped some, particularly in the days and weeks just following Sallie Sue's passing. At Sallie Sue's request at the time of her premonition, the baby was taken in by her brother and his wife. But most everyone in Cypress Creek, roughly eight miles from Beulah, was poor in those days, and they didn't have much to give. So by early November, the children were often hungry and had begun to look like little street urchins from the Dickens books their old grandfather used to read to them when he was alive.

But in the last few weeks, the most drastic change had evolved, climaxing just hours earlier when Ike Hatcher turned on his five-year-old son and threw the axe at him. He missed by only inches as the weapon slashed into the thick pine Johnny was hiding behind.

Maggie had wisely fled the scene, yelling "Run, Johnny, run!"

But Johnny couldn't run. He was paralyzed by fear, suddenly certain that his papa wanted to kill him as dead as his mama. But, why? Had he done something wrong? Why didn't his papa love him anymore? Why did his papa hate his children so?

Like all precious children in every generation who are the innocent victims of self-hate rooted in fear and shame, Johnny would never receive the answers to his unending questions. And like all the other innocent children, the unanswered questions would torment him all the days of his life, particularly the one written in bold at the end of the list, "What did I do that was so bad?"

But within tiny Johnny Hatcher and the brothers and sisters he would always feel responsible for, there was a seed sprouting that would grow into a giant tree from which could be made a raft to take them out from the Sea of Despair. Johnny whispered the seed's name now, over and over again as his heart pounded wildly. The crunch of his papa's footsteps treading closer and closer to his hiding place was a terrifying sound indeed.

"Jesus. Jesus. Jesus. Jesus," he whispered the Name out loud and then silently as the footsteps quickly approached, crunching the dead limbs and undergrowth in Ike's fury to get to the child whose only guilt was to be alive when his mother was dead. Even Ike himself had no idea that at least part of his anger stemmed from the fear of having to raise nine small children with no wife to help him. But Ike didn't know the Name, and so his grief and fear merged with the old childhood shame he had endured from his illegitimate birth and resulted in the sinister narcissism that invites violent rage.

But the Jesus Sallie Sue had introduced to her small son was there that dark day, right behind the tree with Johnny. And He saved him that day and throughout many more days to come.

Chapter Three

Like a flash of lightning on a hot summer night, the news was all over town. Not a week had gone by since Election Day, but the news was not political; it was criminal. More than likely, the entire county knew of the murder before Doc Williams arrived in the wee hours of the morning at the small run down shack back in the field just past Billy Goat's Corner. Corbett Thomas and his boys were waiting on the porch half asleep. Corbett was dozing in the only rocking chair, his two sons and a half dozen cousins and neighbors scattered from the porch to the wagons and buggies pulled up in front of the old weathered shack. Jack Thomas's two sons were keeping watch out by the road to Gander's Fork at their papa's orders, shotguns in hand, alert to any sights or sounds that could hint at more violence to come in the night.

"Who goes there?!" Abe Thomas shouted as Doc began to pull on the reins, easily turning the gentle mare toward the path that led up to the former slave's shack.

"Don't shoot, Abe! It's just me, Doc Williams."

"Sorry, Doc. Guess I've got the jitters out here by myself. Tom was getting sleepy, so he walked down the road a bit to wake himself up. I do believe this is the darkest, hottest November night I've ever seen."

"Where's Corbett and your daddy, Abe?"

"Uncle Corbett's up at the cabin with all the boys keepin' watch. Pa said to tell you he had to get some shut-eye; said he's too old for this kind of excitement."

The old man let out a long sigh, wondering to himself if the day would ever come when he could finally claim he was too old to keep these unholy working hours. Delia's sweet tea had given him the energy boost he had needed just to stay awake for the eight-mile ride to the Thomas farm. The pint Mason jar was lying empty on the seat beside him. Thank God for the old mare, Bertha. She knew every inch of every road on both sides of the Duplin/Onslow County line from Back Swamp to the Northeast Cape Fear River. All Doc had to do was stay put and give the reins a gentle tug when it came time to make a major turn. Bertha took care of the rest of the journey.

The faithful mare slowly clomped past Abe's post, pulling the squeaking, rattling buggy on up the narrow path. The night was still and quiet. It seemed even the crickets and frogs had gone to bed.

"Hey, Doc!" yelled Abe.

"Yeah?"

"Tell one of those lazy rascals to come take my place!"

"I'll do it!" Doc Samuel gave Abe a mock salute and chuckled, wondering if the boy had been at his watch even an hour. Shaking his white head, he asked old Bertha, "What's going to become of this younger generation?"

Evan heard Doc's buggy well before he could see it in the blackness of the night. He reached over and prodded his brother, Ned, then stood up to gently shake his father's shoulder.

"Pa," he whispered, then a little louder, "Papa! The Doc's here. I hear his buggy comin' up the path."

"Alright, son, I'm awake. Why don't you go out and greet our old friend."

Evan ambled down the steps and disappeared into the thick darkness as Corbett stood up and stretched, his arthritic joints snapping and crackling as if they were taking the place of the insects that should have been singing. What would he tell Samuel? The only fact he was sure of was that there was an old colored man lying dead on the kitchen floor just inside the cabin door, the bright red blood from his head wound seeping into the dry pine boards, creating a crimson stain that would memorialize his death as long as the old shack was left standing.

The small cabin, the last of the slave quarters on the old Thomas plantation, was located about a quarter mile from Jack Thomas's home. Jack and Corbett were in their sixties now. Earlier in the evening as they sat on the cabin porch together mourning the old man's passing, neither of them could recall a time when the former slave, old James, hadn't lived there. He had worked on the farm until he was too old for hard labor and then helped the women in the garden and did odd jobs until a day that no one seemed to remember when he began to rock the hours away playing a small hand organ and singing Negro spirituals and old ballads. Generations of Thomas children had been lured to the steps of the old cabin by the plaintive melodies and lively tunes old James pumped out of that small instrument. He had taught many a youngster how to pump the little round bellows in and out to get just the right pitch for the tunes they loved to hear.

Corbett stretched again and scratched his back as best he could, smiling at the cherished memories flooding his thoughts. My, how he had loved to dance the jigs old James taught him when he was a boy, right here on this squeaking old porch. In those days, the black man of indefinite age could pump and dance at the same time—sing, too. Oh, what a time they had! Well, for a while at least, until Corbett's ma found out. Ella Sloan Thomas was a Baptist, and it's a well-known fact in the South that Baptists don't dance; they don't even think about it.

"Now, who would want to kill old James?" Corbett whispered into the night.

Bertha pulled the black buggy up to the edge of the porch as if she recognized Doc Samuel's old friend and knew the Doc would want to visit with Corbett awhile. Ned grabbed her harness and, taking the reins from Samuel, he tied the leather straps loosely to the porch post while Evan jumped from the buggy to help the Doc climb down. Hardly moving a muscle during the eight-mile buggy ride in the middle of the night had left Samuel's joints stiff and swollen. But he would never complain—not then, not ever. Endurance went with the territory.

Samuel held onto the porch rail and climbed the steps before he looked into the weary eyes of his old comrade. "It's good to see you, Corbett, even on such a sad occasion."

"Yes, it's good to see you, too, Samuel." Corbett clasped his old friend's hand tightly.

"Tell me, Corbett. What happened here?"

"Nobody knows. Two of Jack's boys came home late, it being Saturday night, and heard shouting over here, but they couldn't make out the voices. Abe said he went on into the house and was about to get ready for bed when the shoutin' suddenly stopped. It was then he got real worried, wondering why anyone would be yelling at old James, especially that late at night. So he hurried over to the cabin to check on things. He found him right where he's still lying—on the kitchen floor with his head bashed in a pool of blood."

"I'm sorry, Corbett. I know you thought a lot of that old man." Samuel patted his friend's shoulder tenderly.

"Yes, he was special to all of us." Corbett's weary eyes brimmed with tears as he took Samuel's arm to show him into the house. "I sure hated to get you up on a night when you could have got some sleep, but I thought maybe, with your experience, you might see clues that we wouldn't readily observe. Of course, it was obvious that James was dead when Abe found him, but...well, I just wanted you to see him, Samuel."

"Don't apologize, Corbett. I'm glad to be of help."

The two white-haired men stopped still at the bare feet of the dead man. Samuel silently thanked the Good Lord that the old man's eyes were shut. In forty years practicing medicine which, of course, included pronouncing more deaths than he could count, Samuel never got used to the cold, blank stare of death. He hated it—death, that is. Time and again, he'd sit in the old worn chair which he could hardly get out of these days reading his Bible, turning by habit to the verse that read, "O Death, where is thy sting? O grave, where is thy victory?" It was one of those verses that, at times like these, didn't seem to make much sense.

Samuel slowly bent his aching knees to kneel down beside the cold body. "Did it look as if the house was broken into?"

"No, but like most people around here, I'm sure old James never locked his door. More than likely, the doors have never seen a lock, but I'll check."

"Any sign of fighting? Anything broken?"

"No, no signs of anything going on except James's dead body with his skull bashed in."

"What about the murder weapon?"

"We didn't find one. What do you think it was, Samuel?"

"Hmm. It was either a very powerful weapon like the side of a sledge hammer or a mighty strong person using a less potent tool, maybe an iron frying pan or something like that. You can easily see that a sharp instrument wasn't used. It was large and blunt, but terribly hard."

Samuel continued to examine the body. "Hmm...strange."

"What? What's strange?" asked Corbett.

"You told me Abe heard a lot of shouting that ended abruptly just before he ran over here. Isn't that right?"

Corbett nodded. "We all assumed James was arguing with some-body and that somebody must have killed him."

"That's what I thought, too, but...well…there are two problems with that theory. James was hit from behind. Of course, he could have turned around, but that doesn't seem likely. My bet would be he didn't know it was coming. Also, James was an unusually old man. I'd say close to a hundred years old if not more, don't you think?" Samuel continued without waiting for Corbett's reply. "There's no way his voice could have been heard a quarter mile away at his very loudest. That means at least two men were here in the heat of the argument and whether or not old James was involved, he got the bad end of the deal. My guess is that he was dead when the shouting started."

"What else?"

"How did you know there's something else?" Samuel glanced up at his old friend.

"You have that puzzled look on your face I've seen a hundred times before, like you're worried about something you don't understand."

"You got that right. Do you see the expression on old James's face, Corbett?"

"Actually, I've tried not to look too closely."

"Well, either take a look or I can tell you. He's almost smiling. There's just no way he could have had any idea he was about to die a violent death."

Chapter Four

By the time the election results came in on Tuesday afternoon, the weather had turned cold, the fire in the wood stove in Nate's store was blazing hot, the Democrats were in shock and Laney Gresham had slowly and painfully produced a six-and-a-half-pound baby girl. Beulah's Democrats were an angry, defeated lot, but a grinning Nate Gresham stood behind the counter handing out the cheapest cigars he could find to the friends and customers who came in all during the day. Most came by to argue the election results and speculate on who killed old James, but some actually made a few purchases while congratulating the proud papa.

Since Laney's mother had passed on a few years earlier of pneumonia, Nate had sent for Sarah Jane Gresham when his wife's time came. And even though some folks judged her to be a bit young, Hannah had obediently accompanied her mother to the birthing room.

The practical-minded Sarah Jane was not clairvoyant as her daughters sometimes suspected, but she did have a gift. She seemed to see deeper inside a person than most people. She saw who they were and, better yet, who they were meant to be. Within her second daughter, Sarah Jane saw one who was meant to comfort and to heal. She recognized it early on when Hannah took care of the younger girls when sickness came and, more specifically, when Sarah Jane herself needed care after the birth of the two youngest girls. Hannah was a natural-born nurse, and the best thing her mother knew to do to enrich an innate gifting was to follow the Good Book's advice, "Raise up a child in the way he should go and when he is old, he will not depart from it." She saw the way her child should go, and she raised her and trained her the best way she knew how—on the job.

While her mother gently bathed Laney, giving her strict orders to stay in bed for nine days following the birth, Hannah held the newborn baby in her arms, humming contentedly as she wrapped her in the soft receiving blanket she had warmed by the hot wood stove out in the store. Before she laid the little bundle next to the weak but ecstatic mother, she kissed the tiny head one more time, breathing in that special sweet fragrance that only new life can give.

"Here she is, Laney, all clean and shiny now. Smells good, too."

"Ohh, my...," whispered the new mother weakly. "She is beautiful, isn't she?"

"Of course, she is." answered Sarah Jane with a knowing smile. "She's the most beautiful baby in the world." She looked at Hannah and winked.

Laney didn't notice. Her eyes were still glued to her baby's face. "I'll bet all your new mothers say that, don't they?"

"Well, it's only natural that a mother sees her child as beautiful," replied the voice of wisdom and experience.

Hannah was still standing by the bed, smiling down at Laney and the baby. "But she is especially beautiful, isn't she, Mama?"

"Yes, she is child. I'll tell you both a little secret. We midwives seem to have the same distorted vision our new mothers have."

The three females laughed knowingly as Sarah Jane and Hannah gathered up the pans of wash water to take outside now that Laney and the baby were clean and snug and ready for male company. Hannah poured the water into a bucket and pushed open the door to the little sitting room. Making sure the coast was clear of male onlookers, she quickly slipped out the door and hurried down the long porch and around to the back of the store before anyone could see her. When she approached the outhouse, she hurried around back and threw the bloody bath water over the ditch and into the woods.

Her load lightened, Hannah took a deep breath of the cold November air. It felt good. She had been inside too long. Slowly, she strolled back to the house, swinging the empty bucket and humming a livelier tune than what was in her usual repertoire. She felt good.

Better than good, actually. Since her mother had allowed Hannah to help with birthings this past year, her eyes were opening to an entirely new world than that of girlish chatter and what often seemed like silly prattle with her sisters and cousins.

The whole process of birth was frightening, that was for sure, even for girls who were used to helping little ones come into the world. However, the birth was not half as frightening as the tales she'd heard about how the baby was conceived to begin with. That was something she just didn't want to think about—not now, not ever if she could help it. Of course, one day she would have to think about it, but for now, she'd leave those wild speculations to the remainder of the Gresham girls as they giggled while whispering incredible tales of human beings acting like animals in the wild. Certainly, nothing could be further from the truth. She was sure of that.

But helping to bring a baby into the world was another matter altogether. It was nothing short of a miracle—certainly, the greatest miracle of all. Hannah felt especially blessed to be a part. It was as if she had been given a gift. Each time she witnessed the miracle, she felt closer to the God who brought it all to pass. Yes, she wholeheartedly agreed with her wise mother. This was what she was born for.

Hannah rounded the corner of the building that served as home and livelihood for Nate and Laney, pausing again to take another deep breath of the crisp fall air that always filled her heart with an excitement she didn't understand. Like Kate, Hannah well remembered long childhood days when she and her family traveled to the sparsely populated crossroads to visit Uncle Willis T. and Aunt Margaret and her cousins. There had been no more than three or four homes by the road as far as the eye could see. Now, there were houses all up and down the wide dirt road, plus a small schoolhouse, a couple of stores, a post office and a livery stable dotting the flat landscape. There was even a bank now down near the school house, although hardly anyone had money to put in it. Those who did certainly weren't about to trust a banker with their hard earned cash. A Mason jar buried deep in the earth was thought to be much safer…and it probably was.

"Hannah! Hannah!"

She was just about to climb the steps to the porch when she heard Jessie calling her name from down the street. Hannah walked out to the road and waved at the excited young girl running her way.

"Hannah! We just heard about Laney's baby! Mama's coming later, but can I see her now? Please?"

"I'm sure Laney won't mind, but I'd better ask first. Wait right here 'til I get back."

"I'll wait, but hurry!"

Hannah quickly climbed the few steps leading up to the porch and went inside the house. Before Jessie had time to grow too impatient, she was back with the verdict.

"Come on in, Jess. Laney and Mama said you could see the baby, but you can't hold her, just in case you have germs or something worse."

"I don't have germs! Why, Mama would faint if I had a germ!"

"Well, you never know, and we can't take any chances with newborn babies. Just look at her, okay?"

"Okay, but if I run home and wash, can I hold her then?"

"I'm sure Laney will let you hold her when she's ready. Come on in."

Jessie followed her cousin into the small sitting room and on into the bedroom, wondering why, even though they were close to the same age, Hannah always seemed so much older than she was. Although she was quiet and unassuming, Hannah appeared mature and in control. But Jessie wasn't jealous. Actually, she admired her cousin more than she would probably admit. Jessie was happy to let Hannah take the lead in serious matters, knowing that her cousin would gladly follow her when it came to socializing. That was her area of expertise.

"Oh, my, she's just beautiful," exclaimed Jessie quietly as she gazed down at the little bundle in the crook of Laney's arm.

"Well, Jessie, you make the vote unanimous." Laney laughed but very weakly. "We all think she's beautiful."

There was a knock on the door. Sarah Jane walked over to crack it open and peek out to see who was there. "Nate, you can come back in now. Everything's in order, and Laney and the baby are ready to welcome visitors, especially the proud papa."

Nate crossed the small room in about two long strides and quickly pulled up the only chair in the room close to the bed. Later that day, Jessie told her family that he seemed to have a grin stuck on his face so that if someone had come in and told him his store was being robbed, he'd have kept right on grinning. Pulling the baby's blanket away from her tiny face with one hand and grabbing Laney's hand with the other, Nate reached down and softly kissed the baby's forehead. Then he gave Laney a big smack right on the mouth. Jessie giggled aloud and quickly covered her mouth with her hand. Hannah, deeply embarrassed by the sudden show of intimacy, turned away and began to fold the clothes she had taken off the clothesline for Laney earlier in the afternoon. Sarah Jane quietly patted Jessie on the shoulder and motioned for her and Hannah to follow her into the sitting room so the little family could have some privacy.

"You did good, Laney," whispered Nate, staring at his exhausted wife and new baby as if he couldn't get enough of them.

"Thank you much, Nate," she whispered back, glowing like the full moon. "You're not disappointed I didn't give you a boy?"

"What? Are you crazy, Laney? There's plenty of time for boys. I got me a princess!"

"You're a good man, Nate Gresham."

"And you're a smart woman, Miss Laney."

The new mother laughed weakly, more tired than she had expected from her recent ordeal.

"What do you want to name her?" Nate opened the bottom of the blanket to count the baby's toes.

"Well, I was thinking we might name her after your mama and mine—Elizabeth Carolina Gresham. What do you think?"

"Seems to me that's an awful lot of name for such a tiny baby."

"We could name her Elizabeth Carolina and just call her Lizzy. How's that?"

Nate lay his head down next to the baby and spoke softly into her tiny ear. Hmm...Lizzy. Are you a Lizzy, little one?"

At just that moment the baby opened her little mouth wide with a big yawn, delighting Nate and Laney to no end with the confirmation that she was indeed a little Lizzy, happy and content with her new name and her mama and papa. You couldn't have found a happier household in Beulah that day, or even all of Duplin County.

Jessie meandered slowly down the side of the wide road towards home, kicking hard clumps of dirt as she mulled over mental pictures she had saved of Laney and her baby. Nate, too, of course. The romance of it all sent her mind soaring on flights of fantasy. To be married to the man of one's dreams with a beautiful baby to boot was Jessie Gresham's idea of the most wonderful life a girl could possibly have.

Holding her blue gingham frock up over her ankles, she ran to the other side of the wide road, all the while jumping deep wagon ruts and mud holes as if she were playing a game of hopscotch all by herself. She didn't notice Big Rufus Bostic until she found herself in front of the Jackson house on the other side of the road, and then she was so embarrassed she could hardly speak. And that was a first for Jessie Gresham. What if he had seen her kicking dirt and jumping mud holes like a child and here she was sixteen years old? Why, just the thought was enough to turn her face a hundred shades of pink.

"Hello, Jessie," said Rufus, shyly.

"Well, hel...lo....., Rufus," she stuttered.

"Where you goin'?"

Jessie's face lit up again. "Back home. I've been to see Laney's new baby."

"Oh." Rufus wasn't sure young men were supposed to discuss babies and such, and even if it was okay, he had no idea what to say, so he quickly changed the subject before he waded in too deep and couldn't find a way out.

"Hey, Jessie, want to go with me to the Thanksgivin' dance at the River Barn next week?"

Jessie stared up at the tall young man, wondering how in the world she had gotten into such a predicament in such a short amount of time. But at least it was obvious she hadn't made a fool of herself kicking dirt and jumping mud puddles. Oh, yes, she wanted to go to the dance, of course she did, but Jessie had never actually been courting and had no idea if her mama and papa would allow it. Many girls her age were close to marrying, but Jessie's parents were more particular than most when it came to their daughters' future spouses. Kate could vouch for that.

"I'll have to ask Papa."

"Alright. Can I walk you home?"

"*May* I walk you home?" Jessie quickly corrected him.

Margaret Gresham, Jessie's mother, had recently given her daughters a lecture on correct grammar, a subject dear to her heart. She just could not abide what she considered the greatest weakness of the area's population—the mutilation of the English language.

"That's what I said, Jess."

"Oh, forget it, and no, you mustn't walk me home. Papa might not like it."

"Then how will I know if you can go with me to the dance?"

"I'll let you know at church on Sunday, how's that?"

"You know I don't go to church, Jessie."

"Well, it's high time you did!"

And with that, Jessie skipped off down the side of the road towards home but quickly thought how childish that might look. So she slowed down to a stroll and lifted her head high, wishing she had eyes in the back of her head like her mama so she could see if Big Rufus was looking at her. If he wasn't, she was wasting a lot of time acting like a lady when she didn't have to.

Chapter Five

"Hannah," said her mother quietly. Sarah Jane was resting in the rocker by the wood stove while Nate enjoyed a few private moments with his wife and newborn daughter. "The labor was long and hard, it being her first baby, but Laney's actually doing very well. She's just worn out, that's all. So, I'm thinkin' it would be best for you to stay and help her a few days and I'll go on back home where I'm needed the most. Laney and the baby don't need any special nursin', just lots of rest so the new mother can gain her strength back. All the baby needs is to be kept clean and fed. She needs lots of love, of course, but I'm sure Laney and Nate will take care of that. If you were to need me, Nate can send one of the Brinson boys to fetch me. Now, if Laney were to start bleedin' or hurting bad or anything like that, you send Nate over to get Doctor Kennedy fast."

The bright light in Hannah's soft blue eyes spoke louder than words. Her mother's trust was worth more than silver or gold. "We'll be just fine, Mama."

"Of course you will," replied Sarah Jane with a smile.

"But how will you get home?" asked Hannah.

"I sent Jeb word by Clyde Thomas. He was on his way to see Nell. Your Papa ought to be here before long to check on us and see how things are going. He expects to take one of us back to the farm this evenin'. Now, you're sure you'll be comfortable here by yourself?"

"Yes, Mama. I'll do my best to keep Laney in bed as much as possible, and I know how to bind her chest if she gets fever. I'll keep both patients real clean like you taught me, and I'll make sure Laney eats good."

"Let her get up some to keep her blood circulating and all, but make sure you keep her bedded down for nine days. If she does get up, don't let her do heavy work of any kind. She mustn't pull anything inside so as to allow for complete healing before her days get back to normal." Sarah Jane chuckled. "Don't know why I used that word," she said. "That girl will never know normal again as long as she lives."

Hannah laughed as Nate slowly opened the bedroom door and quietly shut it behind him.

"They're both asleep," he almost whispered, still glowing in his new fatherhood.

"That's good," replied Sarah Jane. "They need the rest. Hannah and I'll cook up some supper for you before Jeb gets here."

She pushed herself up from the rocker and reached around to knead the small of her back. "Nate, Laney's doing so good that I'm going to let Hannah stay with her for a few days. If all goes well, and I'm sure it will, Laney will gain strength each new day and be up and tending to this household before you know it."

"That's a relief." Nate huffed a sigh. "She seems so weak and tired. I've been a mite worried, I'll have to admit."

"She'll be fine, Nate."

Sarah Jane started out to the kitchen to begin preparing supper. As she passed the concerned young husband, she paused long enough to lay her hand gently on his arm. "You'll be fine, too, Nate. You're a good man, and you'll be a good father to your children. Lizzy is blessed to have you for her papa."

Tears suddenly welled up in Nate's eyes. Embarrassed, he quickly turned away and began to stoke the fire. The warmth radiated throughout the small room.

Hannah peeked in on Laney and the baby. Seeing they were still fast asleep, she followed her mother out to the porch and into the separate kitchen. In less than thirty minutes, the tantalizing aromas of sugar cured ham and buttermilk biscuits were drifting back down the porch and into the store where Nate was nodding by the fire. It had been a long hard twenty-four-hour labor for him as well,

although he had no idea he was so tired until he plopped down in the
rocker to wait for supper and rest his eyes a spell.

Nate Gresham was a good-looking young man of twenty-seven—
the long and lanky type, Laney always said—and a hard-working
man as well, far from the category of humanity that Greshams in
general disliked the most—lazy people. Lazy was worse than being
a Republican! Not that all Greshams were Democrats, but they were
careful to keep it to themselves if they weren't.

Nate's mama and papa had passed on quite a few years earlier
when the scarlet fever hit, long years before he and Laney were
married or even knew one another. Oddly enough in those days,
Nate was an only child as well. And even though he was a little old
at fifteen to be considered an orphan, his winning personality and
warm smile gained him the hospitality of aunts and uncles on nearby
farms. So for the first few years after his parents died, he migrated
from home to home, working for one Gresham household for a few
months, then moving on to the next.

Though Nate's parents had suddenly left him alone in the world
at a young age, they did not leave him without an inheritance. When
his grandfather, Thomas Gresham, died in 1881, he left an extensive
will, dividing up over twenty-five-hundred acres between his five
sons. Each one must have come into around five-hundred acres or
so, and Nate's father, Edward Gresham, inherited the land between
what was now the main road running through Beulah and the thickets
of Limestone Swamp, a mile or so north.

By the time Nate saved up enough money working for his kin
to start out on his own, he had wisely come to the conclusion that
he was not cut out for farming. He figured the best thing he could
do would be to sell a few hundred acres of his inheritance to his
cousins and use the money to build and operate a small dry goods
and produce store in the midst of the fast-growing community. The
acreage he kept for himself just happened to be in the perfect loca-
tion, smack dab in the center of the community that had slowly
grown to become the small village of Beulah.

About a month before Nate finished building the store, he finally
noticed the pretty green-eyed girl who had been eyeing him for years,
secretly coordinating visits with her Gresham girlfriends to coincide

with wherever Nate was living at the time. The determined young lady had endured many a barn dance and church picnic desperately longing for her Prince Charming to wake up and realize that Laney Hunter was his future Cinderella. Alas, by the time she turned nineteen on April 8, 1898, Laney had almost given up hope…almost. And then, one day, in one split second, it happened. But not the way she had dreamed.

Although the Hunter family lived only a quarter of a mile down the main road to the east, Laney and her father had taken the old buggy to the post office to mail a letter her mother had written to her sister in New Bern. Bill Hunter had promised his only child, born in his latter years, that after they mailed her mother's letter, he would take the day off for her birthday. Whatever she wanted to do from there on out was fine with him. He had been hoping she'd choose fishing for crappie in the river, but when she came to the breakfast table all fancied up, he just smiled and told her how pretty she was. All the way to the post office, Laney pondered her options. She felt like a princess in the new lavender flowered dress her mama had made.

There was always a crowd hanging about the small unpainted building that served the community's postal needs. That particular day in 1898, it being nothing short of the most beautiful spring day Laney ever remembered before or since, the crowd was unusually large. Amos Gresham was the postmaster at the time and Nate, at Amos's wife's request, had stopped by the post office on his way to the store to take his uncle a plate of fried chicken, pickled beets, early squash, and of course, rice and gravy, along with a jug of spring water. Laney had become adept at conniving random meetings with her intended, but on April 8, 1898, at eleven o'clock in the morning, she had no idea that timing and destiny were about to meet head on.

Bill Hunter whistled twice and tugged the reins gently. The gray mare turned smoothly into the muddy area in front of the post office, made even worse than usual by the heavy spring rains that year. The buggy bounced violently a time or two, but the strong mare pulled it easily through the worst of the mud holes and on up to the hitching post in front of the small weathered building.

"Bill! Bill Hunter!" Corbett Thomas was coming out of the post office just as they pulled up. He hurried over to greet Laney's father as quickly as possible, considering his recent bout with rheumatism.

"Good morning, Corbett! Why, I've not seen you in a month of Sundays." Bill reached down to shake Corbett's hand, genuinely happy to see his old friend.

"You're a sight for sore eyes, Bill Hunter. How's Miss Lura?"

"She's a mite feeble these days, but I'm sure she'll perk up now that summer's almost upon us. How's Celie?"

"Oh, she's fine; she's fine. Wish you'd bring Lura to visit one of these nice Sunday afternoons."

"Lura would like that. It's hard to believe we live within a mile of one another and hardly ever get to visit."

Now, all the while her father had been chatting with Corbett, Laney had been tapping him on the shoulder, trying to get his attention so he would climb on down from the buggy while he talked and help her down as well. It wouldn't have been ladylike for her to have climbed down herself, but she was getting further and further behind on her socializing by the minute. But her daddy was paying her no mind at all; so finally, she had been patient as long as she could stand it and quickly decided to take matters into her own hands. She had no idea that Nate Gresham was within a mile of the place.

Pulling her dress up as far as modesty and decorum would allow, Laney held on to the side of the buggy and lifted one leg to step down onto the running board. But about the time her foot was in midair on its way down, her father turned and saw what was she was up to.

"Laney Hunter!" he yelled suddenly, so suddenly it scared her half to death.

She never could remember exactly what happened from that second to the moment she was lying flat on her back in a big mud hole, looking straight up into Nate Gresham's handsome face. But it didn't matter what transpired beforehand because that's when it happened. Nate suddenly woke up and saw her silky, wheat-colored hair streaked with gold all disheveled and floating in the same black mud that smeared her face and soaked her new lavender flowered dress.

In the midst of deciding upon the correct response to the horrendous situation—vacillating between crying, screaming or just pretending she was dead—Nate's sudden revelation broke his face into the most radiant smile she could have ever imagined. And that was the end of that. Laney Hunter just lifted her head out of the mud and kissed Nate Gresham right on the mouth, stunning her already anxious father and sending the remainder of the crowd into belts of laughter or else gasps of disbelief.

The marriage ceremony took place just three months later.

Chapter Six

Even though she had gotten little sleep with a hungry newborn to attend to, Hannah was up before sunrise and dressed for the day. Her attire, the best she had, was a long-sleeved green calico dress, gathered slightly at the waist and flowing to her ankles. It was covered by a clean white apron tied at her waist. If cleanliness was next to Godliness, there was no doubt that neatness followed close behind, her mother often said.

Laney and the baby had taken to nursing as easily as breathing, and so thankfully, one of the concerns of postpartum care was marked off Sarah Jane's list fairly quickly. Laney would be sore, that was to be expected, but the most serious problem, and the most frustrating to the mother, usually came when the baby was either too small or too weak to suck. Lizzy was neither small nor weak, praise the Lord! She looked like a plump little cherub already.

No need to worry about that, thought Hannah as she walked into the kitchen and saw that Nate had already stoked the wood stove and made it ready to cook breakfast.

The door creaked as he slipped in quickly and shut it behind him, blocking out the chill. "Good mornin', Cousin Hannah!"

"Mornin', Nate," she said shyly. "You must be hungry. I'll have breakfast ready in a few minutes."

"Now, Miss Hannah, you didn't come here to wait on me. I'm not about to wear you out so you can't take care of Laney and little Lizzy. You go on in to them, and I'll cook breakfast. I took care of myself a long time before I was lucky enough to wed Laney Hunter."

"That's alright, Nate. The new mother and baby are sleeping soundly this morning, and I'm more than happy to cook breakfast for everybody. Anyway, I'm hungry, too, and I'm not quite as confident as you regardin' your cooking skills."

Hannah actually produced a tiny smile, hinting to Nate that she was teasing. Relieved that the overly serious young woman would actually venture to joke around a little, Nate acquiesced with a smile and told her he'd be minding the store if she needed him for anything.

Hannah quickly and competently prepared the morning meal just as her mother would have done had she been there. She had been cooking since she was ten or eleven and hardly even thought twice about it anymore. Nate had already sliced the smoked ham with the long sharp butcher knife now lying on the side of the cutting block. Placing the heavy black iron pan folks called a "spider" on the hot burner, she laid the ham slices neatly in it, throwing in a dab of lard to help the ham fry a more golden brown and produce stronger flavored gravy.

Glancing out the window toward the old still, standing dark and forbidding across the wide dirt road, Hannah sifted a few handfuls of flour into the long wooden mixing tray used for kneading biscuits or bread. Next, she plopped one large handful of lard into an indention she had made in the flour and then began to pour fresh buttermilk into the mixture. After mixing, then kneading the dough a few minutes until it felt and looked just right, Hannah formed it into a long fat roll and began to pinch wads off the end and roll them into perfectly formed round biscuits. Then she placed the biscuits neatly in the long tin pan. Just before she set the pan of plump biscuits in the hot oven to cook, she added her final touch, her signature, if you will. She pressed the middle three fingers of her right hand gently into the top of each biscuit which, in a matter of about fifteen minutes, was destined to absolutely melt in Nate Gresham's mouth.

The oven door slammed with a loud bang, the biscuits safe inside. Hannah turned to open the kitchen door to walk out on the porch a few minutes before she fried the eggs in the hot ham drippings. She would need to add water later to create the thin ham gravy. The grits were already done and sitting on the stove to keep warm.

"Hmm," she sighed, taking a deep breath of the crisp November morning air, her arms wrapped tightly about her shoulders. She could see the kerosene lamp shining through the windows of the Jackson house across the road and the smoke rising from the chimney. Down the road a bit, signs of early morning life began to emanate from the few houses scattered all along the dirt road, offering Hannah a sense of community she had never experienced growing up on the remote Hall farm.

This is good for me, she thought, suddenly realizing her mother had known that all along. She smiled as she thought of mama and papa and her sisters who were even now stirring about their warm kitchen in preparation for the new day. But she wasn't homesick. No, sometimes she felt a little lonely, but all in all, she knew the Good Lord had prepared her for this, her life's work, and she was satisfied, content to be what she was meant to be. She wondered if she would ever marry and have her own family. Perhaps not. She would just have to wait and see.

The morning stars beamed their brightest and then slowly faded into the dark sky, gloriously upstaged by the first light of dawn. Hannah loved this moment. There was none other like it throughout the day. It was as if God was creating once again—a new day, a new life, a new beginning. She pulled her gaze from the heavens to watch the kerosene lanterns flickering through the windows of the small homes scattered along the road. The lights of man were nothing compared to that of his Creator, she mused. But the light of lanterns and fires flickering in each home gave Hannah opportunity to think about friends and cousins her age who were beginning to find their life partners. Some, like Kate, had married already. But Hannah wasn't jealous. She would accept her lot, whatever it was.

The aroma of freshly baked biscuits interrupted the girl's morning reverie, suddenly reminding her of the tasks at hand. She rushed into the kitchen to the sudden sound of little Lizzy bellowing for her breakfast at the exact moment the biscuits had to be taken out of the oven and the ham removed from the spider. It was then she remembered she hadn't yet fried the eggs Nate had retrieved from the backyard hen house.

"Maybe I'm not as ready to do this on my own as I thought," Hannah mumbled as she pulled the pan from the oven and nearly threw it on the butcher block. She took a rag and pulled the hot spider from the burner and left it there to hurry out on the porch and into the sitting room yelling, "I'm comin', Laney! Don't get up!"

✖

Around seven thirty that morning, Nate was in the store taking inventory when the door burst open and Deputy Sheriff Ben Jones strode in like he was the President of the United States. Abe Thomas and Eck Williams, one of Doc Samuel's sons, followed close behind, looking to be a bit upset by the deputy's attitude but very serious about whatever was going on.

"Howdy, Nate," said Abe.

Eck touched the tip of his hat to echo Abe's greeting, but the deputy just stood there looking like a strutting rooster, slightly overweight and wearing a big hat.

"Good morning, boys," replied Nate. "Did you know I have me a new baby girl?"

All three men softened at that. Even Ben Jones hinted at a smile.

"Congratulations, Nate!" said Abe, reaching out to shake the new father's hand.

"Yeah, Nate, congratulations," said Eck with a shy smile. He had two small children of his own, having married Pansy Weston from Potter's Hill a few years ago.

"I'd offer you a cigar, but I'm all out," said Nate, still grinning. "But you boys look like you're on a mission. What can I do for you this fine mornin'?"

At that, pausing to rethink what they had come to say, the men instantly regained their sober countenances.

"We're here about the killin', Nate," said the Deputy, as loud as he was big.

Nate wasn't sure why they had come to see him, so he said nothing.

Abe filled in the gaps. "Old James...hmm...well, I'll be. I never thought about James not having a last name until right this minute. I guess he woulda been a Thomas, wouldn't he? Him having been a Thomas slave before the War? Anyway, you know that old James was killed two nights ago, Nate—just before the weather turned. Yeah," Abe continued, "he was murdered right there in that old shack he's lived in for no tellin' how many years."

"Uh huh, I did hear about it, boys, but with Laney giving birth and all, I'm sorry to say I haven't had time to think much about it. I sure am sorry to hear he died that way, Abe. He was a good man, and I know your family thought a lot of him."

"Yeah, it was terrible...." Abe paused as if he had more to say but found it too hard. He looked down at the counter. "I'm the one who found him."

Nate wondered if he glimpsed a tear in the young man's eyes, but before he had a chance to think more about it or reply to Abe's sad confession, Ben Jones butted in.

"Now, listen up, Nate. It's a known fact that the men in this community gather 'round your wood stove to talk over whatever's going on 'round here. I want you to be all eyes and ears from now on. Listen to what's being said about this murder. I can't believe you didn't listen to the talk yesterday, new baby or no." The deputy bristled at Nate's obvious neglect of community responsibility.

"Sorry, Ben, but it's not every day my wife has a baby." Nate's smile didn't look too genuine. His eyes were a bit squinted, and his jaw was clinched.

Abe and Eck smiled guardedly from behind the deputy's back while Nate wondered if the county's number two law enforcement officer had ever been happy about anything.

"Give me a bag of those roasted peanuts, boy," demanded the deputy.

Nate quickly obliged. As he handed Ben the small brown bag, he said, "That'll be three cents, deputy."

The rooster puffed up; this time more like a bull frog. It was as if he considered himself too important a person to have to pay. Throwing three pennies on the counter, he turned and strutted out of the store, chomping on a mouthful of freshly parched ground peas.

Eck shrugged his shoulders and followed him out, leaving Abe lingering quietly behind.

"Is he really going to do anything about old James's murder, Abe?"

"I don't know. You never can tell. I guess it's according to who he's talking to. When he's talking to Pa or Uncle Corbett, he's all sympathetic and determined to find the man who did such a terrible thing. But just yesterday I heard him talkin' to some of the other deputies and you'd a thought he was the head of the Ku Klux Klan. He said something like, 'What's the big deal? Another nigger's dead, and it was way past his time.'"

"Yeah, that's what I thought," replied Nate, looking as grim as Eck and Abe by then.

Eck popped his head back in the doorway. "Come on, Abe. We've got to make sure this job's done right."

"I'm comin'. See you later, Nate."

"See you, Abe."

By the time Nate finished the inventory, all the while pondering the early morning visit from the deputy sheriff, his stomach was rumbling from hunger. Wondering what happened to breakfast, he strolled across the porch, entered the sitting room and then walked on toward the bedroom. It was a bit strange having to knock on his own bedroom door, but having seen how easily embarrassed Hannah could be, he certainly didn't want to make matters worse for her while she was helping out.

Tap! Tap! He gently knocked on the door just in case the baby was asleep.

"Come on in, Nate," answered Laney weakly. "Miss Lizzy has eaten more than her fill, and Hannah's cleaning her up. Come see your beautiful princess this morning. It's her second day on earth, you know."

Hannah smiled at Nate for a second and then, with a start, she exclaimed, "Oh, no! I forgot all about breakfast when I came to check on the baby and Laney! You must be starving!"

"Don't worry, Cousin Hannah. I'm a healthy man, too healthy to starve from breakfast being a bit late. Here, let me hold the baby some. I won't hurt her, I promise."

Hannah blushed from head to toe. "I know you won't hurt her, Nate. It's just that Mama says some papas don't know what to do with a tiny baby. Most don't even want to try."

"Well, I do, so you go on and finish breakfast, and I'll nuss little Lizzy and keep a watch on Miss Laney for you, okay?"

"Alright," she answered, somewhat reluctantly. "I'll have food on the table in a jiffy. Better yet, why don't I just bring it in here and you and Laney can have breakfast together? If anyone comes in the store, they'll ring the bell and I'll run help them." Hannah was beaming with her great idea.

"I'd like that, Cousin Hannah. I'd sure like that. How about you, Miss Laney?"

Laney was smiling broadly, her gaze riveted on the picture before her. Her precious new baby girl lovingly held and protected in the arms of her beloved husband. She wondered if it was possible to die of happiness.

Jessie's mama and papa didn't allow her to go to the dance with Big Rufus Bostic as he had hoped, but they had agreed for her to go with her sisters and brothers. Not surprisingly, at the last minute, Margaret and Willis T. had decided to go, too. Dances in those days were community affairs involving young and old alike. Everyone enjoyed them...except a few of the strictest Baptists who stayed home. The square dances were fine opportunities for smitten young people to court under the watchful eyes of their parents and the scrutiny of the entire community.

The excitement in the air exploded as the fiddle player hit the first note of the evening, setting toes to tapping, feet to dancing and hands to clapping. The talented fiddler, along with a couple of guitars and a hand accordion, filled the huge barn with one lively tune after the other, exhilaration rising as the night wore on. Sweating until her straight black hair was wet as water, Jessie danced the night away, first with her cousins and brothers and then with Big Rufus. She had to admit he wasn't the best dancer in the community, but Jessie didn't care about that. She had enough dancing in her feet for the both of them, and it looked as though she set about to prove it right off. Big Rufus just did whatever Jessie did or followed the instructions of old Jule Williford who untiringly called all the square dances. A night like that was what Jessie Gresham was born for. Yes, sir, it was her cup of tea.

That dance sparked a flame between spry little Jessie Gresham and Big Rufus Bostic that continued to burn bright all through the fall during tobacco tyings, pea shellings and quite a few more dances down at the big barn near the river. Her parents, having gone through such a difficult time with Kate, were a bit more lax with their younger daughter, even though they considered her much too young for Rufus Bostic. If he was still interested when she was a little older, they would seriously consider giving their blessing, but not now.

As for Jessie, she gladly admitted she was too young. She would have been apt to shy away from a serious relationship with anyone because of her sister's unhappy situation anyway. She was sure she loved Rufus Bostic, but why be so serious now? There would be plenty of time for all that when she was a bit older. In the meantime, she was free to have fun with Rufus at dances and other social events while enjoying the nearly constant companionship of her sisters, cousins and friends in between. Besides, Jessie Gresham loved to talk, and it was a known fact that Big Rufus wasn't the chattiest fellow in town. She might love him, but that didn't mean she looked forward to days on end with no one to talk to but Big Rufus. Her daddy assured her that the boy would be willing to wait for Jessie if he truly loved her, and Jessie assured her pa that Rufus's love for her was apparent to anyone with one eye and half sense.

Chapter Seven

As Abe Thomas discussed with Nate the morning he dropped by the store with Eck Williams and the deputy sheriff, Ben Jones had absolutely no set values by which he planned to go about the investigation of old James's murder. In explaining his dilemma, one might say his intentions could be summed up in one precise statement: He would coordinate the investigation in whatever manner would best insure his political future. Whether or not that goal led to the truth about James's killer was of little consequence compared to the most important matter at hand—Deputy Jones's career.

"I can't stand that man!" declared Kate. She was standing by the roadside with her hands on her hips, stamping one foot and glaring at the deputy as he strutted away to interview another blissfully innocent potential voter who hadn't a clue about the murder.

"Who does he think he is? And who does he think he's fooling with all that 'poor old James' stuff? He doesn't give a hoot about that old man and anybody with one eye and half sense can see right through him, fat as he is!"

"He's just doing his duty, Kate," said Doctor Kennedy calmly. "Come on in now. I'll need your help in the office today."

"I'll be there in a minute," she snapped, her eyes spitting fire at the deputy as he walked on down the road toward the bank and the barber shop. Then she spun around to glare at her husband's back as he climbed the steps and entered their new house that included two rooms on the front for his medical practice—one for the waiting room and the other for examining patients. For now, his office was anywhere he could find a place to sit down and work on his reports.

"Men!" she exclaimed under her breath, careful that the doctor didn't hear her. Kate already knew just how far to go with her new husband. But she wasn't afraid of him...not exactly. She wasn't about to admit that she was afraid of anybody. But there was no doubt their temperaments were about as opposite as night and day, and she had already pushed him a little too far on more than one occasion. After two months of marriage, it had become obvious to Kate that the doctor, as she would always call him, believed patience was the greatest of all virtues. He took great pride in staying calm and cool no matter what the circumstance. He didn't want his feathers ruffled and was nothing short of stunned to find out, after only three days of marriage to Kate, that his lovely bride excelled in feather ruffling, his and most everyone else's. What's more, she didn't seem to care, and that left a wound in his walled up heart that he was determined never to let her see.

But she really did care. She certainly hadn't expected to and was more than surprised when she realized it. But she did care, even now as he climbed the porch steps, pretending not to know she was angry at him for the simple crime of being a man. Actually, that was the one thought that gave him hope—that the two of them might gain some semblance of a satisfactory, if not happy, life together. At least her anger didn't seem to be directed at him personally but to all men in general. Considering the doctor knew nothing of her railroad man, his theory brought him a certain measure of comfort, believing in time he could prove to her that not all men were monsters as she seemed to believe.

As for Kate, she had no idea why she had elected herself judge and jury over the male population. Every now and then, like right now, she actually embarrassed herself, speaking her piece before she had time to run it through her mind and back to her tongue. Had she taken time to think on the subject even a few minutes, she may have realized that when it got right down to it, even though both her parents had prodded—actually, you might as well say "forced"—her into marrying someone she didn't love, her father always had the first and final say in that or any other matter. Perhaps that was one cause of Kate's problem with men in general.

But no, she didn't hate the good doctor. Problem was she didn't know him well enough to hate him or like him, most definitely not well enough to love him. He had wanted a wife from one of the upstanding families in the community who would help him in his practice and bear his children while being a model of virtue and social grace. That's what he wanted. Kate wanted the railroad man. She figured both of them got gypped.

Her anger slowly turned to resignation as she watched her husband through the open window, knowing he was meticulously preparing his equipment for the patients who would be dropping by throughout the day. By now she was beginning to feel a bit sorry for him, knowing she should be inside helping him get ready for the busy day ahead. But she was too proud to give in just yet, and besides that, she had rather be outdoors than inside the house any day of the week. So Kate put a clamp on her conscience and, with a deep sigh, turned around to see whose horse and buggy was clomping down the road at such a fast pace. But it wasn't a buggy, just a horse and rider.

"Miss Kate! Miss Kate!" shouted young Tom Kennedy, one of the young men from the Sandy Plain community just about three miles or so north of Beulah. "Get the Doc! Hurry!" He was already swinging his leg over the horse as he spoke.

Kate waved from her face the dust stirred up by the galloping horse and ran back towards the house as fast as she could in one of those infernal long dresses she despised, yelling for Doctor Kennedy all along the way. The doctor met her on the porch as she was rushing up the steps, but spotting Tom instantly, he quickly passed her by and hurried to find out what the emergency was.

"Get my bag!" he shouted back to Kate.

"It's one of Doc Samuel's boys, Eck Williams!" Tom's face expressed even more concern than his tone of voice. Breathless words rushed out of his mouth. "He's hurt bad over at the corn mill. Zeb Miller said he pulled his wagon up to the mill for the boys to grind his load of corn and then hung around visitin' a spell 'til the meal was ready and sacked. They helped him load up, and then

Eck walked around the mule. He grabbed the reins, but before he could step up on the running board, that darn mule kicked him side windin'. It's bad Doctor, real bad, and somebody said Doc Samuel is taking care of a young'un over in Back Swamp and can't be found. There's no time to fetch him anyway."

Kate heard the last of the report as she rushed out the door with Doctor Kennedy's black bag and a jug of water. All she could think about was Eck's wife and the two little ones at home in Weston Woods, Pansy's family home place near Potter's Hill. Her heart was pounding as she shoved the bag into her husband's arms and gave him something akin to a loving smile. Surprised, he received it, whatever it was.

"Come on, Doc," urged Tom, holding the mare still for the doctor to mount. "Take my horse, and I'll follow in your buggy. I doubt Eck's got enough time for us to get the buggy ready now."

Tom held the nervous mare while the doctor placed one foot in the stirrup and heaved himself up into the saddle. He wasn't used to this, but he could certainly handle his own in an emergency. He flipped the reins quickly and clucked his tongue, urging the young mare into a gallop as clouds of dust rose once more, blurring Kate's vision and filling her mouth and eyes with the sandy dirt.

Tom was slowly shaking his head as Kate pulled her apron up to wipe enough dust from her eyes to see him clearly. "He ain't goin' to make it, Miz Kate. He just ain't goin' to make it."

She slowly lowered the white apron from her stinging eyes and stared at Tom, her heartbeat accelerating as she grasped what he had said.

"You think Eck's going to die?" she asked, almost in a whisper.

Tom just stood there, staring off in the distance after the doctor, still shaking his head. He had always been a soft-hearted boy. Everybody said he was going to be a preacher some day.

Kate had to rid herself of the sudden sinking feeling in her stomach. She quickly reminded herself that she was the doctor's wife and it was her duty to arise to the occasion no matter what.

"The doctor will do everything he can for him, Tom. You know that."

"I know. But this will take a miracle from the Great Physician Himself."

With both her patients taking a midday nap, Hannah slipped into the store to let Nate know she was going to walk down to Cousin Kate's and see if she had any news about Eck. In a matter of minutes, she had walked the quarter mile to Kate's and climbed the steps to the front porch. Maybe Doctor Kennedy had returned with good news. But even before Kate opened the screened door to let Hannah in, she knew the news wasn't good. She stared into Kate's eyes, waiting for an answer to the question she left unasked.

The fact was, Eck Williams was dead before the doctor arrived, possibly even before Tom left the mill to fetch him.

Kate choked up, desperately trying not to ruin her reputation for toughness by crying in public, even if her long-time confidant was the only one in sight. "Oh, Hannah, he's gone."

"Oh, no, no! What will poor Pansy do? Does she know yet?"

"By now she does. The doctor had Eck's body placed in the back of his wagon with the sacks of meal and sent one of the boys who works at the corn mill to drive him home."

Kate motioned for Hannah to turn back and slowly stepped outside to lead her friend to the swing that hung from the porch ceiling by two long thick ropes. As they eased onto the wooden seat, Kate reached for Hannah's hand and held it tightly.

"Hannah," she whispered, "this terrible tragedy has scared me half to death. I can't tell you all the horrible things that have wandered through my mind since the doctor left to tend Eck this morning."

"I know, Kate. I can hardly bear to think of Pansy and those two little children. And just think of Eck's daddy and mama! Doc Samuel is one of the kindest men I've ever known in my life. This will break his heart, maybe even kill him." Hannah began to weep, dabbing at her eyes with her ever ready embroidered handkerchief.

The stricken expression on her cousin's face frightened Kate even more than she was already. Like Jessie, Kate had always considered

Hannah one of the most stable of the Gresham girls, and she figured if Hannah was upset, everybody should be upset.

"Yes, I know, but you don't understand what I'm trying to say." Kate clutched her cousin's hand tighter, tears flooding her fiery green eyes.

Hannah turned her head to look directly at Kate. She looked confused. "What *are* you trying to say?"

"Kathleen!" The doctor called for his helpmeet before she could think how to answer the question.

"Oh, never mind," said Kate, grabbing Hannah's handkerchief to wipe her eyes. "It was probably just a passing fancy anyway. I'll be right there, Doctor!" Kate jumped up, squeezing Hannah's hand before she let go and hurried to the screened door. "I'll be back in a few minutes," she called over her shoulder.

"Oh, I can't stay, Kate. Laney and the baby will be awake by the time I get back."

The disappointment in her cousin's eyes revealed more than the few confusing words Kate had spoken. It was extremely unusual for Kathleen Gresham Kennedy to share her heart with anyone—other than in anger, that is. But it was obvious she needed to unburden her soul about something, and Hannah didn't want to miss the opportunity to be a friend.

"You haven't seen the baby yet, so why don't you come down to Nate's tomorrow and visit a spell? And maybe, while Laney and little Lizzy rest, you and I could take a walk."

Kate stopped still, holding the door partially open. Her eyes lit up at Hannah's suggestion. "Alright, I'll do that! I've been thinking about baking them a fresh pecan pie. Mama's trees are full this year. Do you think they would like that?"

"That'd be nice, Kate. Nate's a big eater, and Laney's getting her appetite back now that the baby's nursing so well. It seems all three are hungry all the time." Hannah smiled, happy to hear Kate's laughter as her cousin waved good-bye and stepped into the house, pulling the door shut behind her. Hannah could hear the mumble of voices coming from the front room as the doctor gave his young wife a rundown of the supplies that needed cleaning and refilling.

✼

Corbett Thomas heard about Eck Williams' death around noon. Celie went straight to the kitchen, spouting orders to her two daughters as she made a mental list of what would be needed. Although in her early thirties now and rightly considered an old maid by the community, Hepsy still lived at home. So did Millie, but for another reason. She was a mighty young widow with a bunch of children.

Thin as her sprightly little mother, Hepsy rushed to gather potatoes from the bin under the shelter of the pack house and on to the pantry shelves where the canned foods were kept. Millie, the pretty one (well, prettier, anyway), grabbed the hatchet and headed to the hen house. By two o'clock, the buggy was packed with the baskets of food Celie and her daughters had cooked for the grieving family, and she and Corbett were headed towards Doc Williams' house.

The aging man and his wife were wrapped in silence, both deep in their grief and concern for their old friends. It was a beautiful November day, warm with the slightest hint of a chill in the air. Corbett glanced at his wife out of the corner of his eye. As he tugged on the reins and guided the mare off the main road onto Wagon Ford, Celie seemed lost in thought, more than likely mulling over plans to help Pansy and the two little ones. He turned his attention to the road ahead, shaded now by groves of maples and sycamores still holding on to large clusters of brilliant red and yellow leaves. The colorful trees were accentuated by the backdrop of sweet-smelling evergreens. Even though the weather had turned markedly cooler since Election Day, Thanksgiving was sure to be beautiful this year as was the norm for eastern North Carolina.

Corbett felt the slight pressure of Celie's thin body moving closer as the sun played hide and seek with the thick pines and hardwoods. Winter was on its way, that was for sure, and it was going to be a cold one according to the old timers' predictions. Celie unconsciously snuggled closer and threw the old blue and white wedding ring quilt she had brought along over her legs. She looked up at Corbett and smiled faintly, then turned back to her thoughts and the wooded countryside they were passing through.

He didn't have to ask what she was thinking. He knew, even now as his eyes left her thin, almost gaunt, face and turned to the road ahead. Strange, he couldn't remember when he had begun to know what Celie was thinking. Sometimes, he even knew what she was going to say before she said it. It had just happened as natural as morning dew as they had experienced life together day by day, hour by hour, over a period of forty years come Christmas. It seemed like yesterday they had stood by the fire in her papa's house, surrounded by a swarm of Whaleys and Thomases as they said their vows to one another, promising to be faithful as long as they both would live. He had kept that promise, and he knew just as certainly that Celie had, too.

Why, faithful is Celie's middle name, Corbett mused, turning to glance at her once more. Every morning at daybreak when he got down on his knees beside the little table where his old worn Bible lay waiting, he thanked God first of all for this plain little woman sitting close by his side. Corbett smiled, feeling her sharp elbow in his ribs. She must have weighed all of ninety pounds, soaking wet, when they got married, and she hadn't gained an ounce in all those years. Actually, she may have lost one or two. But she was a strong woman physically and, he thought proudly, mentally and spiritually as well.

Yes, Celia Elizabeth Whaley had made Corbett Thomas a good helpmeet throughout their long marriage. She was a good mother, too; a little strict perhaps—at times even a bit hard—but the children knew she loved them as did he. For a few moments, he considered telling her how much he had grown to love and appreciate her through the years. But no, there was no need of that. In the backwoods of North Carolina, it was still the Victorian Age. Besides, Celie knew how he felt. She could read his mind, too. He was sure of it.

Man and wife rode silently along the old dirt road, unconsciously listening to the steady "clippity-clop" of the mare's hooves, backed by a symphony of insect sounds and the call of a flock of geese in formation, soaring south for the long winter ahead. He and Celie had been lucky...*no, not lucky*, he corrected himself. They had been blessed with good health, theirs and their children's. Hepsy hadn't found a husband, and Millie would probably never remarry, but Corbett enjoyed having them around, and Celie obviously appreciated the female company and four extra hands to help with the chores. He had learned long ago to ignore the gossipers and doomsayers. The Good Lord must have a reason for keeping his daughters close at home and who was he to question the Lord?

Corbett and Celie had lost two babies years ago, and though that loss was heartbreaking, it was certainly not unusual. Most everyone Corbett knew had lost more than one child at birth or within the first two years of life. The infant mortality rate was still high, even with good doctors and experienced midwives available. But to lose a half-grown or adult child was another story altogether. It just wasn't natural to bury your offspring as would his friend, Samuel, sometime before nightfall. It went against the order of things. The hurt was too deep to bear.

As he caught sight of the Williams's home place just ahead, Corbett let out a long sigh, not bothering to brush away the tear that trickled down over his high cheekbone and into his bushy gray beard. There was a half-dozen or so buggies and wagons parked this way and that in front of the small house that stood at least fifty yards off the road under the shade of two giant oak trees. Again, he glanced down at Celie, her mouth set in the manner he recognized easily. He doubted she would speak even a few words in way of consolation or sympathy. It was her way to just roll up her sleeves and do what had to be done. Her actions always spoke louder than her words. Corbett envied her ability to know how to help in time of need. But as for himself, he would need words for his old friend—words of wisdom, gentle words, kind words. Gentleness and kindness, he could handle, but words of wisdom? Where were they? What were they? He just couldn't think up any to fit the tragic occasion.

Deputy Ben Jones had used up about all the time he could spare investigating old James's murder. Anyway, he figured nobody cared what happened to the old slave; he certainly didn't. How old was he? Ninety? A hundred, someone said. He'd surely have died before the next spring came round. It was probably a good thing somebody helped him on his way…kept him from suffering so much. Now, all he had to do was figure out how to get Corbett and Jack Thomas off his back. The thought of that impossible task caused his heart to skip a beat or two. Those two aging men had more respect in the community than Ben thought they deserved. They were just old farmers. What did they know compared to someone high up in law enforcement like himself?

The deputy's thoughts continued to wander in that direction as he climbed up the steps to Nate's store once more. The weather had taken another turn over the past few days. It was often said in Beulah, "If you don't like the weather, just wait a minute or two and it will change." The wind had picked up considerably, and now it seemed to push Ben, heavy as he was, up the steps and into the warm store.

Nate struggled to keep from grimacing as he turned from placing a bucket of nails on the shelf to see who had just come through the door. Corbett Thomas and Jeb Gresham were gazing intently at the checkerboard placed between them on top of an overturned pickle barrel. Jessie and Kate's father, Willis T. Gresham, was leaning on the counter talking with Nate about his future plans for making a real town out of Beulah, maybe even dividing up his land into lots when there were enough people around to buy. He figured that would be fairly soon considering the continuing growth of the community over the past year. More folks were coming in every day. At least, it seemed like it. Sarah Jane was out in the sitting room with Laney, Hannah, and the baby, making sure her patient was well enough for Hannah to go home.

Jeb's eyes didn't budge from the checkerboard as he raised his bushy eyebrows to acknowledge Corbett's latest move. "How you doin', Ben?"

Corbett echoed him. "How you doin', Ben?"

"Fine, fine. How're you boys?"

Corbett chuckled. "We're a little past boyhood, Ben."

"Yeah, about fifty years or so." Jeb jumped two of Corbett's checkers and said, "Crown me!"

"Hmm. Ben must have taken my mind off the game." Corbett scowled at the board and grudgingly plopped a red checker on top the one Jeb had just moved to the back of the board.

"Sure, he did," chuckled Jeb. "And I'm a boy, too."

The two men laughed together, pretty much ignoring the fact that Ben had pulled a ladder back chair up to the barrel and flipped it around. He sat down and used the back to lean forward on.

"What's so funny, boys?"

"Nothin', Ben. Nothin' you'd understand, anyway," replied Corbett.

The two men turned their focus back to the game, wishing Ben would leave them alone. The old saying goes that if you ignore something, it will go away. Hopefully, it would prove true.

But that was a little much to expect seeing that Ben was sitting close enough for the two men to feel his hot breath when he opened his mouth to begin his questioning, or rather, his politicking. "Got any more ideas as to who mighta killed old James, Corbett?"

"Nope. Have you?" Corbett moved a checker forward one space and then pulled it back, studying the board one more time before he slid it back to the same square.

"No. Seems nobody from Gander's Fork to Potter's Hill and clean over to Kenansville has heard a word. I even rode over to Back Swamp and Cypress Creek. It's like old James decided he had enough of this world and just did hisself in."

Ben was obviously going somewhere, but before he could ease into his mapped-out plan, Corbett jabbed back.

"Nope."

"No what?" Ben's heart picked up a quicker tempo.

"No, old James didn't kill himself." Corbett jumped two of Jeb's checkers and leaned back in his chair to see what his old friend would do now.

"How do you know that? He might have."

"Nope. Doc Samuel said it was impossible. Try to hit yourself in the back of the head one of these days, Ben."

"Well, you never know."

"Nope. Even if he could have managed to get behind himself and knock a hole in his head, he didn't kill himself."

"How can you be so sure?"

"Because he was a good man, a God-fearin' man. He wouldn't have taken anybody's life, includin' his own."

Ben was clutching the top rung of the chair. He leaned his chin on his hands to rethink his plan.

Jeb pushed his chair back from the barrel table and stretched his arms. "If you're going to keep talking, Ben, we might as well call this game quits. I got to go anyway. That is, if I can drag Sarah Jane and Hannah away from that baby."

Jeb pushed the chair a little further away and stood up, his joints popping and cracking. "Nate! Wrap that bolt of cloth Sarah Jane wants so bad. Wouldn't hurt the woman to get a surprise every twenty years or so."

"Already did, Uncle Jeb. I knew you'd change your mind." Nate grinned, holding out the bolt of soft blue chambray wrapped in brown paper and tied with tobacco twine.

"Didn't change my mind, son. I was going to buy it the whole time she was hintin'. Just didn't want her to know it. You better learn how to do these things, boy." Jeb smiled at his own cunning.

"I doubt I'll ever learn now, not with my little princess holding my heart like a puppet on a string." Nate grabbed the box of supplies Sarah Jane had ordered earlier and started out the door to load Jeb's buggy.

"How well I know. I have five, remember." Jeb was smiling as he clapped his oldest brother, Willis T., on the shoulder and walked back over to the stove to shake Corbett's hand and tell him good-bye.

"We never did get to discuss the election." Corbett firmly shook Jeb's hand, gnarled with layers of calluses made by years of plowing and digging and chopping.

"It'll wait, my friend. Those fellows in Washington sure ain't goin' nowhere."

"We can be sure of that." Corbett laughed, casting a sly glance in Ben Jones's direction.

The deputy was abnormally quiet, but he quickly became aware someone had suddenly opened the door he had been waiting for all along. "Speakin' of elections," he said, "guess you boys heard I may be running for sheriff next go 'round. Sure would 'preciate your vote."

"No, Ben, I didn't hear that interesting bit of news, but congratulations. Hope you good luck." Jeb patted the younger man on the shoulder and turned to the door. It looked like a good time to make a quick exit.

Sarah Jane and Hannah stepped out the kitchen door onto the long porch as Jeb helped Nate cover the box of supplies with a large gray tarp. Laney stood at the door to wave good-bye with Lizzy in her arms. It would be good to have her own home and family completely to herself again. Nonetheless, she would truly miss Hannah's help, and her company. Like her mother, she always seemed to know what to do and when to do it. It had been good to have other women around for a while, even if one of them was only sixteen. She missed her own mother terribly, especially now the baby was here. Little Lizzy would have been her mama's first grandchild. Her daddy, Bill Hunter, had come by nearly every other day, but having Sarah Jane and Hannah around had helped ease the sorrow of her mother's loss even though she would have to face it head on in the days ahead.

"I can't thank you enough, Hannah," Laney was saying. "You're almost as good a nurse as your mama, you know."

Hannah blushed, reaching out to touch the baby's soft face one more time. "I'll miss you, little Lizzy," she said.

Before she could restrain herself, tears were streaming down her cheeks like a pump that had been primed. Laney's eyes were suddenly overflowing as well. Hannah was more embarrassed than ever. All of a sudden, she lost her ability to think what to do next.

"Come along, Hannah," said her mother gently, taking her by the arm. "If we don't get on out of here, you girls will have me blubbering, too. We have to remember that nurses must control their emotions."

Laney smiled through her tears. "Thank you so much, Sarah Jane. I'll never forget how much you've helped me."

"You just take care of that precious gift you've been given, dear girl. We'll be back in town before you know it to check on you. Bye, now."

"Bye, Laney!" Hannah waved and turned toward the wagon, sad to leave Laney and her baby but excited to be going home after ten long days away. She had missed her sisters, especially Nell, and of course she always missed mama and papa when she was away from them. The time away had given her a lot to think about in the weeks ahead, particularly what it would be like to have a husband and children of her own. The secrets Kate had shared two days ago when she came to visit would roll over in her mind for quite some time. One thing was for certain, she wasn't quite as concerned about her newly married cousin as she had been when they were together on Election Day. Maybe Kate would be content with her life after all. Well…maybe.

Back in the warm store, there wasn't much being said. Ben Jones was trying to think of another way to close the chapter on old James's death and get on to more important matters—like his career—and Corbett was hoping he'd just shut up and be on his way. Willis T. had followed Jeb and Nate out to the wagon, assuring his brother that he and Margaret and the children would be out to the Hall Farm on Thanksgiving to have dinner with Sarah Jane, Jeb and the girls. Most of the other Gresham families would be attending as well.

All of a sudden, Deputy Jones made an extremely apolitical-like decision. He decided to be totally honest and lay the issue straight out on the table, not heeding the consequences.

"Corbett, let's be honest with one another. You and I both know there's no way anybody in his right mind is goin' to tell us what he knows about James's death. And hell could freeze over before anybody admitted to foul play."

Corbett was staring at the checkerboard, running his hand over his beard as if he was planning his first move in the next game.

Ben continued, "My point is, nobody gives a hoot what happened to that old nigger so why don't we just let it be? I don't have time to waste tryin' to get people in these parts to reveal something they're not likely to speak of ever, not even on Judgment Day. Come on, Corbett, whatta you say? Let's put this case to rest, alright?"

Corbett was staring at the checkerboard again, still stroking his beard. Suddenly, his hand stopped moving. The glazed look in his eyes caused Ben to wonder if he'd heard his little speech. But then the older man turned to look into the eyes of the younger, and what Ben saw there made him cringe and quickly step back a foot or so. When Corbett began to speak, his normally pleasant personality was nowhere to be seen.

"Deputy, somebody does care about what happened to that old man. I care. Black or white, rich or poor, he was a human bein' and a good one at that. You can walk away from his murder if you want to, but don't expect me or my family to pat you on the back and say, 'Well done.'

"Now," he continued in the same hardened tone of voice, "if you'll step out of my way, I'll bid you a good day and be on my way. It's gettin' mighty hot in here, and there doesn't seem to be enough air for the both of us."

The aging gentleman seemed to have gained about a foot in height as he drew back his shoulders and marched toward the door. Ben Jones was glued to his tracks, stunned by the presence of the Corbett Thomas he had never met.

Chapter Eight

*W*inter, *1900/1901*—Just as the old-timers predicted, the winter proved to be a cold one, even before it was legally winter. Snow before Christmas was rare in these parts, but by Christmas Eve, at least a foot and a half of snow was banked up against the post office steps, and it was still coming down. The sky was filled with fluffy white flakes that floated on the cold air like millions of tiny white parachutes invading the pine forests as well as the vacant fields and countryside.

Many Americans were most likely in church on Christmas Eve, but alas, there was no church in Beulah. Though the small community had evolved from a turpentine camp in the early 1700's, it had only supported a church for a very short length of time, from 1890 until sometime around 1895. The Wilmington Synod of the Presbyterian Church had seen the small village as a mission field and had sent emissaries to seek out a place to build a small house of worship. Willis T. Gresham, Kate's father and owner of most of the land that was later to become an incorporated town, gave an acre of his land to build the simple structure. The building was erected a short distance north of Nate Gresham's store on the road to New Bern, the one that ran through Potter's Hill. Beulah Presbyterian Church didn't last long, though. Its doors quietly closed after only four years. Later, nobody seemed to know why. Or perhaps they just forgot.

Those in the small community who had a mind to attend church on Sunday had only one logical choice, the Baptist Church at Hallsville. The Presbyterian Church in Chinquapin was a longer seven miles south, and the old Grove Presbyterian in Kenansville, the county seat, was across the river about eleven miles to the west. In those days, any place across the river might well have been on the other side of the ocean.

But on this frigid, snowy Christmas Eve, most of the area's children were huddled by blazing home fires listening to grand-parents' stories and hoping for even a small gift in their stockings on Christmas morning. They weren't much into Santa Claus. Most had never even heard of him. The women were preparing pecan and sweet potato pies, and the men were dressing the deer or wild turkeys they had hunted early that morning.

Sarah Jane and Jeb lived a few miles south of the riverside village of Hallsville so they went as often as possible to the small Baptist Church which was established in 1803. It stood rather regally on a small sand hill in the fork between the road that led northeast to Beulah and the one that led east to Muddy Creek. Reverend Aldridge would not be expecting many parishioners on this snowy Christmas Eve—maybe a few families who lived close to the church along the river, but certainly not those who were a few miles away like Jeb Gresham's crowd.

Hannah missed being with her friends in the little church on the most special night of the year. She loved the muffled giggles and excitement gushing from the young girls as they clustered on one long pew dressed in their Sunday best, blushing at the shy glances of the boys squirming in their own pew across the aisle. But most of all, Hannah loved to come to the house of the Lord on the eve of His birthday when the altar was bathed in candlelight and the windows and doors were decked with green wreaths adorned with red holly berries or dried apples. When the small group of worshipers sang the traditional Christmas carols proclaiming the glad tidings, it seemed to Hannah Gresham as if the Lord Jesus Himself filled the little church with His very presence. It was sort of like that cloud of glory she had read about in the Bible. But though she couldn't really see Him, He touched her longing heart and once again, she was assured of God's unconditional love.

Tonight, kept from church by the snowstorm, she stood gazing out the window at the pure white beauty of creation, wondering how a plain young girl like herself could possibly fit into the Almighty Creator's mysterious plan. Hannah considered herself quite simple, really—obviously not pretty like so many of the Gresham girls and neither particularly intelligent nor scholarly. She was average and she knew it. To be a nurse was her one and only dream, but she would have to learn by assisting her mother and other women in the community who shared the healing gifts, not through books and professional training. There was little opportunity for the luxury of higher education in her rural area at the turn of the century. She would have to be what was called a practical nurse in those days, a very descriptive title, to be sure.

A week before Christmas, Kate had invited Hannah to stay with her in town a few days, and as always, Hannah was happy for the opportunity to spend time with her. Doctor Kennedy was out of town, having taken the train from Wallace to Wilmington for a series of medical meetings which would keep him up-to-date on what was new in the world of medicine. Although she was finally growing to appreciate the good doctor her parents had coerced her into marrying, Kate was delighted to have a few days for herself. She had invited Hannah and Jessie to stay with her while her husband was away. For a little while, she was a young girl again, giggling and telling silly tales and sharing dreams with her sister and her cousin.

It was during one of those carefree days that Kate said something surprising. Hannah was still pondering Kate's words, holding them close to her heart as she gazed out the window, quietly watching the fluffy white snowflakes swirling against the black night sky.

"Hannah?" called Sarah Jane. "Nell and I made hot cocoa. Would you like some?" Sarah Jane's keen eyes searched her daughter's face for some clue to her deep silence. Hannah was never chatty like Liza and Frannie, but she was never this quiet either, particularly on a special night like Christmas Eve.

"Yes, Mama, thank you. Are you sure you'll have enough chocolate for the cake you wanted to make?" Hannah reached for the steaming cup her mother held out to her.

"Oh, yes. Your papa stopped by Nate's store when he went into town to get everything he'll need for the hog killing next week. Laney talked him into buying a big chunk of chocolate and some raisins, too. Said he could pay for it after hog killing. While you were off visitin' Kate, the girls and I made a fruitcake, and it's still wrapped in the wine cloth waiting for your pa to cut the first piece." Sarah Jane smiled at her daughter. "We're mighty blessed this Christmas, child."

"Um, hm. It's a good Christmas." Hannah took a sip of the rare hot treat and turned again to the window.

Sarah Jane walked up behind her young daughter. Unsettling as it was to her papa, his second-born was quickly becoming a grown woman. She placed her arm around Hannah's shoulders. "What do you see out there, child?"

"Oh, I don't know, really. It's just so beautiful and...well, sort of mysterious in a way, don't you think?"

"How so?" Sarah Jane's interest was piqued.

"It seems as if God is trying to tell us something, but we can't speak His language — almost, but not quite. Perhaps we once knew it, but we've forgotten. Yet, sometimes I think we understand deep in our hearts if not with our minds."

Sarah Jane nodded slowly, pondering Hannah's words carefully.

Warmed by the hot cocoa and the blazing fire Jeb had stoked a few moments earlier, mother and daughter were silent for awhile, both gazing out the window at the swirling white snow that was coming down heavily now.

Finally, in a low voice so the others couldn't hear, Sarah Jane asked, "And what is He saying to you?"

"Oh, Mama," sighed Hannah, relieved by the question. She turned to look into her mother's eyes. "Kate said that Doctor Kennedy told her to ask me if I would like to assist him with patients from time to time, mainly with birthings. She said his practice is growing fast with the expanding community and he really needs more help than she'll be able to give him with her expecting a baby in early summer." Hannah laughed, continuing, "Kate said the doctor doesn't consider her much help anyway being she's terrified at the sight of blood."

Her mother smiled and sighed, turning back to the window. It was her turn now to stare at the snow. She couldn't see far, just what the light from the window allowed. For a few moments, she seemed to forget what Hannah said. And then, she looked deep into her daughter's eyes. The girl's longing was evident. She would be heartbroken if her parents withheld her dream from her reach. But what would they do without her on the farm?

Clearing woodland for farming was hard work—excruciating, back-breaking work. During the spring and summer months, Sarah Jane, Jeb and the girls worked from dawn to dusk—plowing, planting, chopping, weeding, fertilizing and then harvesting the crops for market in the fall. Their only sons had died in infancy, so all five girls and Sarah Jane were forced to work the fields with Jeb, taking turns in the kitchen to prepare meals and can the fruits and vegetables they raised. Due to the fairly mild winters in southeastern North Carolina, they cleared land when the ground wasn't frozen, chopping down the tall pines and pulling up stumps with the old mule or a borrowed ox. The work was never-ending and much too hard for young women who often grew old before their time. The backbreaking strain of manual labor plus year after year of child-bearing was more than their bodies could tolerate.

The work load would be even heavier without Hannah's help, but the mother again looked deep into the soul of her daughter and knew she couldn't help but give her consent.

"I'll talk to your papa. I'm sure he'll agree for you to help Doctor Kennedy as often as possible. But remember, we'll be needin' you during barnin' season."

"Oh, Mama, thank you!" Hannah, the steady, unemotional Gresham girl, burst into tears, quickly hiding her face on her mother's shoulder. She hugged her tightly as the winter wind whistled around the little house and the falling snow wrapped the earth in a soft white blanket.

Little Johnny Hatcher's feet were nearly frozen. He could hardly feel them touch the ground as he stumbled out of the deep dark woods into the light of the coldest Christmas Day in years. He had to keep walking. If he stopped now, frostbite would completely take over and his blood would stop circulating. Young as he was, the boy was all too familiar with the effects of frostbite and hypothermia. He had seen grown men fall prey to the savage cold, losing a hand or foot, sometimes even a leg, as the result of staying too long in the freezing cold forest.

"Keep walkin', legs," he mumbled through chapped, bleeding lips. He rubbed his thighs with hands nearly as frozen as his feet as he limped along the narrow path that led to Back Swamp Road. He had to keep going. The small cabin was only a few yards from the point where the path met the road. His sisters and brothers would be there waiting for him, wondering what in the world had happened to keep Johnny and his pa in the frozen forest for so long today. Maybe Martha and Maggie would have a pot of soup cooked. Yes, that's what he would think about—hot food! That would keep him going. He could almost smell the pot of soupy rice flavored with the last bits and pieces of an old smokehouse ham his daddy had traded work for. But the hunger he had ignored all day began to tear at his stomach in waves, and before long, he couldn't tell which was worse, the pain and numbness in his legs and feet or the raging hunger in his belly. The cold biscuit Martha had put in his pocket when he left the house at first light was long gone.

He could see the road now and the smoke from the chimney of the little house. Warmth...food...brothers and sisters...home...but no mama. And now he knew that after what had happened in the forest again today, there would be no papa either.

Suddenly, pain worse than hunger or frostbite stabbed the little fellow between his ribs. *Oh, no! What if Papa was there in the cabin? What if he had gone home in his drunken rage and hurt the other children?* And then he prayed the unthinkable prayer, *Oh, God, please don't let him come home again! Not ever...please!*

Johnny prayed hard the rest of the way, silently for awhile and then out loud just in case God might hear him better that way. It felt good to pray, even though he sometimes wondered why he bothered. Mama was the one who prayed all the time and just look what happened to her. Now, it seemed like Martha had taken her place, somehow inheriting Sallie Sue's gift of prayer and more than that, her gift of faith. But Johnny didn't have his sister's faith, at least not consciously. But he always kept on praying if for no other reason than he knew his mama would want him to. He could almost hear her tender voice, riding high and clear on the whistling wind.

"Don't forget your prayers, Johnny."

"Aw, Mama, I'm too tired."

"What if I went days, or even a few hours, without talkin' to you? How would you feel, Johnny?"

"I'd be sad, Mama. Please don't stop talkin' to me." Johnny's bleeding lips formed the words he had spoken as his mother helped him to bed one night not so terribly long ago.

"I'll always talk to you, Johnny. Do you know why?"

"Uh, huh, 'cause you love me."

He could feel his eyes growing heavy now as when she had tucked the warm covers under his little chin and reached over to kiss him goodnight, the fragrance of her soft skin lingering in the air.

He slapped his cheek. He couldn't sleep now. Only a few more yards to the porch steps.

His mother's voice floated back through the cold wind once more. "Yes, I wouldn't withhold my voice from you because I love you, and I know it makes you feel loved to talk with me. And God is like you and me, child. He feels loved when He hears your voice callin' to Him."

The wind calmed and suddenly the dark world was soundless but for the crunching snow beneath his hobbling feet.

Oh, Mama, don't go! Please don't go!

Tears stung his eyes. His cracked lips trembled as he finally reached the bottom cinder block that formed the porch steps. But he couldn't raise one foot high enough to make the first step. Tears freezing on his bright red cheeks, Johnny Hatcher crumpled into the deep snow and drifted to a warm place where his mama wrapped him in her arms and kissed his tears away forever.

Doc Samuel leaned back on the buggy seat and closed his eyes. Old Bertha's reins lay limply across his legs. Only a few more miles and he'd be home for Christmas. Delia would have a cup of hot cider waiting for him, and a few of the children and grandchildren would be there to greet him. He had been gone a week this time. One of the Edwards boys had come down with a high fever that had stubbornly resisted every treatment he had kept up his sleeve for forty years. Nothing had worked, but finally, the fever had broken, and now the boy would be alright. Samuel still wasn't sure what it was but there would be more; he was sure of that. He'd better rest while he could.

His eyes closed once again. His tired body slumped over, wrapped in the heavy quilt Delia had insisted he take with him. He was surely grateful. Two more miles. Bertha could handle it from here. Just a straight line down Wagon Ford Road and around the curve to the old home place. Pansy and the children would be there, of course. It was so hard to see them without Eck but worse not to see them. Little Flora and Bo were only two and four years old with no papa for Christmas. He'd have to fill in somehow, bad as his own heart ached.

Pansy was the youngest in a family of ten children, the baby daughter of old John Gordon Weston who had fought in the Civil War and walked home from Andersonville prison. Her papa had been dead a long time and her mama, too, worn out from childbearing and farming. Samuel and Delia were the only elders she had, and so she had turned to them when Eck was killed by the mule. What else could she do? Samuel was glad, of course. But his own grief over the loss of a son was pushed down and hidden away in deference to the young widow and her two little ones.

Having Pansy and the children around seemed to be cathartic for Delia. Somehow, Bo and Flora helped fill the deep void in her heart left by Eck's death. No matter how badly she felt, physically and emotionally, when those two little ones came running up the path, she lit up like a lightning bug in June. My, how he loved to see that glow. There was no need for a Christmas tree.

Chapter Nine

Spring, 1901—The winter of 1901 seemed unending, but that was due to the unusually cold weather. It seemed like all the men folk and young'uns around Beulah had the same ailment from Christmas to early April. It was called stir-crazy. About the time everybody thought spring had come, the heavens released another layer of snow on the thawing earth. The last one was on April 15. Jeb wrote it down in the Bible.

After that, it seemed the sky was empty and the lengthening days were filled with warm sunshine and soft breezes. The spring rains came and they were welcome as always. By late May, flowers were blooming and cornstalks and bean sprouts were popping through the black dirt in Sarah Jane's garden.

It was on the prettiest day yet that Hannah and Jessie were working alongside their mothers and sisters clearing a small field that Jessie's father, Willis T., had agreed to allot as a cemetery for the entire clan. Aunts, uncles, cousins—most of the Greshams living within ten miles of Beulah had turned out just after daybreak to help clear the land of pine and sweet gum stumps. Those who were not fit for hard labor—like Laney who was still nursing little Lizzy and Kate who was expecting—came all during the long warm day in late May, bringing baskets of food, fresh water and even a keg of lemonade. All in all, by midday, the young people had to admit that even though the labor was backbreaking, it was rather enjoyable, if not downright fun working all together. But that all changed in a Biblical twinkling of an eye, one might say. By 12:15 p.m., the date May 28, 1901 was forever etched in the memories of Beulah's citizens. It registered nothing short of the most frightening day of their lives.

Everyone had stopped work for lunch about an hour earlier. It had been a long time since breakfast, about six hours, Nate guessed, and around eleven most everyone was weak from hunger and exhaustion. Hannah, Jessie, Nell and Kate sat on uprooted stumps and ate much more than they normally would have in public. Young women were expected to eat like little birds, especially when men were around.

"Remember your etiquette, girls," said Margaret Gresham.

"Etiquette, my foot," mumbled Kate. "How can anybody be expected to pull nine hundred pound stumps out of the ground from sunrise to sunset and starve to death?"

"Just be glad *you* didn't have to pull stumps today, Kate," said Jessie teasingly.

Kate blushed, remembering the baby growing inside her body. Concerned about the other girls, she had almost forgotten that her plight today was a rather easy one. Because of Kate's "condition," she had been put in charge of helping Laney and her grandmother, Josephine Hines, with the food. Of course, Doctor Kennedy was exempt from this type of work and was now en route to a nearby farm where Carl Jones had come down with something the doctor hoped wasn't the yellow fever he was dreading.

Children too young to work, anyone under the age of nine, ate quickly and went back to playing hide-and-go-seek among the uprooted stumps and deep holes. The very youngest were already nodding, sleepy-eyed and still, waiting to be put down for an afternoon nap on a colorful quilt laid out under the shade of a sycamore tree.

The girls ate slowly, remembering their manners, as Jessie chattered away and the others managed to get a word in edgewise every now and then. Finally, Kate got up to help Laney gather the leftover food to save for those who might need to keep up their strength later in the afternoon. The other girls quickly resumed the task of digging around the stumps so that the men, with help from the ox, could pull them out of the ground more easily.

Hannah had just stabbed the shovel into the rain-softened ground when all of a sudden, she had an eerie feeling. The hairs on the back of her neck stood at attention as a current of electricity seemed to ripple over her skin, down both arms to the tips of her fingers. Puzzled and somewhat frightened, she was straightening up to ask Nell if she felt anything when she saw the huge, dark black shadow moving stealthily towards her across the field.

"What on earth?" she whispered, too shocked to speak aloud.

By this time, everyone was aware that something strange was happening. They were all looking at one another questioningly, hoping someone would have an answer for the sudden darkness. The smaller children began to cry, some even screaming, running to find their mamas.

"Lord, have mercy!" shouted Sarah Jane, the one who was usually calm no matter the crisis. She gathered Frannie and Susie under each arm as Liza ran up and threw her arms around her mother's waist. Even Hannah and Nell drew close to their mother as if she were a safe magnetic pole. Jeb was off on the other side of the field with most of the men, but he came running right after the initial shock when he heard Sarah Jane scream.

Within seconds, the black shadow had engulfed the earth in an eerie darkness that could be felt as well as seen. It was as if someone had dropped a black veil over the entire earth, enshrouding it in darkness. The closest house, only twenty-five yards or so away, looked dim and ghostly. All the children were crying now, some still screaming because they couldn't find their mamas. Mothers were shouting their children's names above the spine-chilling wail of the old ox that was, at the moment, hitched to the hauling wagon. Roosters were heard crowing like banshees, right in the middle of the day. That was not a good sign. The adults were running this way and that, trying to find their little ones in the chaos of the strange dark gloom.

Other than Willie Hill, the wrinkled old man who drove the ox cart, hardly anyone thought to look at the sky. In retrospect, it was a good thing. His eyes were never the same again. Once the thick blackness enveloped the good people of Beulah, a strange glow seemed to emanate from the earth itself. But it didn't come from the earth, as Willie would later explain. It came from the sky, and only one other person dared look at it.

Ida Wash Sandlin, the old postmistress who had named the village Beulah in 1873, had caught a ride in the buggy with Laney Gresham that day, just tagging along to make sure she knew what everyone was doing and to add her famous pound cake to the noonday meal. While most everyone else in the field, children were now clinging to their parents, suddenly caught their breath in stunned silence, old Ida looked up into the sky to see if her Lord was coming as she suspected. For a minute or two, she was certain her redemption was drawing nigh as the Bible said.

In the midst of the dark sky high overhead hovered a round disk blacker than the surrounding heavens. Circling the disk was a bright light eerily radiating from behind the black circle, hurting Ida's eyes as she stared hard to see the Lord and His angels. Regrettably for Ida, the Lord didn't come that day or in the short time she had left on earth thereafter. The citizens of Beulah had not witnessed the Second Coming as some had hoped—and others had dreaded—but a total solar eclipse, an event that would not occur again in the area for exactly seventy years and two months to the day.

Although no one had a watch to tell the time, they all agreed the eclipse lasted nearly an hour. The faithful sun had always served as the only timepiece for these farmers, but that day, no one could see the sun. In the weeks following, fairly educated men like Doc Williams and Corbett Thomas would hang out at Nate's store and the post office explaining what they had read about solar eclipses, but in the midst of the darkness, no one understood what was happening.

Ida said that, although the Lord didn't come, it was nonetheless a sign in the heavens of some sort. They'd all just have to pray and seek the Lord to know what it was He was trying to say. Then she reminded the crowd about the roosters crowing at noonday. Then she suddenly remembered that the very same thing had happened when she was a small child. Ida stopped talking and started counting on her fingers.

"Oh!" she gasped. "Just what I thought. It happened exactly seventy years ago! Now, mind what I say, folks. It's a sign!"

Adding to the mystery was the fact that the Gresham clan, which made up more than half of the small village's citizenry, had been clearing land for a graveyard. Now, how could you say that was mere coincidence? A graveyard, no less. Jessie said later that she sure was glad they hadn't buried anyone in the graveyard yet 'cause if the Lord had come they would have all been standing around in a cemetery full of resurrected dead people.

But, as has been pointed out previously, the Greshams were anything but a lazy lot, so after approximately an hour of terrifying darkness plus another hour of heated debate as to what had happened, they all went back to work, digging and pulling up stumps. Everyone except Willie Hill, that is. He told Nate he thought he might better walk over to Doc Kennedy's and see if he was back from the Jones place.

Nate took one look at the old man's eyes and said, "Yep, I think that's a good idea, Willie."

Miraculously, Ida Wash was just fine.

About an hour before sundown, Jeb held his gnarled hand up between the sun and the horizon and said, "Time to go home, folks. It'll be dark in a hour."

For a few moments, the entire clan stood perfectly still and silent, gazing intently at the golden globe as it continued its quick descent into the western horizon. Streaks of crimson and brushes of gold mingled with multitudes of soft clouds, graciously escorting the royal sun to its glorious setting.

It was a comforting sight to behold.

Knowing they would be working late on May 28, Sarah Jane and Jeb had planned to scatter their family throughout the houses of their kinfolk in Beulah for the night. Hannah and Nell were to stay with Jessie at Willis T.'s place on the west end of town while Sarah Jane and the two younger girls stayed in Laney and Nate's spare room which Lizzy would sleep in when she was older. Liza boasted that she was spending the night with Cousin Bessie Bishop all by herself. Jeb was happy as a lark sleeping on the fresh hay in the horse barn beside Nate's store.

Hannah couldn't sleep. Neither could Nell nor Jessie, but both finally drifted off and left Hannah alone with her thoughts and fears. Her skin was still crawling after the frightening events of the strange day she would never forget. Neither would anyone else in Beulah.

Pushing Nell's slender body over a bit, she turned over once more and situated her feather pillow more comfortably. Gazing out the window into the clear night sky, she wondered what had really happened today. Even though Hannah knew little about the constellations, the Big Dipper was readily identifiable, and it made her feel safe somehow that the familiar form was always there, connected by an invisible line from star to star. Sometimes, on a night like this, the star-studded dome of the universe overwhelmed her young mind. It was just too awesome, too much to take in. Perhaps Ida Wash was right. Perhaps God had given them a sign.

A scripture came to mind—"What is man, that Thou art mindful of him?"

Yes, Lord, she thought. *What is man? What are we doing here?*

Maybe old Ida was right after all, she thought. Perhaps the Lord was trying to tell them something today. But what? And why couldn't people hear Him? She recalled the feeling she'd had watching the snow on Christmas Eve—the feeling that God was trying to tell her something and she couldn't understand His language.

There was obviously a big difference today, though, even if only in His tone of voice. In the snow, He had whispered softly, lovingly, like a tender father. Today, hiding the sun at the peak of noonday in a shadow of darkness that seemed to cover the entire earth, He had shouted like a man of war. Or perhaps an angry God.

Hannah shivered, but not from the cold. She needed to get her mind on something a little more down-to-earth and, hopefully, a bit more pleasant. She turned over again, this time thankful for her sister's closeness. But then, there were the dogs, barking and howling in the dense darkness of the night. As much as she liked visiting her cousins in town, she hated the long nights after everyone went to sleep and she stayed awake listening to the dogs. They didn't just bark; they moaned and howled like the ghosts in the tales Jessie's brothers told at night to scare the girls. She didn't understand why country dogs never seemed to bark all night. She guessed it was because they didn't have other dogs to bark to. Perhaps the city dogs were communicating somehow with dogs all over town, telling the news, howling together about some dog that had gotten hurt during the day or died. The Bible said all creation is moaning and groaning for the revelation of the sons of God. She never had understood what that meant, but maybe the dogs were doing just that. It sure sounded like it. Strange, the dogs never seemed to be close by, but far off in the distance, creating an eerie and mournful sound that seemed to come from another world...or perhaps a graveyard. She shuddered and pulled the covers up about her neck, even more determined to think of something a bit brighter.

Just another month and she would begin working with Doctor Kennedy—the Doctor, as Kate always said. Odd, Hannah never thought of him as Kate's husband. He was the Doctor, and he and Kate lived in the same house, but that was about it. Of course, the fact Kate was "expectin'" threw a little wrench into Hannah's unrealistic picture, but she was able to deal with that by naively ignoring the facts of life. It's hard to believe that a seventeen-year-old girl who was about to embark on a nursing career, majoring in midwifery, could pretend sex didn't exist, but she did...for as long as she could, that is.

Finally, her tired body overcame her worries and fears, and she drifted off into a dreamless sleep. Even Nell's sharp elbow in her side didn't wake her up.

The next morning at breakfast, the conversation focused on the strange phenomenon the family had witnessed the day before. Just after daybreak, the U.S. postal service man had ridden into town in his buggy and told the men gathered on the porch at Nate's store that what the people of Beulah had seen was definitely a solar eclipse. For over an hour the moon had hidden the sun. Only the glow of the sun had shown around the infinitely smaller moon. The bright glow was called a corona, he said.

"That cain't be," said Willie Hill. "I always heerd the sun is thousands of times bigger'n the moon. How can the moon hide the sun?"

"I don't know, Willie," said Corbett Thomas, shaking his head. "I'm not an astronomer, but I've read about these things, and what we all saw yesterday certainly does fit the description of a solar eclipse."

The talk went on like that for weeks, but by early July when the tobacco fields were still green at the top but turning gold at the bottom, the excitement over the day the world turned dark at midday had about petered out. The county farmers were too busy readying their barns and equipment for the year's curing season to worry about signs in the heavens and such. They just hoped the darkness wasn't a bad omen. The crop that grew best in their soil hardly brought in enough money to provide for their families all year long anyway. They certainly didn't need an omen.

Summer, 1901—To say the least, farming had been challenging for Jeb Gresham. The three older girls and Sarah Jane worked more than their share, that was for sure. It was tough not having boys to help in the fields. They did alright in the spring planting season when Jeb and old Simon took turns plowing behind the stubborn old mule and Sarah Jane and the girls tended the plant beds until the tiny green sprigs of tobacco were ready to replant in the long rows of the broad fields. But when it came time to crop the big golden leaves one leaf at a time in the hot July and August sun and then haul the sticky piles back to the barn so the women could string the leaves onto splintery slender sticks, Jeb longed for the boys he and Sarah Jane had buried long ago.

But there was a lot more work to be done. At the end of every hot and unbearably humid day, after the girls and Sarah Jane had strung the tobacco neatly onto the long sticks, it was Jeb's job to see that those sticks, heavily weighted down with tobacco, were hung on the rafters in the top of the barn. That took a lot of climbing and a lot of heavy lifting. Old Simon Hall always helped him, but the former child slave was about the same age as Jeb or older and had about the same amount of energy leftover from his younger days.

And then, there were the long hot nights when he and Simon took turns sleeping under the shelter at the barn, making sure the fire didn't burn too hot or too low so the golden leaves would cure an even deeper shade of gold, filling the atmosphere from the barn to the house with an aroma that smelled better to Jeb than Sarah Jane's roses. The fragrance of cured tobacco in July and August meant food on the table in the cold days of January and February. It meant schoolbooks, pencils and paper in the fall and clothing for the family throughout the year. It meant that when he called all the girls into the sitting room around the first of September and traced each foot on a piece of old newspaper, they would have shoes on their feet for the coming winter. Yes, cotton was somewhat worth planting and might reign supreme further south, but tobacco was soon to be King in eastern North Carolina, and no one would deny that fact.

Oh, Lord, why did you take my boys? asked Jeb for no telling how many times in the past twenty years. He straightened his back in the density of the tobacco row, the giant sticky leaves flapping him in the face as sweat dripped down his wrinkled brow. Clucking his tongue to the mule, urging it a little further up the row, Jeb called out to Simon, "How much more you think we can get in today?"

"Don't rightly know, Mistah Jeb. If'n we had some hep, I b'lieve we could be done with this here field by nightfall."

Jeb stood with his hands gripping his overall straps, thinking on what Simon had said. "Well, that's neither here nor there 'cause we don't have any help. Let's get this truck up to the barn. Those women will be caught up and out of something to do if we don't hurry up. Don't want 'em to sit idle."

Simon climbed up behind the mule on the wagon seat. The wagon that Jeb called a truck was piled high with greenish gold tobacco leaves. He clucked a couple of times for the mule to speed up, but she didn't seem to have a speed other than slow, so she just clomped on through the thick jungle of tobacco plants. Jeb followed close behind to make sure the precious cargo didn't fall by the wayside.

Back at the barn, Jeb saw he had guessed correctly. The women were almost done with the previous truck of tobacco. The younger girls and Simon's daughter, Queen—who wasn't quite right—handed three or four leaves at a time to Sarah Jane or Simon's wife, Swanee, who stood on one side of the truck and Nell or Hannah on the other side. The handers paced the work so the stringers could rhythmically take a handful of tobacco in one hand and quickly wrap the tobacco twine tightly around the stems with the other hand and flop it securely over the stick. Like clockwork, the women did this all day, stopping only for a minute or two as the stringer took a stick tied with heavy tobacco off the horse—a wooden rack set up to hold the stick on a horizontal level—and laid it in a neat pile ready for the men to hang in the barn at the end of the day. Other than the noonday meal, which Sarah Jane and Swanee had prepared before daylight, they took only one short break in midmorning and another in mid afternoon, drinking cool water from the overflow near the barn and resting a spell in the shade of the giant oak tree. The best they could hope for was the breeze of a thunder storm that, hopefully, wouldn't quite make it to the barn.

The rain was needed desperately, needless to say, but there were two reasons Sarah Jane prayed there would be no thunderstorms while they were barning. Number one, she was scared to death of lightning. She had all the faith in the world until the sky lit up with jagged bolts of electricity, and then it was if she was all by herself hiding under the kitchen table the day the Yankees came and everybody else had gone to Hallsville. That was the day she went back to wetting her pants at ten years old. Lightning and Yankees inspired the kind of prayer the apostle Paul called "unceasing." But today, July 25, the only storm that blew in was Lula Belle Aldridge.

Lula Belle was Jonas Aldridge's wife and Jonas, a highly educated man, was not only the pastor of the Baptist Church in Hallsville, he was head of the Hallsville Academy and infamous for his strict discipline and impeccable moral character. Lula Belle, on the other hand, was well known only for her big mouth, although if anyone had taken the time to get past her mouth, her much bigger heart would have been fairly obvious.

But there was one thing she did that tested Sarah Jane Gresham one step short of lightning storms and Yankees. Lula Belle, who had never worked a day in the fields in her life, had the habit of riding by the barn in her nicely attired buggy, all dressed to a tee right up to a gray, wide-brimmed hat decorated with a red rose whether it was summer or winter. Ignoring the fact that *she* was being ignored, Lula Belle would rein in the mare, which was by that time up to a very dignified trot, carefully climb down from the buggy seat and walk over to the barn shelter as if she had been invited. And then, "The Mouth," the name she was unaffectionately called in private (a la behind her back), would start moving as she walked around the big truck of tobacco, talking first to one and then the other, asking questions about who was doing what these days and every now and then brushing the dirt from the flopping tobacco leaves off her clean starched and ironed dress. Then, she would usually take her seat for awhile and proceed to share all the news she could remember—and that was quite a bit—with the women who were hard at work.

Yes, Lula Belle Aldridge was a trial Sarah Jane found hard to bear. For one thing, Sarah Jane hated gossip, and for another thing, she considered it the rudest thing in the world for somebody to come for a visit all dressed up in their cleanest and finest clothes and just stand around and watch her and the girls working and sweating in the dirty, grimy environment of a tobacco barn. What's more, it was obvious that Lula Belle didn't just happen by on her way somewhere. Jeb's barn wasn't on the way to anywhere unless she wanted to see the tiny community of Chinquapin, and there was nothing there to see except old G.B.D. Parker's store and the river which, by the way, she could have seen in Hallsville. The only other option was the Presbyterian Church, and Sara Jane knew for a fact Lula Belle wouldn't be caught dead there. It would have helped Sarah Jane's opinion of Lula Belle if the woman had just been honest once in a while.

Alright, Lord, I'll try harder to like her. Sarah Jane resigned herself under a mighty strong twinge of guilt. Lula Belle *was* the preacher's wife. But come to think of it, nobody liked him much either, not personally anyhow. Jonas Aldridge was as aloof and downright unfriendly as Lula Belle was a social butterfly with the mouth of a mockingbird. Now, if you were a man, and there were a lot of men around, and if you were educated enough to join Jonas in a theological debate, and no man in Beulah was, you might have found him rather amiable at times. But the university graduate and self-professed authority on anything of a Biblical nature had few peers in the entire county. Not that there were no educated men scattered about the county, there were. Sadly, they just happened to be Presbyterians, mostly descended from the Scots-Irish settlement of 1736. If there was anything Jonas could not abide, it was a sprinkling Calvinist. But all the churches in the county were to some degree Calvinistic, from Presbyterians to Baptists to Primitive Baptists—or Hard-shell Baptists, as Sarah Jane called them.

Sarah Jane was just beginning to realize she wasn't listening to a word Lula Belle was saying. She had long ago decided that a body was left no true choice in life but to figure out religion for one's self, especially if one was a woman. Women didn't seem to fit too kindly into the theology of the sons of Adam. If the daughters of Eve were to be forever blamed for the sins of not only man but all of mankind, it seemed logical to Sarah Jane that they would just have to figure a way out on their own. Ironically, according to the way she read the Good Book, the man Jesus was the way out.

She smiled, her features softening as she flipped the gummy golden leaves back and forth across the wooden stick, her fingers calloused from years of working with the cutting tobacco twine.

Now, there was a real man, she thought.

Most every day, in the early hours of the morning around first light, Sarah Jane sat in her rocking chair on the porch when the weather was good or by the fireplace when it was cold, reading the red words in her Bible over and over again. They were words of life to a woman hungry not only to feel the presence of God, but desperate for genuine answers to life's daily problems as well. She was a practical woman, as were most in her day, and she wanted something real, something that worked. She was looking for truth, not a bunch of religious double-talk.

The red words were full of practical wisdom for daily life, the kind of hard life the women around Beulah had obviously been allotted. Of course, there were the Psalms and Proverbs, a veritable wealth of wisdom, but the young Jewish man who according to the apostle Peter and Sarah Jane Gresham, was the Son of the Living God, had the answers to all her questions...even if more often than not He seemed to keep some of them to Himself.

As she sat in the porch rocking chair reading His words, "Consider the lilies of the field, how they neither toil nor spin, and yet Solomon in all his glory was not arrayed like one of these," Sarah Jane would often lift her own eyes to the fields beyond the little house, and her heart would warm at the sight of wild pink phlox and purple anemones dancing in the sunlight of a brand new day. And then she would lean back in the rocker and close her eyes, whispering, "Thank You, Jesus. Thank You for clothin' my girls and me and Jeb. Thank You for the food on our table and the cannin' You gave me the strength to put up for the winter. Thank You for five girls whose hearts are turned in the right direction, even if they stumble now and then just as we all do. Thank You for the land. Thank You that my rheumatism isn't as bad as it could be. Thank You, Lord. I thank You."

Chapter Ten

The best thing about barning season, according to Sarah Jane's female brood, was that Willis T. often allowed his oldest girls to "hep" out in an emergency, as Simon would say, and an emergency came up almost every week when there was more tobacco in the field than could possibly be cropped before the week was out. If the golden leaves were left even one day too long in the field, they would burn in the scorching sun. It was during such times that Jessie and her sisters, Mollie and sometimes Kate, and a few of the other Gresham and Bishop cousins, the city girls, climbed up on their Uncle Jeb's wagon and giggled all the way to the old Hall farm Sarah Jane had inherited from her daddy.

Now those girls could beat the band. You'd have thought they were competing in a prize-winning contest to see who could talk the most and work the fastest. The stringers flip-flopped the tobacco faster and faster in rhythm with the constant chatter and laughter shared around the truck of yellow-green tobacco leaves.

There was one big disappointment on some of those days. Usually, Willis T. could spare one or two of his sons, but if not, the oldest girls, Hannah and Nell—and before her marriage, Kate, too— were sent to the field to help Jeb and old Simon with the cropping. It wasn't that they minded working in the steamy jungle of sticky tobacco plants under the scorching sun; it was just that they missed all the fun at the barn with the other girls. All except Kate, that is; she liked doing man's work away from all the female silliness. Thankfully, Jeb very kindly gave them more breaks than he and Simon took themselves, so the cropping girls would hurry back to the barn, gulp down a few dripping mouthfuls of cool spring water and get in on ten or fifteen minutes of news from town. If there wasn't much news, they might hear a few of Swanee's funny tales before they hurried back to the field.

Even Hannah's new job assisting Doctor Kennedy didn't exempt her from barning tobacco. From late May (the day of the eclipse, actually) through the Fourth of July, Hannah had stayed in town alternating her place of residence among Jessie's house, Nate and Laney's and Kate's. Her first priority was to learn what the doctor would expect of her when she was needed.

It was not to be a fulltime job, however. Most doctors in those days made house calls to the homes of the sick or wounded where the follow-up care was provided by the women in the immediate family. Hannah's job description was mainly to help with birthings; therefore, Doc Kennedy preferred she simply be called a midwife, and she meekly submitted. Nevertheless, she told Kate in confidence that she had much rather be called a nurse than a midwife. Kate nodded in agreement and said that Hannah wasn't anyone's wife, praise the Lord. She never could understand what the word midwife meant exactly. It seemed to her that "midmother" might be a more fitting title.

But now, Hannah was back in the field snapping the giant leaves from the stalk about three at a time, one after the other. She then flipped them under her arm where she carried her hot sticky load until she had enough to pile it neatly on the layers of tobacco in the truck. The girls wore Jeb's long-sleeved shirts over their dresses when they cropped. That made the job even hotter but less sticky. Back and forth, back and forth, all day long in the hot scorching sun of July and August, they snapped the big gold leaves from the stalks and piled them in the truck.

There was only one chance for reprieve, short of a rogue storm, that is. Jeb always arose long before day, wolfed down the filling breakfast Sarah Jane placed on the table and then hurried off to the barn that had been filled with tobacco a day or two before. He climbed up on the barn rafters to hand the sticks of cured tobacco down to Simon who then laid the sweet-smelling leaves in neat piles waiting to be loaded up to take to the pack house. Dirt and dust flew everywhere, covering the two men with a sticky mess in the hot humid barn long before the sun came up.

After the cured tobacco was piled on the wagon and taken to the pack house where the women would later pull it off the sticks and tie it in bundles to take to market, Jeb would walk out to the field with old Simon and stand there watching as the sun came up. When the field came into focus in the clear light of dawn, Jeb might state matter-of-factly, "It ain't ready."

Old Simon would nod his head and reply, "Nope. It ain't ready."

Then, they would go back to the house and tell Sarah Jane and Swanee, who were already busy preparing the noonday meal. The girls were quietly eating their breakfast and getting ready for another day at the barn or in the field.

"Not ready," said Jeb to Sarah Jane as he cracked the screened door and peeked in.

"Nope, ain't ready," nodded Simon in agreement.

"Then we'll start tyin' today, girls," said Sarah Jane. "No sense lettin' the work get ahead of us."

Now, you may have thought the girls would have groaned and moaned about more work, but this was 1901, and these were farming people. They didn't know any other way of life. Actually, it was good news. The opportunity to sit in chairs or on overturned barrels all day, maybe even an old rocker, under the shady shelter of the pack house and sweet gum trees didn't come around very often. It was almost fun to tie the sweet-smelling bundles, taking turns standing up to break the twine and rip the leaves from the sticks. No doubt about it, tying was an easy job compared to barning.

That's where they were the day Jessie was quiet...under the shelter of the pack house. She had spent the night with Hannah thinking she'd be needed at the barn the next day, but now the women—Sarah Jane, Swanee, Queen, and all five girls plus Jessie—were busy tying tobacco and chatting every now and then about most anything that came to mind. Nobody said too much that day, having caught up on all the news the day before when a small herd of Beulah cousins had helped out at the barn.

It was nearly noon when Sarah Jane casually asked Jessie how her mama was and didn't get an answer. Assuming Jessie didn't hear her, she asked again, a little louder, "How's your mama, Jessie?"

"Hmmm?" the girl slowly replied, her eyes glued to the tobacco in her lap.

"I asked how's your mama, child?" Sarah Jane glanced at Hannah who raised her eyebrows, understanding exactly what her mama's look meant.

It meant, "What ails her?"

"Oh…Mama's fine. Said to give you her respects." Jessie went back to tying tobacco, much slower than usual, Hannah noticed. Jessie was fast at everything she did. Her hands usually moved as quickly as her mouth.

"Is there anything wrong, child? Do you feel poorly?" Sarah Jane was getting a little worried. She had never seen Jessie Gresham quiet, much less wordless.

"No…, I'm fine. I…I just have a lot on my mind, I guess you'd say."

Now all the women and girls were glancing back and forth from one to the other. If Jessie had anything on her mind, it was bound to come out her mouth.

Hannah was in the process of making a decision to ask Jessie about it later when they were alone when the object of everyone's attention suddenly blurted out, "I'm going to marry Big Rufus Bostic; just thought y'all would want to know."

Stunned beyond words, they all froze with their mouths open, staring at Jessie who, oddly enough, looked more serious than she had ever been in her life.

"What did you say, Jessie?" asked Nell quietly.

"I'm going to marry Rufus Bostic. I've decided I love him and he's the one I'm going to marry."

"Has he asked you, Jessie?" said Sarah Jane gently.

"Not yet, but I can tell he's just about to pop the question." She smiled impishly. "Haven't y'all noticed he follows me around like a big ol' hound dog all the time?"

Liza giggled, standing up to put a new stick of tobacco on the wooden horse. "I've noticed," she said. "He looks like he's mourning over you, like you died or somethin'."

"Liza," said Sarah Jane sternly, "why don't you take Susie and Frannie up to the house and start settin' dinner on the table. We'll all be up in a few minutes."

"Oh, Mama, I never get to hear the good stuff," moaned Liza. She was terribly disappointed, but she didn't dare disobey her mama. She'd been in enough trouble lately. Grabbing Susie by the arm, she took Frannie's hand and started off down the path, stamping her feet a little just to make sure they were all aware of how unhappy she was about her plight. Not hard enough to raise Sarah Jane's ire, though. If there was anything her mama couldn't abide, it was outright rebellion.

Sure that Liza and the younger girls were out of earshot, Sarah Jane asked, "Now, Jessie, why are you suddenly so serious about getting married? You have plenty of time for that. Hannah's not married yet, and you're younger than her."

"Yes, but I just know it's time, that's all. Rufus is considerably older than me, you know, and I can tell he's more than ready to settle down and get married." Noting the concern in her aunt's eyes and suddenly thinking of her close relationship to her own mother, she added, "Now don't worry, Aunt Sarah Jane. I'm going to talk to Mama about it Saturday afternoon. I thought it'd be better for her to speak to Papa before I do."

"Yes, I think so, too," said Sarah Jane, wryly.

"I decided it last Sunday, but I haven't told anybody yet," said Jessie, seeming rather pleased with herself.

Sarah Jane wasn't yet over the initial shock, and now she was dealing with the knowledge that Jessie hadn't yet talked to her mama about marrying Rufus Bostic. Added to that disturbing news was the even more amazing fact that Jessie had first thought about all this last Sunday and had kept it a secret until today which was Thursday. Put all that together and the concern was bad enough, not even considering what Willis T. Gresham would have to say about it.

"Girl, you better stay right where yo at," said Swanee, deftly twisting the twine around the dried tobacco. "Yo got a nice house, fine clothes and everything yo needs. Why, yo don't even have t' work in 'baccer 'less yo wants to. Why on dis here earth yo want to go and git marrit?"

"I love him, Swanee."

"You cain't live on love, chil', 'specially when dem babies start a'comin'."

Hannah and Nell blushed, quickly looking back to the tobacco in their hands.

Jessie frowned, her bottom lip poked out in a pout. "Wish I hadn't told y'all. Wish I'd kept it a secret."

"Oh, Jessie, honey, we want the very best for you because we love you. You're just like one of my girls, child, and I want to see you happy as much as I want my own children to be happy. I certainly didn't mean to hurt your feelin's."

Sarah Jane wasn't sure if the love-struck girl was listening by that time. Jessie seemed off in a world of her own, a feat of amazing ability for a sociable girl like herself. Rising from her chair for only the second time since daybreak, Sarah Jane rubbed the small of her back and stretched her neck. She brushed the dirt and grime off her apron as well as she could and then walked over to the black iron bell that was hanging from the corner of the shelter.

Dong! Dong! Dong! Three times she hit the iron bell, informing Jeb and Old Simon it was time to come to the house and eat the noonday meal.

By the time the entire crew had washed the black stickiness off—or at least as much of it as they could get off—at the hand pump on the end of the porch by the kitchen, Liza had spread a table full of food she had heated in the oven, still slightly warm from the morning biscuits. There were collards, colored butter beans, corn on the cob, back bone meat and the inevitable pot of rice and gravy to go with it all. She pulled the cornbread out of the oven just as everyone sat down to fill their growling stomachs and enjoy the much-needed reprieve.

Nothing much was said for quite some time. Everyone was too hungry to talk. But as the bowls of fresh vegetables finally settled down on the table and the edge was taken off their hunger, a few comments flowed here and there, increasing as the food began to disappear.

"Well, Jessie," said Jeb, stabbing another cob of corn with his fork, "sure is good to have you at our table today. Glad you came to help out."

"Thank you, Uncle Jeb," she replied, daintily wiping her mouth. Her mother's etiquette lesson hadn't gone unheeded.

"I hear you're playin' the piano at the Baptist Church these days." Jeb took a crunchy bite out of the corn cob, golden butter dripping down his stubbly chin and onto his plate.

"You're behind the times, Uncle," replied Jessie with a giggle. "I've been playing the piano in church for two years now. I alternate with Cousin Sallie Hines."

Jeb put the stripped cob back on his plate and grinned. "I never could keep up with the news."

"She plays real pretty, Papa," said Liza. "You'd hear her if you came to church more often."

Jeb's mouth twisted to one side as he glared at his daughter, quickly deciding what he wanted to say was better left unsaid.

Liza successfully ignored her papa's eyes and sipped her water, wishing for sweet tea.

Sarah Jane made a quick decision as well. She thought it best to change the subject. "Have you heard anything more about the murder investigation, Jeb? It's been months since old James was killed and as far as I know, nobody's been arrested."

"Nope, not a word." Jeb turned and shouted to the black man sitting on the porch with his wife and Queen, eating their dinner. "You heard anything about old James's murder, Simon?"

"Nope, nary a word," answered Simon, sopping what was left of his cornbread in the gravy.

"I heerd tell dey wus a'givin' up," said Swanee.

Queen didn't say anything.

"That's what I heard," said Sarah Jane. "Nobody cares who killed that old man. It's a cryin' shame."

Jeb finished his second plate of back bone and collards and, as usual, got up and left the kitchen before anyone else had finished eating. In two jerks of a sheep's tail, he was coming back down the porch yelling, "Sarah Jane! What'd you do with those land deeds I brought home from the courthouse last Tuesd'y?"

Jeb slammed the screened door and stood there in the middle of the kitchen floor glaring at his wife, impatiently waiting for an answer. Sarah Jane placed both hands on her hips and stared out the window, her back turned to Jeb. She didn't answer him.

"Well? Where are they, woman?"

Slowly, she turned around. With a frustrated sigh, she finally replied, "Jeb Grissom, I have *not* seen any deeds."

"Sure you have! I put them on the dresser the minute I got back. You've put 'em up somewhere, and now I'll have to take a whole day off to go back to the courthouse and pay somebody to copy 'em again. Why cain't you just leave somethin' be? You're always puttin' everything I need away somewhere!" His voice was getting louder and louder, his face red as a beet.

By now, the girls could tell that Sarah Jane was trying real hard not to, but she was about to lose her temper—something that didn't happen very often around their house and definitely not in the presence of company. No one dared move a muscle, every eye wide in amazement.

"Jeb, I'm telling you *one more time*. I did *not* see any deeds, and even if I had, I would *not* have moved them from the dresser!"

"You put 'em up somewhere, and you'll just have to find 'em. Now stop what you're doin' right now and help me, you hear?" Before he got the last word out of his mouth, Jeb was out the banging door and on his way back to the living area of the house, a man on a mission.

Sarah Jane glared at the door for a moment or two. She was livid and the girls knew it. They still sat there without daring to move. Slowly, she turned back around and calmly resumed washing the plates and forks.

"Aren't you going to help Papa, Mama?" asked Liza.

"No," she answered calmly, her cheek twitching. "Your Papa'll be back in here in a little while with the deeds which he will find right where he put them. Mark my words."

The women were finishing up when Jeb's footsteps were heard coming down the porch on his way back to the kitchen. Again, the screened door banged, and Jeb went straight to the table where he spread out the papers and sat down to compare one deed with the other. He didn't say a word about where he found them. In fact, he didn't say anything at all. He acted as if the papers had never been lost in the first place.

Sarah Jane had a look on her face the girls very seldom had the privilege to see, or misfortune to see, according to the way you look at it. She walked over to the table and faced Jeb head on.

"Where'd you find the papers, Jeb?"

"Hm? What'd you say, woman?" You could tell his mind was on his business and nothing else.

"I asked you where you found the papers." She had a hand on each hip. Her mouth was set in a straight line.

"Oh, yeah…the deeds. I remembered I had put 'em in the bottom drawer with my long underwear for safe keepin'. Didn't figure I'd need my underwear in this heat." He didn't look up but continued to scan the papers, adjusting his wire-rimmed glasses as he read.

"Jeb Gresham, you owe me an apology," she said emphatically.

"Huh?" He looked up then, surprised at his even-tempered wife's tone of voice. "Apology for what, woman?"

"You know what for," she continued, looking madder than a wet settin' hen by now.

"I don't know anything of the sort," said Jeb, exasperated as could be. "What did I do?"

"You fussed at me for something I didn't do, as usual, and then, when you found the papers right where *you* put them, you didn't even have the gall to say you were sorry for blaming me. *That's* what you did!"

He gathered up the papers from the table and quickly folded them into the long pocket in the breast of his overalls. "Don't know what you're fussin' at me for," he said. "You must've got up on the wrong side of the bed this morning." And with that, he slammed the screened door again on his way out.

Glaring at the trembling door, Sarah Jane threw up her hands and let out a word that on a scale from one to ten would probably have been a one if anyone else had said it, but considering it came out of Sarah Jane Hall Gresham's mouth, it sounded as if it had passed ten a long time ago.

Jessie stared wide-eyed and speechless. The two older girls gasped, Liza clasped her hand over her mouth to suppress a giggle and little Susie cried, "Mama! That's a bad word! The Good Lord doesn't like that word, Mama."

"The Good Lord is as frustrated with your papa as I am, Susie Gresham!"

They all stared at their previously sainted mother. But Sarah Jane offered no repentance. She just said, "Let's get back to the pack house, girls. We're a'wastin' good daylight doing nothin'."

Chapter Eleven

The best thing about tobacco tying time was not only that it was rather easy work compared with barning, but it was another fine time for neighbors to take turns helping one another and get some visiting done. Sitting under the shelter of the pack house in old wooden rockers from the porch, or overturned barrels, the women and children—and oftentimes the men—chatted for hours while they tied the dry cured tobacco in bundles for Jeb to haul to the tobacco market in Kinston. That's what the Greshams were doing a few days later when Kate, who was thrilled at the opportunity to stop being a doctor's wife for one day, sat back in her rocking chair, rubbed her swollen belly, and asked teasingly, "Jessie, when are you and Rufus Bostic going to get on to some serious courtin'? I saw y'all walking down the road by Nate's store Sunday afternoon, and you weren't even holding hands."

All eyes were on little Jessie except her own which were darting back and forth from one face to the other while she tried hard to remember who she had told about her marrying Big Rufus. Evidently, she had forgotten to mention it to her sister.

Before she could think up something to say, which in this situation was unusually difficult for Jessie Gresham, Liza exclaimed, "Courtin'?! Why, Kate, they're getting married, don't you know?"

Kate looked as if a powerful contraction had suddenly hit her and she might be producing a baby any minute. Holding onto her belly, she stuttered, rather loudly, "Wha…what are you talking about, Liza?"

But before Liza could answer, Kate turned to Jessie and asked even louder, "What is she talking about, Jessie Grissom?"

Jessie, never at a loss for words, glanced sharply at Hannah for help, but Hannah was staring at the tobacco she was tying as if she was doing some kind of delicate needlepoint or something and intended to give it her full attention. Nell, who always avoided conflict if at all possible, wasn't a bit of help, and when Jessie got to Sarah Jane's face, it was easy to see what she thought about the situation. Her pragmatic aunt's eyes said, *Time to face the music, child. See what a mess you've gotten yourself into?*

By now, Kate was standing with her heavy load. "Jessie Grissom, I think you and I better take a little walk. I feel the need of some cold water from the spring, don't you?"

"Yes, Kate, I sure do. I'm real thirsty."

Jessie was a good actress, but the problem was that her older sister knew her like a book and Jessie knew she did. There would be no hiding the truth or coming up with a good cover story. But she did have one hope. Kate had experienced so many problems of her own when her parents had forced her to marry Doctor Kennedy that Jessie was certain she wouldn't tell her mama and papa. Not yet, anyway.

Later, the only details Jessie told Hannah about her walk with Kate was that her older sister had begged her over and over again, "Don't do it, Jessie. Don't get married now. You're too young. You don't know what you're gettin' into."

Although she didn't say much, as usual, Hannah couldn't help but agree with Kate. In her heart, she was convinced that Jessie was just longing for some excitement in her life. She was forever looking for a new adventure, and the silly girl, optimistic to a fault, seemed to think that getting married was like going to the county fair every night for a week or two. Kate told Hannah later that as enjoyable as her little sister was to be around, she was just plain naïve when it came to the serious matters of life.

"She's also a little short on common sense," said Kate with a sigh, tears welling up in her eyes at the thought of merry little Jessie walking through the prison gate called matrimony.

Well, by the time Saturday came around bold little Jessie Gresham had lost her nerve, and it ended up being two weeks before she got around to telling her mama she was going to marry Rufus Bostic. She might as well have kept the news to herself considering her mama's reaction. Grabbing the funeral parlor fan (the one engraved with the phrase, "Gone, but not forgotten") she had kept as a remembrance of her recent trip to Wilmington for her great aunt's funeral, Margaret Gresham slumped into the porch rocker, fanning herself as fast as she could, moaning, "Ohhhh, ohhhh." Then she cried, "Don't tell your papa, child. Don't tell your papa!"

"But I love Rufus, Mama," said Jessie, looking determined as ever. However, there was something about the way her mama's eyes rolled back in her head that caught Jessie up short, causing her to think she might better hold off on the wedding a bit. If the news was about to kill mama, there was more than a slight chance that papa might decide to kill Big Rufus — or worse, Jessie Gresham.

So that's the way it was from tobacco tying time in late August and early September to the harvest festival near the end of October. In the meantime — just a few days after the revelatory day at the barn — Sarah Jane and Hannah helped Kate bring a seven pound, two ounce boy into the world. Sarah Jane said Kate's bones must have been spaced just right for childbearing because her labor was only about nine hours and that was fairly short for a first baby. Doctor Kennedy named him Albert.

The day was made even more exciting when the drummer stopped at Nate's store and told everybody that President McKinley had been shot. It was a terrible thing, even to the Democrats who'd get no relief because Teddy Roosevelt was now president and some people thought him to be more Republican than McKinley.

Jessie hadn't said another word about getting married, and her mama acted as if she'd never heard a thing about it. Margaret was as good at pretending as any other southern woman. Sarah Jane warned her girls to keep it to themselves, and Kate certainly wasn't about to bring the subject up. She was occupied with a newborn baby anyway. Knowing Jessie, they all figured she had probably forgotten about it herself and moved on to a new plan to alleviate any boredom she might be experiencing.

Then came the harvest festival at the schoolhouse. It was as close as Beulah ever came to having a fair in those days. The big Duplin County Agricultural Fair was always held in Kenansville, the county seat, and it was a humdinger of a day for people who worked from sunrise to sunset six days a week. But the harvest festival in Beulah was almost as exciting. There were all kinds of games that day — horseshoes, checkers, dunkin' the school principal and one-legged races, to name a few. There was even a turkey shoot, with real live turkeys, which the men had practiced up for all year. The women from miles around brought their famous jellies and jams, cucumber pickles and pickled watermelon rinds to be judged for first, second and third prizes. All the labeled jars were placed neatly on a long table, guarded carefully by a covey of mighty competitive females, old and young alike. There was a cake contest, too, but everybody knew that Ida Wash Sandlin's pound cake would win first place. She always won. Myrtle Jones, the best cook in town other than Ida, said every year that the only way anyone else would ever win the cake contest was if Miss Ida's redemption drew a bit more nigh.

The younger children were bobbing for apples and playing catch all over the place while their more senior siblings strolled around the grounds trying to catch the attention of someone of the opposite sex they had taken a fancy to. Every now and then one of them would stop by the kissing booth to see who had the nerve to pay to kiss Miss Lucy Hill, the new school teacher. She was surely pretty enough, but it seemed to the boys a sin to kiss a school teacher, and so most of them kept their distance and watched for the bachelors like Arnold Lanier to boldly step up to the booth and put a nickel in the jar. Arnold had just built a little store at the other end of town with a scandalous pool table in the back, and they said he was out looking for a wife to help him run the place. Of course, Miss Lucy Hill didn't know that she was on trial when she kissed him. But she must have passed the test because later in the day it was said that she closed her kissing booth early and took Arnold's arm as he led her over to the big tent to see who won the prize ribbons.

The Gresham girls turned out en masse. Jeb's five, Willis T.'s four, and all the other cousins, all dressed up in their Sunday-go-to-meeting finery, gathered in a huddle at the opening of the tent like a flock of chirping bluebirds in early spring. And that was when Jessie, chirping the fastest, saw what almost caused her to faint right then and there.

Rufus Bostic was standing beside a giant oak tree, his shoulder resting against the trunk as he gazed cow-eyed down into the face of Delphie Mae Jackson, a fairly pretty girl two years older than Jessie—a nice girl, to boot. Now, what on earth was Rufus doing talking to Delphie Mae? Jessie's first thought was to try to think up some practical reason for the suspicious encounter, but in another moment, after seeing the look Delphie Mae was giving Big Rufus with her moist brown eyes, Jessie's heart just sunk right down into her stomach. She quickly closed her eyes and clamped her hand over her open mouth, hoping she wouldn't throw up right there in the middle of the jam and jelly. When she opened her eyes, every Gresham girl in the crowd was staring at her because she had stopped chattering right in the middle of a sentence. Most of them just thought little Jessie must be a mite sickly, but Hannah and Kate, her baby bundled in her arms, had seen the direction Jessie's gaze had taken. They were both heartsick for the young girl.

Neither of them wanted to embarrass Jessie so Kate, more talkative and quicker to make decisions, said, "Sister, you look a mite under the weather. Don't you want me to walk you down to the doctor's house and let's sit on the porch a spell? You can nuss the baby awhile if you want to."

"N...no. I'm alright, really I am." She seemed to pull herself together. "Anyway, I want to see if Mama wins first prize again this year with her strawberry preserves."

She quietly left her spot at the tent door and took a seat on a bench closer to the front where the contestants eagerly awaited the judges' decisions. Margaret won again which was the only spark of light in Jessie's dark day.

It was a heartbroken Jessie Gresham who slowly walked home at the end of that beautiful autumn day, alone and dejected. She left the other girls still hanging around, innocently flirting and laughing with some of the local boys, carefully watched by hopeful mamas and anxious papas. Well, it may have been vice versa.

"I'll show Rufus Bostic," Jessie muttered into the cool October air.

It was hardly a month later that everyone in Beulah heard the news that Big Rufus Bostic was going to marry Delphie Mae Jackson. Thank goodness only close friends and family knew about Jessie Gresham's vow to marry Big Rufus, and most of them pretended they'd never heard such a thing, particularly her mother who was more thankful than ever she had possessed the common sense not to tell Willis T. So nothing else was said about Jessie's love for the boy, not until the day of the wedding, that is, and the one who said it was Jessie herself.

Now, as Jeb had been reminded back during barning season, Jessie played the piano at the Missionary Baptist Church in Hallsville. It was the only church around Beulah, actually, and the church Delphie Mae Jackson attended as well. So, as was fairly common in those days, at the beginning of the Sunday morning service, Reverend Aldridge announced that Rufus Bostic and Delphie Mae Jackson would be getting married immediately following the service. Then, he graciously invited the congregation to stay for the happy occasion.

And everyone did stay, including Jessie Gresham who was seated on the piano bench during the entire sermon. It was a mighty long sermon, and her back was beginning to ache something terrible, but when Jonas Aldridge said, "Amen," Jessie straightened her shoulders, carefully placed her hands on the piano keys and began to quietly play.

And then she began to sing…not so quietly:

I'll deck my brow with roses; my true love may be there.
The gems that others gave me will shine within my hair.
And even those that know me will think my heart is light
Tho' my heart may break tomorrow, I'll be all smiles tonight.
I'll be all smiles tonight, love; I'll be all smiles tonight.
Tho' my heart may break tomorrow, I'll be all smiles tonight.
And when the room he entered, his bride upon his arm,
I stood and gazed upon him as though he were a charm.
And then he smiled upon her as once he smiled on me.

They knew not what I suffered; they found no change in me.
And when the day is over and all have gone to rest,
I'll think of him, dear Mother, the one that I love best.
He once did love me dearly and ne'er from me would part.
He sought not to deceive me; false friends have changed his heart.
I'll be all smiles tonight, love; I'll be all smiles tonight
Tho' my heart may break tomorrow, I'll be all smiles tonight.

Slowly and deliberately, Jessie Gresham lifted her slender fingers from the piano keys and laid her hands in her lap. And then, with head held high and mouth set in something just short of a smile, she turned to watch Rufus escort Delphie up to the pulpit, looking as if he had seen the ghost of his recently departed mama and might pass out any minute from the terrible fright. Delphie, although rather perplexed as to why Jessie had chosen such an odd song for the occasion, smiled innocently up at her betrothed, assuming he was reacting like any other nervous young groom on his wedding day.

As for the others in church that day who knew of Jessie's plans to marry Big Rufus—namely her mama, Kate and Hannah who was staying in town to help Doctor Kennedy—well... suffice it to say that her mother nearly had a fainting spell and almost fanned herself into a bad case of pneumonia. Hannah was totally mortified, stiff as a board with tears locked in her eyes. As for Kate, well, after she got over the initial shock, she held her baby close to her heart and tried her best to look as if the smile on her face was for the happy bride rather than the audacious little sister still sitting primly on the piano bench. She had never been so proud of anyone in her entire life.

And that was that. Jessie never spoke of Rufus Bostic again.

But before barning season came round the next year, she was married to her distant cousin, Clancy Whaley.

"She was as determined to get married as Kate was *not* to marry," Sarah Jane told Jeb after hearing the news.

Kate was heartbroken. She had believed all the time that Rufus Bostic's indiscretion had saved her little sister from an early prison sentence. But it was not to be. The cell door clanked, and the key might as well have been thrown away forever.

But Hannah had high hopes for Jessie and Clancy, assuring Kate quite often that unlike herself, Jessie might actually like being married. And she was right. Jessie had a lot more in common with her new husband than she ever had with Rufus Bostic, Clancy being her distant cousin and all. And then, to her great delight, Jessie's papa built the newlyweds a house right beside his own, there on the west end of the village where she could visit back and forth with her family and walk down to Nate's store and Kate's house any time she wanted to. Yes, Jessie was a happy young bride whether Kate liked it or not.

There was a lot of marrying going on in and around Beulah in 1902. In early spring, Nell surprised everyone but Sarah Jane by quietly announcing that Clyde Thomas had asked her to marry him and she had agreed. No one knew if she was happy about it or not, and Jeb figured they'd never know; that was just the way Nell was. But one Sunday afternoon in the middle of May, his oldest daughter, the prettiest of Sarah Jane and Jeb's girls, dressed up in her new Sunday-go-to-meeting frock and slowly walked with her papa out to the flowering crabapple tree in the front yard where Clyde Thomas and the preacher were patiently waiting. The three youngest girls pranced and skipped behind the silent bride, giggling all the way.

Nell was dressed in the paper white dress her mother had lovingly helped her make, her soft brown hair pulled into a braided bun at the base of her neck. Liza had made a wreath of wildflowers for the bride's hair. In her hands, she carried a lovely bouquet of Queen Anne's Lace, gathered that morning from the ditch bank at the edge of the woods by Frannie and Nell, all in a twitter on their oldest sister's wedding day. Sarah Jane and Hannah followed up the more lively section of the procession, silently praying that Nell would have a good life with Clyde…that he would be good to her.

It was a sad time later that day—after a wedding dinner of fried chicken, string beans, rice and ham biscuits—when Clyde helped Nell up onto the wagon seat and timidly took his place beside her. Jeb placed her small carpetbag of personal possessions in the back of the wagon along with a large pine box, Nell's hope chest. It held the quilt she had made out of colorful fabric scraps, the dresser scarves and a tablecloth she and Hannah had painstakingly crocheted out of tobacco twine, plus a partial set of pewter plates Sarah Jane had inherited from her own mother and carefully saved for the first daughter who married.

When Clyde clucked his tongue to the mare and said, "Giddy-up," Nell, with her usual shy smile, turned to wave good-bye to her family, all of whom were in tears by then. Even the excited younger girls were hit with the realization that their little family was breaking apart for the first time. Their lives would never be the same again.

Susie, strangely enough, was affected more than the others, weeping uncontrollably. Soon, they found out why. All of a sudden, she ran over to Hannah and threw her arms around her sister's waist, crying, "Oh, Hannah, you'll be next! Don't leave us, Hannah! Please don't leave us!"

That did it. Everybody went to crying—some, like Liza and Frannie, loud as holy rollers and others more quietly like Sarah Jane and Hannah. Even Jeb turned aside to hide a few silent tears that were trickling down his leathery face.

Sarah Jane wondered if she was crying more for herself or for Nell, the daughter who had never strayed far from hearth and home. She had depended on her...more than she realized. Now, with Hannah in Beulah most of the time helping Doctor Kennedy and Nell gone to live with the Thomas crowd, there would be only the three youngest to help with all the chores. Of course, they weren't so young anymore; it was just that she couldn't help but think of them that way.

Liza was sixteen now and a hard worker, but her mama had one of those feelings the girls mistakenly called premonitions that her middle child would be married before long. Frank Carroll just happened to show up everywhere Liza was for the past few months, and it seemed like every time she turned around, he was sitting in the porch swing looking at Liza like a sick puppy. Liza seemed to love every minute of it.

All of a sudden, standing by the side of the road near the crabapple tree, someone pulled the string and turned on the light in

Sarah Jane's brain. Of course! Why hadn't she thought of that before? Even though his family owned quite a bit of land, the Carroll boy had an older brother who stood in line to inherit the home place and a lot more acreage than Frank. It was the custom for the oldest son to stay at home and help work the land, preparing to inherit the farm when his papa passed on. That meant that even though Frank Carroll would probably come into some land of his own, he wouldn't have a house and all the out buildings, barns and equipment he would need to get a good start farming.

So, while the girls dried their eyes and drifted off to one place or the other to mourn their loss, Sarah Jane took a deep breath and relaxed, watching the dust cloud that was still swirling down the road from the wheels of Clyde Thomas's wagon. Thank the Good Lord, Liza wouldn't be leaving home…and thank Him even more that Jeb Gresham was about to get a full-grown son to help him in the tobacco fields. The sooner, the better.

Chapter Twelve

"Well, howdy-do, Miz Laney," said an unfamiliar voice. Laney was stacking a few dozen small boxes of tacks on the shelves behind the counter with one hand. With the other, she held Lizzy on her hip, rocking gently back and forth. The toddler had been irritable since yesterday afternoon and wouldn't eat. She had a fever, too, and it was rising steadily. Laney shifted the little girl to her other arm and turned to look at the man with the friendly voice.

The fellow was in his early thirties, she guessed, with a smile as pleasant as his voice. But she certainly couldn't say his looks were particularly pleasing. Shah, she couldn't even say he was fair to middlin'. The stranger was downright homely, as her mama used to say. But if she hadn't been staring him in the face no more than twenty-four inches away, she'd have never noticed he was homely. His winning personality and broad smile made up for his lack in good looks. Laney Gresham decided she liked him right off the bat.

"What can I do for you, fello…hey! How did you know my name?" Laney's eyes widened as she stared into the kind face while she moved Lizzy back to her side, shifting the whining child to her other hip. She kissed her forehead one more time. It was hotter now, that terrible dry hot that causes a mother's heart to skip a beat or two.

The man ignored her question, staring at the baby with noticeable concern. "Is she sick?"

"Well, I thought it was just a little stomach ache, but now she's hot with fever." Laney was obviously getting more worried by the minute.

"Mister, if you'll just tell me what you need, I'll get it real quick so I can lock up and take little Lizzy down to Doc Kennedy." Laney looked as if she might cry. "I do hope he's in Beulah today," she added.

"Well now, why don't I hold the baby so you can close up? I can come back another time for supplies." The man was smiling at Laney as if he had known her all his life.

She couldn't imagine allowing a stranger to hold her baby, but something about the fellow made her feel safe. It was like there was a glow of peace about him, and she didn't know when, if ever, she had seen such compassion in a man. She decided to trust him right then and there.

"Alright," she said, holding the toddler out to the stranger, fully expecting to have to pull her back when Lizzy started screaming in fright.

But much to Laney's surprise, Nate's chubby little princess patted the strange fellow's smiling face, cooing with pleasure. Speaking softly to the child, he held her gently in his arms, and before long, she rested her little head against his chest and closed her fevered eyes.

Laney followed him out the door onto the porch and had just turned the key in the lock when she heard the man say, "Here, you are, Laney. Your daughter will be fine now. When she wakes up, give her something to eat."

Grateful for his help in locking up, she took the baby from him, smiling down at the sweet little face as she continued to sleep peacefully in her mother's arms. "Thank you for helping me, Mister... ah...what did you say your name wa...." She looked up.

He was gone. Just like that.

"Well, I'll be," said Laney.

She carried Lizzy to the edge of the porch and looked up and down the dirt road. The man was nowhere to be seen. She eased herself down into the rocking chair so as not to wake little Lizzy and just sat there for a few minutes trying to figure out what could have happened to the stranger. She had only taken her eyes off him for a few seconds after he had handed Lizzy back to her. There wasn't enough time for him to get down the porch steps, much less to walk off out of sight.

But she didn't have time to think on the mystery; she had to get Lizzy down the road to Doc Kennedy's office. Rising carefully from the rocker with the toddler in her arms, Laney gently pushed back the soft blonde curls that had fallen across Lizzy's eyes.

Suddenly, she froze. The little girl's forehead was cool as a cucumber. There was no sign of fever. Laney looked closer. Her skin was back to its healthy pink glow. Lizzy was sleeping peacefully for the first time since yesterday afternoon.

Laney sat back down in the rocker. *What in the world?* she thought. How could the baby's fever drop that quickly? It was impossible. The child's head had been burning up only seconds ago. She sat there a few minutes, still as a mouse, staring at Lizzy's peaceful face.

Suddenly, she remembered what the man had said when he handed the sleeping child back to her, *"Your daughter will be fine now."*

"Lord, have mercy," she whispered in awe, staring down at the sleeping child. "I do believe you and I have had a visitation, baby girl."

Laney was beside herself with excitement, but she didn't want to wake Lizzy who was resting peacefully. She sat perfectly still, gazing at the baby's face, touching her stomach and back which were just as cool as her forehead.

"What if he was an angel, Lizzy?" she whispered. "Maybe he was *your* angel. Maybe it's his job to watch over you. Maybe...oh!" she gasped. "Oh, my!" The hairs on the back of her neck stood up like on the day of the solar eclipse.

Holding the little one as gently as she could, Laney fished the giant brass key out of her apron pocket and tried to fit it in the hole in the lock with one hand. The lock kept moving back and forth, slipping out of her grasp. She was about to give up and walk around back to see if there was a window open that she could crawl in when she heard someone coming up the steps behind her.

"Nate!" she whispered loudly. "Here, take the key and unlock the door, quick."

"Where've you been?" he asked, easily fitting the key into the lock.

"Nowhere," she answered, pushing past him in a hurry.

"Well what were you doing locked out of the store?"

"I wasn't locked out," she yelled, if a person can yell in a whisper.

Before he could untangle his confusion and think what to say next, Laney had glided through the store to the sitting room where they kept the family Bible. She was holding the baby in one arm and flipping through the giant pages when he caught up with her.

"Hold Lizzy," she whispered excitedly.

Taking the little princess in his big arms, Nate reached down and kissed her forehead as she snuggled into her papa's embrace.

"Thought she had a fever this mornin'."

"She did," replied his wife, her forefinger coming to rest on the passage of scripture she was searching for.

Nate gently nuzzled Lizzy's plump little neck. "She seems fine now. Doc Kennedy must have some mighty powerful medicine."

Laney suddenly plopped down in the rocker, silently reading the passage one more time before she gazed up into Nate's eyes and said, "I didn't take her to the doctor, Nate. He came to us."

"Well, that was mighty nice of him," said Nate, genuinely grateful for the doctor's kindness.

"Not Doc Kennedy, Nate," said Laney, glowing like a full moon over the ocean.

"You mean old Doc Samuel got this far into Duplin on his rounds?"

"No, it wasn't Doc Samuel either." About that time, Laney realized she was still whispering, but now she couldn't manage to raise her voice to a normal level. Her skin was still tingling, her eyes brimming with tears of awe.

"Laney, you look weird," said Nate. "And you sound weird, too. Are you sick?"

"No, I'm not sick. I'm fine. I'm real fine. In fact, I've never been better in my entire life." She reached down and picked up the large black Bible.

"Listen, Nate."

She read slowly, her voice quivering, "'And He told them to give her something to eat.'"

Nate stared at his wife, waiting for further explanation, still wondering if Laney had caught the fever.

"Who's 'he'?" asked Nate, his face crinkled in a frown.

"Jesus," whispered Laney, her glow growing brighter by the minute.

"Jesus?"

"Yes, Jesus."

He stared at her until Lizzy began to squirm in his arms, slowly waking up from her restful nap.

"Nate, at first I thought the man was just a man, but when he held her and the fever went away, I thought he was an angel sent to watch over our baby. But then I remembered what he said and when I found it in the Bible, I knew for sure. He wasn't an angel, Nate— that would have been miracle enough—but he wasn't an angel."

Nate's mouth fell open, and if he hadn't been holding little Lizzy, he would have put his arm around Laney and tried his best to calm her down. But, problem was, she wasn't upset a bit. She was happier and prettier than he'd ever seen her in his life, even on their wedding day.

And then, as Lizzy opened her eyes and beamed a smile straight into her daddy's eyes, Laney said, "Jesus came to our house today, Nate, and He took Lizzy's fever away."

And then, before he could catch his breath, she added, "Well, I guess we'd better give her somethin' to eat."

And with that said, Laney got up and hurried out to the kitchen to get a small bowl of chicken and pastry for the child that Jesus had held in his arms and healed.

Now, you might imagine how long it took that story to get around Beulah. A couple of hours, more or less. Ida Wash Sandlin, who was getting very close to meeting her Maker, said the Lord hadn't appeared in Beulah only to heal little Lizzy Gresham, even though that act of divine mercy was wonderful indeed. She said His visitation was one more sign from heaven, the second after the eclipse. There would probably be a third, she said, now that there had been two. And then, to add what to her was unquestionable validation to her prediction, she said, her long right forefinger pointed at her listeners, "The first two signs were exactly one year apart to the day."

Some people, totally uninterested, just ignored the whole thing. It was obviously an overly worried mother's imagination, not worth their valuable time to even discuss such silliness. And then there was Reverend Aldridge and the intelligentsia like him in Kenansville and at Richlands Academy who, in their hearts, hid a secret wish that the story was true but could not allow themselves to believe it. Miracles and supernatural occurrences came to an end with the death of the twelve apostles, they believed. The dispensation for such things had closed nearly two thousand years ago, adding that the apostle Paul had clearly said, "These things shall pass away."

But there were a lot of people in the community—the majority in fact—who took Lizzy's miracle to heart. There were some who readily believed and others who added the event to the top of their list of reasons to believe. Strangely enough, Lula Belle Aldridge fitted into the second category.

Now you might think the issue would have caused a bit of a problem in the Aldridge household, and you would be correct... except for one other strange thing. Lula Belle kept her thoughts to herself. She had no choice, really. Jonas Aldridge's book of immovable theological opinions included only one chapter on women, and nothing in it allowed Lula Belle the right to disagree with her husband, particularly on a subject that was obviously too theologically complicated for her weak and uneducated female mind to understand. Submission was the sixty-four-thousand-dollar word and the only one Reverend Aldridge seemed to have on the subject. Of course, his definition of submission was on another page of Webster's Dictionary under the word *obedience*.

So the night the news wound its way to the neat little parsonage by the Cape Fear River, an uncharacteristically quiet Lula Belle listened patiently to her husband's diatribe about the silliness of

Beulah's uneducated citizens as long as she could stand it, and then she went to bed.

The following day, she did a lot of thinking.

The day after that, two days after the visitation, she asked Reverend Aldridge if he'd need the buggy that day, and when he said no, Lula Belle and Rahab, the mare, quickly headed to Beulah.

Laney carefully cut three yards off a bolt of navy chintz for Lula Belle, excitedly sharing the only firsthand account of the miracle story available. (The preacher's wife had always believed in going straight to the horse's mouth if at all possible.) The former chatterbox stood mutely by, her eyes roving back and forth from Laney to the chubby little girl playing about her ankles, glowing with health and vitality. Laney was so happy to be telling the story one more time, plus busy cutting and folding the fabric, she didn't pay much attention to her captivated audience. So by the time she handed Lula Belle the brown parcel tied with tobacco twine and announced, "That'll be a quarter," she had missed the collection of tears in the preacher's wife's eyes. It was only after the door closed behind Lula Belle that Laney realized the woman hadn't said a word.

"Well, I'll be," said Laney.

Out on the porch, the well-dressed lady, still handsome at forty-nine though a bit on the plump side, clutched the brown package in her arms and leaned against the porch post. Her heart was racing, and it was all she could do to hold back the tears. It had been so long, so very long ago.

She took a deep breath and gulped her exposed emotions back into their safety deposit box in her wounded heart. The horse whinnied, wondering why it was taking her so long to climb up into the buggy seat and get going.

"You're right, Rahab," Lula Belle said aloud. "It's time to go."

The horse seemed to sense what she said, stamping her feet in anticipation.

Lula Belle loosened her grip on the post, flecking of old white paint, and carefully descended the steps just in time to see Sarah Jane Gresham's slightly smiling face, which carefully hid the dread that had suddenly gripped her at the sight of Lula Belle Aldridge coming down the steps of Nate's store.

"Mornin', Lula Belle," said Sarah Jane, one grain short of cheerfully.

"Good morning to you, Sarah Jane," replied Mrs. Aldridge, her voice still a bit quivery.

Sarah Jane quickly sensed that something was awry, but as usual, she wisely kept it to herself and proceeded on up the steps, hoping to avoid at least a half hour of Lula Belle's gossip. But the woman didn't say another word which caused Sarah Jane's curiosity to soar so high she felt forced to turn around and take another look at Lula Belle. She might be sick, and if she were, Sarah Jane certainly didn't want it on her conscience that she hadn't asked about her and offered some word of comfort.

There she was, perched on the buggy seat as prim and proper as ever but, surprisingly, a bit slumped, causing the proud woman to look rather humble as she sat with the reins in her gloved hands staring at Rahab's rump.

What in the world? Sarah Jane just stared for a few moments.

"Lula Belle?" she called quietly.

"Yes?" She was obviously aware of her surroundings, but it seemed she had no energy to move, not even her eyes.

Sarah Jane pulled up her skirt and quickly stepped back down to the ground and walked over to the buggy, watching her former nemesis all the while. But, surprisingly, something changed in Sarah Jane during the short moments it took for her to get from the porch to Lula Belle's buggy. Later, she would think it strange, but at the time it didn't seem strange at all. The fact was that Sarah Jane Gresham didn't dislike Lula Belle Aldridge anymore. In fact, she felt drawn to the woman. Why? She wasn't quite sure, but in Lula Belle's demeanor that day, Sarah Jane saw something she not only recognized but was deeply familiar with. Its name was Grief.

"Lula Belle, would you like to come sit on the porch a spell?"

Sarah Jane's voice was gentle and caring. Something in her tone gave her new friend the strength she needed to force her body to move. She slowly turned her head to look into Sarah Jane's face, now filled with nothing but compassion.

"N...no, not today," she said, her voice halting and almost inaudible. "But...but perhaps another time. Could we do that?"

"Of course we could. You just send me word to come to you or, better yet, come out to the farm any time."

Sarah Jane reached into the buggy and patted Lula Belle's gloved hand. But before she could draw back, the now humble Mrs. Aldridge grabbed Sarah Jane's bare calloused hand and tearfully whispered, "Thank you, Sarah Jane. You don't know how much this means to me."

And then she was gone, flipping the reins and clucking her tongue to Rahab who was obviously thrilled to be on her way once again. Sarah Jane gazed after the buggy, amazed at her own change of heart and even more amazed at the sudden change in Lula Belle Aldridge.

She was still standing there when Jeb yelled from down the road, "What's wrong with you, woman? Forgot where you're goin'?"

Chapter Thirteen

Summer, 1902: Romantic weddings and one astounding miracle had surely ushered in the warm flowering spring of 1902, but the summer that followed was quickly recorded as one of the most miserable in recent history. One day in late June the weather was pleasantly warm and breezy, a perfectly lovely summer day; the next it was ninety degrees in the shade with no sign of a breeze within fifty miles or so, not even at Topsail Beach. Laney and Lizzy weren't the only hot folks in Beulah. Even the oldest citizens like Ida Wash Sandlin couldn't recall a hotter and more humid summer in their entire lives.

Now, if it was ninety in June, one might imagine how high the thermometer soared in July and August during barning season. However, it wasn't just the incredible heat, pushing the little red line on the thermometer up and up and up, which brought about the misery; it was the insufferable humidity. The air was so thick Jeb said he could have eaten it with a spoon and choked for sure. It was a wonder the barometer in Nate's store didn't explode. It was hard to breathe—worse for anyone afflicted with any type of bronchial disorder like asthma or emphysema. Old and young alike passed out in the tobacco fields from heatstroke. Entire families rose earlier and earlier, marching to the fields way before dawn with lanterns in hand, hoping to get as much tobacco as possible into the barn before the unrelenting sun reigned high in the noonday sky.

It was in the middle of the heat wave that Ida Wash Sandlin took leave of Beulah. Well, not just Beulah. Actually, she left this world for her reward in the next, happy at last for the opportunity to meet her Redeemer and ask Him a few questions she had on her mind.

They said her last words were, "I'll see if I can find out what the third sign will be, and if I can figure out a way, I'll be sure to let y'all know."

Then she laid her head back on the pillow, closed her eyes and peacefully exhaled her final breath.

As luck would have it, being she died in a heat wave—although Ida Wash didn't believe in luck but in the sovereignty of the Almighty—she passed away late Saturday afternoon and was buried in the early hours of Sunday morning before the church bell rang. Jeb Gresham said she couldn't have picked a better time to go. If it were not for Sarah Jane and the girls, he'd a mind to leave himself, hot as it was.

Day after day, night after night, Laney wiped sweat from her face and neck, stopping work every now and then to give Lizzy a cool bath or to let her play in a bucket of water on the front porch. Nate said more than once that she shouldn't be wasting water like that. The river was getting mighty low, and if the river was drying up, it meant the wells were drying up, too. But Laney couldn't bear to see the little girl covered in sweat, her chubby cheeks red as a freshly picked strawberry.

If the truth were told, Laney was probably much more miserable than her merry little daughter. In the middle of such an intensive heat wave, just the feel of a few drops of water splashing from Lizzy's bucket onto her hot clammy skin was like a reprieve handed down from heaven.

As was expected of her, Hannah stayed close to home that summer, cropping the ripe tobacco leaves alongside her papa and Simon, pacing herself so as not to get overheated. Jeb kept jugs of spring water in the back of the wagon, easily accessible to the croppers working steadily behind. Trudging back to the spring through the long humid rows, fighting the sticky tobacco jungle to get a drink of water was much too risky.

Hardly anyone led a social life that summer. After long workdays in the overwhelming heat, there was no energy for other activities. Sarah Jane and the girls were usually in bed before darkness settled in, and it seldom took Jeb long to follow suit. He and Simon took turns sleeping at the barn to keep the fire regulated. On the nights old Simon kept watch at the barn, Jeb usually crept into the bedroom trying not to wake Sarah Jane and grabbed a quilt out of the cedar chest. Clutching it against his sweating bare skin, he quietly eased out the screened door and made himself a pallet on the porch, taking care to place the quilt where his sweaty body would catch the breeze if one should happen to blow in from somewhere.

But there were no breezes to speak of — not from late spring to the first week in September. Little rain either. But come September there was a change…a drastic change. However, the weather that arrived suddenly and unheralded wouldn't exactly have been described as breezy, and the word rain was definitely an understatement.

Throughout the day, September 5, 1902, Jeb and Simon worked on the two farm wagons Jeb owned, making sure they were ready for the thirty mile trip to haul the gigantic bundles of cured tobacco to the market in Kinston. One of the wheels needed a lot of work, so other than making sure the pack house — filled with the year's crop of tobacco — wasn't sweating, the two men pretty much kept their focus on repairing the wagon wheel.

Sometime during the day, about one o'clock Jeb would later recall, old Simon suddenly stopped working for a moment or two and looked off into the sky, squinting his eyes as if straining to see a bit more clearly. Then the corners of his mouth dropped, forming a somber frown. His ageless chocolate face seemed puzzled like something strange was going on, a mystery he couldn't quite solve.

Jeb was watching him out of the corner of his eye. "What is it, Simon? What's wrong?"

"Don't rightly know, Mistah Jeb." Simon continued to gaze off down the road as if expecting someone…or some *thing*.

Jeb stood up then, holding the hammer in one hand and a large greasy wrench in the other.

"Air mighty still," said Simon.

"Been still all summer," replied Jeb, "so still I wouldn't know a breeze if it hit me in the face."

"Hmm," muttered Simon. He closed his eyes, not moving a muscle.

Jeb waited, watching Simon like a hawk.

"Tell me," he said.

"Weather's a turnin'. Goin' to be a storm, Mistah Jeb. A bad un, and it ain't goin' to wait for nobody." Simon took a deep breath and turned to Jeb. "Better git ready."

Throughout the remainder of the afternoon, the two aging men worked diligently to get all the farm equipment either in the barn—packed in with the cow, the mare, the mule and about twenty chickens or so—or under the barn shelter. The cats and dogs would find refuge under the house. The hog pen was about a quarter mile from the barn in the edge of the woods. Thankfully, the gigantic sow had produced an amazing litter of pigs in the spring, twelve in all, and they were all fattening nicely. Jeb looked over towards the woods for a minute and then, heaving a deep sigh, he turned back to the tasks at hand. All those hams and pork chops would just have to take care of themselves. There was nothing else to do.

Only once did Jeb take time to regret he hadn't already hauled the dried tobacco to market. But, realistically, he knew there hadn't been time. The women had just finished tying the first load two days earlier. The wagons couldn't have made the thirty-mile trip without repairs.

When Jeb walked up to the house, a little more briskly than usual, to warn Sarah Jane and the girls that a storm was coming, he wasn't surprised to find her standing on the long porch, gazing into the sky with just about the same look on her face as old Simon.

Before he could open his mouth, she said, "Storm's comin', Jeb, a bad one. I feel it in my bones."

He just nodded. There wasn't any need to discuss the matter, too much work to do.

By late afternoon, the sky was painted an ominous gray. Like Elijah of old, every now and then Simon ambled over toward the stripped tobacco field, empty stalks standing like sentinels waiting for the storm, and stared out towards the horizon watching for a cloud the size of a man's hand. About six o'clock, he spied the cloud. By quarter to seven, the skies over Duplin County looked as if they had been invaded by the principalities and powers of darkness, the murky clouds swarming violently. They seemed to fight one another as they swiftly gathered for some predetermined apocalyptic event.

Swanee joined Simon at the edge of the field and studied the sky. "Sure hope this ain't Miz Ida's sign number three."

And then the wind picked up—out of nowhere it seemed. Suddenly, the tin roofs on the house, the barn and the pack house began to make a strange rumbling sound. The mare whinnied in the barn, and the cow began to moo, loud and long. Sudden gusts nearly knocked Jeb down as he made his way from the barn to the house, yelling for Simon and Swanee to go get Queen and come up to the house to wait out the storm.

Simon could barely hear him above the roaring wind. He raised his hand to let Jeb know he understood and quickly went on his way to gather his family. Ducking his head against the force of the wind, he headed off, his gait much faster than usual, toward the little cabin at the edge of the woods behind the tobacco field.

Jeb was about ten yards from the house and Simon was about halfway to the cabin when two major events occurred simultaneously: Number one, the rooster started crowing, and number two, the vicious clouds in the heavens attacked the earth with torrents of rain. There couldn't have been more during Noah's flood, and unfortunately there wasn't an ark in sight. Old Simon set off in a run then, his heart racing, trying to think of a way to get Swanee and Queen up to the Hall house before the worst of the storm hit. He knew in his knower that this was nothing compared to what was coming.

Back to number one, the rooster's crowing. Like Miss Ida, all country people believed in signs, even the folks who hardly offered a prayer to the God who gave them. These humble farmers believed the Almighty not only set the heavenly hosts in perfect order so man would know when to plant which seed, when to expect the harvest and how to navigate strange lands and seemingly endless seas, He also programmed animals uniquely to give man certain signs upon occasion. Now when a rooster crows just before dawn, man knows the new day is arriving and it's time to rise up and begin the day's work no matter if he feels like it or not. And when the rooster, after having lorded himself over a flock of hens and biddies all day, returns to his roost at dusk, man knows night is imminent and it's time to stop work and rest. But when a rooster crows during the day, well, that's another story.

Back to number two, the torrential rain. Sarah Jane was waiting at the screened door when Jeb's feet hit the porch. For a split second he turned around to survey his beloved farm, hoping against all hope that at the very least the pack house would be left standing by morning. Those golden leaves were like money in the bank, and they were all he had.

"Get in this house right now, Jeb Grissom!" ordered Sarah Jane. "I'll get you some dry overalls so you can change in the kitchen."

"Simon," whispered Jeb, his eyes haunted. "They'll never make it back."

Sarah Jane's face fell. For a moment or two, he thought the toughened woman was going to cry. But then she grabbed his hand—a very unusual gesture even in private—and said, "The woods, Jeb. They might be better protected there under the trees."

"There may not be any trees left by mornin'," said Jeb quietly, his face drawn.

Slowly, he turned away and took off his floppy soaked hat. He walked over to the window, but he couldn't see out. The rain was coming down too heavily. It formed a dark gray wall impenetrable to the human eye.

The wind began to howl ferociously around the old farm house as if it were beating the boards with a gigantic whip. Before long, the aged beams and rafters began to creak and squeak and moan. The tin roof made a high pitched zinging noise. The torrential rain beat the tin with such force and noise it was hard to hear what anybody said in the house. But nobody was saying much of anything anyway.

As was mentioned earlier, Sarah Jane Gresham had two fears: lightning storms and Yankees. Therefore, she had a couple of storm rules that were fearfully and obediently followed by Jeb and the girls: Sit down and shut up. That was about it. So they did. The girls pretty much stayed huddled together in the sitting room or on the black iron bed the three of them shared. There was no way to get from the main house to the kitchen without going out on the porch, so Sarah Jane and the girls had stored food and water in the sitting room for the long night ahead.

About fifteen minutes after Jeb changed into dry overalls, there came a loud pounding and banging on the door. It sounded as if the door was going to come crashing in any minute. Jeb lifted the bolt out of the lock and the door burst open. A powerful gush of wind and rain was accompanied by Old Simon who quickly propelled Swanee and Queen into the sitting room. They were all soaked to the bone. At their heels was Jeb's old hunting hound, Jake, who looked like he had been drowned in the river and pulled out just in time.

The girls were delighted. Susie and Frannie clapped their hands. There had never been an animal in Sarah Jane's house before. The girls skipped about after Jake who nervously ran around in circles shaking water all over everybody. Sarah Jane tried to help Swanee and Queen dry off while Simon told Jeb about the multitude of pine branches that were lying all over the place. The girls chased Jake, and the old hound began to howl with the wind. He was obviously terrified, and the girls' excitement and all the jabbering weren't giving him much comfort.

"That dog's got to go!" yelled Sarah Jane above the din.

"No, Mama, no!" cried the girls.

"He might get hurt in the storm!" Susie whined.

"Now look," said Sarah Jane, determination in her eyes, "I'll give that ol' dog five minutes to calm down or he's out the door. He'll be fine under the house with the other dogs. If the house blows down, he won't be no worse off than we are. You girls go on back to your room and settle down, and maybe Jake will do the same."

Liza and Frannie sadly shrugged and turned to do as their mother said. Susie, thinking up a plan to get the dog back to the bedroom, watched Jake pace the floor and hassle like he was about to have a heart attack. Finally, she sadly turned and joined her sisters. The dog didn't offer her much hope.

Susie was right. Old Jake kept pacing in circles, his long tongue hanging out the side of his mouth dripping drool. You'd have thought he was trying to catch his tail. He alternated between hassling and howling, pausing every now and then to trot over to the door and listen as if he hoped the storm had died down. Even with the three girls back in the bedroom, the small sitting room felt packed and stifling hot with five adults and the hound dog that seemed to have lost his mind. The white of Queen's eyes grew bigger and bigger and even perpetually peaceful Simon began to fidget, gradually losing his tranquil state of mind.

Finally, Sarah Jane stood up and said, "Jeb, either that dog goes out or I do. Now who do you want to sleep with the rest of your mortal life?"

Normally, Jeb might have stood his ground a while longer—old Jake was his prized quail-hunting hound—but the dog was about to drive him crazy, too. It was as if there was a worse storm inside than the raging one outside. Sadly compliant, he motioned to Simon to unbolt the door while he grabbed Jake by the collar and pulled him towards the driving rain. Surprisingly, the fear-crazed dog ran out the door like a streak of lightning and was under the house before Simon could fight the wind to shut the door. Perhaps he thought the quiet company of his fellow canines was better than the chaotic atmosphere the humans were creating.

Within the hour trees started crashing to the ground, near and far. The old house shook to its foundation with every crash, feeling like an earthquake had been added to their woes. It was about that time that Sarah Jane said she thought it would be a good idea if they all prayed together, specifically thanking the Good Lord that there were no trees close enough to fall on the house—other than the ancient gigantic oak she was sure couldn't be felled. It had stood at least a hundred years and had even endured the Yankees, so why should it fall now?

She couldn't get Hannah and Nell off her mind either. Nell hadn't said anything yet, but Sarah Jane was sure her oldest daughter was already expecting her first baby. It wasn't healthy to experience a lot of trauma when a woman was in the family way. She wasn't even sure where Hannah was tonight, at Jessie's new house or with Kate and Doc Kennedy. Yes, it was time to pray.

She asked Simon to lead the prayer. Even Sarah Jane's faith seemed to pale in comparison to the former slave's. Everyone acknowledged it, even Jeb. But at the very moment of Simon's powerful "Amen," a bolt of jagged lightning streaked earthward from the storm-tossed sky, lighting up the dark house as if it were the middle of a sunshiny day. The bright light was accompanied by the loudest noise any of them had ever heard. It sounded too much like a Yankee cannonball to Sarah Jane. That was when the topmost portion of the ancient oak, hit hard by the lightning bolt, fell full force onto the kitchen roof and crushed it like it was made of match sticks. As if each one had seen the same vision, in an instant they knew what happened.

Swanee, in her slow drawl, her heart beating a lot faster than her mouth was moving, quietly remarked, "Simon, yo don't pray s' good."

The whites of Queen's eyes looked like giant white buttons stuck on her dark face. Simon looked as if he might cry. Jeb was still as a statue—Sarah Jane, too, her mouth wide open.

And then, slowly, her expression transformed. A soft smile flooded her face. In awe, she looked straight at Simon and said, "Oh, but he did, Swanee. He prayed mighty powerful."

"Sho'nuf?" asked Simon, still stunned and a bit confused.

Sarah Jane's smile broadened. "We're still here, aren't we?"

"Hm," said Simon, "I sees what yo means, Miz Mary."

Then Simon grinned, too, his white teeth shining in the dark. Swanee wiped the sweat from her forehead and began to chuckle while Jeb relaxed his shoulders and let out a long sigh of relief. Queen finally got the message and began to laugh, too. All of a sudden you'd have thought they were holy rollers, clapping and singing and praising the Lord. The rejoicing went on a few minutes, and then, right in the middle of a loud "Hallelujah!" from Swanee, Sarah Jane remembered she had three daughters in the back bedroom. Or so she hoped.

"Oh, no!" she gasped. "Jeb, the girls!"

They both jumped up at the same time like someone had poured a powerful dose of Haticol down their throats. Pushing Jeb aside to get through the doorway, Sarah Jane ran through the room she shared with Jeb and arrived panting at the curtained-off passage into the back bedroom. And there, all huddled together on the weighted-down feather bed, were Liza, Susie and Frannie...in shock, silently awaiting the news that the world had ended and they were the only ones left alive. Or worse, the Lord had come for his own and left them behind. Let me tell you, the rejoicing in the front room was nothing compared to that in the back when Sarah Jane softly called, "Children, are you alright?"

Other than finding their daughters safe and sound, the greatest rejoicing came around first light when the winds finally calmed and the heavy rain slowed down to normal. Sarah Jane begged Jeb to wait, but he couldn't stand it another minute. Plopping his still damp fedora on his gray head, Jeb turned to Simon and said, "Might as well face the music."

Now, you've never seen two happier men in your entire life as were Jeb Gresham and old Simon Hall on the morning of September 6, 1902. And for only one reason. Although the old barn's tin roof was somewhat slanted, tilted quite a bit off to the side, actually, it's frightened occupants had fearfully accumulated in the driest corner and all was well. However, the pack house, filled with its golden treasure, was still standing...roof and all. Not a leak in sight. The tobacco was safely kept in the midst of the storm.

Sometimes Jeb Gresham didn't quite see eye-to-eye with the Creator, not understanding His mysterious ways, but that morning Jeb was as full of thanks as old Simon. They pushed the splintery, creaking old pack house door open and stared speechless at the piles of golden leaves, nice and dry and ready for market. When old Simon fell down on his knees, Jeb was right there beside him, not embarrassed a bit. Yes sir, he was a thankful man.

All in all, like Sarah Jane said, the damage wasn't as bad as it could have been. A lot of people fared worse, that's for sure. Jeb figured it would take him and Simon about three weeks to saw up the oak branches in small enough pieces to be lifted off the ruined kitchen and then build the roof and damaged walls back to what they were before the storm. Since there was no way to cook—the iron wood stove was somewhere underneath the rubble—Sarah Jane and the girls planned to help clear the yard of broken tree limbs and mostly unidentifiable flying debris during the day and stay at her brother Will's house about a mile down the road to Hallsville at night. Will always said his sister never had time to visit, and now she did. His wife agreed. It would be nice to have Sarah Jane and the girls around.

Distant neighbors and church family brought food during those first few days when they heard Sarah Jane was without a cook stove, but most everyone in a fifty mile radius of Beulah had more repairs and clean up to do on their own land than was humanly possible. It would be months, perhaps years, before the area looked normal again. Jeb was still burning gigantic piles of tree limbs and rubbish at Thanksgiving.

The Presbyterians said, "It was predestined."

The Hard-shell Baptists said, "Whatever's going to be is going to be."

The Missionary Baptists said, "To the work, to the work, we will labor 'til the Master comes."

And they all did...no matter what they believed.

Chapter Fourteen

Winter, 1903: From the fall of 1902 throughout Christmas and early winter of 1903, Hannah delivered—or helped Doc Kennedy deliver—babies and more babies. She could hardly believe her good fortune. She was almost nineteen years old and had already helped deliver more babies than she could remember. Whenever she took the time to sit down and make a list of "her babies," she would inevitably forget one or two. There were at least ten or eleven just within the nearby Gresham clan. Cousin Kate was expecting her second. Kate's sister, Adeline, had recently given birth to a new little Sandlin out on Gander's Fork Road and happily as a lark, Cousin Bessie Bishop had produced a fat little baby boy with Hannah and Sarah Jane's tender care. That's not even counting Nell and Liza. By the way, Liza ran off one Saturday evening and came home married to Frank Carroll, the act of which shocked both Hannah and Nell but pleased Sarah Jane to no end. Her girls had made a good start on filling the countryside with Carrolls and Thomases.

Just before Christmas of 1902, Laney presented Nate with another little princess, tiny Mary Alice Gresham. Other than being so small, she was a replica of her two-year-old sister, Lizzy. Nate and Laney were happy but Lizzy Gresham was ecstatic. It was all Laney and Hannah could do to keep her from dragging the baby around like a rag doll.

Outside the clan there was Emmy Brinson, the meek little wife of Theophilus Brinson. Remember him and his brother, Uz, the town drunks? Well, Emmy was a sweet girl whose heart was simply bigger than her brain. She adored Theophilus, whom she lovingly referred to as Theo Honey. Theophilus was a nice looking man when he wasn't passed out in a ditch somewhere. He wasn't dumb either. As Jeb had remarked to Nate on the last Election Day, those Brinson boys could have made something of themselves if the drink hadn't gotten them first. It was a sad situation, most of the time ignored by sweet Emmy who in the winter of 1903 gave birth to her fifth child, regardless of the lack of household income at present.

But that glaring fact was not ignored by Sarah Jane Gresham. If there was one thing she could not abide, it was a man who constantly begat babies with little or no means of taking care of them. It was a sin; that's what it was.

With anger simmering in her steel blue eyes, she gently bathed the tiny newborn and then Emmy. A few minutes earlier, she had sent Hannah back to stay with Cousin Bessie for the last few days of her confinement. It was a good decision considering the state of affairs in the Brinson household. The present situation called for someone with years of experience and a strong constitution, and Hannah had neither as yet. Sarah Jane possessed both.

The light in the three-room cabin was dim; the small windows covered by burlap sacks Emmy had tried to make look like curtains and failed. The early January day was cold, too. The hot coals in the wood stove were almost burned out. The other four children, ranging in age from two to six like little stepping stools, ran in and out the door looking worse than little orphans in their tattered clothes and bare feet.

Now, keep in mind that hardly anyone living in and around Beulah had money in those days, or since, for that matter. Most people were considered what was called land poor. They owned land—some quite a bit of land—but there was little cash money for development or expansion. It was all most folks could do just to keep their families warm, fed and clothed...and that was hard enough. But because of his drinking, Theophilus Brinson couldn't manage even that.

Sarah Jane had ordered Theophilus, almost sober today, to ride out to the farm and ask Jeb if he could trade some work to cut firewood in the woods behind their house, assuring him that Jeb would be glad to haul Theophilus and the wood back to town in his wagon.

But when Sarah Jane had finished bathing Emmy and the baby and had tidied up the bedroom that looked as if it hadn't been cleaned up since the hurricane in September, she hurried out on the porch to see if Theophilus had come back with the firewood. Even with all her busyness, Sarah Jane was feeling a bit chilled herself.

Well, lo and behold, there sat Theophilus on the top step, whittling away like he didn't have a thing in the world to do, humming all the while, "Oh, my darlin' Nellie Gray."

"Theophilus Brinson!"

The anger in the midwife's eyes wasn't just simmering now; it was up to a hard boil.

"Huh?" said Theo Honey.

"What *are* you doin'?!"

"Makin' the young'uns a toy to play with. How do you like it?" Smiling proudly, he held up a small wooden horse for Sarah Jane's approval.

She felt like knocking it out of his hand. Theophilus excelled at whittling; everybody knew that. But if he'd reproduced a Michelangelo, she would have been just as angry.

"Theophilus Brinson, you're supposed to be cuttin' firewood to keep your wife and young'uns warm!" She had more to say, but she was boiling over now and so was careful to guard her tongue which, as the Bible said, was the unruliest member of the body.

The calm, only slightly tipsy young man, with half-naked children hanging all over him, asked innocently, "What's the problem, Miz Sarah Jane? Is Emmy alright?"

"No! She's not alright! She's cold, and so are your children! And there's nothing in the pantry to cook for supper!" Her lip was quivering. Taming her tongue was going to be harder than she had first thought.

"Theophilus Brinson!"

"Huh?" he replied rather dejectedly, disappointed she hadn't complimented his new creation.

"Did you know the Bible says that a man who won't take care of his own is worse than an infidel?!"

"No, ma'm," he sighed.

"Well, it surely does. You don't want the Good Lord to judge you an infidel, do you?"

He thought a minute and then pulled a small bottle out of his overalls. "What's an infidel?" he asked, followed by a little swig from the bottle.

"Oh!" she shrieked, exasperated to the end of her endurance. But she couldn't stop now. She was on a roll.

"An infidel is an unbeliever, Theophilus Brinson! It's as bad as you can be when you stand before the Great White Throne. The Bible also says…."

He interrupted her, his speech slurring a bit by now. "The Bible alsooo saysss that a man is to multi(hiccup)ply and replen-ish the earth, thankey ma'm."

That did it.

"Get up from there you….oh!" All of a sudden she saw eight sad and frightened little eyes staring at her from inside the ragged screened door. In the midst of her anger, Sarah Jane hadn't realized the children had disappeared, led by six-year-old, Theo, Jr. who had whispered, "Papa's goin' to git a whippin', sure as shootin'."

Her heart just melted, even for Theo Honey. She'd have to find another plan. This one just wasn't working.

Chapter Fifteen

Spring, 1903: Throughout the previous sweltering summer of 1902, Jeb Gresham's barns had been conspicuously absent of Sarah Jane's once dreaded visitor, Lula Belle Aldridge. Sarah Jane had chalked up her lack of appearance to the insufferable heat wave while admitting to Jeb from time to time that she almost missed the obnoxious woman. She didn't mention the odd encounter between the two of them at Nate's store soon after Laney's visitation last spring. Lula Belle had been in such a strange state that it somehow seemed to be an invasion of her privacy to speak of it.

And then there was the terrible September storm that abruptly ended the heat wave. Consequently, Beulah's typical autumn season was changed dramatically. With each and every family member's nose to the grindstone, clearing the land of scattered debris from destroyed buildings and repairing what was salvageable, there was no time left for the area's annual fall social events—not even the harvest festival. By the onset of winter, with houses repaired at least enough to stay warm throughout the cold stretch, a collective exhaustion had set in. Never had the citizens of Limestone Township been overjoyed to see winter come, but that year the seasonal reprieve was welcomed with open arms and hymns of praise.

Thus, by early spring of 1903, nearly a full year had passed since Sarah Jane invited the distressed Lula Belle to come sit on the porch a spell. Lo and behold, today of all days, about two hours after Jeb left for Hallsville to help O. W. Scott build his store back, the familiar horse and buggy came trotting down the dusty road. Sarah Jane was gathering the wash off the clothesline when she spied the dust cloud, and for some strange reason, she knew who it was long before she ever laid eyes on Lula Belle. Thankfully, she beat the dust storm to the house with the cumbersome clothes basket under arm and even managed to wash her face at the pump and smooth back her wispy graying hair before her guest pulled the buggy under what the hurricane had left of the giant oak in the front yard.

"Lula Belle, what a nice surprise." Smiling sociably, Sarah Jane pulled up her skirt and walked down the steps and out to the buggy, hands extended to help her guest down.

"Sarah Jane, I hope you don't mind such an unheralded interruption in your workday, but I woke up this morning just knowing this was the day to accept your invitation to visit a spell. I hope you remember; it's been quite a while."

"Of course, I remember, and I'm glad you've come." She took the seemingly nervous woman by the arm and led her towards the porch. "Make yourself comfortable in the rocker, and I'll fetch us some cold water from the pump. You look like you're in need of some refreshment."

"Yes, thank you. I'm mighty thirsty. Looks like we'd better pray for rain."

In a few minutes, Sarah Jane was back with two glasses of water and a tin plate holding two slices of golden pound cake.

"Oh, my, what a nice treat! I wasn't expecting such a generous welcome on a regular weekday." Lula Belle took a bite of the cake and rolled her eyes at how good it was.

"Actually, your timing is perfect. Hannah came home yesterday and asked that I make her a pound cake."

"Hmm, it's so good! Now that Miz Ida Wash has gone on to glory, you'll be sure and win the cake contest at the harvest festival next fall, Sarah Jane."

Her hostess laughed. "Oh, I don't know about that. There are more good cooks around Beulah than you can shake a stick at. I doubt my pound cake is any better than the rest."

As the old yellow cat's tail swished back and forth, the rocking chairs creaked in a rather off sync rhythm. Miraculously, the rockers missed the cat's tail every time while the cat seemed to totally ignore the danger its tail was in and pretended to patiently wait for a crumb to fall from Sarah Jane's hands. As is the nature of felines, nobody would have ever known she was anxiously waiting for a snack. Her eyes slowly closed and opened. Her breathing, too, was paced and even as her tail played Russian roulette with the rocking chair.

While the two women finished their cake in silence, the cat, with hidden envy, watched them politely lick their fingers. Graciously conceding defeat for now, she slowly stretched out on her side. With a sigh, the cat closed her tired eyes for a short nap, her long tail victorious in its contest with the rocker.

Sarah Jane rested her head on the high-backed chair and, like the cat, closed her eyes. But she quickly reminded herself that it was a dangerous thing to sit still, much less close one's eyes in early afternoon, particularly when one was worn out from the morning's chores. It was about that time she noticed how abnormally quiet Lula Belle was. She figured if this visit was going anywhere, she had better be the one to jumpstart the conversation. However, in the manner of southern women, it wasn't polite to go straight to the point, especially considering that whatever was on Lula Belle's mind was perceptibly a matter of the heart.

And that's why, not because she really wanted to know, she casually asked, "How's Reverend Aldridge, Lula Belle?"

"He's fine, just fine. His rheumatism was bothering him back in the winter, but since the weather turned warmer, he's been fine, just fine."

"I can fully sympathize with the Reverend. My old joints fare much better in warm weather for sure." She looked down at her knotty knuckles, pleased to be able to stretch her fingers out to full length today.

Lula Belle was gazing out across the yard towards the buggy as if she had forgotten something she should have unloaded. She was rocking a little faster now. The creaking was getting louder, and before long the old yellow cat's head popped up to see what was disturbing her nap. With a terribly condescending look at Lula Belle, she slowly plied herself from the floor boards and stretched so hard her back made a perfect arch. And then, as if haughtily rejecting the women's company altogether, the cat daintily pattered down the steps and out to the shade of the ancient oak tree where she curled up in a ball and pleasantly drifted back to sleep, far away from the presence of lowly human beings.

Sarah Jane could tell her guest was working up the courage to share what was lying so heavy on her heart. She just needed a little more prodding.

"And what about the rest of your family, Lula Belle, how are they?" Sarah Jane knew perfectly well Lula Belle Aldridge had no family other than the Reverend's highfalutin kin down in Wilmington.

Her plan—it had come to her in a split second with no fore-thought at all—worked powerfully. Tears streamed from the dark-circled eyes Lula Belle had tried that morning to camouflage with a few dabs of zinc oxide. It was the newest thing in face powder which the pastor's wife ordered from Sears & Roebuck so no one would know about it. It seemed to the poor woman that she hadn't slept a night since the visitation last spring. And now, here she was, crying like a baby on Sarah Jane's front porch.

Sarah Jane kept on rocking, biding the time. Lula Belle would get it all out now that the plug was pulled.

"I ah…well, I'll have to be honest and admit that I was well aware you would be alone today." She sniffed into a delicately embroidered handkerchief. "I heard Jeb was helping O. W. Scott, and then I bumped into your girls on their way to the river with your brother, Will."

"Uh, huh. He came by to take the girls swimmin', and against my better judgment, I let 'em go." Sarah Jane shook her head, still worried about her uncharacteristic decision. It was much too early in the year to go swimming in the Cape Fear. For one thing, the water was too cold, and for another, the current was too strong even though the spring rains were slow in coming.

"Please forgive me for deliberately ruining your day, Sarah Jane. I'm sure you were looking forward to some time by yourself."

The soulful expression on Lula Belle's face pricked Sarah Jane's heart to the core. Once again, she easily recognized the familiar pain of sorrow and grief, and though physical expressions of sympathy were rare between such toughened women, without thinking, Sarah Jane reached out her hand to pat the woman's shoulder.

That did it. Lula Belle went to sobbing. Her dainty little hand-kerchief was soaking wet in no time at all, and before long, she had succumbed to the unthinkable: She wiped her eyes and nose on the sleeve of her fine dress. Had she not insisted on dressing up all the time, the woman would have been wearing her apron like Sarah Jane, and there would have been no lack of something to dry her eyes with.

"Oh, m…my," she stuttered between sobs. "I certainly d…didn't plan on behaving like this. You m…must think I'm being awful silly."

"No, Lula Belle. A woman with an arrowhead in her heart the size of yours is not silly." She paused a second, then added, "And if I had to guess, I'd say it has something to do with the Reverend. Am I right?"

"Y…yes, you are. You are quite correct in your assessment of the situation. That's why I…I felt you were the one I could talk to, Sarah Jane. I've always noted you to be a wise woman."

"No, I'm not wise, more like good at puttin' two and two together. Common sense, maybe, but not wisdom. Wisdom belongs to people like Solomon, and Solomon, I'm not.

"Well, whatever you have, I'm in need of it."

Sarah Jane's distressed visitor took a deep breath and straight-ened her shoulders, her hands clenching and twisting the now pitiful-looking handkerchief. The pain had been there so long, locked up with the key thrown away, the woman had no idea how to let it out without losing what dignity she had left. For a short while, the longing to share her heart with someone who might be able to help waged a violent war with the one coping mechanism Lula Belle had developed over a lifetime—namely, pride.

Finally, she gave in. One hand flew from the handkerchief in her lap to her forehead as if to shield her eyes from her listener's gaze. But then, just as quickly, she threw both hands up in the air and blurted out, "I don't love my husband, Sarah Jane!"

It was all her hostess could do to stifle the laughter that bubbled up in her throat. *Only God loves your husband,* thought Sarah Jane with a wry twist of private humor.

But she didn't say it. She said, "There are a lot of women in your shoes, Lula Belle." Her thoughts jumped straight to Kate who, even though she had apparently resigned herself to her fate, still begrudged her parents' choice of a life-mate for their rebellious daughter.

"I know," replied Lula Belle with another long sigh, "but he's the preacher, and I'm the preacher's wife! I'm supposed to love him."

"Well, *supposed to* is a long way from reality in my opinion. Needless to say, I know more women than you could count who didn't love their men on their wedding day but grew to love them through the years. I'm sure you could name a few yourself."

"Yes, I could. Quite a few." Lula Belle let out a loud sigh, almost a huff. "I thought that's what would happen between us. I thought… no, I expected that one day I would wake up and find myself lying next to a sweet, kind man and I would suddenly realize I loved him with all my heart and he loved me, but…but that didn't happen."

Lula Belle looked away, her gaze resting on the old yellow cat that was just now stretching from her nap and assessing the territory, wondering what to do next, if anything. Sarah Jane wondered when Lula Belle was going to get around to the crux of her problem. To be sure the woman hadn't just figured out she didn't love her husband after thirty-four years of marriage.

"I'm not making much sense, am I?" Lula Belle looked straight at her hostess for the first time since the conversation had turned serious.

"Not yet," replied Sarah Jane.

"It's not just that I ought to love him and I don't; it's that something happened a long time ago that killed what love I might have had for him."

With that confession, Lula Belle seemed to mature right before Sarah Jane's eyes. Although she was obviously still in despair, there was a focused calm about her now. She had lost that agitated, nervous spirit that was vexing her so.

The truth will set you free, thought Sarah Jane, waiting patiently for the remainder of the story. Everybody has a story, she often told Jeb.

Lula Belle leaned peacefully back into the rocking chair and then suddenly stopped rocking altogether. She turned away again, sighing. "When Laney told me about the visitation, it all came back. No one knows it around here, Sarah Jane, but I had a child once, a little over a year after the Reverend and I were married."

Her eyes began to take on a dreamy look. A soft smile began to form around her thin lips. Sarah Jane watched in awe as the seemingly self-absorbed Lula Belle turned into a tender mother before her very eyes.

"The birth was terribly long and difficult, but you know better than anyone that most first babies are hard to come by. We lived in Wilmington at the time, so there was a doctor in attendance who, thankfully, saved my life and that of my precious baby. My folks were living down in Charleston, but an elderly aunt lived close by. She moved in with us until I was finally up and about. I don't know what I'd have done without her. The Reverend didn't like her, of course."

Lula Belle breathed a deep sigh and closed her eyes for a moment. "It's a long story," she said softly as if apologizing.

Her listener patiently waited for her to go on.

"The Reverend was disappointed that the baby was female. Oh, he didn't say anything, but I could see it in his eyes the first time I saw him looking at her. At first, I felt like I had let him down, but then I prayed about it, and I felt as if the Good Lord was as happy as I was that we had a little girl. I remember reading Psalm 139, the one that says God forms us in our mothers' wombs and that we're 'fearfully and wonderfully made.' Remember that passage, Sarah Jane?"

"Yes, I do. I read it quite often." Sarah Jane glanced at Lula Belle out of the corner of her eye and gave her guest one of her dry smiles. "And I do sympathize with your plight, Lula Belle. Don't forget, I gave Jeb Gresham five girls."

Lula Belle actually laughed. "Well, I decided fairly quickly that the Reverend would just have to get over whatever disappointment he was feeling. As for me, I was thrilled to have a little girl. I was an excellent seamstress, so she would have beautiful dresses and bows in her hair and lovely embroidered handkerchiefs. She would go to school, of course, and I even talked the Reverend into sending her to one of the best female academies in Wilmington when she was older."

Turning to Sarah Jane, Lula Belle added sadly, "I left out a major detail about the birth. I was never to have any more children, so my little Bonnie was the light of my life, you see."

The light of love and the darkness of loss were both embedded in the storyteller's eyes at that moment. She almost smiled, but the darkness won, and a dark shadow crept over her countenance.

Sarah Jane perceived what was coming, but the suffering woman needed the healing that came from the telling of it, so she quietly waited, the rockers conspicuously stilled.

"She was about the age of Laney's little Lizzy at the time of her visitation when I began to notice that something was wrong. For awhile, I didn't tell anyone, particularly not the Reverend. He didn't pay the baby much attention anyway. His days consisted of long hours teaching at the academy and performing the duties of an assistant minister at the First Baptist Church on the weekends. But before long, there was no doubt in my mind we would need to confer with a physician. She should have been taking steps—walking, actually—and she wasn't even crawling proficiently.

"Finally, I told the Reverend. He immediately called in the best doctor in Wilmington, and I'll have to say that, for a little while, I saw the love and kindness I had longed for in my husband's eyes. But it was not to last. In retrospect, I believe he determined to harden himself against the pain of losing his only child, but in doing that, he hardened his heart towards me and everyone else as well.

"The doctor conferred with highly respected colleagues from Charleston and Richmond, but in the end, the prognosis was the same: My beautiful daughter would not live to celebrate her second birthday."

There were no tears now—just that resigned look of loss which had become so familiar to Sarah Jane through the years. A mother who lost a beloved child was forever marked.

Lula Belle's hands rested in her lap, her eyes staring vacantly into the distance. Slowly, she turned back to Sarah Jane and quietly ended her story.

"The pain of losing a child is more than a mother can possibly endure...." Lula Belle's eyes implored understanding from her listener, and Sarah Jane responded, her head nodding slowly in agreement. She had buried two of her own.

"I prayed so hard, Sarah Jane. As Bonnie became weaker, I sat by her bedside and searched the scriptures. I found passage after passage in which Jesus healed people, lots of people and many of them children. Oh, Sarah Jane," she cried, "I desperately wanted to believe that He would heal my baby. And so I went to my husband, the preacher of the Word, and I read him the scriptures I had discovered, and I asked him to pray with me that God would heal our daughter."

She glanced down at her hands, and again she began to twist the wrinkled handkerchief. When she looked back at Sarah Jane, there were new tears in her eyes.

"Do you know what he said?" she whispered, her lips quivering.

Sarah Jane just shook her head, her eyes filled with the empathy of one who has lost.

"He said that Jesus healed when He was on earth, but that was almost two thousand years ago, and the so-called 'power gifts' ended with the deaths of the apostles." Tears were streaming down Lula Belle's cheeks as she whispered, "He said God's way of healing our baby was to take her to heaven."

The two women sat in silence a few moments, both pondering what Lula Belle had said.

And then, quietly and gently, Sarah Jane asked, "Don't you think that's true in some cases, Lula Belle?"

The woman looked carefully into her new friend's eyes, searching for hidden meaning. "Yes, I understand that to be true, and I did at the time. And it may be God's way in some cases. But, you see, the Reverend resigned himself to the fact that Bonnie was to die...no, no, it wasn't necessarily her death; he resigned himself to the conviction that God couldn't, or wouldn't, heal her."

And then she added, with more pain in her eyes than before, "But worse than that, he imparted his so-called doctrinal principles to me, and I believed him. I gave up and...and we buried our little

Bonnie on the coldest day of the year. The only thing colder was my heart…towards God as well as my husband."

It was Sarah Jane's turn to sigh now and sigh, she did, again and again. *Lord, have mercy*, she prayed silently, *so many hurtin' people, all alone in their pain when they could be leanin' on Your everlasting arms but for the interference of some high and mighty expert in religion!* She shook her head slowly back and forth, her mouth set in the straight line her daughters knew meant something was needling her to anger. But she wisely held her temper. Lula Belle didn't need that.

"So you see, Sarah Jane, when Jesus came to visit little Lizzy Gresham and healed her, all those memories rose up in me like an erupting volcano. And then, just before you greeted me so kindly on the porch that day, I suddenly became aware that my thirty-two years of unbelief had come to an end…just like that."

Lula Belle reached over and touched Sarah Jane's hand. The older woman received the token of kindness and appreciation with a smile and a squeeze.

"I'm glad I told you my story, Sarah Jane, and I thank you for being such a good listener. It's done me a world of good." A genuine smile formed on the woman's face for the first time that day. "I guess I've finally forgiven the Reverend, even though I thought all those years it was God who had done me wrong. My insides feel clean, like I've had a real purging."

Sarah Jane took both Lula Belle's smooth hands—the well-groomed ones she had once despised to look at—and gripped them tighter. "You'll be alright now, Lula Belle. And who knows, maybe you might find some love left in your heart for that high and mighty old man you live with."

Their laughter rang in the spring breeze as if the giant oak branches the storm left behind were hanging full of wind chimes. Even the old yellow cat turned to glance back at the lowly humans on her way to see what the chickens were doing. They were still laughing when Will's wagon rolled up the road with Sarah Jane's three wet girls, Frank Carroll and a few cousins hanging off the sides.

Liza shouted, still shivering, "It weren't too cold, Mama!"

❃

In a small rural farming community like Beulah, the excitement and grief of each and every birth, death and marriage was felt by one and all. However, an event even more far reaching occurred in late March of 1903. Willis T. Gresham died. Even though he was eight years older than Jeb, Willis T. was only sixty-two years old.

His death was a shock to everyone but for no one more than Jessie Gresham Whaley. Her daddy had built her and Clancy a house right next to his because that was exactly where she wanted to be. He had meant the world to her. And now she stood like a little lost bird in the middle of her mother's parlor while her brother, William Lewis, broke the terrible news to the family. Of the immediate family, only Jessie, Clancy and Margaret were there when he arrived. Jeb had come to visit his brother, unaware that Willis T. had gone to Kinston the day before. Before he got to the house, William Lewis had sent Willie Hill to contact the others. By the way, Willie could still drive a mule even though his eyes were never the same after the eclipse.

"Where's your papa, son?" Margaret asked cheerfully when William Lewis walked through the front door.

Willis T. had gone to Kinston to sell a load of bacon. He was to meet his son and have a late dinner at Hotel Tull where they planned to spend the night and drive the wagon back to Beulah together the following day. Willis T. died of a heart attack during the night.

It took William Lewis a long time to get the awful words out of his mouth. He was as stunned as he knew his mother and siblings would be. His father had waved good-bye to his wife yesterday morning, excited as usual to launch a new business venture. He was healthy as a horse, or so everyone thought. Now, William Lewis was bringing Willis T. Gresham home in a casket.

Margaret swooned. Jessie was too shocked to go to her. Awash in his own sorrow, Jeb didn't know who to go to first, Jessie or her mother. But Clancy was standing at Jessie's side so Jeb rushed over to Margaret while giving orders to William Lewis.

"Get the smelling salts, son."

Within the hour, Adeline, Kate and their other brothers were notified and the entire family gathered in the once happy home of their childhood. Willis T. and Jeb's four brothers and one sister arrived one by one as well as Nate and Laney, Sarah Jane and all the local Gresham cousins. Of course, the entire citizenship of Limestone Township came by all through the day and night to pay their respects and mourn the loss of Willis T. Gresham.

It seemed that in every conversation Jeb overheard, before and after the funeral the following day, someone mentioned Willis T.'s grand plan to make an actual, incorporated town out of Beulah. His brother was a visionary, that was for sure. Jeb was content to farm his land without thinking much about anyone else. Just providing food and clothing and a roof for his family fitted the definition of success to him. But when his older brother went off to fight the Yankees at nineteen, he had come home with broader dreams in mind. Most southern men had returned from the most gruesome war in American history feeling totally defeated—which they were as a whole. Nonetheless, Willis T. Gresham was not defeated. He had just begun.

Chapter Sixteen

Summer, 1903—The rain Lula Belle Adridge had prayed for didn't come for quite a while, only a few quick showers here and there. Water might as well have been gold in Duplin County that spring and early summer. Jeb Gresham even took to driving his old rickety wagon to the ever-receding river to haul back as many buckets and any other kind of containers he could find full of the precious liquid commodity. He was just making sure the tobacco beds were kept irrigated. It took everybody—Jeb, Sarah Jane, Nell, Frannie, Liza, Frank, Simon, Swanee and Queen—to keep the small plants from burning up in the beds before they had a chance to grow to maturity, ready to be transplanted in the fields.

The work was exhausting, another time-consuming task added to an already overloaded workday. The girls weren't young'uns anymore, and they were well aware of the seriousness of the situation, but Jeb still caught himself yelling all during the early morning hours when the water had to be hauled down the long dirt rows by human hands, "Be careful now! Don't spill it! There's not a drop to be wasted! Hurry up, Susie, the waterin's got to be done long before the sun gets high! If you keep messin' around, the wet plants will scorch in the noonday heat! Come on, girl!"

Not only were the tobacco fields dry but so was everything else for miles around. Sarah Jane's garden thankfully received some of the water brought up from the river for the tobacco plants, but not much. They were still bringing enough water up from the well for drinking and cooking, but Sarah Jane had noticed that very morning that the water was looking a little murky and that meant mud was mixing in from the bottom of the well. As for baths, well, suffice it to say the weekly Saturday night ritual had become a luxury of the past.

"It's sort of like eatin' spring onions," Jeb assured the girls, "if everybody eats 'em, nobody smells any different than anybody else."

One Saturday morning in June, after looking out over the tobacco fields and asking old Simon to pray for rain (Jeb still couldn't shake his "whatever's goin' to be is goin' to be" philosophy), Jeb packed the two younger girls in the back seat of the buggy, helped Sarah Jane into the front and set off to Beulah. The females were to visit their kin while he gathered up supplies at Nate's store and had the mare shoed at the blacksmith's.

All along the long dusty road from Hallsville to Beulah, Jeb and Sarah Jane watched the fields go by. Many were filled with long neat rows of stunted tobacco plants, but some were peppered with cornstalks that should have been much higher by now. The long green leaves were beginning to curl from the lack of water, the edges already turning a crispy brown. The cotton fields didn't look too bad. The prickly plants seemed to take the drought much better than corn and tobacco.

Jeb shook his head, and Sarah Jane whispered many a prayer on that journey. Even the girls were unusually quiet, subdued by the worry etched in their parents' faces. As long as they could remember, their lives had been ruled by the crop in the field. Whether fresh in the summer or canned in the winter, the food on the table was from the garden. Any meat the family had the luxury of eating was raised and slaughtered right there on the farm. Feed for the animals plus meal for cornbread, and even the southern staple, grits, came from the corn Jeb planted in early spring. The shoes on their feet, the clothes on their backs, the supplies and tools necessary for life, taxes on the land—all that and more came from the golden tobacco leaves and the blades of corn now drying up in the fields.

Total dependence on the land spilled over to the few who chose not to farm as well. Nate's store provided all kinds of dry goods—tools, nails, flour, fabric, sugar and everything else necessary for life on the farm. Stores were a year-round business. All during the planting and growing season, however, men like Jeb Gresham made their marks on tickets which Nate and Laney put away in a cigar box until fall when the tobacco and corn were hauled to market. Only then did the relieved farmers come to town with cash in their overalls' pockets to pay their debts.

And so the rains that finally came in late June were welcomed as a gift from God by most everybody but the worst of the heathen like old Cranky Mosley. It was said he stood in his tobacco field in the middle of a storm and dared God to strike him with lightning. He didn't last too long after that. Doc Kennedy couldn't figure out exactly what was wrong with him.

The following Sunday morning—it started raining on Friday around noon—the congregants of the Hallsville Baptist Church, the Hallsville Presbyterian Church and the Potter's Hill Primitive Baptist all sang, "There shall be showers of blessing; showers of blessing, I plead" to the top of their mostly unharmonious voices. The Baptists and Presbyterians made a much louder joyful noise, considering they enjoyed the accompaniment of a piano. The Hard-shells didn't believe in musical instruments, the lack of which usually caused their songs to drag slower and slower. But they sang loud enough for heaven to hear anyway.

Now it was Lottie Moon Mission Day at the Baptist church, and the women had prepared nothing short of a feast for the noonday meal. Since it was a special day and since everyone was rejoicing over the rain, there was a lot of singing to be done. So by the time the last song was well into the fourth verse, Jeb's stomach was growling something fierce. Sarah Jane gently laid her hand on his knee, a serious warning for him to sit still and not get up before the last amen. It just so happened that the visiting quartet was singing, "Jesus took my burden and left me with a song," when Jeb brushed Sarah Jane's hand away and whispered, a bit too loudly, "Well, all I can say is I just hope He didn't leave'em another'n."

One might be wondering how the Baptists enjoyed a feast on the church grounds in the rain. Well, miracle upon miracles, the rain let up long enough for the women to set out huge platters of fried chicken, bowls of fresh green beans right off the vine, newly dug boiled potatoes, spring cabbage and squash, ham biscuits and more cakes and pies than anyone could count. The men had stretched a makeshift banquet table of chicken wire from one pine tree to the other. It was a sight to behold and smelled even better than it looked.

Jeb thought he might starve to death before the preacher finished asking the blessing, which was way too long to leave hungry sinners saved by grace standing around mouthwatering mountains of tempting fried chicken. He thought he might better have a word with the preacher after dinner to remind him that a blessing is supposed to be short and sweet. Sermons should be left for the pulpit.

It seemed like everybody in Beulah and Hallsville showed up for the celebration that Sunday in June of 1903, even folks who seldom set foot inside a church door. Sarah Jane figured that since Theophilus was in the middle of a long drunk, his family might be going hungry, so she invited them to the banquet. A few of the high and mighty did snub their noses at the likes of Emmy Brinson and her brood, but all in all, most everyone was kind and neighborly, obediently following the Golden Rule as best they knew how.

Hannah was the only child of Jeb and Sarah Jane Gresham absent from the early summer celebration. Sarah Jane missed her terribly. Her second oldest had always loved dinners on the grounds. Hannah's deep love for the church had always flowed over into all its activities, which included anything of a corporate nature within the community considering the church was the only communal institution around. It had even served as the school until a couple of years ago when one was built on Hall land just fifty yards or so down the road. Built on a sand hill in the fork between the road to Beulah and the road to Muddy Creek, the small clapboard church with its bell in the yard instead of in a high steeple overlooked the Hallsville community like a beckoning and protective haven of rest…which it surely was.

In later years, as is true of all communities everywhere, the citizenry of Limestone Township would inevitably become divided, but oddly enough, not by social standing or financial success, or even education. The people of Limestone separated according to which church they joined. It was as if each denomination created its own little pasture, unconsciously erecting a high fence around it with no gate in sight. But in 1903, a year after the Hallsville Presbyterian Church was founded and four years before the old Hallsville Baptist congregation planted a daughter church in Beulah, the Lord's flock was united—at least in a broad interpretation of the Christian faith. Its politics, as mentioned previously, was another matter altogether.

After all bellies were filled to satisfaction and the men drifted off to discuss crops and politics, the older children ran off to play hide-and-seek and other toy-less games while the littlest ones lay down to rest on quilts spread beneath the shady branches of the ancient river oaks. The courtin' age crowd, anywhere between twelve and twenty, quickly divided into twosomes—that is, if they managed to avoid the eyes of ever-watchful mamas and papas. Some of them sneakily meandered from the populous for a hand-holding walk down to the sandy river bed. The women, naturally, began cleaning up the mess and packing up what was left of the dinner into baskets or buckets.

Sarah Jane had just fitted the only leftover slice of pound cake into the top of her bucket and was standing beside the chicken-wire table wiping her hands on her big white apron when she slowly turned to see what else needed to be done. But instead of more work, her gaze rested on a sight made for sore eyes. Just a few yards away, Reverend Aldridge stood holding Lula Belle's hand, helping her up into the buggy. Now, that wasn't so strange. Most men of any descent upbringing whatsoever would have done that, and the Reverend had more than his share of good upbringing. What was odd was that when Lula Belle took her seat and settled in for the ride—their destination eluded Sarah Jane considering the Aldridges lived just a few yards from the church and certainly didn't need a buggy to get home—the Reverend didn't let go of Lula Belle's hand. He just smiled up at her as if she was a new bride, and Lula Belle blushingly gave him a sweet smile in return.

The power of forgiveness, Sarah Jane mused with a sigh of relief, *is truly amazing.*

She pulled her gaze away from the touching scene and scanned the thinning crowd for Jeb. Some of the folks planned to stay longer and have a sing, but knowing it would get them home late and certain that Jeb would be itching to get back to his own front porch, Sarah Jane was ready to pack up the buggy and head out. She was tired, too, and although the day had been a delight for one and all, this Sabbath had certainly not been restful. Monday morning was coming painfully early no matter what.

Her searching eyes finally found Jeb leaning against a pine tree talking with his brother's widow, Margaret. She was dressed in black from head to toe and would be until her year of mourning was up next March. Jeb's head was covered with the same floppy hat that he wore to work in the fields all during the week. Sarah Jane caught his eye in a second and waved that she was ready. Nodding in her direction, Jeb turned back to Margaret and spoke a few more words of comfort.

"Thank you, kindly, Jeb," she said tearfully as she squeezed his hand and turned away.

Sarah Jane was thinking how peaked Margaret was looking these days when her ears caught wind of a loud racket that wasn't coming from the crowd who had gathered on the church steps. Ira Hines was playing his guitar, leading about ten or so of the most harmonious in a few gospel songs, but they all hushed when the noise reached them.

"Giddy-up! Gee! Whoo-ee! Haw, now, haw!"

"What on earth?" Sarah Jane wondered aloud, turning towards the dirt road from whence all the noise was coming.

It was Sonny Boy Batchelor, slapping his thighs and hollering at himself as if he was his own horse. The strange man of unidentifiable age was dressed in ragged overalls with no sign of a shirt on his back or shoes on his feet. He was running—trotting might be a better description—so fast dust would have been flying had it not been raining since Friday. Instead, mud was splattered all over his overall legs and his great big feet, and more was being applied as Sonny Boy managed to hit every mud hole in the road.

"Well, I'll be," said Jeb who had ambled over to Sarah Jane to help her load up.

His wife just stood there, staring at the wild-eyed man who thought he was a horse. "I've heard of Sonny Boy Batchelor half my life, but this is the first time I've ever laid eyes on him," she said, in awe.

Jeb nodded. "They say he never stops runnin'." Jeb scratched his head without taking his hat off. "I say he's bound to rest sometime."

"To be sure," agreed Sarah Jane.

All of a sudden, Sonny Boy screamed, yelling something that might have been "Ow!" but went on and on, sounding more like a mule braying or perhaps a donkey. The crazy man was obviously in pain. Instead of trotting now, he was jumping up and down and running around in circles, still braying like a hound at full moon.

Jeb, along with Ira and a few more men, went running towards Sonny Boy, wanting to help but a mite scared of the notorious horse man. Just before they got to him, Jeb spotted the problem sitting on a porch step across the road from the churchyard.

"Jiggs Hall!" shouted Jeb. "You put that rifle down!"

"I ain't shootin' real bullets at 'em!" ten-year-old Jiggs shouted back with a big grin.

"I don't care what you're shootin'!" yelled Jeb. "You hurt the man!"

"He ain't a man! He's a horse, more'n likely a mule. I was just havin' me some fun anyway." Jiggs was still grinning.

Ira Hines drew up to his full six feet about the time he got to the porch where young Jiggs was reclining rather proudly, leaning back on his elbows with his rifle in hand. Deliberately standing as close to the boy as he possibly could so as to hover over him even taller and bigger, Ira spit out, "Boy, I better not *ever* catch you doin' such a thing again! You understand?"

"Yeah, yeah." Jiggs was a little scared, but he didn't think Ira would actually hit him or anything. The fun of it all was well worth a little risk. His real worry was that Jeb or Ira would tell his pa, and naturally, that was exactly what came up next.

"When your pa gets home, I'm going to pay him a visit, boy." Ira's eyes were flashing fire.

"D...don't tell my Pa, Mister Ira. He'll whip me good. I won't do it again! I promise!" The mischievous boy actually sounded rather repentant.

Ira looked madder than the devil a moment longer, but then his big heart relented. "Alright, not this time, but you'd better believe

I'll go straight to your pa if I ever even hear tell of you doin' such a thing again."

"I won't."

Jiggs looked for a minute as if he might cry, but the minute Ira and Jeb turned away to walk back over to the churchyard, his rather chubby freckled face broke into another grin, the same kind he had expressed a few minutes earlier when he shot the pebbles at the crazy man. Thankfully, by that time, Sonny Boy had calmed down and trotted on off down the road towards Beulah.

All in all, it was a rather exciting conclusion to the day's celebration of rain and the church's dedication to foreign missions. However, as Jeb clucked his tongue for the old mule to get on home, he turned to Sarah Jane and commented, "I don't know why we need to go to China. Seems like there's a mission field in the churchyard if you ask me."

Chapter Seventeen

Summer, 1903: The blessing went on and on. In later years, the summer of '03 was considered to be the most pleasant as well as the most productive anyone could remember, even the old timers. Everything seemed to go right, weather included.

As Jeb said, "It weren't too hot, and it weren't too cold," which was agreeably followed by old Simon's, "Yep, yo right, Mistah Jeb. Ain't too hot, ain't too cold. It be jest right."

Although Duplin's farmers had feared a summer without rain, after the weather turned in June Duplin County's rich black soil stayed moist and pliant throughout the long farming season, producing in the fall a bountiful harvest whether tobacco, corn or cotton. Sarah Jane's garden continued to produce basket loads of vegetables well into September when the bright blue morning glories played hide-and-seek up and down the bean poles and among the drying cornstalks.

On lazy Sunday afternoons, the wide beach on the Northeast Cape Fear River at Hallsville was filled with the happy summer sounds of splashing water, yapping dogs and the laughter of children. Young mothers sat with their babies on quilts spread close to the sprinkled shade of the tall pines but not too close for fear of red bugs and biting ants and other such unseen varmints.

About halfway between the old plank bridge that hovered high above the river and the deep dark Gar Hole, some of the local boys had climbed up onto what was left of an ancient river oak and tied a long tight rope to one of its strongest branches. So in the midst of all the splashing, yelling and laughing, a cry could be heard above it all as a brave young soul screamed, "Get outa the way!" just before swinging out on the rope and plunging bottom first into the depths of the river. It was as fun as fun could be.

Yes, all was well in Beulah throughout that entire farming season...except for one thing. Jeb had begun to notice that old Jake, the prized hunting dog who had survived the storm of '02, was acting a bit strange. The old dog had always followed his beloved master everywhere, even to Beulah when there was room in the wagon, and sometimes when there wasn't. On many a trip to town, Jeb or one of the girls would glance back down the road, dust flying everywhere, and spy old Jake trotting down the wagon ruts, tongue hanging out and tail a' wagging, happy to be following his people no matter how far they were going.

Most of the time, if there was room, Jeb would rein in the mule and yell, "Come on, you old dog!" And no matter how old or tired he was, Jake stopped dead still for about two seconds, pricked up his floppy ears and grinned, at least that's how Susie described it. And then, all of a sudden, that old dog changed gears and high tailed it up the road. In no time at all, he had jumped into the back of the wagon and flopped into his favorite traveling position, his head resting on the tail gate. He was just a'hassling.

But lately, old Jake hadn't been jumping in or out of anything. In fact, Jeb had noticed he seemed afraid to jump, even if it was only from the wagon to the ground. The dog would just pace about inside the wagon, whimpering as though trying to tell Jeb about something that was troubling him. At first, Jeb just walked on off and left him up there, thinking the old dog was getting mighty ornery or maybe even lazy. He'd come down when he got hungry enough. But finally, whatever was wrong, Jeb felt sorry for the dog and gave in. The hound was heavy and clumsy in his arms, but he lifted him down from the wagon and from then on, from most anywhere Jake got himself stuck.

"You're some huntin' dog," he said, shaking his head doubtfully. "I'll be totin' you over ditches come huntin' season."

And then one day in late August, Simon and Jeb were taking a mid-afternoon break near the spring at the edge of the woods. The cool water, spouting up from the rich ground like Old Faithful, had refreshed the two men somewhat, and they began to entertain themselves by throwing sticks for old Jake to fetch. At first, the only unusual thing the dog did was instead of running off after the stick like a bullet shot from a rifle, he would pause a second and prick up his ears. Then, he was off in the direction the stick went. Problem was, he might find it and he might not.

"Somethin's wrong with that ol' dog," muttered Jeb.

"Yep, somethin's wrong with that ol' dog," replied Simon, nodding his white head in agreement.

And then came the clincher. On his way back to the two men, carrying a stick in his drooling mouth, Jake ran smack dab into a big pine tree. Stunned for a second or two, he dropped the stick and flopped down on the thick pine straw, whimpering a bit mournfully.

Jeb and Simon rushed to his side, each of the toughened old farmers murmuring sounds of comfort to their old friend whose problem was obviously more serious than they had previously thought. Kneeling down beside the old dog, Jeb rubbed his neck and patted him reassuringly. He didn't feel so assured himself.

Simon sat down and leaned back against the pine tree for a while, sadly watching his old friend ignore the inevitable. He hated to say anything, but they had always been truthful with one another, and this was no time to change their ways, so he finally said, as kindly as he could, "Ol' Jake done gone blind, Mistah Jeb."

"Yeah, well...maybe not," muttered Jeb, almost in tears but determined not to let it show.

"Sho, he be. Dat's why he done run into dis here pine tree."

"He just didn't see it, that's all."

Simon scratched his tight snowy locks; his eyes squinted in a frown. "Dat's what I said Mistah Jeb. Dog's blind."

Jeb heaved a big sigh and quit his kneeling position to sit beside the dog on the sweet-smelling pine straw. He scratched the old dog's ears and neck with all the love he had in his heart. Jake had been his faithful companion for nigh on to fifteen years. Suddenly, he turned away, but not in time for Simon to miss the tear that was trickling down his leathery cheek. It was too much for Simon, the former child slave who had always been mighty tenderhearted.

"I run into a tree one time," he said, his gaze on old Jake.

"Huh?"

"I sed I run into a tree one time."

Jeb wondered if Simon was as bad off as Jake. "What's that got to do with Jake?"

"Well, suh," said Simon, "I run into a tree and we knows I ain't blind, so maybe he ain't blind. Maybe he just befuddled like I wuz."

Jeb smiled a little at that, appreciating Simon's attempt to modify the dire prognosis for his sake. "Nah," he said, sadly shaking his head. "You were right the first time. I've been sittin' here thinkin' about how he's been actin' for a long time now. It's like a puzzle come together all of a sudden."

Simon nodded, brushing back his own tears with the back of his hand. "Want me t' take care of it for yo, Mistah Jeb?"

The normal thing would have been to put the old dog out of his misery, saving him from more suffering than either he or his master could bear. But Jeb couldn't let old Jake go, not yet.

"He ain't so blind that he cain't follow me around and get some pleasure out of life. He still eats good. He ain't sick exactly. We'll just have to help him out a bit. No more fetch games and such as that. As much of a blessin' as he's been to me, it won't hurt me none to pick him up when need be. He's probably been livin' more by smell and hearin' than by sight for a long time now."

Simon nodded, relieved to be spared the dreaded task.

Jeb gave Jake another pat and rose to his feet, straightening out his stiff legs. Immediately, the old dog got up and smiled, tongue hanging out and tail wagging. He happily lopped between the two men as they headed back to the pack house where Sarah Jane and the girls were tying tobacco.

About a week later, Jeb called for old Jake, and he didn't come. He searched the farm, his heart heavy, for over an hour. He found the dog lying peacefully in a particularly profuse bed of blue morning glories. Jake's eyes were closed. His faithful heart was at rest.

It was right after Jake's sad demise, but having nothing to do with it, that Laney Gresham decided she wanted to get baptized. Now, there wasn't a church house within five miles of the village, and that sad fact posed a few difficulties to Beulah's citizens of faith—one of them being hardly anybody got baptized in a timely fashion.

Some people, like Laney, grew up in homes where everybody believed in Jesus and tried their best to live their lives according to the Golden Rule, "Do unto others as you would have them do unto you." And then, there were others who—in the midst of drunkenness, meanness, pride or whatever type of sinful lives they were leading—suddenly or not so suddenly experienced an encounter with the Almighty, faced inevitable accountability and thereby shed their past sins like ragged old clothing. And then they began new lives; they really did. Anybody who didn't fit into either category was just tolerated as a sad fact of life by those in the other two categories.

Now, since Laney Gresham certainly fit in the first category, having been raised in a home where everyone believed, one might readily assume she had already been baptized and needed nothing further since her sins were washed away. But not so, at least in Laney's mind. She had been baptized as a baby and had always taken her faith for granted. Since the visitation, however, Laney had come to the conclusion that baptism should be a personal decision and a very special event, a milestone one could look back on as a new beginning.

After talking to Nate about it for some and listening to him say, "That's just fine, Laney," over and over again, she had him take her and the two children down to the river one fine Sunday afternoon so she could get baptized.

"But what about a preacher?" asked Nate as he carefully placed four-year-old Lizzy in the back buggy seat and lifted Mary Alice up to Laney.

"Well now, Nate, just who is it that's going to wash away my sins and make me new?" She settled herself comfortably and held the sleepy baby against the bodice of her best blue muslin dress.

"Jesus, I reckon," replied Nate, confused as he always was in the middle of one of Laney's wild ideas.

"Right," she said adamantly as if she was the one proven to be in the right. Needless to say, he still didn't know what she was talking about.

And so the little family headed out to Hallsville and arrived in the midst of a beautiful Sunday afternoon in early September, just before the weather turned and chilled the flowing river too cold for swimming. Nate reined in the mare and tied her loosely to a tree. Then he helped Laney and the children down from the buggy. Lizzy, although sleepy at first from the long ride, happily rode on her papa's shoulders down the winding sandy path that led to the river's edge while Laney trudged through the deep sand carrying the baby.

She hadn't expected there to be so many people. Being town folks confined by a store, she and Nate didn't get to the swimming hole very often. She had no idea so many bodies would be vying for a place in the water so late in the summer.

As Nate lifted a happily squealing Lizzy from his shoulders and placed her down on the sand, he looked around and commented, "You might find a preacher here after all, Laney."

She slowly nodded her pretty head as if in a daze, then handed the baby over to Nate as she assessed the situation. Shading her eyes with one hand, the other rested on the hip bone which usually held a child.

Turning back to Nate, she spoke in a very decisive tone, "Over there, Nate, where the river bends and goes into the woods. There's hardly anybody swimmin' there, just a few big boys." She reached down to take Lizzy's hand and lead her over to the chosen baptismal font.

Lizzy reached up to take the baby's tiny hand in hers. "Come on, Mary Alice. Mama's goin' to get dunked."

"Wait!" Nate looked at Laney as if she were crazy. "That's the Gar Hole. You can't get baptized there."

"Why?" she asked, both hands on her hips now.

"Well, first of all, it's deep and dark and probably very cold. Second of all, do you know what a Gar is, Laney Gresham?"

"No, what's a Gar?"

"It's a big fish with sharp teeth; that's what it is," replied Nate worriedly. "I'd rather not take my wife home missing a few bites of her flesh or maybe a finger or two even if her sins are washed clean away."

"Well, I'm sure if the Good Lord loves me enough to die for my sinful self, He'll surely protect me while He's cleaning me up!" She turned with a huff and marched off towards the Gar Hole, leaving Nate behind to manage both children while following his determined wife through the deep sand.

It was on the way to the Gar Hole, hardly noticing anyone along the way, that Laney caught a glimpse of a hand waving near the shade of the woods. Then she heard a voice calling, "Laney! Nate! Over here!"

Although her mind and body had one goal in mind and that was to get to the baptismal waters as quickly as possible, she did pause a second to see who was inviting her into their company. Recognizing Sarah Jane, Jeb and Susie, Laney raised her hand high and waved back. And then she had a wonderful idea. Her mama had died right after Laney and Nate got married, and her papa was ailing too badly to go anywhere these days, so other than Nate and the girls, she had no congregation to witness her baptism. So with just as much determination as before, she trudged up the sandy incline towards Jeb Gresham's crowd and invited them to her baptism, just like that. Nate and the little ones were still bringing up the rear, wondering what she was doing now.

Although it did seem rather odd, the invitees quickly acquiesced. Helping one another to their feet, the growing baptismal party again headed off to the baptismal pool, sort of like the Israelites marching towards the Jordan. When they got there, the little group of attendees stared at the deep dark water a few minutes and then turned to stare at Nate, wondering what was next. He didn't know, of course, but Laney did. She had planned this for a long time.

After asking the few swimmers very nicely if they would mind moving to another place to swim for awhile, Laney Gresham took off her shoes and stepped into the edge of the water and then turned back to the little congregation. They were all standing a little further back from the white ripples of the river's strong current.

"Let us all sing one verse and the chorus of the hymn, *O Happy Day*," she proclaimed rather elegantly.

Nate smiled then. This was the woman he loved, and he was proud of her...whatever she was doing. As they all joined in the song, he hugged the baby in his arms and squeezed Lizzy's little hand.

"O happy day, happy day, when Jesus washed my sins away!" They joyfully sang the refrain over and over until Laney motioned them it was time to move on. By this time, many of the Sunday river goers nearby had heard the singing and were inquisitively making their way towards the baptismal fountain.

It was a bit hard to stand still with the water lightly lapping about her ankles and her feet sinking in the wet sand, but she did. Standing tall and making sure her blue muslin dress was neatly in place, Laney clasped her hands together at her chest and began to speak.

"As y'all know, Jesus visited our home a while back, and He healed our Lizzy. Nate and me will be forever grateful; there's no doubt about that. But it got me to thinking about a lot of things, one of which was that there was never a moment in my life when I consciously decided to follow Jesus—to make Him Lord of my life, as some folks say. I'm told my Mama and Papa had me baptized as a newborn baby, but I'm sure that was just a little sprinkle. I'm also sure at that point in my life I had no particular sins to speak of. But now that I'm twenty-some years old, I have a bunch of sins behind me, and the great possibility of even more in front of me. I guess you can understand why I have come to the conclusion that I'm in terrible need of a Savior."

Nate was still thinking how much he loved the woman, and Jeb's crowd was hanging onto her every word as more onlookers drifted over to the river's edge where the pretty woman stood in the water addressing her audience.

"Now, I don't have much of an education, but I can read. And during this past year and a half, Nate can vouch that I've been reading the Bible as much as I can. You see, I want to do this thing right. I read that when a person becomes a real believer, allowing Jesus to be first in her life, the next thing to do is make a public announcement. I think the Bible calls it a 'public profession of faith' or something like that. Anyway, the next step is to be baptized. I figured both could be done all together and save time.

"So that's why I'm standing here in this cold water talking like this. I've made my public announcement, and now I'm going to be baptized." Laney was glowing as she continued, "My former and future sins and my entire sinful nature will be washed down this river and into the ocean of God's forgetfulness. I thought about bringing some soap since some of my sins are ground in so deep, but I figured if the Lord Himself went down into nothing but clear water, who am I to argue with that?"

Laney turned and waded out toward the treacherous dark waters of the Gar Hole. Nate quickly let go of Lizzy's hand and handed little Mary Alice to Sarah Jane. The old song says we have to cross Jordan alone, but he would just have to change that, today, anyway. His wife wasn't going into that deep water all by herself. He knew she wouldn't wait for him if he hollered so he high-stepped it through the shallow part until he caught up with her. She seemed pleased to see him, and with a beaming smile, she gratefully grabbed his arm and held on.

Back at the riverside, Susie's eyes were brimming with tears. Jeb wondered what in the world had gotten into her.

"Was Jake baptized, Papa?" she whispered loudly, her voice quivering.

Jeb frowned. This entire scenario was emotional enough without bringing up ol' Jake. "No, child, he weren't baptized. You don't baptize dogs. Now hush, girl."

"But why, Pa? How's he goin' to get to heaven?" Although she was trying her best to whisper, the distraught girl was getting louder and louder.

"Hush now," said Jeb one more time. "We'll talk about Jake later." He let out a heavy sigh and put his arm around Susie's shoulders, trying to be of some comfort to the girl even if his own heart was still aching something terrible over the old dog.

Laney figured the water was deep enough so with Nate's help, she turned and faced what was now a fairly large crowd. "Well," she began, "since Jesus is the one washing away my sins, and since I'm the one making the decision to let Him do it, I figure I'll just dunk myself in this river and He'll be faithful to do what He said He'd do. So, in the Name of…."

"Laney! Laney Gresham!" a voice called out from the back of the crowd.

Laney opened the eyes she had just closed and removed her hand from her nose. With the other, she gripped Nate's arm tighter and strained to see who was shouting her name.

It was Reverend Aldridge. He was coming towards the water, Lula Belle following close behind. When he got to the water's edge, he stopped and said—humble in tone but loud enough for her to hear as well as everyone else—"Mrs. Gresham, I would be greatly honored if you would allow me the privilege to conduct your baptism. I've listened to your testimony today, and I've heard about your unusual encounter. I have come to the conclusion that you are a worthy candidate for baptism. Would you allow me the honor to step into the River of Life with you and to baptize one who has seen the Lord with her very own eyes?"

Laney smiled and held out her hand. It took Jonas Aldridge a little longer to fight the strong current to where Nate and Laney stood holding on to one another, but when he got there, he realized he hadn't experienced such a surge of well being in a long, long time. He was a tall man, clad in long dark trousers, shirt, vest, coat and tie which when wet, weighted him down considerably. But when he placed one large hand on Laney Gresham's back to support her—the other holding tightly on to hers—and gently laid her back in the cold dark water of the Gar Hole, Jonas Aldridge felt the surefire power of love and forgiveness like he had never felt it before. In the blink of an eye, he went under the cleansing tide with her and just as suddenly, both so-called saint and sinner burst from the depths with shouts of joy and smiles that were brighter than the sun.

Nate hugged his crazy wife, happier than a lark and soaked to the bone, as he led her out of the river and into the embrace of a worried little Lizzy who wrapped her arms around her mama's legs and wouldn't let go. Sarah Jane and Jeb walked over to offer congratulations and a rare kiss on the cheek while Susie poured her worries about Jake out to Liza and Frank who had drifted in with the crowd.

After Nate dried Laney off, she took the baby from Sarah Jane, shifted her to one hip and pulled the leg Lizzy was holding onto around to thank Reverend Aldridge. But he wasn't there. She looked around for a second and then spied him still out in almost waist deep water, baptizing people, one by one, in the Name of the Father and of the Son and of the Holy Ghost. She smiled the prettiest smile Nate had seen since the day they both fell in the mud hole at the post office — the day he fell in love.

As Jeb turned to go, leaving Sarah Jane chatting with Lula Belle like they were old friends, Susie caught up with him and gripped his hand as if she were a little girl again. She didn't say a word, but she knew her pa was grieving Jake, too, and she thought perhaps he needed a little comfort as well.

They walked hand-in-hand a few minutes as the light of the September sun began to dim through the lofty pine trees. There was a sudden slight chill in the air, heralding the advent of autumn, and Jeb thought about Laney and the others and hoped they had brought something warm and dry to put on.

"I sure wish Jake had been baptized so he could go to heaven," Susie murmured sadly.

"Well, girl, I've been thinkin' about that," said her pa.

She looked up into his face expectantly. "You have?"

"Yep, I have." He took a deep breath as if this was the most serious subject he had ever discussed with his youngest daughter. It probably was.

"Do you remember the story about old Elijah, the one where he went up to heaven in a fiery chariot?"

"Uh, huh," she replied, a bit confused.

"Well, have you ever seen a picture of a chariot going anywhere without a horse to pull it?"

"No, Pa. I guess not."

He could tell she wasn't getting the picture, not yet. "And do you remember the story you girls love to hear your mama read about Jesus comin' out of heaven ridin' a big white horse?"

She got it then. Her big brown eyes, set in a sweet but rather homely face, filled with tears of happiness this time as she stopped in her tracks to ponder what her papa had said. Her face lit up from dark to light, even as the early shadows of evening fell across the land.

"Oh, Pa!" she exclaimed in whispered awe. "If there are horses in heaven, there must be dogs, right?"

He paused and pulled off his fedora to scratch his head for a second. "Looks that way to me. Don't see why not."

Susie sighed as deeply as a child can. Awed by her pa's picture of animals in heaven, she was ready to rejoice over Jake by telling everyone she knew. She suddenly let go of Jeb's hand to run back to the crowd down at the river.

Jeb quickly reached out and caught her by the sash of her dress. "Wait a minute, girl!"

"What is it, Pa?"

"Well, I'm thinkin'," he began, glancing nervously over at Reverend Aldridge, "just thinkin' that we should keep this between ourselves, just you and me. We're the ones who miss old Jake the most, right?"

"Yes, Pa," she said, in awe for the second time in about five minutes. It was truly amazing to think that she and papa would share a secret nobody else would know.

He looked down at the satisfied girl and gave her a wink and a smile. And then he glanced back at the crowd coming up from the river and smiled again.

Chapter Eighteen

Spring, 1904: With more babies on the way, Hannah was as close to being happy as she knew how to be. Very seldom did she stop now to think about having a family of her own. She was too busy helping others bring little Greshams and Halls, Sandlins and Gradys, Quinns, Hunters, Laniers, Bratchers, Kennedys, Brinsons and Jacksons into the world. Sometimes, when she placed a newborn into its smiling mother's arms for the very first time or when a proud papa got so excited he forgot decorum and hugged Hannah in his enthusiasm, she couldn't help but wonder and hope and wonder some more.

And so it was that in the spring of 1904 Doctor Kennedy called Hannah into his office from the porch where she and Kate were swinging the children and told her he had recommended her for a job if she wanted it. A colleague of his in Kinston was looking for someone to take care of a patient of his, an older woman of means who was recuperating from a fall.

"A nursing job?" asked Hannah quietly, almost reverently.

"Yes," replied the doctor, "this would be fulltime nursing for at least three months."

He continued to explain that Hannah would be required to live in the house with the patient, sleep in the room with her or a room close by and take all her meals with the family. It was a wonderful opportunity for Hannah, but before she made a decision, she would need to take into consideration that she would be given no time off to speak of during the three months or so it took the patient to fully recover. There would be no coming home. As for her work with

Doctor Kennedy, he would miss her, he kindly assured her, but if she was serious about nursing, this would be a fine opportunity to practice her skills and learn much more than he could teach her at the moment.

Hannah agreed not to make a hasty decision. Quickly, she exited his office to go back and tell Kate what the doctor had said. Not surprisingly, Kate already knew about the offer, but the doctor had ordered her to secrecy until he had an opportunity to speak with Hannah himself.

Surprisingly, she had kept the secret, but only because Kate wasn't too thrilled about the idea. Not only was Cousin Hannah her lifelong friend, she was a close confidant as well. With the doctor totally focused on his practice and her with two babies and a house and garden to care for, Hannah's visits were looked forward to with the highest anticipation. All of Kate's sisters were producing babies one after the other, understandably preoccupied with their own husbands and households. She would miss Hannah terribly.

But after a long talk with Sarah Jane and Jeb and a whole lot of prayer, Hannah arrived at Kate's house one day in early May with news of her decision. One look into her eyes told Kate all she needed to know. The doctor was pleased even though he would surely miss his dedicated young midwife. He had come to depend on her more than she was aware. A young woman of her sensitivity and skills who had no personal life to keep her from assisting when needed was hard to come by.

So, early on Saturday morning, May 15, just after her twentieth birthday, Hannah Gresham climbed up into Jeb's old buggy and settled down beside her papa for the long ride to Lenoir County. All her sisters were there to see her off, this being a rather unusual occasion for a woman in the Gresham clan, or any woman for that matter. Liza carried a baby in her arms, and Nell's two little boys clung to her skirt tail, one with a thumb in his mouth, watching grandpa coach the lazy mare into a more respectful attitude. Susie and Frannie—young women themselves now—sorrowfully waved good-bye, grieved to see their sister go. As for Sarah Jane, her smiling eyes said it all. Her swelling pride in the daughter she had trained so well was evident for all to see.

It was almost nightfall when the haggard mare pulled the buggy to the front of the large Victorian house on Queen Street in Kinston. Lights were twinkling through the tall parlor windows, revealing a large cozy room appointed with elegant mahogany furniture and upholstery. There were even oil paintings on the walls and lovely stained-glass panels in the front door. Hannah could see silver candlesticks on the mantle, wine-colored velvet draperies lining the large windows and low-burning flames in the inviting fireplace. The country girl had never seen such beauty and finery. One of her Gresham cousins had recently built a large two-story house on the road through Beulah across from Willis T.'s place, and although Hannah had thought it a mansion, it was just a plain, two-story square house compared to this.

Jeb slowly climbed down from the buggy seat, every muscle and joint in his body stiff and aching from the long ride. He tied the reins to the hitching post and turned around to pull Hannah's bag from the back of the buggy, calling resignedly as he went, "Come on, girl. Let's get you inside."

But Hannah couldn't take her eyes off the house. It was painted a soft mauve with white trim. The white wooden trim work had been skillfully carved into curves and curlicues at each connecting point under the eaves. The parlor walls jutted out in a semicircle from the rest of the house. The window itself curved to fit the outer wall. Glowing with light, the beautiful stained glass entryway was situated beside the protruding parlor but set back about six feet, allowing for a wide verandah across the front of the remainder of the house.

It was beautiful…and it was the future, welcoming her with all its loveliness and peaceful warmth. Others may not have considered hers an exciting future had they known, but when she alighted from her papa's buggy that evening, she knew she was walking into her destiny…and she was glad.

Now there were some days when Hannah went about her nursing duties for Mrs. Mosley as contented and happy as a busy beaver building a dam. Those were most days, actually. But then there were others when she was so homesick she longed to hide in a corner somewhere and cry her eyes out. And Hannah Gresham was not a crier.

Having been in terrible pain the first week of Hannah's employ, the elderly lady didn't pay much attention to her young nurse's emotional state. If the truth be told, she showed very little personal interest in her at all, and that was certainly understandable. However, after a while, bones mending and pain gradually diminishing, the kind and gentle lady reverted to her normal state of mind and began to wonder about the rather homely but highly proficient young girl who cared for her so well.

Their days together had taken on a rather pleasant flavor, actually—quite enjoyable for both to some extent. Mornings were filled with the usual activities of a sick room. Around 7:00 a.m., Hannah helped her patient sit up in the bed and then gently washed her face and hands while Mrs. Mosley's daughter-in-law brought breakfast in. It was well into the third week of Hannah's employ when Mrs. Mosley noticed that Hannah's breakfast was set aside and growing cold while the girl helped with hers. From that time on, the kind lady urged Hannah to eat, suggesting it would be lovely for them to have breakfast together in the mornings. When Mrs. Mosley was able to sit in a chair, the daughter-in-law or the maid, Polly, placed the tray on a round pedestal table between two dainty chairs near the window. Sitting there at the small mahogany table beside thickly pleated floral drapes with matching wallpaper, it seemed to the rural farm girl—poor in comparison but not deprived of life's necessities—that she was a princess only recently connected with her lost identity.

But Hannah was not raised to act high and mighty, and so after a few days of delightful pretense, she shook off the fairytale attitude that had so easily beset her and wrapped herself once again in the plain robe of common sense and practicality. It fit her much better.

Nevertheless, the days with Mrs. Mosley were pleasant enough. Her patient wasn't a whiner or a complainer; in fact, she was just the opposite. Hannah realized early on that the well-bred southern lady would never dare ask for anything unless she felt it absolutely necessary. That left it up to her nurse's sensitive nature to discern when to do what. It also left time in the afternoon and late evening for Hannah to write letters to her family and keep up with her crocheting, a hobby she had enjoyed since childhood. The long needle, a ball of tobacco twine (she couldn't afford nice thread) and whatever piece she was working on lay on the table by the window throughout the long summer days. If Mrs. Mosley drifted off to sleep or rested peacefully in her chair by the window, the movement of Hannah's fingers with the needle and twine was constant. By Christmas, she hoped to have a small gift for her mother and sisters as well as the cousins whose quickly multiplying babies had put a damper on their own crocheting time. A dresser scarf, a doily-like cover for a chair arm or back or perhaps a small table cloth would be under someone's Christmas tree—if they had one—wrapped neatly in brown paper and tied with doubled twine.

The fact that she loved her work as she did, as well as the kindness she received from the gentle lady, combined to form a strong sense of satisfaction and growing contentment. It stopped, however, just short of contentment. The weekly letters from home—always one from Sarah Jane and usually a few quickly written notes from one of her sisters or cousins—were filled with news of weddings, babies and more babies within the Gresham clan and throughout the Hallsville and Beulah areas. As always, Hannah was delighted for the young brides and mothers, but nothing she did could prevent that sad, lonely feeling creeping into her heart as she read the happy news. And although Hannah Gresham was one of those women who hardly ever showed their feelings, always on one even keel when others are going up and down, Mrs. Mosley was old and wise enough to read the young woman's thoughts as she watched her reread the letters day after day.

"Hannah, dear," she said one afternoon as she woke from a nap. Her young nurse was sitting by the window reading a letter that had just arrived. "Have you good news from home?"

Hannah let the paper rest in her lap and turned to smile at her patient. "Yes, ma'm; it is good news. One of my Bishop cousins is going to have another baby. It's her third."

"That's nice," replied Mrs. Mosley. She studied the girl as Hannah folded the letter and placed it neatly back in the envelope. "Come sit by me a moment, would you, dear?"

Hannah quickly rose and placed the envelope in the personal carpetbag she kept on the floor beside the large walnut wardrobe. She pulled a straight back chair beside the bed and straightened her patient's covers.

"Do you need anything?" She had noticed that the elderly woman had been looking a little poorly the last couple of days, and she was concerned.

"Oh, no, I'm fine. I just wanted to speak with you about something personal, if I may."

"Of course," replied Hannah, rather puzzled.

"Well, my dear, I hope I'm not invading your privacy, but I thought that perhaps I might give you a bit of well-earned wisdom for the days ahead. If you don't mind, that is." Mrs. Mosley was a lady of fine southern gentility, and no woman of her pedigree would dare cross a personal—or geographical—boundary line without full permission.

"You feel free to say anything, Mrs. Mosley," said Hannah, reassuringly. It was obvious she meant it.

The old lady smiled. Even on her sick bed, her white hair was elegantly coiled in a high loose bun. The pastel blue bed jacket set off her fading pale blue eyes, causing her to look much healthier than she really was. A soft slender hand reached out for Hannah's calloused one and held it tenderly.

"Don't worry, dear. I believe there is a husband God has chosen for you out there somewhere. But not just any old brutish man. You deserve someone kind and gentle, someone who will put your welfare before his own." She squeezed Hannah's hand in her weak grip.

Hannah blushed, embarrassed by the personal attention and intimate words. But she quickly pulled herself together and smiled gratefully, gently pressing Mrs. Mosley's hand in response. Tears leaked from her eyes and began to run down her face. She didn't know what to say. No one, other than her mother, had ever talked to her of such things before, and even Sarah Jane hadn't said much. It just wasn't done in her neck of the woods.

Mrs. Mosley was thoughtful for a few moments, obviously trying to make sure she would say the right thing. Her lovely wrinkled face, pampered by years of daily creams and herbal concoctions, crinkled into a worried frown. "But, my dear Hannah, if there isn't someone for you…if there truly is not, I want you to know that you are one of the most special people I have ever known. The lack of a partner in life does not mean you are less in any way. The gifts you have been given are great blessings, for yourself and for others as well. You are a giver, and you have much to give."

The soft weary eyes locked with Hannah's own for a moment. And then she asked tenderly, "Do you understand, child?"

"Yes, ma'm, I understand," whispered Hannah tearfully, reaching for the ever-present handkerchief in the pocket of her white apron.

Mrs. Mosley smiled. She pulled her hand back and laid it on her chest. "Well then," she said, "we need not speak of this again. But I want to assure you that I am always here for you if you need someone to listen."

"Thank you, ma'm," Hannah murmured, releasing the burden of her soul through one long sigh now that she had blotted her eyes and wiped her nose.

The old woman closed her eyes. The young one rose from the chair and began to busy herself straightening a room that was perfectly neat already.

They never spoke of it again.

Hannah left home to nurse Mrs. Mosley in early spring and by midsummer, her patient had mended sufficiently from the fall to leave her in the care of her family. Nevertheless, the Mosleys, and Doctor Parrott as well, had urged Hannah to stay on until the first of September, their mother's age adding to their concerns for her full recovery. And so, Hannah stayed on.

But come September, when Doctor Parrott came around for his final prognosis before releasing the young nurse, he suggested a discussion with Mrs. Mosley's son and daughter-in-law and asked Hannah to join them in the parlor. While she sat quietly on the wine velvet Victorian sofa listening politely, the good doctor informed them all that even though Mrs. Mosley had mended well from the fall, her heart was weakening daily. In his professional opinion, the beloved old lady did not have long on this earth.

Though greatly saddened by the news, Hannah was not surprised. Her experience helping Sarah Jane tend the sick and broken, plus her service to Doctor Kennedy, had given her an extra sense about such things. Although the signs had been clear, until the pronouncement came from the doctor's mouth, Hannah had tried to put them out of her mind. But now, they all had to face reality and make decisions in the patient's best interest. And according to the Mosleys and Doctor Parrott, the very best for Mrs. Mosley's last days would be for Hannah to continue on as her nurse until the end.

Hannah's heart was torn. She had grown to love the dear old woman like a beloved grandmother she had never known. But her own family's plan had been for her to return to Beulah in early September, the most enjoyable time of the year to be on the farm, the mild season everyone called Indian summer. All the women, young and old, would be gathering at pack house shelters to finish tying the last loads of tobacco while catching up on the goings on in and around Beulah and Hallsville. It was pea shelling time, too, when farmers' wives would throw parties and invite everyone around to come help them shell the field peas that were already turning red and purple in the fields. And although she considered herself too old (and some might have said, too proper) to splash around in the water, she looked forward to the year's last gatherings at the river as well.

Pleasant thoughts of fun and friends and the family she so sorely missed were filtering through her mind while the good doctor and the Mosleys stared at her, waiting for an answer. But then, thinking fondly of the dear old lady upstairs and how terrible it would be for her to have to get used to another nurse in her last days, Hannah's conscience won the day. She lifted her head and gave them an affirmative nod. Their kind expressions warmed her homesick heart, but they weren't the same as just one glimpse of her mama's face.

She slowly rose from her place on the velvet sofa. "Mr. Mosley?"

"Yes, Miss Gresham?" he quipped.

Mr. Mosley had served in the army in his early years, and although a kind gentleman, he had retained that rather stern look and posture of a commanding officer which sometimes caused Hannah to tremble slightly in his presence. She thought of him as "the general" in private, yet she took courage this time and spoke up. Kate would have been proud of her.

"As you know, I have not seen my family since early spring, and it's now the end of September. I wonder if it would be possible—with the doctor's permission, of course—for me to go home for just a day or two." She wanted to say more, but all her energy was needed to fight back the tears that were poised on the precipice of her eyelids.

The doctor, the son and the daughter-in-law all stared at Hannah, each touched by the girl's heartfelt plea, but more than that, by the guilt of their own thoughtlessness.

Mr. Mosley was the first to speak. "Please forgive us, my dear girl. Of course, you may go and visit your family."

His wife joined in. "Yes, of course, Miss Gresham. I will be happy to attend to Mother while you are gone. I will ask Polly to work longer hours, and I'm sure she will agree."

It was all Hannah could do to hold back the tears, but she did. It helped to finger the handkerchief in her pocket like a security blanket as they discussed the situation.

"Now, that's settled," said Mr. Mosley as if the troops had just saluted his command. "But how shall we get you to Beulah and back again in a few days?" His right hand went to his mouth. He crooked his forefinger under his nose and rested his chin on his thumb in deep thought.

Doctor Parrott's face brightened. "I know," he said. "There's a fine tenant family living on my farm just now, and one of the boys broke his arm recently. There isn't a whole lot he can do, but he can certainly drive a wagon. I'll ask him to escort you home, child."

"That's a grand idea, Doctor Parrott," said Mr. Mosley, clasping his hands behind his back in satisfaction.

His kind but rather distant wife smiled in agreement as Doctor Parrott reached for his hat and cane. "I'll send him first thing in the morning, Miss Gresham. You can pack your bags and say your farewells to Mrs. Mosley."

"Thank you, sir," said Hannah rather feebly. The whole thing had worn her out.

"Oh, Miss Gresham?" said the doctor as an afterthought.

"Yes, doctor?"

"If those fine Duplin vineyards produced a good sweet wine this past year, perhaps you might bring a jug or two upon your return... for my wife's Christmas fruitcake, of course."

"Of course, Doctor. I'll be happy to."

Hannah quietly climbed the stairs to the second floor bedroom and tiptoed over to Mrs. Mosley's bed. Finding her patient still awake, Hannah gently told her about the conversation in the parlor (not the part about her predicted demise) and quickly assured Mrs. Mosley that she would return soon with renewed energy and vigor for the days ahead. Naturally, the dear lady gave Hannah her blessing, wisely reading her own prognosis between the lines. Hannah was able to get to bed fairly early because packing didn't take long. She only had the one carpetbag lying beside the walnut wardrobe in Mrs. Mosley's bedroom.

And so it happened that shortly after daybreak on a beautiful September day in 1904, "the general" placed the carpetbag in the back of the wagon and helped Hannah Gresham climb up onto the high seat not too close to Elbert Waller. The wagon rumbled down the cobblestone street past the rows of lovely Victorian homes and finally over the Neuse River Bridge into the Indian summer countryside. As the sun rose higher over the eastern horizon, the fragrance of fresh falling pine straw and late wildflowers filled the warm morning air. The leaves on the hardwood trees were still green, but they had that dry look, heralding the change of color soon to come. All in all, it was a wonderfully pleasant day to travel, adding to Hannah's joy in going home.

The girl's only thoughts were of hearth and home, the longing for her family building to the bursting point as she settled in for the long, thirty-mile rumbling wagon ride to Beulah. Only once or twice along the way did she actually turn to look at the quiet young man beside her who was holding the reins and clucking every now and then to head the mare first one way and then the other. After they got out of town, there was very little clucking. It was a fairly straight road from Kinston to Beulah, and there wasn't much need of any driving expertise to speak of.

Elbert Waller was a fairly young fellow, perhaps four or five years older than Hannah. He wasn't tall, but he was thin. He had that thick jet black hair and rather gaunt look of many of his Welsh ancestors, sort of a young Abraham Lincoln look. Sitting high on the wagon seat, the two made quite a contrast. Some might have said Hannah was a little on the plump side. She was fair-skinned with pale blue eyes and rather thin wheat-colored hair which she wore in a tight burn at the base of her neck. Yes, in looks they were definitely opposites, but thankfully, both seemed to be shy and quiet, and it didn't take long for each to note that the other didn't expect a lot of conversation.

They might not have spoken three sentences to one another after the brief introduction at the Mosley home had they not experienced a rather strange road hazard along the way. Along about Potter's Hill, they came across Lem Weston's wagon, jackknifed in the middle of the farm-to-market road. He and one of Samuel Williams' boys, Cloudy—they said he was born on an unusually cloudy morning— were doing everything in their power to persuade a gigantic hog to walk up a ply board ramp and get back into the wagon. Lem and the Williams boy had been hauling the hog to the market in Kinston when the animal suddenly got nervous and somehow managed to break the high railing Lem had carefully nailed up early that morning. Hogs are usually rather calm creatures—downright lazy, actually—so no one had expected such a thing to happen.

But the reason Elbert and Hannah broke their fast of silence to chat a bit, and even to laugh a little, was the sight of Lem Weston running around that huge hog commanding it to get back in the wagon. He jumped up and down, in and out of the wagon crying, "Suey! Suey!" And then, when it was obvious the dumb animal wasn't budging, Lem jumped down and started begging it to move. His audience of three wondered if he might start crying any minute.

There was no telling how much that hog weighed, but Lem even tried getting behind the stinking thing and pushing 'til he was red in the face. The Williams boy stood a safe distance away and stared at the entire debacle. He had no idea what to do.

Actually, the two witnesses in the wagon didn't start laughing until later. Elbert left his passenger in the wagon long enough to help Lem out. He quickly grabbed an ear of dried corn from the back of his own wagon and threw it to Lem, shouting, "Get in the wagon and hold out the corn!" Lem did, and the giant hog lifted its snout and snorted loudly a time or two and then slowly ambled up the ramp into the wagon where Lem quickly dropped the ear of corn, clanked the rails shut and jumped back down to the ground. Elbert and Hannah watched as he shouted at the Williams boy to come help him loop extra rope all between the rails and tie them down.

With a wave to Elbert and a loud, "I thank you, now!" Lem jumped onto the wagon seat and said to the Williams boy, "Get in, boy! We're gonna be late!"

With one arm in a sling, Elbert grabbed the side of the wagon with his free hand and pulled himself onto the seat. It was about the time the two wagons passed in the sandy dirt road that it hit both Elbert and Hannah how funny the whole thing was. They politely held their laughter until Lem's wagon was a few yards behind them, and then the shy farm boy and the demure young nurse burst into laughter. From then on they felt more at ease, and eventually, they talked enough to find out a little about one another. By the time the wagon reached Beulah late in the day, Hannah Gresham and Elbert Waller were what one might call "comfortable" together. Comfortable enough that Sarah Jane struggled to hide a questioning smile as she welcomed her daughter home again. Jeb didn't notice anything. He was just glad someone had brought her as far as Beulah.

Chapter Nineteen

*F*all, 1904—It had been nearly four full years since old James was murdered in the wee hours of a hot November morning just after Election Day 1900, and nobody knew any more about it now than they did before it happened. Furthermore, hardly anybody cared, other than Corbett Thomas whose father had been the old slave's master in another lifetime. Corbett's boy, Evan, and his growing family had been living in old James's cabin for awhile, waiting for I. J. Sandlin's crowd to vacate the large farm house Evan had recently purchased near Corbett's old place close to Beulah. Mr. I. J. Sandlin was building a large general merchandise store in Beulah, a skip and a jump from Nate's. I. J. had married Kate and Jessie's older sister, Adeline. Corbett had heard I. J. say he'd have horse stables and chickens and the most modern plows and anything else you could think of, including readymade clothing.

Lessie, Evan Thomas's wife, couldn't wait to get out of that old shack. Every time she walked into the kitchen—which was no telling how many times in a day, considering she was the slowest moving woman Corbett had ever seen—the hair rose on the back of her neck. She did everything in her power to keep from looking at the ghostly, telltale stain on the kitchen floor. But like a magnet, it drew her eyes every time. Evan and Lessie had tried everything, even lye and sandpaper, but nothing was powerful enough to remove old James's blood from those pine boards. Corbett thought it might be some kind of a divine memorial for the old man, unquestionable proof of a life wrongly taken and a mystery left unsolved. The blood would remain as long as the shack was left standing.

Once a year, on the ninth of November, Corbett climbed into the buggy and slowly rode along the muddy road to Billy Goat's Corner where he turned the mare into the path that led to the old slave graveyard, far behind the cabin at the edge of a thick pine forest. Most of the grave markers—the few that remained—were so weathered the carved names were illegible, but Corbett had laid a large smooth river stone at James's head and carved his name and the date of his death with a fine chisel. Sometimes, he stopped to pick a wildflower or two that had been hidden well enough to escape the frost and laid them gently atop the grave. Then, he stood with hat in hand and said a prayer of blessing for his old friend.

But this particular day in September of 1904, Corbett wasn't headed out to old James's place. Weighted down with grief, he loaded the buggy with a few gifts from Sarah, including a pack of her special Johnny Cakes and a jar of the summer's cucumber pickles, and headed out for another grave on Wagon Ford Road. His old friend, Samuel Williams, the beloved doctor of east Duplin's ailing citizens, had passed on to his reward in the middle of July. Corbett missed him something terrible.

Back in July, when he and Sarah arrived at the Williams home place for the wake, Owen, one of Samuel's youngest sons, took Corbett aside and told him what happened the day the doctor died. Owen had married Pansy, his brother Eck's widow. Eck was the one who got kicked by the mule and died.

"I tell you, Mr. Corbett, it was the strangest thing. My baby girl, Nettie—who's not much more than two years old, you know—well, she was playin' out in the front yard that day. Pa had been gone for days, tending to that Thigpen boy who fell off the barn rafters over near Cedar Fork. Did you hear about that?"

"No, no I didn't."

For a second, Owen looked as if he had forgotten one story and was into another, but then he switched gears back to where he started. "Well, about ten o'clock that morning, Nette came in the house just asmilin', telling Pansy and Ma that Pa-Pa had come home. And then, she held out her little hand and showed them a dime, a shiny silver dime. She smiled and giggled, saying over and over, 'Mine! Pa-Pa give it to me. Horsie come home.'

"Well, of course, Ma and Pansy knew she was tryin' to tell 'em Pa had come home in the buggy and brought her a dime, which weren't unusual at all. He always brought Flora and Bo and Nette somethin' if he could. So Ma went out to welcome Pa home and see how he was. She weren't thinkin' about nothin' 'cept how glad she was he'd been paid in cash for a change.

"But the strange thing is, Mr. Corbett, Pa weren't nowhere to be seen. And that's when Ma hollered for Pansy to come outside. Then, they both walked over to the barn where Pa kept the buggy under the shelter when he was home. Pansy was a totin' Nette who was still sayin', 'Pa-Pa come home.'"

Owen paused a moment, his face crinkled up in a frown. He looked about as puzzled as anybody Corbett had ever seen. He just shook his head from side to side and then let out the air pent up in his lungs.

"Mr. Corbett, when they rounded the barn, there weren't no buggy in sight. All the young'uns went to lookin' for him, but he just weren't there." Owen was shaking his head back and forth again, still stumped at the mystery of the whole thing.

Corbett joined his wonderment, just as mystified, waiting anxiously for Samuel's boy to go on with the story.

"Well, Mr. Corbett, long about midnight that night, Ma heard the old buggy rattlin' up the path to the house. She laid still a few minutes, listenin' for the sounds of the horse and buggy movin' on towards the barn shelter as usual. Then she got up and went to fetch some milk for Pa to drink when he got to the house. He always said it helped him sleep better when he was so tired.

"But Pa never came in. Ma sat at the kitchen table for awhile, thinkin' he'd be in any minute. Finally, she called for me, and I pulled my pants on and walked with her out to the barn." Owen took a deep breath and swiped his eyes with the back of his hand. "And there was Pa," he said sadly, "sittin' up in the buggy just like he was drivin'. Ol' Bertha was still hitched up, eatin' hay like she was mighty happy to be home. Pa's eyes were closed, but that weren't unusual. He always said he slept from the time the buggy turned onto Wagon Ford Road until he got to the house. Said old Bertha knew the way good as he did, and he might as well get some shuteye while he had the chance.

"But we both knew, me and Ma. We knew he was dead. As Pa always said when one of his patients died, his spirit just weren't there. It was like he just shed his old clothes and went on to a better place where nobody ever gets sick."

Owen leaned back on the porch step and blinked the tears from his eyes, scratching his head. Then he just sighed and sat there staring at the ground, shaking his head. It's hard for toughened working people to grieve. They want to do something…but there's nothing to do.

It was a strange story indeed, and Corbett never failed to play it over in his mind when he rode out to check on Delia. Their last child and only girl, Penny, had married a boy from Hallsville just last year, and Corbett figured that Samuel's lonely widow would probably go to live with her or one of the boys before long. The farm would be too lonely for her now.

The day after Corbett took Celie's gifts to the Williams place and checked on Delia, he climbed back into the buggy to make another dreaded visit. On this particular sunny September day, he was going to his brother's farm, and he planned to give Pete Thomas a piece of his mind. Corbett and his older brother, Will, had seen how Pete treated that little Hatcher boy, and they were planning to put a stop to it.

And then there was Celie. Quite contrary to his character, Pete took the boy to the newly formed Myrtle Grove Free Will Baptist Church near Quinn's Store every second Sunday just like the other church goers in the area. Knowing her brother-in-law only too well, Celie had watched to see how Pete treated the boy when he thought no one was looking. She didn't miss a thing.

Since that telltale day, Corbett thought he'd never hear the end of it. She had pointed her boney finger in Corbett's face just the day before and stated emphatically that if he didn't do something, she was going to. That old fool, Pete, had already run his own children off but at least they were old enough to make their own decisions. Johnny Hatcher was only nine years old and looked much younger. The boy could only do whatever he was told.

But Corbett didn't know what to do. He had watched the boy just as closely as Celie, and to tell the truth, he was just as concerned. The little fellow had nowhere to go, and he and Celie were too old now to take on another child to raise. Celie had said, "Just go get him, Corbett! We'll think of something to do with him. Maybe he might want to go home now, who knows?"

Corbett doubted that. He couldn't tell which man the boy dreaded most, the devilish Pete Thomas or his own pa who was evidently meaner than the devil himself. Just yesterday, after Celie's boney finger almost poked him in the eye, Corbett had hitched up the mare and ridden the short mile to Doctor Kennedy's house. He knew it was an opportune time when he spied Hannah Gresham and Kate in the porch swing. Hopefully, the two women could put their heads together with the Doc and come up with some good advice.

It was no use, however. Even though all three were certainly sympathetic to the cause, their replies were the same. No one would ever be able to prove the eight Hatcher children were being abused. A father held the right to make his children work, and during whatever work each did, they were sure to get hurt every now and then. Doctor Kennedy just shook his head in that calm manner he maintained no matter what and went back inside to see a patient. Kate was fuming as Corbett expected. She was a lot like his Celie. It was Hannah Gresham who surprised him. Jeb's girl was known to be as calm and steady as the doctor she worked for. But her soft blue eyes had hardened quite a bit as she listened to her papa's friend tell as much of Johnny Hatcher's story as he knew. Actually, it looked as if fire was coming out of little blue ponds of water.

Corbett's heart dropped as he drove in sight of his brother's ramshackle house. Speaking of the devil…there was Ike Hatcher, stomping down the steps with the little boy following close behind. Evidently, Johnny's pa had work to do, and he needed the boy to help him. Corbett knew it wasn't out of love Ike had come for his boy.

He pulled on the reins and stopped right there in the middle of the road. Shrugging his tired shoulders, Corbett watched the scene unfold before him. Celie wouldn't be happy to hear this; that was for sure. Corbett and Will might have talked some sense into their cantankerous brother, but there was nothing they could do with Ike Hatcher.

Ike pushed the boy in the other direction and never noticed Corbett's buggy in the distance. Corbett sat there long enough to see Pete hobble out the door. The old Confederate soldier just stood there, yelling at Ike and the young'un. Evidently, he wasn't too happy to lose his help, even if the help was a malnourished little boy. Although he got little to eat at Pete's table, the little fellow kept himself going by guiltily stealing handfuls of dried fruit or grain from the storage bins in the barn when he knew old Pete wasn't looking. All in all, the boy had fared better with mean old Pete Thomas than with his own pa.

Corbett didn't know how long he sat there, but finally, he flipped the reins. Pulling the mare around, he eased her into a slow walk back down the road to his own house while Ike Hatcher headed in the opposite direction with his boy. He figured he'd take his time getting home. Celie would be waiting anxiously to hear what he had done about Pete and the boy. He grimaced. She was going to be mad as fire and sorely disappointed. He didn't much blame her.

The Mosleys had agreed that Hannah could have three days at home to visit her family and friends. The two days it took to travel to Beulah and back to Kinston made five days of vacation in all, the longest the Mosleys felt they could do without her, considering their mother's declining health. In later years, Hannah Gresham would look back on those days as five of the happiest of her life.

When she arrived in Beulah, where Sarah Jane and Jeb were to meet her at Nate's store and take her home to the farm, there were no thoughts of love or marriage or anything like that in Hannah's mind towards Elbert Waller. There was, however, a tiny speck of interest in a man, and that was something she had never experienced before. Because of it, her steps seemed lighter and there was an uncommon gaiety in her voice.

The first of the three days were spent with her mama and papa on the farm. Nell came one day with her two children. Of course, Liza and Frank were living with Jeb and Sarah Jane, so they were on hand with one baby on Liza's hip and another in her slightly protruding belly. It was obvious soon after Hannah went to Kinston that Frannie and Ira Hines were made for each other, and Susie's wedding day wasn't too far off. She had met a boy from Warsaw at the Duplin County Agricultural Fair in Kenansville last fall, and he seemed to be a good match for Jeb's animal-loving youngest daughter.

Their lives were different now; that was for sure. But when all five girls sat around the big round pine table eating Sarah Jane's pecan pie and laughing and talking, their little ones running in and out of the kitchen, banging the screened door, it was as if they were all little girls again. They forgot all their troubles and concerns that day. When Jeb came to the house for the noonday meal, he walked through the door and said, "You girls are a sight for sore eyes." His brood had come home to nest, and he was a happy man.

As for Sarah Jane, well, she might as well have been in heaven. Glancing around the table again and again, her smiling eyes glowed at the sight of all five daughters together. She couldn't help but think of her oft repeated arguments with Theophilus Brinson. She almost laughed aloud. It seemed Theophilus wasn't the only one to multiply and replenish the earth. She and Jeb were doing a pretty good job themselves.

The second day, Jeb drove Hannah into Beulah to visit Jessie and Kate and all the other Gresham kin who lived there. The plan was for her to stay overnight with Jessie. Jessie's house would be home base as Hannah launched out from there to visit with every cousin in the entire clan. Sarah Jane and Susie promised to ride into town with Jeb on the third day to join Hannah at Laney's table for dinner—the large noonday meal, not the light evening meal southerners called supper.

Jessie left her toddler next door in the care of her mother and walked down the wagon-rutted road to Kate's house linked arm-in-arm with Hannah, feeling footloose and fancy free once again. As usual, she chattered away about anything that popped into her mind, delighted to have her cousin, who had always seemed more like a sister, home again.

Jessie had so much to tell she didn't notice anything different in Hannah at first. The girl was humming a lot, but Hannah's humming wasn't unusual. It was a habit she had developed early in life, and nobody paid it much mind anymore. But all of a sudden, Jessie became aware that her normally very solemn cousin was humming a different tune, so to speak. Instead of her favorites, like *What a Friend We Have in Jesus* and *Near the Cross*, Hannah was humming more lively songs like *Send the Light* and *Every Day with Jesus is Sweeter than the Day Before*.

It was just as they were climbing the porch steps to greet Kate—who was waiting in the swing with a young'un on each side—that Jessie's mouth flew open—open wider, that is—and her eyes lit up like the Fourth of July.

"Why, Hannah Grissom!" she said, laughing. "You sly little fox, you!"

Hannah seemed to pay her no mind, reaching down for the smallest child of the two she had helped bring into the world. She turned around and sat down beside Kate in the swing, studying the baby to make sure he was healthy and strong. In the process, however, Kate didn't miss the slight blush on her old friend's cheeks. She eyed her good, wondering what Jessie was talking about. As usual, it didn't look as if Hannah was going to say anything or even acknowledge Jessie's prattle.

Kate turned back to Jessie who had found a seat on the low brick and cement support beside the porch steps. "What are you talking about, Jessie Grissom?"

Jessie was grinning from ear to ear, her thin little face—a bit more plump since the baby came—glowing like the September sun. "Hannah's got a fellow, Kate! I just know it!"

Kate turned again to Hannah who was now smiling at the toddler playing hide-and-seek around his mother's swelling middle. It was a known fact that her cousin had the most amazing way of ignoring anything she didn't want to discuss. Kate was about to have a fit to know about the fellow she now equally perceived was hiding away somewhere in Hannah's life. Nevertheless, being the older, wiser and definitely craftier of the two sisters on the porch, she also perceived that their cousin was in one of her usual clammed-up moods. And, she also knew that as much as Hannah loved Jessie, she would never risk sharing the secrets of her heart with the chatterbox of the crowd. Not that all the Gresham girls didn't chatter, of course.

So she wisely said, "Aw, Jessie, you're always thinking up some romantic notion about anybody and everybody who's not hitched yet. When Hannah has any such news, she'll tell us."

And then Kate quickly changed the subject and invited them into the house to see the photograph some itinerant photographer had made of the Doctor and his family; the photograph in which Kate looked as ill as a hornet.

After a few glasses of lemonade along with a happy hour of light, comfortable conversation, during which Hannah told her cousins about the Mosleys and their lovely home, Jessie got up to take her leave. Regretfully, she had to get back to the baby. Her mother was to preside over the Ladies' Temperance League that evening and needed time to prepare herself. Just before she walked out the door, Jessie, that knowing glint in her eye again, looked back at Hannah and smiled.

I'll get it out of her, she thought, *even if it takes me all night. Kate's not pulling the wool over my eyes!*

But by the time Hannah and her mama and papa sat down to eat fresh field peas, sweet corn, roast pork, rice, gravy and biscuits with Laney and Nate the next day, her two curious cousins knew only that a nice young gentleman had driven her home and would be coming back to get her in the morning, soon after breakfast. That bit of knowledge wasn't much, but it made Jessie one happy young woman. At last she had something on Kate because it just so happened that Hannah was staying at Jessie's house and she'd be the only sister to meet the young man when he came for Hannah in the morning. Kate wouldn't get to lay eyes on him.

However, much to her dismay, her older sister, a child perched on each hip, determinedly arrived at Jessie's house just as Elbert Waller was guiding Doctor Parrott's mare and wagon up to the front porch. Thankfully, Jessie managed to suppress her anger at Kate as well as all her girlish giggles until later while she offered the young man a polite welcome and a brown paper bag of ham biscuits to eat on the long drive back to Kinston.

Elbert shyly accepted the gift with only the hint of a smile.

He's not too sociable, Jessie thought. *But neither is Hannah. They might get along just fine.*

As for his looks, she judged him a bit short of handsome…quite a bit short. He certainly didn't compare to her Clancy; that was for sure. *Oh, he don't look too bad*, she thought, *but he might look a lot better if he'd just perk up a little.*

Kate greeted Elbert just as gravely as he greeted her. She was studying deeper things than Jessie was. Though not of her own accord, Hannah had managed to escape the inevitable plight of all women longer than anyone in the clan, and Kate hoped she wasn't headed down a sorrowful path now. She studied every move and facial inflection the man made, tucking away her insights for later when she would set up her own judgment day. She silently prayed that Cousin Hannah would listen to her well-formed advice.

As usual, Hannah ignored them all, and as placidly as was her character, she accepted Clancy's help climbing up into the wagon and bade them all a sad farewell. She wasn't thinking about Elbert Waller or romance or any of that silly stuff; she was thinking how long it would be before she could come home again. Bravely wiping a tear from her eyes with her embroidered handkerchief, she waved good-bye amid shouts of "We'll see you soon!" from Kate and Aunt Margaret and "Take good care of her, Mr. Waller!" from Jessie's smiling mouth.

It was a long ride back to Kinston.

Chapter Twenty

*F*all, 1904 — Pea shellings were always a part of community life in the pleasant pre-autumn days of September, but this year it seemed mandatory to Sarah Jane that she call for the biggest pea shelling anybody ever heard of. Her help was dwindling fast, even with Liza and Frank living with her and Jeb on the farm. Liza and Nell were head over heels in babies to tend to, and Susie would be leaving soon. There was no telling what Frannie would do. It'd be just like the family clown to think it'd be the funniest thing in the world to run off and get married. But Ira Hines was a mighty strong Baptist, and Sarah Jane doubted seriously that even Frannie could talk him into doing something so unreligious.

And so it was on the second Saturday in September, soon after Hannah went back to Kinston, that at least a dozen of her Hall kin and half the Gresham clan joined the community's young folks — they were looking for any excuse to get together — and they all ended up at Sarah Jane and Jeb's farm. The oldest women sat in the few porch rockers and homemade caned chairs with big pans of field peas on their apron-clad laps while younger ones plopped down on the porch or the steps or anywhere they could find a fairly comfortable spot. Some of the very youngest spilled over into the yard and out under the giant oaks.

Jeb and Simon had hauled dozens of baskets and tin buckets laden with long green and purple peas from the field and spread them out under the porch so they'd stay cool. It wouldn't do for the peas to sweat. They'd sour before the folks could get them shelled. Jeb figured he had done his job for the day, but Sarah Jane promptly caught up with him and handed him a pan full of peas big enough to beat the band. He just sighed and went off to find himself a quiet place to shell his peas, tend to the pig he was cooking and think about what he wished he was doing—fishing.

Laney and her girls had come early to bring some extra pans and help Sarah Jane get everything ready. Nate would tend to store business and hitch a ride with Jessie and Clancy after he closed up. Laney had transported Nate's fiddle safely folded in her wedding quilt because she knew he'd forget it if it was left up to him.

Now, little Lizzy Gresham absolutely loved visiting her great Uncle Jeb's farm. Even though the small village of Beulah—perhaps fifty people in all—wasn't exactly what one might call a metropolis, it was still confining to a four-year-old compared to the freedom of life on a farm. Laney kept Lizzy and little Mary Alice in the store with her most of the time, assuring the children they were too small to be let loose in the road with horses and mules all over the place.

Other than just being free to run and play most anywhere she wanted to, the best part about the farm was the extensive animal kingdom. The only pets Lizzy had in town were an ill-natured old tabby cat Laney boarded to keep mice away and a few mangy dogs that wandered into town every now and then, begging for a free meal.

But Uncle Jeb's farm was a virtual animal wonderland. Old Jake was gone now, but there was a whole slew of jittery hunting dogs plus a couple of black and white Sooners which Jeb swore were descended from a British royal pedigree. Why he thought that, nobody knew. Nobody believed him, either…other than Susie, that is. And then there were cats, bunches of them. It seemed the old yellow feline who usually stayed somewhere near Sarah Jane's feet, was now the grandmother of litter after litter of kittens, every size and color one could think of. Lizzy walked around with kittens in her arms half the day. Mary Alice, almost two now, toddled behind her big sister with her thumb in her mouth. Every now and then, Lizzy paused long enough to let Mary Alice pat the kitten she was carrying. It didn't take Lizzy long to wear the tiny girl out. When Laney walked out to the barn to check on them, Mary Alice had snuggled up to Lizzy and three fluffy cats. With one hand curled behind the thumb in her mouth and the other gently stroking the orange cat Lizzy had named Pumpkin, Laney's baby was quickly drifting into dreamland.

Gathering Mary Alice into her arms, Laney whispered, "You need to rest, too, Lizzy."

"Oh, Mama," she whined, "I've not visited the cow yet and Uncle Jeb said there's a bunch of new pigs."

"Well, alright. But come up to the house after awhile so you can rest before the pig pickin'."

"I will, Mama."

The cows and horses and pigs were a bit too big and scary for her to play with. But the chickens were fun. There was a pen in the backyard filled with Sarah Jane's prized bantams, but the huge flock of regular old hens and biddies and two proud roosters were free to roam about the yard as they pleased. And for some reason, it seemed to be all children's greatest delight to chase those squawking fowls to no end. Lizzy was no different. Her greatest ambition was to see one of those fat hens take off and fly. They had wings so she didn't see why not. Sadly, the old biddies only managed to flap those powerless appendages and make a terrible racket while she ran along behind them calling out, "You can do it! You can do it! Why don'tcha just fly!"

Long before the crowds started flowing in, Lizzy had just about worn out every two-legged creature on the farm and was now working on the four-legged ones. Wondering out to the barn to see what the mule was doing, she spied old Simon huffing up the path. She ran to meet him, curious as to what was in the pail he was carrying.

"What you got, Uncle Simon?" she asked, struggling to keep up with him and see what was in the bucket at the same time.

"Worms." Simon seemed to be in more of a hurry than usual.

Lizzy's brown eyes grew big and round as the full moon. About that time, the old colored man and the small blonde girl arrived back at the barn where Simon sat his load on the ground. Lizzy squatted down beside the bucket that looked to her to be filled with nothing but black dirt. Simon was looking for something high up under the barn shelter.

"There's worms in that dirt?" Lizzy inquired, amazed at the thought.

"Sho is, a lot a worms."

"What you goin' to do with those worms, Uncle Simon?" She was trying to muster up enough nerve to put her hands in the dirt to see if Simon had lost his worms. It sure looked as though he had.

"Goin' fishin'."

"Oh," she replied. "Do fish like worms?"

"Yep."

"Are you sure you got worms in this bucket, Uncle Simon?"

"Sho 'nuf."

"But ain't you goin' to the pea shelling?"

"Nope." The white-haired old man was tying new fishing line on his cane pole, pulling it taut to make sure it would hold when the biggest crappie in the Cape Fear caught hold of his hook.

"Aunt Sarah Jane's goin' to be mad as fire." The little girl's face twisted into a worried frown.

"I ain't goin' to tell her." Simon placed his pole over one shoulder and stooped down to pick up the bucket of worms. About halfway back up, he stopped and looked Lizzy in the eyes. "And yo ain't neither, is yo?"

Lizzy giggled. Her little hand flew up to cover her mouth. "I won't tell. I promise." Her gaze went back to the dirt in the bucket which now seemed to be moving in one spot.

"I see one, Uncle Simon, I see one!"

Simon sat the bucket back down for her to get a closer look and then fiddled around in the dirt until he caught a wiggly plump worm. He lifted it up for Lizzy to examine. Her eyes were filled with delightful wonderment as she hesitantly reached out a small finger to touch the fascinating creature.

But about that time, the worm fell off Simon's finger, and the old man stood up and told Lizzy he'd better hurry or Swanee and Sarah Jane would surely find something for him to do and he'd never get a chance to go fishing. And that would be terrible because now was the time to go fishing.

Simon hurried off towards the road which he planned to cross well out of sight of the house where the women were. Then he planned to sneak through the dried cornfield to the woods and the river beyond. Lizzy ran after him as fast as her short little legs would go.

"But Uncle Simon, how do you know it's time to go fishin'?"

"God tol' me," he yelled back.

Almost out of breath, she caught up with the aging old man and tugged on his overalls. He stopped and looked down into her little face, all aglow with something akin to adoration. For a moment, she just stared up into the kind old face. And then she said, her voice filled with amazement, "God talks to you, Uncle Simon?"

"Sho, He do," replied Simon, matter-of-factly.

"Out loud? You mean to tell He just looked down from heaven and did this?" Lizzy promptly placed her tiny hands around her mouth like a megaphone and yelled, "Time to go fishin', Uncle Simon!"

"Well, yep and nope." Simon sat the bucket down and scratched his head.

"God ain't ever talked to me," Lizzy whispered sadly.

"'Course, He do, chil'. De Lord talk to ever'body."

"I ain't heard Him."

"Now, Miz Lizzy, yo of all de folks know de Lord talk to us. He done walk smack kedab into yo pappy's store and heal yo little self two year or so back."

"I know, but you see, I was little then and now I just cain't seem to remember it." Lizzy's little face crinkled into a worried frown again.

"Oh, don't worry yo little self 'bout dat, chil'," said Simon, his tired old eyes filling with tears. "Yo remember in yo heart, little Miz Lizzy, and dat's jest as good. It might be eben better considerin' good folks' hearts are bigger 'n der brains. Bad folks has big brains and itty bitty hearts." Simon thought a minute, scratching his white head again, a habit which seemed to help him think better. "And den dere's de folks what has little hearts *and* little brains. Dere de scary folks."

She brightened somewhat at that line of thinking and slowly nodded in thoughtful agreement. Then she turned back towards the barn and raised her little hand to wave good-bye to Simon. Suddenly, she thought of something.

"If He didn't holler at you, how *did* God tell you it was time to go fishin'?"

"Well, now, dat's easy," Simon said with a grin. "He done sent me a yeller butterfly, jest yestidy."

Lizzy perked up at that, her eyes brightening.

"Yo see, chil', God talk in wondrous ways. Don't let nobody ever tell yo de Almighty don't know but one tongue."

Simon set the bucket down one more time and took a seat on it for a second. He knew if he squatted, he'd never get back up. "You see dat sun up de sky, Miz Lizzy?"

She squinted as she lifted her head. "Yep," she said.

"And you looks up at de stars and moon at night oft times, ain't dat right?"

"Uh, huh. My Papa knows the name of some of 'em," she said proudly.

"Well, me and Mistah Jeb, we does our plantin' and nearly all de farmin' by watchin' de signs in de sky. Dat's de way God tells us when to plow and when to plant. So, yo sees, chil', way back when God made everythin', He was decidin' where to put it all and how to let His chil'ren know what to do and when to do it. After He got all the workin' times figured out, He said to Hisself, 'Now, how is I goin' to tell old Simon when de fish are bitin'?'"

Simon put his fist under his chin, his thumb and forefinger scratching the white stubble thoughtfully. Lizzy did the same, gazing up at Simon, waiting to hear what the Lord decided.

"Well, chil', de Good Lord thought up somethin' nice, real nice. He said to Hiself, 'I'll jest make yeller butterflies, but I'll only send 'em when it's time to go fishin'. Then, ol' Simon'll know.'"

Lizzy nodded soberly for a moment, letting the old man's words sink in. And then a smile filled her face, as bright as the sunshine.

"God sure is smart, ain't He, Uncle Simon?"

"Yep. He sho' 'nuf is."

The little girl turned back toward the house, and in no time at all she was skipping down the path, yelling, "Bye, Simon!"

The old man waved at the merry little girl. She had stalled his fishing but blessed his tender old heart. Then, with a little difficulty, he rose from his seat on the bucket and headed off towards the pine forest and the river that was calling his name.

Nate arrived about the time the umpteen bushels of peas were all shelled and the older women were helping Sarah Jane boil them in jars. The young folks had scattered about the yard, stretching and chatting and enjoying the long anticipated reprieve. All the smaller ones, like Lizzy and the baby, were fast asleep, scattered about on all three iron beds in the house or on quilts spread out under the shady oaks. Jeb and the men folk were moving everything around in the big barn, preparing for feasting and dancing, in that order.

Every woman there had brought a dish of some sort, but the highlight of the banquet would be the pig pickin'. Jeb and Simon had started before sunrise. They dug a barbeque pit in the ground behind the barn, far enough away so there was no danger of flying sparks catching the barn on fire. Then, they filled the pit with oak logs that would burn slowly all through the day, cooking that sweet pork until it was so tender and tasty it would melt in your mouth. Jeb had gone back and forth from shelling peas to turning the spit 'til he was more tired than if he had plowed all day. The fact that Simon had snuck out on him to go fishing didn't help matters a bit.

But by sundown, when the no telling how many dozen jars of field peas were boiled and sealed and put away, the sweet smoky aroma of that tender pig meat was causing stomachs to growl and mouths to water. Sarah Jane, Laney, Swanee and the other twenty or so women set out the various dishes on a long piece of ply board Jeb and Simon had nailed on top of two saw horses. There were field peas in abundance, of course, plus a poor people's version of potato salad, jars of hot peppers and vinegar and more kinds of bread made from corn meal than you could shake a stick at. Corn pone, cake cornbread, fried cornbread and that thin kind Sarah Jane made in the black iron spider that was so thin and tasty it broke off in chips in your mouth. To top it off, there were gallons of sweet tea for the special occasion. Nate's last orders from Laney had been not to forget the big chunk of ice he had promised to bring.

And speaking of Nate, just before the salivating crowd bowed their heads for Jeb's short-and-to-the-point blessing over the feast, he leaned over to Laney and said, "Save me a plate for later. You know I can't fiddle on a full stomach."

And fiddle, he did—way into the night, which for a farming crowd is not as late as in some places. At first, after the pig was picked fairly clean, everybody experienced a great deal of difficulty just moving around, much less dancing. But finally, after the fine feast settled a bit, the leftovers were put away and Nate's fiddle got wound up, the young folks began to twirl and swirl around the barn floor in time to the lively tunes that seemed to get faster and faster. About that time, Simon—he had snuck back into the crowd just in time to eat—joined the one-man band with a small hand accordion that he pumped in and out 'til the sweat was running down his face. He didn't have time to mop his eyes so he could see what he was doing, so every now and then, Swanee would come up behind him and quickly soak up the sweat with an old rag. He just kept right on pumping. When they progressed to Jeb's favorites, the train songs, it sounded like Simon and Nate were conductors on two trains running right through the barn, bound for Beulah Land. That's when Jeb's toes got to tapping.

Old man Williford from down the road at Jackson's Crossroads had come to call the square dances. His quiet little wife watched silently from the sidelines. However, much to Jeb's surprise, the shy little lady joined in for the third dance and kept right on going as long as her husband. The fellow seemed to borrow energy from somewhere for such occasions and just kept right on calling and clapping 'til Nate and Simon were plumb give out. Every now and then, Nate looked at the grinning, wiry little man and shook his head, fearing the fellow might last all night.

Jeb stood near the barn door where he could keep an eye on the hot embers in the fire pit and watch the festivities at the same time. He didn't say much—didn't need to for all the noise—except that one time when Sarah Jane walked by with one of Liza's babies in her arms. He looked at her and yelled, "Always wondered why they call this square dancin'. It's as round as anything I ever saw." Sarah Jane looked at him like he was crazy and kept on walking.

About nine o'clock everybody was, as Simon said quite often these days, plumb tuckered out. The dancers were drifting about searching for a post to lean on or maybe a keg or bucket to sit on. Nate and Simon were more than ready to wind down, and after old man Williford performed a much appreciated little solo dance of his own, still smiling and laughing and clapping, he sort of tap danced over to his sweet little wife and took a seat. Simon slowly got up, joints popping and creaking, and joined Swanee and Queen in the corner by the horse stall.

Nate laid his bow down for just a second to wipe his face and gulp down a drink of the cool water Laney brought him from the pump. As he wiped his chin with the back of his hand, he looked at her and smiled from the inside out. Taking a deep breath, he tucked the fiddle back under his neck and laid the bow gently on the strings. Once more, he looked at Laney and smiled. She knew exactly what his smile was saying. *This one's for you, Laney Gresham.*

The sweet haunting melody flowed from Nate's heart to the place where the bow caressed the strings, filling the barn and everybody in it with a feeling of warmth that went all the way down to their toes. The courting folks cast furtive glances at one another while the little girls looked at Laney and giggled softly.

Pleased as punch but embarrassed because she knew everybody else knew Nate was playing directly to her, Laney moved back a ways and found herself an empty space to enjoy her man's love song. She beamed a smile back at him that would have lit up the night sky had it not been full moon, and then she leaned her head back against the log wall and softly hummed along with the fiddle.

Beautiful dreamer, wake unto me,
Starlight and dewdrops are waiting for thee;
Sounds of the rude world, heard in the day,
Lull'd by the moonlight have all passed away.
Beautiful dreamer, queen of my song,
List while I woo thee with soft melody;
Gone are the cares of life's busy throng,
Beautiful dreamer, awake unto me!
Beautiful dreamer, awake unto me!

As the bow slowly came to rest on the final long sweet note, Laney beamed Nate an even bigger smile. Then she closed her eyes and sighed, knowing what was coming next. Nate's eyes were closed, too. The bow began to move again, slower this time, and the old familiar strains of her favorite hymn, *Rock of Ages*, filled the air, touching the hearts of everyone in that old barn—no one more than Laney. She wiped her eyes more than once before the bow grew still again, the last note lingering softly in the sweet quietness. And then, just as Nate's audience thought he was holding that last haunting note as a finale to the evening, the bow began to move once more. Slowly, back and forth, back and forth, the bow gently lighted on the strings. Circling each and every listener in its warm embrace, the sweet, sweet sounds of *Amazing Grace* poured out of that fiddle and floated throughout the barn and straight up to heaven. You'd have thought angels were singing along.

Jeb looked over at Sarah Jane and almost smiled. It was a mighty fine pea shelling.

Chapter Twenty-one

*F*all 1904: Just a few weeks after Sarah Jane's pea shelling, entertainment of an altogether different variety came to town—a tent revival. Beulah had never had one. Oh, there might have been a circuit-riding preacher who came through town every few years, but not a real bona fide tent meeting in a real tent. The preacher and his crew, which consisted of his wife, brother-in-law and six children ranging from two to fourteen, took their time setting up the portable meeting hall they promised would hold at least seventy-five people standing up and maybe fifty or so sitting down. It took about two days to get the thing up, but that gave everybody in town time to get used to the idea and to get somewhat acquainted with the preacher and his family. A few local folks even jumped in and helped for an hour or so.

The first meeting just happened to be on a Thursday night in early October when days were still fairly warm and nights were getting rather chilly. While the preacher and what help he could get worked on setting up the big tent, the preacher's younger children were sent around town and into the countryside handing out leaflets advertising the revival meetings. So on that first night, Thursday, a few of Beulah's bravest and most curious citizens set out to the tent a few yards off the main road. It stood rather majestically in the fork where the road to Hallsville comes into town and meets the road to the corn mill. It was only a tenth of a mile from Jessie's house, and although she and Clancy couldn't hear the words, the sounds of happy singing and clapping and shouting drifted onto their back porch where Jessie stood straining to see and hear what was happening in and about the big tent. When the singing stopped, which was much later, she could hear a sound coming from the tent she knew to be the preacher, and every now and then a loud "Hallelujah!" or "Amen!" erupted from the congregation in the midst of the fiery sermon.

Well, three nights of revival meetings went by before Jessie's curiosity got the best of her. The holy rollers, as her mother called them, seemed to be having a good time, and if there was a good time going on anywhere, Jessie was determined to be in the middle of it. So on Sunday, riding home from the new Presbyterian Church in Hallsville with her parents, Clancy and the baby, Jessie mentioned that she just might attend the tent meeting later that evening.

Margaret Gresham looked at her daughter as if she'd gone stark raving crazy. "Jessie Gresham! We are *Presbyterians!*"

"But we used to go to the Baptist Church," replied Jessie in self-defense, "so why can't we visit the holy rollers?"

"Well, for one thing, we only attended the Baptist Church because there wasn't a Presbyterian Church nearby. But the main reason is that those people are loud and terribly undignified," huffed Margaret.

"But Mama, what if the Lord is with them?" Jessie was as serious as she could be.

"Well, He may be, but even if He is, He will be with us come third Sunday, and I'm sure He will be thrilled to have a little peace and quiet."

Jessie didn't say another word but by the time she and her mother let the issue lie, she was more determined than ever to find out what was so exciting that would cause the Lord Himself to need some peace and quiet. It wasn't too hard to talk Clancy into letting her go. He was as easy going as she was strung tight as Dick's hat band. She put the babies to bed early, grabbed her black shawl as she went out the door and quickly glanced over towards her mama and papa's house to make sure no one was watching. Then she walked as fast as she could over to the big tent where the singing and clapping were already in full swing.

Jessie quickly slipped inside the tent flaps and took her seat in the back where there were only wooden buckets and kegs set around for seats. Towards the front, there were real wooden benches placed evenly to form an aisle down the middle that led up to the podium where the preacher stood singing his heart out. Most everyone in the little congregation was standing, some singing and some not because some knew the words and some didn't. Jessie's feet soon began to tap with the rhythm of the lively songs, most of which she had never heard before—neither in the Baptist nor the Presbyterian Church.

Before long, the more sprightly songs had subsided and the preacher—Jessie thought he had an extremely nice baritone voice— began to sing, "Rock of Ages cleft for me. Let me hide myself in Thee."

Jessie could sense the gradual change in the atmosphere. She took a deep breath and relaxed a little. No one had paid her any mind so far. For the first time, she let her eyes roam about the tent to see who was there. Not surprisingly, there wasn't a Gresham in sight. There were a few Baptists and more than a few Free Will Baptists like Corbett and Celie Thomas. Jessie noticed they were sitting mighty stiff and still, listening intently to everything that was going on more like they were in school than church. She had a feeling the Thomases were trying to make up their minds what they thought about the holy rollers, too.

About two rows from the front, Jessie spotted Emmy Brinson and a few of her children scattered up and down the pew. Emmy's tired, dark-circled eyes almost glowed as she sang the last words of the song, looking as if she meant every word. A smile seemed permanently etched in her face. She picked up the smallest child and held him in her lap while she settled down to hear the preacher's message. It was obvious to Jessie that Emmy Brinson was happy to be there.

But the big surprise sat a few children down from Emmy, his sober eyes glassy—not from liquor, but tears—as he gathered the two children on either side closer and held their hands. His normally unruly hair was combed neatly to the side and held in place by more than one dab of Brill Cream. The white shirt Jessie was surprised to see him wearing was buttoned at his Adam's apple, and although he looked as if he might choke any minute, Theophilus Brinson was as dressed up for church as anybody. In fact, he was a nice-looking man. He looked kind of new, Jessie mused.

The preacher talked about the same as the Presbyterians and Baptists, except maybe a little louder—certainly no longer than the Baptists. It seemed to Jessie there was something kind of special about the man, but she couldn't put her finger on what it was. He seemed to have a mighty long list of rules to live by, that was for sure, but all denominations espoused a lot of "thou shalt nots," even Presbyterians. By the time he said the final amen, she still wasn't sure what the special thing was, but she was pretty sure of one thing: The man seemed to possess a mighty strong love for Jesus. Added to that, he expressed true compassion for all the people in that tent, particularly when many of them got up and started drifting towards the front for him to pray for them.

About that time, Jessie decided she'd better get on home. She quietly slipped out and walked briskly past the mules and wagons and buggies. Pulling the black shawl tighter about her shoulders, she hurried back towards home, thinking hard all the way. As the sounds from the tent faded into the distance and Jessie rounded the edge of her garden where the only crop left to pick consisted of a few orange pumpkins, she came to the conclusion she was glad she went, no matter what her mama said. It was nice, and she certainly had come away with a lot to think about. Nevertheless, like her mama said, they were Presbyterians and always would be. Anyway, the harvest festival was coming up, and the day's festivities would surely be followed by a big dance down at the River Barn. This was definitely not the time to change religions.

The tent didn't stay long in Beulah. Although Beulah's citizens were of the opinion that quite a few came every night, the attendance wasn't as good as the preacher had hoped. Considering the small population of the village and the distance folks scattered around the countryside were forced to travel, the meetings were actually rather well-attended. Nevertheless, the preacher had a family to feed, and a few coins each night plus a dozen eggs or a pound of bacon just wouldn't do. And so the preacher, his faithful wife and brother-in-law and all the children sadly pulled up the tent pegs and set out towards Richlands, ten miles to the east of Beulah.

Now mind you, just because there were not enough attendees to sufficiently fill the offering coffers didn't mean that the short-lived revival produced no fruit to speak of. Why, Theophilus Brinson was fruit enough even if he had been the only ripe one plucked from Beulah's thorny vines. Of course, nobody believed he had changed, not for months. The sloppy drunk had been through sober spells before and not once had his sobriety lasted beyond a few short weeks. But this time something was different, perhaps two some-things. Number one, never before had Theo Honey experienced a heart-to-heart meeting with his Savior; and number two, Emmy was praying for all she was worth that the change was real and lasting.

And it was. Theophilus Brinson, as Jessie had perceived, was a new man.

Lots of other folks were blessed by the revival as well, and there was even talk among some of starting a new church in town...a holy roller church in some folks' opinion, although Jessie told Kate she hadn't seen any rolling to speak of. Unfortunately, there were not enough people and finances to start either a Baptist or a Presbyterian church, much less this strange new version of Christianity. And so it was many years later that enough holy roller folks came together to form a congregation and build a little church.

In the meantime, the traveling preachers continued to roll into town and out again. Hardly a year went by that hammers were not heard banging steel pegs into Beulah's rich black soil while the locals watched a big tent take form. For some, like Theophilus Brinson, a night or two inside the mobile sanctuary became a life-changing experience. For others, it was a welcome social event to save them from the dreary boredom of rural life. The third group, like Margaret Gresham, ignored the big tent as if it didn't exist at all.

Chapter Twenty-two

*F*all *1904:* It was a fine Saturday in Beulah—the first Saturday after the very last loads of cured tobacco, cotton and corn had been hauled to Kinston and sold in the markets up and down Queen Street. Farmers' overall pockets were filled with more money than most Duplin farmers were likely to see at one glance in a lifetime. Compared to more prosperous areas of the country, it wasn't much to speak of, but thankfully it was enough to buy the staple supplies needed to get a family through the winter months.

Like Sarah Jane's, most homemakers' pantry shelves were lined with jars of field peas, butter beans, tomatoes, corn, pickles and various jellies and jams to last the family until the spring-planted gardens started producing in June and July—that is, if they were rationed well throughout the year. Dry corn had been taken to the local corn mill and ground into meal to make cornbread that would be cooked a variety of ways. The golden nuggets also were ground into that famous southern staple, grits. Barrels of whole kernels had been set aside to make hominy. It tasted rather bland but was known to be extremely nourishing.

However, products like flour for biscuits and a special cake or pie, baking powder, the coveted vanilla extract, cane sugar and Jeb's great delight, coffee, had to be purchased while in Kinston although Nate's store in Beulah had become more of a grocery market since Sandlin's opened.

Shoes were next on the list. Some farmers like Jeb who had only five children or less, loaded everybody up in a wagon in mid-autumn and took their families into town to try on shoes for cold weather.

But others—mainly those who had too many children to get them to town at one time—gathered up old paper anywhere they could find it and traced each child's foot and then wrote his or her name in the drawing. Then the father took all the "feet" to I. J. Sandlin's new brick store and bought shoes for the entire family. If anybody's feet grew out of his or her shoes before spring, it was just too bad. The child would have to bear the pain of tight shoes or the worse pain of the cold ground. Or, he could hope and pray the next oldest child would grow out of his shoes at the same time and pass them down. Growing children never wore shoes in the summer, so if the new shoes would just last until late spring when the ground turned warm, parents were greatly relieved.

An unusual number of women were in Nate's store that Saturday to buy wool or flannel fabric to make one basic winter dress for Sundays and special events for the older girls—the younger ones wore hand-me-downs—and one new flannel shirt for the older males in the family. Fabric was purchased only if there was any money left after winter sustenance was secured. If a child was lucky enough, the one new shirt or dress was worn for school as well. New overalls were only for the older boys, but the younger ones were certainly not jealous about that. The scratchy stiffness of new overalls wasn't worth the glory of having something new.

On this particular payday Saturday in the fall of 1904, the dirt road through Beulah was an abnormally busy thoroughfare. Nate's store was filled with shoppers coming in and out all day. By mid-afternoon, though Nate was still going strong, Laney was exhausted. The baby and Lizzy were taking naps, and Nate was talking to a drummer who was late delivering an order of sewing paraphernalia.

Just as she was stifling her third yawn, Laney heard the man say, "Did you hear about the hangin'?"

Suddenly, she was wide awake with no hint of a yawn in sight. Eyes wide, she turned away from the shelf where she had been placing skeins of yarn and stared at the drummer who seemed overly excited to spread the dire news.

Nate, as surprised as his wife, was saying, "Why, no, Henry. What hangin'?"

"Be right back and tell you the whole story…much as I know of it, anyhow." Henry hurried past the waiting customers and out the screened door to retrieve another load of wares from his wagon.

Everybody—Celie Thomas, Kate Kennedy, Jeb Gresham and Emmy Brinson—heard him. Their heads popped up like a gaggle of choreographed geese. Every eye in the store followed the drummer as he rushed outside and back in again lugging a great big box of heavy flannel. Henry noticed he had everyone's full attention about the time the door banged behind him, but he was out of breath from carrying the box of flannel up the steps, so he set it down on the floor in front of the counter. Then he stopped and leaned on a table piled with overalls so he could catch his breath and get on with the story.

"Well," he said, hassling a little, "they say that two men from over in Onslow—mighty young for doin' something so mean—were brought in day before yesterday for robbing G.B.D. Parker's store in Chinquapin. Sam Brinkley was running the place that day, and they say one of the boys kept his attention by telling him funny stories and jokes and such while the other one came up behind him and whacked old Sam on the back of the head with an iron frying pan. Parker said it was one I sold him back in August. Then those two boys robbed Parker's cigar box dry. Said they took two hundred dollars! Well, Sam lived just long enough to describe his killers, so Ben Jones was hot and heavy on their trail before you could say Jack Rabbit. He's running for sheriff, you know."

Henry paused long enough to take a deep breath and for Kate to roll her eyes and say, "We're all well aware of that fact, Henry."

"Well, you'll never believe it, but Ben and a few of Chinquapin's hunters and hounds ran those boys down before nightfall. They were fixin' to jump on a raft at North East and hightail it downriver to Wilmington. Figured they'd get lost in the crowds down there, I reckon."

Henry paused again and placed his right hand on his chest. "Mind if I sit down to finish telling the story, Nate? It's been a busy day, and I'm plumb tuckered out from just telling the news everywhere I go." He chuckled. "Guess I should a charged everybody like that newspaper down in Wilmington."

Nate laughed and motioned Henry to one of the ladder back chairs near the wood stove. His audience—Laney and Nate, Celie Thomas, Kate Kennedy, Jeb Gresham and Emmy Brinson—didn't move a muscle. They had been in the right place at the right time, and none of them was about to leave before the end of the story, even if it took all day.

Laney walked out to the back porch and poured a dipper of water in the pump to prime it and then pumped fresh cool water into a tin cup for Henry. He was mighty thankful, but his impatient audience thought it took him a ridiculous amount of time to get the water down his parched throat.

Just before Kate quipped, "Spit it out, Henry!" he continued.

"Ben and his boys hauled Sam's killers off to Kenansville in a wagon, and because G.B.D. Parker is such a well known and wealthy citizen of Duplin, they were tried the very next day. Ben said one of the boys kept whining, 'We didn't mean to kill 'im. Just wanted to knock 'im out long enough to get the money.' The other one kept saying, 'Shut up, you lunatic!'"

More customers were coming in the store now, supposedly to purchase something. However, there was such an atmosphere of mystery and excitement in the air, each one immediately stood aside and waited to see what was going on. Well, hear it, in this case. Anyway, it was getting hot and crowded, so Nate edged his way by Henry and propped the front door open with a brick. That helped right much.

"You know," said Henry, "I never did think too much of Deputy Ben Jones, but that boy might be smarter than I thought. He said that by the time he hauled his prisoners to the jailhouse in Kenansville, it was like a bell rung in his head. It took him a while to think it through, but then he suddenly remembered that was how old James was killed on the Thomas place. Remember, y'all?" He glanced at Nate and Jeb, but it was Celie Thomas who reacted the strongest. She gasped aloud, and her eyes about popped out of her thin little face. Jeb reached up and scratched his head under the brim of the floppy fedora.

"Well, I'll be," said Nate.

At that moment, Corbett Thomas walked up the steps and into the store to find out why Celie was taking so long. He was ready to get on home.

"Take a seat, Corbett," said Nate, "you'll be wantin' to hear this more than anybody."

"You sure will," said Jeb.

"Yep, Ben figured it all out," continued Henry. "Of course, the prisoners denied it when Ben and the other deputies started questioning them. Said they didn't know anything about old James. Never even heard of him." Henry paused to take a deep breath.

"Well, Ben got another idea in that head I thought was mostly empty. While they locked up the one that had been telling the other one to shut up, Ben took the whiney one aside and said, 'Boy, I hate to be the one to tell you this, but you're going to get hung no matter what for killin' Sam Brinkley. So you might as well get yourself right with the Lord and come clean about old James. By sunrise tomorrow, you'll be seeing the Almighty or the Devil, and I wouldn't want to be seeing the Devil if I was you.'"

"Ben said the boy started tremblin' somethin' terrible, but he didn't say anything then. He just hung his head and let'em lock him up, still shaking like a leaf in the storm of '02. The jailer said it got worse all during the night so that by sunrise that boy was a mess. Couldn't even eat his breakfast; just threw up all over everywhere."

Laney gagged. She was pregnant again. Nate looked at her and said, "Miss Laney, you better go lie down a spell. You look kind'a puny."

"Believe I will," said Laney. "Tell me what happened soon as you can."

The cool of the bedroom and the softness of the quilt was a welcome respite. She curled up and dropped off to sleep before the story continued. Laney never had been known to be the most curious woman in Beulah.

"Go on, Henry," said Nate. "What happened next?"

"Well, just like Ben said, the judge tried the boys yesterday afternoon, and the hanging was set for sunrise." Henry paused a minute in thought. "You know, it was sort of like that story in the Bible." He thought some more.

"What story?" asked Corbett, more than eager for Henry to get on with the tale.

"The one where Jesus is on the cross with two robbers on each side, remember?"

Everybody nodded, even Kate, though she couldn't help but roll her eyes and hope the man wasn't going to stop and preach a sermon.

"Ben said the robber who kept telling the other one to shut up never did act sorry about any of it, even killin' Sam Brinkley. Yes sir, he was a mean man. But the whiney boy who had shook all night and threw up looked worse than a dying calf in a hail storm when Ben pushed him up to the gallows. So you see, he was like the other robber hanging beside Jesus, remember?"

Everybody nodded again.

"Right before the hangman opened his mouth to ask if they had anything to say, the whiney boy started talkin' so fast you couldn't a got a word in edgewise. Said back in 1900, he and his partner— now standing there with a noose around his neck still saying, 'Shut up!'—had robbed a little store in Back Swamp and were lookin' for a place to hide out for the night. They thought that old shack James lived in was empty, so about midnight they broke in. 'Course, the door weren't locked. They were searchin' the kitchen for somethin' to eat when old James heard 'em and got up to see who was in his house besides him.

Those boys pulled the same trick they used this time on Sam Brinkley. One of 'em kept James's attention by telling him they were lost and thought the shack was empty—which was the truth for once—and they'd be obliged if James would let them sleep there for a few hours. When they saw somebody lived there, the boys' thievin' instincts rose up, and they figured they'd stumbled on some-body else to steal from. The whiney boy said they only meant to knock him out long enough to search the house, but his partner was more heavy-handed than he realized. They skedaddled when they saw old James's blood runnin' out of his head."

Tears were filling Corbett's eyes, and even Jeb and Nate were a little glassy-eyed. Most of the women were dabbing their faces with their handkerchiefs except Kate and Celie who were seething—madder than fire.

"I hope they got what was comin' to 'em," spit Celie through clinched teeth.

"Yep, they did," replied Henry. "Reverend Aldridge was there to pray for their souls. So soon as the whiney boy was done repentin', the Reverend climbed right up to the gallows and laid his hand on the boy's head. And then, so's everybody could hear, he hollered, 'Today, you will be with Jesus in paradise!' I'm telling you the truth, that boy stopped shaking then and there, and right before they dropped the floorboard he looked up to heaven and smiled. Ben said it was the best hanging he'd ever been to.

"Well, that's about it, folks. Guess I'll vote for Ben now. He might not be such a bad sheriff after all." Henry looked out the door at the sky and jumped up. "Dang it, I'll never make it to Chinquapin before the sun goes down!"

"You can stay in our loft, Mr. Henry," said Emmy. "It's not much, but we'd be glad to have you."

"Why, that's mighty kind of you, ma'm. I've stayed worse places than a warm loft. I'd be obliged." Henry followed Emmy out of the store waving good-bye.

Nobody moved for a few moments. Corbett couldn't speak, and Nate was in about the same shape. Finally, Jeb said, "Well, it's finally over, Corbett."

Corbett nodded with a slight smile. He knew everyone would understand if he didn't stay to discuss the matter. He was just too overcome, and besides that, he had a lot to think about. He sure wished the boy who repented could have been saved. But his life wouldn't have been much good on a chain gang, he reckoned.

Corbett looked at Celie and said with his eyes, *Come on, let's go home.*

She laid down the needles and thread she was going to buy and said to Nate, "I'll come by first of the week and get what I need, alright?"

"I'll put these under the counter for you, Miss Celie," replied Nate.

Kate and Jeb brought their purchases to the counter and paid Nate. Not a soul mentioned the hanging. There was no need. It was finished business.

Before news of the unusual hanging had time to spread throughout Duplin County, Election Day 1904 rolled around. Once again, a couple of voting booths were set up near the schoolhouse and a fairly large area of ground was roped off for the crowds who came all day to vote, argue politics or just to socialize and keep up with the news.

Somehow, Deputy Ben Jones managed to show up at every voting arena in Duplin that day, and you can imagine how much he bragged about solving the mystery of old James's murder and bringing the killers to justice. Kate said he was worse than a rooster now—more like a peacock which she had never seen but had heard to be terribly proud.

By the end of the day, there had been less arguments and would-be fights than usual, considering everybody figured Teddy Roosevelt would win, him being the incumbent and all. The Republicans crowed a little, but that was about it. Interestingly enough, the most arguments were about Ben Jones. Like Henry, the drummer, quite a few people had changed their minds about the cocky deputy when he brought in Sam Brinkley's and old James's killers. But some, like Corbett Thomas and Jeb Gresham, kept their mouths shut and voted against him anyway. Kate told Jessie this was the first time in her life she wished she could vote.

In a private conversation later that day, Jeb said to Corbett, "It was a pure accident Ben found those boys. If they hadn't been stupid enough to do the same thing to Sam Brinkley, he'd never 'a found 'em."

"That's the truth," replied Corbett. "Ben's no smarter now than he ever was. I was glad to hear he's developed a little compassion though."

Jeb nodded. "Yeah, but I'm not votin' for 'em."

Corbett's eyes twinkled, and Jeb knew exactly what he meant.

When the election results came in, Ben Jones was still a deputy.

Chapter Twenty-three

*W*inter *1904/1905:* One cold evening Nate and Laney sat close together by the wood stove, Nate pouring over the ledgers for the store. "It don't look good, Laney."

Everybody should have been paid up by December, but as usual, there were quite a few regular customers who had hit on hard times—which means worse than usual—and had left Nate with a hefty sum on the books.

"I'm mighty sorry they're having troubles, but how are we going to pay our own debts?" Pushing the green ledger back on the table, Nate shook his head and sighed. He closed his eyes and leaned back in the chair.

He looked to Laney as if he were hoping the numbers in the book would right themselves before he opened his eyes again. She was sitting by the wood stove in the oak rocking chair Nate had made her for a wedding present, darning socks and stockings and sewing a button on a new winter dress for Lizzy.

"Our little girl is growing up fast," she had remarked to Nate just that morning. But rather than accepting the casual remark for what it was, the nostalgic musing of a doting mother, Nate took it as a reminder that more provision was needed for his growing family. He was happy about the new life Laney was carrying in her belly…he really was. But deep down inside—actually, not too deep tonight—he was worried…really worried.

One of his oldest customers had come by the store early that morning and leaned over the counter to gain Nate's attention as privately as possible. "Just came by to let you know I ain't got no money to pay up, boy. But take my word, when I come to town for supplies 'bout once a month, more 'n likely I'll give you a few dollars if there's anythin' left."

The old fellow seemed perfectly satisfied that he had taken care of the problem and that Nate should be happy to hear that he "might" get a few dollars every now and then. But at least the man had said something. There were more of the same who never even mentioned their mounting debts.

Nate opened his eyes and stared at the ledger. Nothing had changed.

Slowly, Laney laid her thimble and thread on the table by the oil lamp and leaned down to place Nate's socks back in the darning basket. And then, she leaned her head back in the tall rocker and closed her own eyes for a minute or two. Nate knew she was praying; that's what she always did. But he couldn't seem to shake the worry demon off his back long enough to even pray. Placing his elbows on the table, he rested his head in his hands.

And then he heard Laney speaking softly, "It's alright, Nate. God always calls someone else to pray for us when we can't seem to pray ourselves."

He didn't move a muscle. "That's nice, Laney, and I thank you kindly. But you're in as big a mess as I am. I always think mighty highly of your prayers, but...well, you know what I mean." His voice almost cracked.

She smiled. "My prayers are no more powerful than yours, Nate, but I wasn't speakin' of myself."

He slowly lifted his face from his hands and looked over at his sometimes mysterious wife. "Huh?" was all he said.

"Someone's prayin' for us, Nate, and He's got a good spot so's God can hear Him real good." Her face was flooded with a smile by now, that glowing smile he loved so much.

But he still didn't understand. His own countenance was scrunched into an inquisitive frown. This time he couldn't even manage a "huh?"

"The One who healed our Lizzy and washed all my sins away, He's prayin' for us, Nate. And He don't even stop to sleep or eat."

My, how he loved that woman.

✌

That was early December of '04. By Christmas, Nate had decided to take Laney's advice and take his burdens to the Lord and leave them there. Until the end of the year, anyway. Then, he and the Lord would have to get back to the ledger.

Christmas Eve didn't bring a big snow like in '03, but it sure was cold. Like the previous year, however, it was a good Christmas. Not materially speaking, mind you. *Good* in Beulah meant that most everybody was fairly healthy and nobody went hungry. A few angels of mercy always saw to that.

To most everybody's surprise Theo Honey was still sober, so his and Emmy's brood were warm and well fed. His brother, Uz, was sleeping in the loft during the cold spell. Emmy didn't have the heart to leave him out in the cold, even if he was drunk. Thankfully, Uz was a sleeping drunk and not a fighting one.

It seemed the one who suffered most was Sonny Boy Batchelor, the man who thought he was a horse. But even Sonny Boy was fairly comfortable in the empty stall he had staked out in Sandlin's stables behind the new brick store.

About two o'clock on Christmas Eve, Susie Gresham was out on the porch filling her arms with a load of firewood when she spied a horse and buggy coming up the road through the deepening snow.

Now, where would anybody be goin' in this kind of weather? Curious, but also mesmerized by the lovely scene of a horse prancing through white snow pulling a black buggy, Susie smiled and leaned against the porch post. But the firewood began to make painful dents in her thin arms. Knowing no one in her family was expecting company, she turned back to the screened door and yelled for papa to come open it. When she stepped into the warm sitting room, shivering from head to toe, Jeb took a few pieces of oak from her aching arms and carefully tossed them in the fireplace atop the hot embers. Then he relieved Susie of the remainder of her heavy burden and piled the logs neatly in the wood box.

It was then that both Jeb and Susie heard a horse snorting and a bell jingling outside. Susie hurried to the steamed window and wiped it with her apron. The old glass was still a bit blurry so she ran to the door and cracked it open.

"Shut that door, young'un!" snapped Jeb. "You're a wastin' heat, girl, and we don't have many oaks left on this old farm."

"Oh!" gasped Susie, her hand over her mouth. "It's Hannah, Pa! Mr. Waller's brought her home for Christmas!"

Before Jeb could think what to do, Susie ran outside yelling, "Call Mama, Pa!"

He was glad Hannah was home, that was for sure, but he certainly hadn't planned on company for Christmas. It was the last thing he wanted.

Sarah Jane had heard the commotion and was now carefully stepping across the icy porch towards the steps. Susie was waiting by the post, clapping her hands in glee. By this time, Liza and Frank were trudging through the snow, coming back from the barn where they had made sure the livestock was safe and sound for the cold night ahead. At the sight of Hannah stepping down to the snowy ground with Mr. Waller's help, Liza took off running, leaving Frank shaking his head in wonder that he had married such a headstrong girl.

While Liza and Susie hugged their sorely missed sister and Sarah Jane beamed with happiness, Frank came idling up and nodded to Mr. Waller who nodded back with no smile in sight.

Frank walked on up to Elbert and said, "Let's get this rig to the barn. You're not goin' anywhere tonight."

Mr. Waller nodded again and followed Frank's slow gait back to the barn, the mare and buggy following close behind.

"Dang it!" said Jeb, under his breath. It sure seemed mighty coincidental that the Waller boy was the only one who ever brought Hannah home. But he'd think on that later. Tonight, he was more concerned about his privacy and the occupancy of his warm feather bed.

The women were all coming in the door hugging and smiling and laughing, so he put on a partial smile and welcomed his daughter as best he could, happy the Waller boy would be out in the barn for a while.

Hannah's homecoming was the best gift her family could have received that Christmas, and since none of the adults would get anything anyway, it was their only gift. Sarah Jane continued to beam a powerful smile at her girls as they all sat around the fire shelling pecans for tomorrow's pies and listening to Hannah's account of the last few days' activities in Kinston.

With tears in her eyes, she told of Mrs. Mosley's passing and the fine wake they had for her there in her own beloved home. It seemed to Hannah that everyone in Kinston came, and they were all rich. Compared to her, of course, they were. She said the Mosleys, knowing Hannah would like to be home for Christmas, had released her a couple of hours after her patient left this earth, but the young nurse had insisted on staying for the service to honor the old lady who had become so dear to her heart.

Doctor Parrott attended the funeral, naturally, and he assured Hannah that Elbert Waller would be happy to drive her on past Beulah to the Gresham farm so that she could be with her family on Christmas Eve.

"Thank you, Doctor, but I think I should just stay here until the weather breaks. There's no way he could get back to his own family before late Christmas Day," she replied worriedly.

"Oh, don't worry about the cold, Miss Gresham. I'm sure Polly will heat you a plenty of hot bricks to wrap in a couple of quilts, and you'll be warm aplenty. And don't worry about Elbert, Miss Gresham. He has no wife and children to share the excitement of Christmas Eve. And," he continued with a twinkle in his eye and a chuckle, "I am certain he'd rather be with a nice young lady like yourself than to be stuck at home with his ma and pa."

Hannah blushed from head to toe, totally mortified. As she turned to rush up the staircase to her room, the good doctor shouted, "I'll speak to Elbert when I get back to the farm, Miss Gresham! Now don't you worry. He'll be calling soon after first light."

She didn't go into all that with her parents and sisters. She just said Mr. Waller was kind enough to drive her home and that he would leave first thing in the morning. Sarah Jane said, "No, he won't! He'll stay for Christmas dinner, that's what he'll do!"

Liza grinned knowingly as Susie giggled. Then they caught each other's eyes and giggled some more. This time Hannah was able to revert back to her time-tested habit of ignoring whatever was going on that she didn't want to be a part of.

But Sarah Jane wasn't going to leave the subject of Mr. Waller quite so quickly. "What does Mr. Waller do for a livin', child?"

"Oh, he's a builder, Mama. He builds houses and barns and most anything, I guess. His brothers farm for Doctor Parrott and build, too. He said the men in his family have been builders for generations." She didn't dare raise her eyes, but looked at the pecans in her pan as if they were the most interesting nuts she had ever seen.

So Elbert Waller stayed for Christmas, and all went fairly well. Even Jeb enjoyed his company considering the young man hardly ever said anything and therefore required little attention. Sometimes, he even forgot the black-haired fellow was there. Hannah was happier and much more talkative than usual, surprising her mother and sending her sisters into giggling fits from time to time. Liza and Frank's children made the day, of course, as all children do at Christmas time. Everybody had made something for them from Jeb's whittled toys to Hannah's crocheted sweaters.

Again, it was a good Christmas in the Gresham household, even though Jeb failed to hunt down a turkey and Sarah Jane had to cook chickens instead.

Nate drove out early on Christmas Eve to fetch Laney's pa to town. She was worried about him staying by himself in such cold weather, she said; and anyway, the children needed a grandpa on Christmas. It was a time for family. Nate's last instructions were to bring home a little tree if he found one along the way, and that's exactly what he did. Lizzy and Mary Alice were beaming as they danced around the little pine, decorating it with popcorn Laney had strung as well as a long string of brightly colored buttons they borrowed from the store's inventory until after Christmas.

Yes, it was a good week, but by the time Old Christmas rolled around twelve days later, Laney seemed to be spinning in circles. In spite of the biting wind, folks kept coming in and out the store all day; some to buy a few supplies and some just to warm by the fire and visit a bit on their way to somewhere else. It was too cold for the girls to go with Nate to take her pa back home like they normally did, and that's why Laney had to tend the store, mind the children and do the cooking all by herself and her over five months in the family way. She knew Nate was hoping for a boy this time and for his sake, she hoped so, too. But down deep, she didn't really care. Her girls were mighty special.

By nightfall—which was unusually early because it was not only one of the shortest days of the year, it was cloudy and dark and looked like snow—Laney was completely exhausted and more than ready for Nate to get on home and let the girls follow him around awhile. She planned for him to lock up and put everything away. Maybe he would put the girls to bed and tell them a story, too. If so, she'd have a few minutes to sit down by the fire and prop her swelling feet on the wooden stool.

She lit the kerosene lamps and stoked the fire and still Nate didn't come. Darkness fell fast. The girls were chasing each other around the fabric table and behind the long counter, playing hide-and-seek with all the energy in the world, just like it was ten o'clock in the morning. And they weren't quiet about it, either.

"Lizzy! Take your sister and go wash up. I'll get your supper soon as I lock up." Laney glanced out the rather large frosted window one more time before she turned the big brass key and walked back to the counter to hide it in the cigar box by the cash drawer where anybody could have stolen it if they had a mind to.

Lizzy stopped in her play and looked at her mother with pleading eyes. "Cain't we wait for Papa? 'Member the story Grandpa told us 'bout the animals bowin' down to Jesus on Old Christmas?"

"I remember, but you girls need to eat your supper and get ready for bed." Laney ran her hand over her swelling belly. *Come on, Nate,* she thought. *I've just got to get off my feet a minute.*

Four-year-old Lizzy looked up at her mama, and then, like children sometimes do, she realized something was not right. "What's wrong, Mama?"

"Oh, nothin'. I'm just tired, that's all." Laney patted Lizzy's golden ringlets and walked over to sit in the rocker by the wood stove. Mary Alice, who was always a step or two behind Lizzy, peeped out around her sister and giggled, thinking her mama was playing hide-and-seek with them. Laney picked her up, laughing, and just as quickly kissed her little pink mouth and set her back down beside Lizzy.

"Help Mary Alice to wash up, will you, sugar? There's water in the pitcher on the washstand in the other room if it's not frozen. I'll just rest a bit, and then I'll get your supper."

A little after midnight, Nate was beating on the door, his cold hands wrapped in the flannel Laney had forced him to take as an extra precaution against the cold. He could see the smoke from his breath in the light coming from the window, and if he'd been in his usual good humor, he would have walked in making a joke about his insides catching on fire. But any humor he might have had earlier had frozen a good while back down the road.

"Hurry up, Laney!" he yelled, banging again.

Startled from her sleep, Laney got up as quickly as she could lift her heavy body and stumbled towards the door, calling, "Hold on, Nate, I'm comin'!"

Nate Gresham came rushing through the open door along with a gale of frigid wind, blasting Laney's little nap right out of her head. Suddenly wide awake, she helped Nate get out of his coat and overalls and nearly frozen gloves, and then she pushed him down in the rocker by the fire with nothing on but his damp long johns.

"Stay here while you thaw out. I'll get you something hot to drink."

It was much too cold to walk out on the porch to get to the kitchen, so Laney just reached outside quickly for the milk she was keeping in a jug on the back porch and poured some in a pan to warm on top of the wood stove.

"Got any more of that chocolate we had for Christmas?" Nate's eyes had thawed so quick there were tears running down his cheeks.

"Sure do." She smiled and patted him on the back.

"Well, throw a chunk of it in that pot, if you don't mind." He grinned, rubbing his hands together as the heat finally got through to his bones.

"I'll pour more milk in a minute. The girls will want some after supper."

Suddenly, Laney stopped dead still, the chunk of chocolate still in her hand. Slowly, she let it sink into the pan of milk and turned to look at Nate.

It was right then that he asked, "Where are the young'uns?"

"Huh?" she whispered.

"Where's Lizzy and Mary Alice?"

This time her voice sounded more like a whimper. "I don't know."

"You don't know?"

She drew in a deep breath and held it, her eyes darting about the room. Maybe they were hiding again. "Lizzy? Mary Alice? Come on out, now! We're not playin' a game!"

Nate hadn't been concerned until then. Laney had never lost the young'uns before, so he had no reason to think she had lost them now. But the fright in her face scared him half to death. He jumped up, looking thin as a rail in his long underwear. Nate went to searching under tables and behind the counter. Laney ran into the sitting room and bedroom, holding her heavy belly, looking under the bed and in every corner. The little girls were nowhere to be found.

Just before Laney thought she might faint, Nate took her by the shoulders. "Did Lizzy say anything? She give you any hint of where they mighta gone?"

"N…no. Oh, Nate! I went to sleep, and now I've lost my babies! Oh, Lord, where are they?" Laney's eyes rolled up so far Nate didn't know if she was praying or passing out, so he gently pushed her into the rocking chair and said, "Don't worry. They're around here somewhere. You sit tight and pray, and I'll find 'em."

Nate's coat and overalls were still wet and half frozen, so he ran into the bedroom and grabbed the quilt off the bed and threw it around his body. Then, he pushed his feet into his old boots, without tying them, and rushed out the door against the icy wind. Just before he slammed the door behind him, Laney jumped up as best she could and yelled, "Lizzy did say somethin'! She said she wanted to see if it's true the animals bow to Jesus on Old Christmas!"

Nate looked back at her like she was crazy for a second, but then he remembered the story Laney's pa had told the children on Christmas Eve. It would be just like a child of Laney Gresham's to go out on the coldest night of the year to look for praying cows and such. He clutched the quilt with one hand and waved to Laney with the other. Then he was off to the new stables behind I. J. Sandlin's store, clad in nothing but his long underwear. His shoulders were warm, but his long legs were freezing.

And that's where he found Lizzy and Mary Alice Gresham...in the stable. They were kind of scared of the big old cow, and though the horses looked mighty friendly, they might as well have been dinosaurs to the small girls. And so, Lizzy had taken little Mary Alice by the hand and chosen the best option available. They snuggled up to a couple of stray dogs and a lazy old cat to await the appointed hour. When Nate walked in, his babies were fast asleep. He got down on his knees right then and there. First, he thanked the Good Lord for keeping his little princesses safe, and then he wrapped them in the quilt and lifted both girls in his arms. His backside was cold, but his front side was mighty warm.

"Papa," whispered Lizzy, sleepily. "Did you seem 'em?"

"See what, princess?" whispered Nate, struggling out of the stable with his cumbersome load.

"Did you see the animals bow to Jesus?"

"No, honey, they didn't bow. I'm sorry." His breath was making white circles in the air. His heart was pounding.

"Uh huh, they did bow, Papa. We saw 'em, me 'n Mary." And then, even the frigid air couldn't keep Lizzy awake. Like her little sister, she was in dreamland in no time at all.

Nate could hardly move any part of his body other than his feet, but if he could have, he would have shaken his head in awe. Instead, he just kept on walking until he got to the porch where Laney met him all bundled up, ready to go out and search for her babies like the mail man...come rain, hail, sleet or snow.

She quickly pulled Nate and his heavy load in the door and carefully took little Mary Alice from the quilt while Nate tried to untangle Lizzy and not wake her. Neither mama nor daddy said anything for a while. Nate was almost gasping for breath when he got inside. The cold was hurting his lungs, but finally, his breathing began to slow down, and he felt better. He was still standing there with Lizzy on his shoulder trying to figure out what to do when the quilt dropped to the floor. By now, he didn't know whether he was hot or cold, but according to his backside, he was still cold.

Laney sat in the rocker by the fire holding her youngest close to her heart as well as her big belly, silently thanking God that her babies were safe and sound. She looked up at Nate and Lizzy and smiled.

"Well?" she said.

"Well, what?" asked Nate.

"Did the animals bow?"

He still couldn't move his arms or hands; they were full of Lizzy's warm little body. He just looked at his crazy wife and nodded. His legs were shivering.

She smiled again, and he didn't feel the cold anymore.

Back in a stall at the far end of Sandlin's stables, unseen by Nate and his girls, the man everybody thought was crazy was still on his knees. His eyes were closed; his body unusually relaxed. A sweet smile covered Sonny Boy's rugged face as the longed-for-peace seeped into his tormented soul.

Well, mad as she was, Celie Thomas knew full well there would be no way to take little Johnny Hatcher away from his cruel papa, not unless someone could prove Ike had physically harmed the little boy to the point of putting his life in danger. Of course, nobody knew about the incident in the woods with the axe, and children don't usually tell on their mamas and daddies, no matter how bad things get. By the time Celie prodded Corbett with her boney finger 'til he ran down the boy's whereabouts, Ike had gathered his scattered brood and hauled them off to Kinston to work in the cotton mills.

That was the day sixty-two-year-old Celie Thomas, thin as a rail and light as a feather, picked up the heavy axe and walked by a bunch of mighty nervous chickens to the wood pile behind the barn.

About thirty minutes later, there was a pile of split kindlin' at her feet under which lay the apparition of Ike Hatcher. She stopped and wiped her sweating brow with the hem of her apron. Then she did something no one had ever seen her do. She sat down on the wood-pile and cried her eyes out.

Chapter Twenty-four

*S*pring, *1905:* Another hard winter behind them, the folks around Beulah and Hallsville stretched their dormant muscles and began to move their arms and legs a lot faster by late March and early April 1905. Fields were plowed and made ready for spring planting, seeds were planted in covered tobacco beds, and the women were just waiting for Good Friday so they could plant string beans and potatoes.

It was Sarah Jane's favorite time of the year. Nothing pleased her more than a buggy ride to church in Hallsville on a Sunday morning, passing field after field of neatly plowed rows of clumpy black dirt. In many areas, the dark soil was filtered with white sand that eased outward from the riverbed. When the sun rays hit the ground at just the right angle, it looked as if there were diamonds sparkling out of the black earth. Why, every mound of that Duplin soil looked as if it was just waiting for a seed to nourish, longing to create new life that would provide for the hard working folks who took such good care of the land. Sometimes, Sarah Jane chuckled under her breath, thinking she probably worshiped more on the way to church than when she got there.

Often, Jeb would glance over at his unusually quiet wife and ask, "What're you smilin' about, woman?"

She'd just smile a little wider and say, "Oh, nothin'."

He figured it was just a woman thing, but unbeknownst to Sarah Jane, her husband was usually thinking pretty much the same thing, and like her, he would never think to express his thoughts out loud. Men didn't talk about such things, not even preachers.

Most of the fields were separated by long stands of long-leaf pines that spread all the way back to the dense pine forests behind the plowed land. The contrast of the tall green trees standing guard over the waiting dark soil against a background of bright blue sky was truly a sight to behold. Sporadically, cross-shaped white dogwood blossoms peeked out from under the pines, adding a cheery atmosphere to the landscape. Every now and then, a small pink rosebud tree sang out, "Look at me! Look at me!"

It was such a peaceful experience, even with Liza, Frank and the children sometimes packed in the back seat, usually chattering away about anything and everything. But this particular early spring Sunday morning, Sarah Jane was experiencing a bit of interference in her special worship time. It seemed like every five minutes, Liza asked, "Mama, have you heard....?"

Sarah Jane was in the middle of repenting for wanting to turn around and wring Liza's neck when she heard her daughter say, "Mama, have you heard what happened in town yesterday?"

Repenting done, Sarah Jane let out a big sigh—almost a huff— and grudgingly replied, "No, Liza, I've not heard a word, and I doubt I want to."

"Oh, yes, you do, Mama! Jessie told me all about it when Frank took me into town yesterday. Have you heard about it, Pa?"

"No, but I'd be willin' to bet I'm afixin' to," he said. His sigh was definitely a huff, a loud one.

"Well, here's what happened," began Liza, totally oblivious to her audience's lack of interest. "I reckon y'all know that Arnold Lanier and the schoolteacher have been courtin' ever since they met at the kissin' booth at the harvest festival. Well, Jessie said that Arnold—you know what a reputation he has for being hotheaded— well, he walked out of Nate's store and found Jarvis Mercer talking to Miss Lucy Hill real cozy-like, and of course, he figured right then and there that something was going on between the two of them, and he got madder 'n a wet settin' hen. But Jarvis just happened to take his eyes off Miss Lucy long enough to see Arnold comin' down the steps—you know how big Arnold is—and so Jarvis took off running as fast as lightnin'. By that time, Arnold had his gun out, which of course got Jarvis to runnin' even faster. Jessie said he ran so fast, he ran out from under his hat! That was a good thing 'cause Arnold was aimin' at Jarvis's head, and the bullet went through the hat instead of Jarvis's brain.

"Well, Jarvis ran right into Sandlin's store—probably thinking Arnold wouldn't chase him inside with a gun—and Arnold ran right behind him, probably madder 'cause he missed Jarvis's head and hit the hat instead. Jessie said the only thing that saved Jarvis Mercer's life was that Owen Williams was in Sandlin's to buy seed for Pansy's garden, and knowing Arnold's temper and Jarvis's reputation, he was quick to figure out what was going on and so he stepped in between the two long enough for Jarvis to hightail it out the back door.

"Well, Arnold aimed the gun at Owen and yelled, "Get out'a my way, Owen Williams!"

"But Owen stood there just as calm as a cucumber. Now you know how small he is compared to Arnold Lanier, don't you? Well, Owen said, 'Now, Arnold, you don't want to shoot me, do you?'

Suddenly, there was nothing but total silence coming from the back of the buggy; no sounds but the clippity-clop of the mare and the grinding noise of the wagon wheels.

Jeb looked over at Sarah Jane, his face all squinted in a quizzical expression. She raised her eyebrows in return and then turned around to face Liza with a frown.

"Is that it, girl?"

"Well, I noticed you and Pa didn't seem very interested, so I decided to keep my news to myself. After all, what's the fun of tellin' an interesting story if nobody's interested?"

Her mama couldn't tell if Liza was truly offended or just trying to pull some reaction out of her mama and daddy. She was like that. If her third daughter was on stage, she wanted nothing short of the full attention of her audience. Giving in to Liza wasn't something Sarah Jane ever had a mind to do, but this time it seemed she had no choice. Not if she wanted to know the end of the tale anyway. For a second or two, she considered waiting until she got to the church yard where somebody would surely spread the news, but finally, she turned back around and said, "Alright, Liza, you have our full attention. What happened next?"

"Not much, really. Arnold just sort of wound down with Owen being so calm and collected and all. Jessie said he stuck the pistol back in his belt and shook his head a time or two. Then, he just turned around and walked out of Sandlin's onto the street like nothing had happened. We don't know what he said to Miss Lucy, but Jessie's goin' to try to find out. Jarvis ran home, I reckon, but some said he asked one of Jesse's brothers to send him to the Grissom Cave a while. Everybody in the store gathered around Owen like he was a hero, but you know how shy he is. He just meandered through the crowd and paid for his seed and got out of there. That's about it, far as I know."

By that time, they were passing the graveyard and Jeb was tugging on the reins, reminding Nellie to turn into the churchyard where she could rest a couple of hours. Sarah Jane sat still as a statue, still staring ahead with her mouth open when the children started clamoring down from the buggy. Jeb came around to help her down. There wasn't much to say in response to Liza's story, so she just looked into Jeb's eyes and slightly shook her head. He took her by the arm and said—with a slight grin—"Bet the preacher won't have a sermon as excitin' as that."

Except for an occasional trip to Kinston to nurse someone in the Mosley family, Hannah was now back in Beulah working with Doctor Kennedy on a regular basis. Sometimes she was homesick for the beautiful house in Kinston and the sweet old lady who once lived within its walls; nevertheless, there was just nothing like being home. She tried hard not to think about Elbert Waller any more than she could help, but alas, his dark eyes penetrated her thoughts more often than not. During all the long buggy rides between Beulah and Kinston, the two had developed a relationship of sorts which neither could have identified if anyone had asked. Jessie asked, of course, but Hannah knew how to ignore her.

It was only when Elbert said good-bye last Christmas that Hannah realized he felt something more for her than that of a fellow traveler. Naturally, he didn't say anything, but there was a look in his eyes she hadn't noticed before. It was as if those dark eyes, almost hid under black bushy eyebrows, looked deep into her soul; and then, lo and behold, he smiled. She wished Jessie could have seen Elbert smile. He looked almost handsome. Since that day, Hannah Gresham had held a secret hope in her heart that maybe she wouldn't be an old maid nurse after all.

She didn't see him again until early March, not long after Arnold Lanier shot Jarvis Mercer's hat, when he came to fetch Hannah on orders from Doctor Parrott. The doctor's hardworking wife had come down with springtime pneumonia, and Doctor Parrott was determined to provide her the best of care. Miss Gresham would certainly nurse her back to health if anyone could. He had assured his sons and daughters of that.

And she did. However, she was also given the opportunity to nurse something else…her slowly budding relationship with Elbert Waller. If you'll remember, the Wallers were tenant farmers for Doctor Parrott over at Falling Creek, and so for the first time in Hannah and Elbert's unconscious courtship, they had opportunity to see one another on a fairly regular basis. Quiet and timid, Mr. Waller found all sorts of excuses to walk over to the Parrott home place. He often came with a jar of preserves from his mama, deer meat or quail from one of his regular hunting expeditions, or perhaps one of his own mama's famous blueberry pies. Sometimes, he came just to sit on the porch in the evening, talking hunting dogs with Sam, Doctor Parrott's son who was about Elbert's own age.

Most of the time he didn't even speak to Hannah, just nodded in her direction and then went on to do whatever he had supposedly come to do. She'd smile politely and say, "Hello, Mr. Waller." That's about all the courting they did until a few days before Doctor Parrott decided his dear wife was well enough for Hannah to head back to Beulah.

It was a lovely evening in mid April, warm for that time of the year. Hannah was sitting in a rocking chair on the piazza beside Doctor Parrott enjoying, as usual, his tales of interesting medical cases. It had become Doctor Parrott's habit to add quite a bit of medical information to his reminisces in order to further Hannah's nursing education.

That particular evening, the good doctor was just winding up his most exciting tale yet when, out of the corner of his eye, he spied Elbert Waller ambling up the path to the house with a rifle on his shoulder and a half dozen quail on a string. He knew Elbert would just nod at Hannah and then ignore her for an hour or more due to his extreme shyness. For that reason, the doctor quickly invented a plan. He slowly rose from his rocking chair and, with aching joints, climbed down the steps to greet his new guest.

"Evening, Elbert."

Mr. Waller just nodded and mumbled something like, "Evenin', Doc."

"What you got there, son?"

Elbert finally made it to where the doctor was waiting at the bottom of the steps. Instead of a verbal reply, he just handed the quail to Doctor Parrott and nodded again.

"Well, thank you kindly, Elbert. I can smell 'em frying already."

He took the string of quail from Elbert and smiled graciously. "Tell you what, Elbert, I think I'll just take these birds inside so Dove can clean 'em and get 'em ready to cook for tomorrow's dinner. Why don't you sit here on the pi'za and keep Miss Gresham comp'ny for a few minutes while I'm gone?"

Elbert was looking down at his feet and nodding so he didn't see the twinkle in the good doctor's eye. Hannah did, however, and she blushed so badly she had to fan herself with the bottom of her apron.

"Are you hot, Miss Gresham?" The twinkle was growing brighter by the minute.

"Y...yes, sir," she stuttered. "It's mighty warm for April."

"That it is. Uh huh, that it is, Miss Gresham." With that, Doctor Parrott disappeared into the house where he stayed much longer than a few minutes.

Slowly, Elbert climbed the steps and took his seat in the rocker beside Hannah's. Never have you seen a more miserable, confused soul in your life. And never have you seen a more embarrassed one than Hannah Gresham. Nevertheless, after about five long minutes of silence—except for the crickets—Elbert actually said something.

"Nice evenin'."

"Yes, it is."

Five more minutes went by. Twilight was beckoning, and Hannah was tired. She had been up since daybreak, and if Mr. Waller was just going to sit there in silence all night...well, she might as well go in and get on to bed. She got up as gracefully as she knew how and took one step to get past Mr. Waller to the front door.

"Wait, Miss Gresham," he said, clear as a bell.

"Yes, Mr. Waller?"

"Ah, ah...if you don't mind, could you sit a spell longer?"

Elbert was looking at his feet the whole time, but laying that aside, actual sentences were great progress in Hannah's opinion. "It's getting' late, Mr. Waller, and to tell the truth, I don't much feel like just sittin' here."

"Well, I, uh...I got somethin' to say. You mighta noticed it sometimes takes me awhile to get my words out."

"Yes, well, I have noticed that. Alright, I'll stay a while longer." She sat back down in the rocker, not knowing whether to be glad or sad.

After a few more minutes, during which time Doctor Parrott peered out the door a half dozen times, Elbert sort of muttered, "Miss Gresham, we been knowin' each other for nearly a year now...." He glanced up quickly to see if she was listening. She was, so he went on. "And I, uh...I believe we could make a good life together. I know it don't seem likely, but I'm a hard worker and usually make a fairly good livin' buildin' houses and barns and such...'cept in bad weather."

Elbert glanced up at Hannah's face again, and miracle of miracles, he didn't turn away this time. She didn't either. But Hannah wasn't quite sure she was being proposed to, and Elbert had run out of words to say. Finally, he remembered some and said, "Will you marry me, Miss Gresham? I ain't much, but I'll make you a good life-mate, I think."

Hannah's rocker froze in mid rock. This was the day she had believed would never come. And yes, she had grown to feel something towards the man—something special. But was it really love? And if so, did she love him enough to live with him the rest of her life and have his children? At that thought, the blushing started again, and this time, it was Hannah who looked down at her feet. Elbert just kept staring at her, waiting for an answer.

When the heat in her face had pretty much died down, she lifted her head, and this time, it was Hannah's blue eyes that looked deeply into his. *Yes*, she thought, *I can live with him the rest of my life. I'll just have to deal with the hard part as best I can.*

"Yes, Mr. Waller, I'll marry you." She gave him a kind smile.

"I do 'preciate it, Miss Gresham, I sure do." Her gave her something kin to a real grin and added, "I'd be obliged if you'd call me Elbert, Miss Gresham."

She didn't say anything. It wouldn't hurt for him to call her Miss Gresham a while longer. It was the respectful thing to do.

Kate would have been so proud.

Doctor Parrott didn't hear the tender but rather unromantic proposal; however, he had his ear at the crack in the door when the couple's conversation continued. After listening a few minutes, he chuckled to himself, thinking, *I knew there was more to that boy than nods and yes sirs.*

"Yo git away frum dat door, Mistah Doc Parr't! Ain't none a yo biz'nez what dem young folks sayin'."

Even though twilight had almost faded into the blackness of night, he could see the glint in old Dove's angry eyes. He knew better than to argue with her. She had been with Doctor and Mrs. Parrott nigh on to forty-five years, and nobody, absolutely nobody, had gotten the better of her yet. Turning towards the stair case—which looked more like an unscalable mountain peak every night—he muttered under his breath, "You don't know as much as you think you do, old woman." Then he chuckled out loud.

"What yo laughin' at, Mistah Doctor?"

"Oh, nothing, Dove, nothing at all." Dove had no idea how much interfering the good doctor had done to get Hannah Gresham and Elbert Waller together, and he was determined to enjoy the fruits of his labor no matter what she said. In fact, he was so pleased with the outcome, the climb didn't seem quite as painful as usual. He went to bed and woke up the following morning a satisfied man.

In the meantime, Elbert and Hannah slowly but surely discussed quite a bit of what had been locked in both their hearts for years and years. Mostly, Elbert talked about his love for building and how proud and happy he felt when a project came to completion. Although he came from generations of builders (hence, the name Wall-er), the men of Elbert's family were forced to fall back on tenant farming when times were hard. Since the War Between the States, hard times were in the majority. However, Hannah's young man had a dream, and that dream was to build and build and build some more. Hearing him talk, she began to think of Elbert as more of an artist than anything else. That would explain his melancholy nature somewhat.

About an hour after Doctor Parrott climbed the stairs, Hannah— as satisfied with nursing as she was—had caught the dream and was busy thinking about how to incorporate Elbert's talents into the growth of Beulah. She had listened many times to Uncle Willis T. share his plans to divide his land—which covered the majority of the village of Beulah—into lots people could afford. As simple as Hannah was, it didn't take long to figure out that the folks who bought those lots would need someone to build their houses.

And so, when Elbert and Hannah said goodnight to one another, they were about as excited as two melancholy phlegmatic souls could possibly be.

One day before Elbert was to take Hannah back to Beulah and on to her papa's farm, Jeb Gresham showed up at the Parrott home. He arrived only minutes after daybreak. Hannah was with Mrs. Parrott, assuring herself that her patient was strong enough to resume her many daily duties. As a doctor's wife in a fairly large town, she was not only mother, overseer of two houses—the home place and a comfortable Victorian on Queen Street near the Mosleys—she was required to meet the community's expectations of bustling Kinston's most beloved physician. Pleased with her patient's progress, Hannah had just taken a seat at the breakfast table when Doctor Parrott entered the room with his hand on Jeb's shoulder.

"Look who's here, Miss Gresham," he exclaimed. Somehow, the look on his face didn't quite match the cheery tone of his voice.

"Papa!" Hannah was at once both thrilled and confused. She met Jeb about halfway across the room and threw her arms around his neck, an unusual expression of emotion on her part. For a few seconds, she just enjoyed the comfort and security of her papa's embrace. And then she remembered the confusion.

Drawing away but not too much to leave the comfort of his presence, Hannah asked, "What're you doing here, Papa?"

Before Jeb could think how to answer her innocent question, Doctor Parrott intervened. "Now, Miss Gresham, can't a loving father visit his daughter from time to time without a legal excuse?"

"Of course, he can," replied Hannah, smiling happily. Linking her arm in Jeb's—another unusual show of affection in the Gresham family—she led him to the dining table which was filled just short of overflowing with large bowls of grits, fried eggs, country ham, sausage, biscuits and jars of strawberry, grape and pear preserves. There were even two jars of mouth-watering apple butter made from the farm's own apples.

"Boys," said Doctor Parrott to his four sons who were trying to eat their breakfast and listen to what was going on as well, "this is Miss Gresham's father, Jeb Gresham. Say good morning, boys."

All four boys swallowed the food each had in his mouth and echoed one another with a polite, "Good morning, Mr. Gresham."

"Thank ye, thank ye," replied Jeb. Hannah noted that his floppy old fedora was in his hand rather than on his head. That was an uncommon occurrence for sure.

Dove walked in from the kitchen. "Move over, chil'ren!" she commanded with a shake of the butcher knife. "Yo boys make room fo Mistah Grissom here. He prob'ly starvin' t' death adrivin' all dat long ways frum Limestone. Yo mama 'n papa done teach yo boys better 'n dat." Thankfully, the rather rounded chocolate-skinned women with the butcher knife turned back to the kitchen and started hacking a few more pieces of cured ham so there would be more than plenty for the guest.

"You better move over, boys, or Dove will be back in a minute with that knife, and she won't be swinging it at the ham." Doctor Parrott chuckled and slapped Jeb on the shoulder.

Somehow, Jeb managed to make small talk with the good doctor and his sons until they all finished breakfast. Hannah, still sensing something was not quite right, sat still and proper—which meant very quietly—while the men talked about the ins and outs of the spring planting and lit up the fine Cuban cigars the doctor surprisingly provided.

Finally, when the doctor's sons pushed back their chairs one by one, asking to be excused to head on out to the fields, Jeb turned to Hannah and said, "Girl, I've come to bring ye home."

Surprise written on her face, Hannah asked, "Why, Pa? You didn't have to come all this way during spring plantin'. Mr. Waller was planning to take me home tomorrow."

Her soft blue eyes searched the face she knew so well. Jeb looked down and fingered the old hat in his lap, wondering how to answer her questions. Before he could think up something to say, Doctor Parrott saved him once again.

"Miss Gresham, why don't you take your papa out to the pi'za. No one will disturb you there."

Hannah glanced back and forth from one man to the other, wondering what was going on. Bearing in mind his regular intervention in her life, it was evident Doctor Parrott knew the purpose of Jeb's visit, and that fact added greatly to her anxiety.

Jeb got up and placed one hand under Hannah's elbow, another rare occurrence. The doctor walked behind them to the front door and said, "I'll be out to bid you farewell when you're ready. We'll miss your daughter immensely, Mr. Gresham. More than likely, Mrs. Parrott is already sniffling."

Jeb nodded his thanks and took a seat in the rocker by Hannah, the same seating arrangement that she and Elbert had enjoyed the previous evening. But there was nothing enjoyable about today's conversation.

"What's wrong, Papa?" Hannah's eyes were glassy, heralding tears to come.

"Well, girl, it's like this…." Jeb paused to take a deep breath. Slowly, he let it out. "Your mama…."

Hannah clasped her hand over her mouth and uttered a slight gasp. "Something's wrong with Mama?"

"No, no. Don't worry about your mama. She's fine."

"Tell me, Papa." Tears began to spill over her pale cheeks.

"It's Laney and Nate's knee baby, Mary Alice."

Hannah drew a quick breath and waited for him to continue. Her eyes asked all the questions.

"She's a sick young'un, girl. You know better 'n anybody that Doc Kennedy's been waitin' for this a long time, hopin' Beulah'd be spared, but…well, Mary Alice has the yellow fever. You got such strong feelin's for those young'uns, seein' you helped deliver 'em and all. Me and your mama figured for sure you'd be wantin' to get back and help out, not to speak of the fact that Laney's been askin' for ye. Here time's here, you know." Jeb finally looked up from the hat he was twisting in his lap. He seemed as torn up as Hannah.

For a few moments, Hannah just stared at her pa, thinking how strange he looked without the old fedora on his head. Jeb was going bald, and she hadn't known it until now.

"Take me home, Papa," she whispered. "Laney'll need me. Nate and Lizzy, too…'specially Lizzy." She paused to stifle the cries that were welling up as quickly as the tears in her eyes. "My bag is already packed. It's upstairs in my room."

Jeb nodded sadly. "I'll get it." Standing up, he took Hannah's hand and helped her to her feet and out to the old buggy. Then he turned and went back to fetch her bag and say good-bye to Doctor Parrott.

The two said very little on the way back to Beulah. There was nothing to say. Hannah knew very well the ravages of yellow fever. Even though there had been no epidemic in southeastern North Carolina since the Wilmington epidemic of 1862 when a blockade runner brought the disease into port, there had been isolated outbreaks from time to time. By now, Mary Alice was sure to be suffering from a terrible headache accompanied by nausea and vomiting. Her tongue would be furry, and her pulse rate erratically fast and slow. A high fever was the hallmark of the first stage of yellow fever.

Alternating between praying and planning how to nurse the precious little girl she had helped bring into this world, Hannah didn't take time to give in to her emotions until late in the day when old Nellie pulled the buggy past Willis T.'s cotton gin and Hannah spied the back porch of Nate's house and store. Laney was standing beside the pump, her belly filled with her hopes of a boy for Nate. She held a large enamel dish pan down by her side. It was obvious she was there to pump fresh cool water to bathe her sick child, but Laney just stood there looking off into the distance as if she had nothing to do.

Hannah knew the signs well. A mother in shock, overwhelmed with the possibility of losing a child, was at the same time burdened with household chores and farming which only added to her exhaustion. Oftentimes, she coped with her ordeal by pretending all was well. This seemed to be the case for Laney now, and it was the sight of the pitiful young mother she loved that released the deep sob from Hannah's heart.

Jeb didn't know what to do. Actually, it shocked him to think that he'd never seen his second oldest daughter weep before, and now here she was as torn up as Liza could be during one of her rampages. Wishing Sarah Jane was there to assuage their daughter's tears, Jeb tried hard to act like he didn't notice her crying. Fact was, he wanted to cry himself. He could just picture that tiny, curly-headed girl toddling after Lizzy with a thumb in her mouth and a rag doll in her other hand. She was never outgoing and talkative like her four and a half-year-old sister, but she had a sweet smile for everyone and the deepest blue eyes Jeb had ever seen.

"Now, girl, I know this is hard for ye. But you know Nate and Laney and those little ones'll be needin' you to stay strong for the next few days...maybe a month. You never can tell."

Both father and daughter refused to acknowledge what might cause the need for Hannah's services to come to an end. There was no need to speak of that now.

Hannah retrieved the embroidered handkerchief from her apron pocket and blew her nose louder than she had blown it in her entire life. "I know, Papa. I'll be alright by the time we get there."

And she was. The calm, sure stability which was to become the hallmark of Hannah Gresham's nursing career was born that day in the spring of 1905. One day earlier, the happy young woman had been planning to ride back to Beulah with her husband-to-be to share the news of their engagement. Now, she was riding into her beloved little village wrapped in a dark shroud of grief, praying the inevitable would never come to pass.

✄

When Hannah walked past the wood stove in Nate's store and through the open door into the sitting room, her eyes immediately caught her mother's across the small room which was filled to over-flowing with Gresham women. Instantly, she understood the message in Sarah Jane's look. It was the same as Jeb's, *Be strong, child.*

Hannah nodded, gulping back the lump that was still lodged in her throat. None of the women spoke other than a soft acknowledgement of her presence. She didn't dare look at Kate or Jessie, certainly not at Nell.

Margaret, Jessie, Kate, Nell, Cousin Sallie and a few others slowly vacated the packed room. They had been discussing when to set supper on the table when Hannah walked in. Margaret, still dressed in her black mourning clothes, took charge while Hannah and her mother entered the sick room. There on the bed lay the tiny form of little Mary Alice Gresham. Hannah could hardly see her, wrapped as she was in the quilts the doctor hoped would force her body to sweat out the fever.

Nate and Laney were sitting on the bed, one on either side…just sitting there staring at the small form under the quilts. Suddenly, Hannah lost all sense of how to approach the heartrending situation. She stood there inside the door, wondering if it would be alright to hold her mother's hand.

But Sarah Jane left her side and stole softly across the small room toward the iron bed Laney had painted white. She had explained to Nate that little girls should have something bright and dainty to sleep in. Placing her hand gently on Nate's shoulder, Sarah Jane said, "Hannah's here and supper'll be ready in a minute. You need to eat, son."

Laney was the first to look up. With dark bags under her reddened eyes, she slowly stood and reached out her arms. Hannah quickly moved to her side and caught Laney's thin body, heavy with child, as she fell into her arms. That's when Laney Gresham's last spark of energy failed and she fell apart.

Sobbing uncontrollably, she tried to talk. "I...I pray...prayed Jesus would heal her like He did Lizzy. Why, Hannah? Why won't He heal her?"

Hannah held her tightly, terribly troubled now by the feel of Laney's boney ribs. "Shhh, now, we'll talk about that later. You need some sleep and good food so you'll have the strength to take care of Mary Alice. Come on, let's get you to bed...Nate, too. Mama and I will look after the baby while you rest."

For a moment, Hannah thought Laney was going to refuse. She turned to one side as if to go back to her child but the lack of food and sleep finally overcame her, and Laney just sort of wilted in Hannah's arms. Sarah Jane rushed over to help Hannah lead the worn out mother into the other bedroom which was only separated from Mary Alice by a curtained off doorway.

As they laid Laney on her bed and covered her with a light spread, Sarah Jane said quietly, "I'll go fetch a small cup of the chicken and rice soup Margaret made. Every time Laney wakes up, I'll force some down her throat."

Hannah nodded. In the natural it didn't look as if Laney would wake up for a long, long time. But you never could tell about mothers. Sometimes, they were known to hear the suffering of their children while in a deep coma. She tenderly brushed Laney's soft curls back from her face and whispered, "Sleep tight, Laney. You'll need it more than you know." And then she turned back to Mary Alice and her daddy.

"Nate?" she called quietly. He hadn't moved since she came in.

"Cousin Hannah? That you?"

"Yes. I've come to help, Nate." It was bad enough to watch a mother grieve, but to see a tender man like Nate Gresham was more than Hannah could bear. Hopefully, she could get him to lie down beside Laney and rest awhile.

"That's nice," said Nate, still staring at his tiny girl.

"Nate, I'm sorry to ask questions 'cause I know you don't feel like answering, but has Doctor Kennedy said what stage of the fever she's in?"

"Yeah." He looked as if he couldn't bring himself to speak the words. Finally, he replied, "Doc said it's the first stage but...but it's as bad as he's come across. Maybe because she's so little. Our Mary's always been on the small side. Never did have that plump look Lizzy had at this age."

Like Laney when Hannah first saw her on the back porch, Nate was abnormally calm. It was as if Mary Alice was going to be fine even if the doctor had warned them of the opposite.

"Where is Lizzy?" Hannah asked quietly as she moved closer to Nate.

"Lizzy? Oh, she's over at Cousin Kate's playin' with the young'uns." He finally sighed and stretched a little as if the thought of Lizzy playing somehow brought him out of his trance-like state.

"Nate," said Hannah, gently touching his shoulder, "has Lizzy been exposed?"

He still didn't look up, just nodded. "The Doc's young'uns, too. That's why he and Kate asked Lizzy to stay at their house. Their two boys and Jessie's and Nell's came to Mary Alice's birthday dinner day before yesterday. Nell and Clyde's house is quarantined. Jessie and Kate's, too. Doc said there's no tellin' where it came from. Could be the whole village has been exposed. Laney sent word for her pa to stay home."

Hannah shivered. "Well, let's hope it's just one of those isolated cases." She patted Nate's shoulder.

For the first time since she arrived, he wrenched his eyes from Mary Alice's face and looked up at Hannah. "I know," he said.

She understood exactly what Nate meant, and for the first and only time in her entire life, Hannah put both arms around a man not her papa nor her husband and gave him a quick hug. "Come on, Nate. You need to sleep as bad as Laney. Go lie down for awhile, and I'll take care of Mary Alice. Mama will be back in a minute with some soup for both of you. Maybe I can get some down Mary's throat."

He looked unconvinced, though wavering. Finally, he said, "Alright. But promise me you and Sarah Jane won't leave her for a minute."

"Oh, Nate, you know Mama and me better than that. One or both of us will be with her around the clock. If one of us leaves, it'll only be to see to Laney."

He wanted to lean down and kiss Mary Alice goodnight, but something told him he'd never be able to leave her if he did. Nodding gratefully to Hannah, he stepped through the curtain and crawled into bed beside the wife he loved so dearly. He was never ashamed of his feelings for Laney, but if he had known the curtain had caught on a nail giving Hannah an unsolicited view of the bed, Nate would have tried hard to keep from crying. But he didn't know, and the sight of a grown man—one she loved and respected—as he wrapped his arms around his sleeping wife and sobbed as if he'd never stop caused Hannah's heart to break.

❊

Nights became days, and days became nights. No one in Nate and Laney's house seemed to be able to tell the difference. One of Margaret and Willis T.'s boys—the drummer—had come to help Nate in the store. Margaret decided he'd be the best choice considering he knew the merchandise so well. Hannah and her mama finally forced Nate into a normal schedule of sorts if for nothing more than for him to get some exercise. He was sleeping a few hours at night as well.

Bill Hunter continued to stay away due to Laney's insistence. Her papa had been feeling poorly since Christmas, and she sent him word to take no chances on getting the fever by coming into town to see Mary Alice. She missed him something terrible, but he would have to stay away.

The second stage of yellow fever—the one during which the patient seemed to improve—came and went quickly. But it did offer an opportunity for Lizzy to come home and keep her sister company for one short day. In childhood innocence, Lizzy plopped down on the bed and chattered so much there was no need for Mary Alice to respond other than with a few grateful smiles for her big sister's presence. Once, she was able to lift her arms and hold them out to Lizzy for a hug.

Lizzy squealed in delight. "Oh, you silly girl! You're m' best friend, 'member?" And then she gave her sister a big smack on the cheek which caused Mary Alice to beam.

That was when Laney almost fell apart. But by the grace of God, she held on. The following day, Mary Alice slipped into a coma, and Lizzy was sent back to Kate's house.

The misery of her heavy load and its imminent arrival would normally have kept Laney awake half the night, but when either Hannah or Sarah Jane helped her up from Mary Alice's bed and into her own, she usually collapsed into a deep sleep right away. Sometimes, she even slept through the rooster's crow.

"At least she'll make it through the birth now that she's sleepin' and eatin' some," Sarah Jane commented as she and Hannah stood by the doorway after putting Laney to bed.

"Thank the Good Lord," replied Hannah softly.

Their identical unspoken thought was, *If she doesn't get the fever.*

With a heavy sigh, Sarah Jane turned back to Mary Alice. She walked over to the dry sink and poured fresh water into the bowl from the pitcher. Reaching for one of the clean rags Hannah had washed and hung on the line to dry early that morning, Sarah Jane stepped quietly over to the bedside and eased down onto the bed beside the little girl. The stiff rag softened instantly in the cool water.

Sarah Jane Gresham was known for giving the best baths of anyone around Beulah, and she had passed that gift onto Hannah as well. Nevertheless, little Mary Alice didn't know she was getting a bath from the best.

But perhaps she does know, Sarah Jane mused. She had always believed that sick folks imprisoned in comas or in the delirium of fevers were much more aware of their surroundings than most people gave them credit for. And so, as she tenderly bathed Mary Alice's frail and burning body, Sarah Jane spoke softly to her. She told the girl how happy her mama and papa were the night she was born and how special she was to Lizzy and the other children in Beulah. And then she began to hum as she washed the tiny girl, *Jesus loves me, this I know; for the Bible tells me so.*

When Hannah came into the room, she knew instantly that her mama was praying for Mary Alice. The older woman had paused in her labor of love. One calloused and arthritic hand was on the girl's head and one lay gently on her chest. Hannah's heart fell. She had seen her mother pray for the sick many times through the years and had come to easily recognize the signs of deep concern in Sarah Jane's manner and countenance. Her mother was not only worried, she was resigned.

Sensing Hannah's presence, Sarah Jane looked up. Her eyes were filled with the terrible but solemn sadness of one who has faced death too often to see it as anything other than an unwelcome but natural part of life that humans are forced to suffer. Nonetheless, as she and Lula Belle Aldridge had discussed a year ago, the death of a child was altogether different, and that fact showed now in Hannah's mother's eyes. She didn't have to say anything. But Hannah did hear something, and it didn't come from her mother. It was the death rattle.

She unlocked her gaze from Sarah Jane's and walked quickly over to the bed, desperately hoping the sound had come from some-where else. It hadn't. Lizzy's little sister was no longer writhing or moaning from pain and fever. She lay perfectly still. Her golden hair—made curlier by the dampness from the fever—clung to her forehead and the sides of her pale little face. Her tiny mouth was open, and the last sounds Nate's smallest princess would ever make were the most terrifying any parent could possibly hear.

The sound of Nate's voice behind them startled both women. "Get Laney."

Sarah Jane and Hannah quietly left the room as Nate took Sarah Jane's place beside Mary Alice. Reaching under the clean white sheet, he took his baby daughter's small hand and lowered his head to tenderly kiss each tiny finger as he had the night she was born and every night since. Gulping back sobs that he refused to allow now for Laney's sake, Nate laid his head on the feather pillow and whispered, "Papa loves you, baby princess. Always remember that, you hear?"

Although groggy from her own coma-like sleep, when Laney looked up into Sarah Jane's eyes, she knew. With the look of a helpless wounded animal, she whispered, "Help me."

Braced on one side by Sarah Jane and at the back by Hannah, Laney staggered into the other room. Nate's eyes were closed, his body cuddled up to his daughter's tiny frame, his lips still nestled close to her ear. Laney motioned for Sarah Jane to help her lie down on the other side of their dying child.

Imbued by the miraculous strength God grants parents in anguish, Laney and Nate lay beside their baby. From time to time, Nate reached across the small form and held his wife's shoulder or tenderly touched her face. Sometimes, Laney wept as if her heart would surely break. Most of the time, they lay still and calm. Every now and then, when Laney's strength allowed, she whispered a prayer. Her prayers, however, were very different now, consisting mainly of short sentences thanking God for loaning Mary Alice to her and Nate, if only for a short while.

"Lord, I just want to remind you that our baby won't eat much except grits with a little butter and biscuits and jam. Never could get her to eat anything green. Maybe you can. Or if you don't have time to feed the little ones, maybe one of those bright-colored angels could help. Mary Alice just loved those pretty angels in the picture book we got from the drummer."

Hannah turned to leave the room. This was too much. She was too close to this family to maintain a professional manner. Nate heard her steps and lifted his head.

"Cousin Hannah?"

"Yes?"

"Send for Lizzy. She'll be worse if she don't get to say good-bye, and I don't want her to see her sister after her spirit goes. I want Lizzy to remember Mary Alice alive."

Hannah glanced at Laney. She nodded in agreement and whispered, "Hurry."

When Hannah looked over at her own mother, the look in Sarah Jane's eyes confirmed the urgency. Within minutes, Hannah was back with Lizzy who was as confused and frightened as all children are in such situations.

"Why can't I play with Mary Alice? I'm tired of stayin' at Cousin Kate's."

"Now, Lizzy, you know your little sister has been very sick."

Thankfully, the child asked only one more question on the short walk back. "Can I stay home now?"

"Yes, child. You can stay home now."

Just after Hannah ushered Lizzy into the sick room, Sarah Jane caught her daughter's eye and motioned for her to leave the room. Again, Hannah understood. It would have been an insensitive invasion of the little family's privacy to stay. She was glad. As trained and established as she was as a practical nurse, Hannah was well aware that standing by while Nate explained to Lizzy that her sister and favorite playmate was going to heaven would be the straw that broke the camel's back.

Margaret had easily guessed what was happening when Hannah rushed out to bring Lizzy back, and the look on the two women's faces as they vacated the sick room readily confirmed her suspicions. "Come sit down, both of you. Lula Belle and I will fix you something to eat and drink."

At the quizzical look on Sarah Jane's face, Margaret said, "Lula Belle's been here since sundown. Said she had a feeling."

Sarah Jane nodded and let out a heavy sigh. "I don't know about Hannah, but I couldn't eat a bite, Margaret. I do appreciate it, though."

Hannah shook her head slightly in agreement. She was afraid to speak. The thin thread that held her emotions together was sure to break if she did.

Margaret left the room, and in no time at all was back with two glasses of lemonade. "Here, drink this. You need your strength, too. I doubt any of us will sleep tonight."

Hannah and Sarah Jane gratefully accepted the rare beverage. Margaret sat down in Laney's rocker by the cold wood stove. Leaning her head back, she closed her eyes. Into the wee hours of the morning, all three women kept a silent vigil, intermingling prayers with sips of the cool lemonade. Every now and then, Hannah reached in her apron pocket for the ever ready embroidered hand-kerchief and dabbed at her eyes. Lula Belle waited in the rocking chair out in the store.

It was at first light when the morning stars were still shining brightly in the dark sky that Nate slowly opened the bedroom door. There was no need for words.

One week after Lizzy worked nearly half a day planting a clump of pink thrift on her sister's tiny grave, she stood silently with her papa beside an even smaller burial place. It seemed as if the entire Gresham clan plus Bill Hunter and everyone else around Beulah was there. Everyone but Laney, that is. She didn't have the strength to get out of bed.

Six hours earlier, with Sarah Jane and Hannah alongside, Doctor Kennedy had delivered Laney of a four pound, one ounce boy. He was stillborn. With hardly any strength left, physically or emotion-ally, Laney had suffered through the long labor bravely. Still in the first days of shock, there was only one light of hope in her thoughts of a future without Mary Alice. Nate would have a boy. She was sure of it.

And he did. Owing to the young mother's debilitating weakness and exhaustion from grief, Laney passed out after the final push. When she awoke, Nate was sitting beside the bed holding her hand. There was no sound of a baby's cry, and the midwives were nowhere to be seen. Doctor Kennedy stood in silence by the door, his coun-tenance solemn. A kind man and dedicated to his patients, he had insisted on being there when Laney was told the baby died.

Laney's eyes looked back at Nate, imploring him not to speak the words he had to say. She weakly removed her hand from his and reached up to place it over Nate's mouth. "No," she whispered.

Tears instantly spilled from his reddened eyes. He held her hand against his mouth and kissed it over and over again. For a few moments, she lay there staring at Nate like he was crazy. And then she collapsed. It was too much.

At the graveside, Nate came out of his trance long enough to hear Reverend Aldridge speak the final words from the book of Job, "The Lord giveth and the Lord taketh away. Blessed be the Name of the Lord."

For weeks afterward, Laney lay in her bed, dazed and too weak to even turn over. Nate walked around like a zombie, and little Lizzy followed him around screaming in tears or asking the normal questions of a frightened, grieving child. Hannah had to remind him often that the child he had left needed him now more than ever. At those times, Nate would lift his little princess up in his arms and hug her tightly.

His answer to her questions was always, "I don't know, princess. Your mama knows about these things. When she's better, we'll ask her."

"When will she be well, Papa?"

"I don't know that, either, baby." He kissed her forehead, ruffling her curls with his big hand.

"But I miss my Mama!" Lizzy wailed. "And I miss my little sister! Can I go to heaven and play with Mary Alice, Papa?"

Nate clutched her body tighter in his arms. *Oh, God, no! No!* He wanted to scream. He wanted to run away. He wanted to go to heaven himself, but he knew that was impossible. Who would take care of Laney and Lizzy? Somehow…someway, he had to get through this nightmare.

Nate repositioned Lizzy and sat down in Laney's rocker. *Oh, dear Jesus,* he prayed silently, *I never have kept company with you like my Laney, but I just want you to know that I really do believe. I believed Laney right off when she said you came to the store and healed Lizzy. I surely did. But you didn't heal Mary Alice, and that scares me somewhat. But, Lord, I don't have time to worry about that now. Laney's in bad shape and so is Lizzy, and I don't know what to do. If you don't mind, I need some help down here.*

He held Lizzy against his chest and pushed the chair into a slow rock. In no time at all, she was fast asleep. Gathering her up in both arms, thinking how much she had grown, Nate stole softly across the pine floor that had recently developed a creak and pushed open the door to the bedroom Lizzy had shared with her sister. For the first time since Mary Alice died, he laid her big sister on their bed and tucked her in. When he turned from giving her a kiss, Laney was standing in the doorway.

Nate's mouth flew open. For a few seconds, he could only stare at her in shock. She was obviously weak and white as a ghost, but a tiny fleck of the beloved sparkle that identified her as Laney Hunter Gresham was there in her eyes. Only two long strides took him to the door where his wife held on for dear life. Nate gently gathered Laney's thin body in his arms as if she were made of fine porcelain. She was his treasure for sure.

"Nate?" she whispered into his chest.

His voice was low and broken as he whispered back. "I'm right here."

"Please don't die."

Tears running down his face, Nate looked down and took her face in his hands. "I won't die. I promise."

Looking up at him, her face awash with tears, Laney asked, "You prayed for me, didn't you, Nate?"

Only half surprised seeing the question came from Laney Gresham, Nate replied, "Yeah... yeah, I did. For Lizzy and me, too." He stroked her hair and ran his fingers over her cracked lips wishing he could make them better. "We'll make it through this together. I just know it."

Laney smiled.

Chapter Twenty-five

*S*ummer, 1905 — It seemed to Hannah as if the world stopped spinning when Nate and Laney lay the small bodies of their two youngest children to rest in Beulah's black earth. For two entire days after little Nathan Gresham's funeral, she totally forgot about Mr. Waller. When his memory returned, it was accompanied by a fear that rippled through her body like a shockwave. What if they were to have a child and then it died? Would she survive the loss? What about Mr. Waller? Was he strong enough to endure such grief and come out stronger on the other side? Was she? Maybe her life would be better lived alone, helping others bring babies into the world.

Those questions and more throbbed in her mind as she took out pen and paper to write the man no one knew she was betrothed to marry. There was nothing to do but ask him to wait awhile. He would certainly understand that Hannah's close relationship to Nate's family was reason enough to place their plans on hold. She wouldn't need to add that questions and doubts were barraging her mind like a swarm of big fat bumble bees. She was glad now they hadn't told anyone. There would be ample opportunity to ponder her thoughts without the loving but nagging questions about when she was getting married.

It was the most difficult letter she ever had to write. The melancholy Mr. Waller would be sorely disappointed, and if she had judged his character correctly, he was sure to think she was trying to let him down gently even though her explanation of the need for postponement was clearly stated. She started over three times. Finally, she signed her name and laid the pen aside.

❊

Throughout the summer, Hannah traveled back and forth from Beulah to the Gresham farm, helping Doctor Kennedy when needed, tending to Laney and working in tobacco the remainder of the time. Nate begged her to stay with them when she was in Beulah. He said it helped Lizzy ever so much to have Hannah close by. Hannah was their rock, Nate said. She was, of course, pleased with the compliment, but at the same time she held strong doubts as to its credibility.

She was sitting in a rocking chair on Nate's porch with Lizzy in her lap when the mail carrier came riding into Beulah. A nice breeze was blowing, and the scent of Laney's pink petunias tickled their noses. The Mercer man with a long white beard always looked to Hannah as if he came straight out of her mama's big Bible, like an Israelite on his way to the Promised Land. If the truth be known, she was a little afraid of him. But Lizzy wasn't.

"Howdy, Miss Gresham," he said in greeting, a wad of chewing tobacco in his leathery cheek.

"Good mornin', Mr. Mercer."

Lizzy hopped off Hannah's lap and hurried out to meet the old man. "You goin' to the post office, Mr. Mercer?"

"Yep, sure to be, Lizzy. Wanna help?"

"I sure do. Me and Hannah don't have nothin' to do." Lizzy's little face was squinched in a serious frown.

"Well, thanky ma'm, I can fix that, sure as shootin'. Now, go on and ask your pa, you hear?" Mr. Mercer leaned over the side of the buggy and spat at least an ounce of tobacco juice straight down into the dirt.

Lizzy paused in flight to watch the amazing feat and then rushed into the house yelling, "Papa!"

Before Brock Mercer could work up another good spit, Lizzy was back with the happy news that her pa said it'd be fine to ride to the post office with Mr. Mercer and help him sort mail. Of course, she couldn't read which both she and Mr. Mercer knew quite well, but she loved helping anyway.

Just before they rode away, Lizzy stuck her curly head out of the buggy and yelled, "Want to help us, Cousin Hannah?"

"Not today, child. You go on and enjoy yourself. I have plenty to do."

Hannah had always loved to see Lizzy smile, but these days it was like the sun coming out after months of continual rain. The sad news of the day was, there would be more rain ahead. The little girl didn't know it, but the brother or sister she was hoping for would never come. Doctor Kennedy had mercifully waited a good three months after Mary Alice and Nathan died to reveal his dire prognosis, and even then he only spoke to Nate. It would be up to Nate to judge whether Laney could handle the news or not. So far, she hadn't been told.

Just that morning, Nate had spoken to Hannah. "It's a known fact that Laney has more than her share of faith to take her through all this, but I just don't think she's strong enough yet, do you?" He went on without waiting for a reply. "She's just got to start eatin' better. The few bites she takes couldn't keep a bird alive."

"She'll be fine, Nate. Like you said, her faith will take her through. Not many folks have seen Jesus face to face and I'd be willin' to bet—if I was a bettin' woman, which I'm not—that your wife was given a bigger dose of faith than she realized during that visit. Not to mention that she's always been mighty spiritual in an odd way. Now, don't worry, you hear?"

He nodded and finally gave her a crooked smile.

Hannah smiled back. "I'll try harder to get her to eat more. I promise."

Now, waving at Lizzy as Mr. Mercer drove the buggy away, Hannah's thoughts turned to her own personal concerns...or concern—Mr. Waller, that is. He wrote seldom. As he had confessed to Hannah in early spring, it was hard for him to get his thoughts out in words. She understood his dilemma owing to the fact that she often experienced the same problem. So Hannah wrote Elbert at least once every few days, and he wrote her a short note every Lord's Day.

Thankfully, she had convinced her young man that she wasn't calling off the marriage, only postponing it for a while. Elbert's letters—notes, one might say—were mainly pleas for Hannah to set a date, often bringing up the fact that his building contracts and the responsibility of helping his pa on Doctor Parrott's farm might cause a problem. If she'd just go ahead and tell him something, anything, he could work out a schedule of sorts.

Even so, Hannah didn't know what to say. Everything had seemed so simple that night on Doctor Parrott's piazza, but now...well, now complications had set in like dark clouds over a tobacco barn. Never in her fairly short life had she been so confounded about anything. And never had she even considered talking over personal issues with anyone. Now, she sat quietly, slowly rocking and humming, longing for a listening ear whose mouth she could trust.

The screened door opened, interrupting Hannah's thoughts. Laney's deep sadness was evident these days, rather like a part of her apparel. Nevertheless, as Nate often noted, if you looked deep enough, the sparkle was still there. Slowly, she made her way to the rocker beside Hannah.

Hannah hoped she wouldn't get up and go right back inside like she often did. It would do Laney good to get some fresh air and sunshine. The young nurse was good at keeping company with folks who couldn't talk or didn't want to which was the state Laney was in most of the time. She was in for a surprise when the grieving mother began to speak.

"Ohh, this breeze feels good." Laney's drawl was slower than usual. Her extreme weariness showed in her voice as well as in her body and spirit. Resting her head on the back of the rocking chair, she closed her eyes.

"It does feel good," replied Hannah. "I think this is the most pleasant barnin' season I can remember." She paused in thought a moment and then continued, "Mama always says everything in life is part of a stage within a cycle—like seasons, I guess, or like the weather within a season. For a few years, we have a lot of terrible storms, sometimes, one right after the other. And then we have a few years with no bad storms at all which makes us forget how horrible they can be."

Laney nodded, seriously pondering what Hannah said. She wondered if death came in cycles. In her life, it certainly had. Within six years, she had lost her mama and two children, and she had a feeling her papa wasn't long for this world. But she couldn't think about that now.

"What about you, Hannah? What cycle are you in?"

It was obvious to Hannah that Laney's questions were more than light conversation. They were straight from her heart. Perhaps Laney was the ear she had been wishing for.

Hannah's light blue eyes seemed to bore into hers. "If I share something with you, will you promise not to tell a soul? Not even Nate?"

"Your secrets are safe with me, Hannah…you know that."

Laney's voice seemed to have decreased in volume since the death of her babies. Sometimes, it was hard for Hannah to understand what she said. Her last words, however, were clearly understood.

And so, Hannah haltingly told Laney the story of her growing relationship with Elbert Waller and his subsequent proposal. Sharing from her heart was difficult for Hannah, almost as difficult as it was for Elbert. Folks around Beulah accepted life as it came without much thought or planning beyond next year's farming season. There was neither time nor energy to speak of feelings and such as that. Besides, it just wasn't done.

"There were no doubts the night Mr. Waller asked me to be his wife," said Hannah. She paused, looking at Laney rather oddly.

"What caused your feelings to change?" Hannah's listener's eyes were filled with compassion like the old Laney.

Hannah studied Laney in silence a few moments. She'd have to be careful how she answered that question. Her voice was as soft as Laney's when she finally confessed. "After Mary Alice and Nathan passed on, I became afraid…afraid that if I lost a child, I wouldn't be able to get through it."

Laney's eyes brimmed with tears. Her lips trembled.

"I'm so sorry, Laney," Hannah cried softly. "I shouldn't have told you. I'm so sorry." She looked as if she was about to burst into tears.

"No, no," Laney assured her in slightly broken words. "You're only being honest, and I need that right now. I want to hear your troubles, and I want to help you like you've helped me. I'll be fine."

Hannah took the handkerchief from her apron pocket and dried her eyes. Taking a deep breath, she explained her concerns to Laney who more than likely understood her fears more than anyone in the county at the moment. It felt good getting it all out, almost as if she was no longer totally responsible for the decision she'd be forced to make.

Laney reached over and patted the hand lying on the arm of the chair. "Hannah, owing to the fact that I don't know much, I don't usually give folks advice. So I don't want you to take what I'm about to say as advice, just as a few things I've come to see a little clearer since that day Jesus came to visit. Understand?"

Hannah's mind, Baptist through and through, didn't really grasp such a mystical sounding statement, but her heart did. Anyway, she trusted Laney and would take whatever she said as good advice no matter the forewarning.

"Tell me," she whispered.

"Well, here's the way I see it. You and me have a lot in common. More than anything, we were both born in a small farmin' community in the South that fifty years later is still sufferin' from the terrible effects of war—poverty in particular. We've never had a lot of worldly goods, just enough food to eat and clothes to keep us warm. Other than nursing trainin' with your mama and Doc Kennedy, you've had no education at all and neither have I. Oh, I went to school a few years, and I'm sure you did, too. So we can both read and write, and I can add tickets in the store.

"What I'm tryin' to say, Hannah, is that we're both simple people born in a simple place and time. There's very little time or energy for dreaming big dreams and making plans to see the world and such as that. We'll probably never see one of those really fancy dressed women in the catalogs Henry brings every now and then. We sure won't see one of those dances they call bal-a or something like that. Like I said, in a nutshell, we're simple people."

Hannah nearly started crying then, thinking Laney was telling her to give up her dream of a family of her own. That's why she was surprised at what her listener said next.

"Simple people have simple dreams, honey. Simple for God to work out anyway. I've watched folks pass up the answers to their prayin' or wishin' or whatever they did right when the answers were starin' them smack in the face. They got to worryin' and, I'm tellin' you the truth, girl, worryin' kills faith to believe dead as a doornail. 'Cause you see, darlin', when God puts somethin' in your heart and leaves it there, growing bigger all the while, it's not really a dream as such. In His eyes, it's real. And while we're holdin' it tight, He'll figure out some way to make it happen. Do you understand what I'm sayin'?"

Hannah nodded. "I think so." She gazed down the long dirt road towards the small schoolhouse and sighed.

"Well, I said I wouldn't give advice, but I will say this. Please don't give up the dream God's tryin' to bring to pass just because you're afraid. We're all afraid of the future. Just think…what if Nate and me had decided not to have babies because we didn't know ahead of time what might happen?"

Hannah looked back at Laney with a troubled expression. There was obviously no answer to the probing question.

"Listen good, Hannah Grissom. If we'd done that, if we'd never had our young'uns, just think what we'd a missed. These blessed five years of lovin' Lizzy and her lovin' us back. Watching her grow and learn and change from a baby into the sweet little girl she is. And Mary Alice, what if we'd never had her? What if we'd missed her giggles and the sight of that serious little face of hers when she was ponderin' somethin' that seemed too deep for us to understand?"

Laney laughed. It sounded like music to Hannah's ears, like sunshine in a shower of rain. She couldn't help but smile as tears trickled down her cheeks.

"You know, I used to wonder if our baby girl was especially close to the Lord. She seemed more connected than the rest of us somehow." Laney's voice trailed off into silence.

Finally, having lost the laughter in her voice, she spoke again. "More 'n likely, you're probably wonderin' why a baby born into the world dead could a been a blessin'. But he was. I knew him just as good as I knew Lizzy and Mary Alice. For nine long months, I carried him in my belly and talked to him and felt him move around. Our Nathan was special. He was Nate's boy."

Laney wiped her eyes with the hem of her apron. Looking over at Hannah, she said, "Even though I never got to suckle him or sing him to sleep at night, he was worth it. All the pain. All the sorrow. Life is worth it all, Hannah. It's a gift from God, you know.

"So the advice I wasn't goin' to give you is this: Shush your fears and reach out for the Good Lord's answers to your dreams and hold 'em tight. Thank Him and praise Him every day for the life He gave you to live. He won't give it to anybody else, you know, even if you don't live it. He's good and kind. You may not understand all His ways, but He won't trick you, Hannah. I was sorely tempted to believe that when my babies died, but when I came back to life after Nate's prayers, I knew it wasn't so."

Laney grew quiet and still. Hannah was actually surprised she had spoken so long. Laney had talked little since her collapse even though she was obviously growing stronger physically. Doc Kennedy told Nate that her quiet demeanor was a common symptom of trauma and grief. In due time, her ability and willingness to speak would be restored along with her health.

"You're overtired, Laney. Let's get you to bed."

Hannah stood up and took her patient by the arms, lifting her slight body out of the rocking chair. They had only gone a few steps when Nate came through the door. Seeing the shape his wife was in, he tenderly lifted her up in his arms and headed through the sitting room to their bedroom.

"I'll stay with her a little while," he called back to Hannah. "You watch out for Lizzy when Brock Mercer brings her back, alright?"

"Of course, Nate. I'm afraid it's my fault she's so worn out. I'm so sorry."

"Now, don't worry about that. I was watching through the door, and I've not seen Laney that alive in all these months. I was sorely tempted to go to the door and listen to see what she had to say." Nate smiled as he carried his wife through the door to the bed.

"Thank you, Lord," whispered Hannah under her breath. "Thank you for keeping Nate from hearin' what we said out there."

Chapter Twenty Six

*F*all, 1905 — At summer's end, having helped Nate's household regain some small sense of normalcy, Hannah decided to accept another job from Doctor Parrott in Kinston. Although Laney would be grieving the loss of her children each and every day of her life, after five months she was eating fairly well and strong enough to tend to most of her daily chores…some of the time. Other days she had spells of going into that trance-like state that scared Nate half to death. But when he went over to her and took her in his arms, she'd slowly come back to him.

And so, after saying a tearful good-bye to Laney — Lizzy wouldn't come out — Hannah climbed into Corbett Thomas's buggy and set off for Kinston. Down at the post office, Jeb had heard Corbett say he had business in Kinston and asked if Hannah could catch a ride. Even though he was well aware Hannah Gresham was not a chatterbox, Corbett was glad to have the company. Actually, he was just as happy about that particular aspect of her character. Living in a house where he was the male minority, a day of peace and quiet riding through the autumn countryside was a welcome reprieve.

September had come again to eastern North Carolina. All along the long dirt road, bright blue morning glories wound their way up dried cornstalks and trickled down over ditch banks, mingling new life with the drying wild flowers. Morning glories on earth, added to the blue sky and white clouds overhead, caused the neutral pre-autumn canvas to come alive before Hannah's eyes.

Some folks said fall was the saddest time of year — the dying season — but Hannah saw it differently. It was the season for winding down for sure, but not dying. Autumn was for celebration. The hardest work of the year was over. The harvest was in and pantry shelves were filled. The smell of fresh pine straw and dry wild-flowers floated in the air along with a hint of coolness, assurance that the insufferable humidity of a Duplin summer was past.

As Hannah joggled along in the buggy seat beside her papa's friend, she decided that autumn was a lot like a Saturday afternoon before the Lord's Day. By noon, folks in Duplin had finished the week's regular work, mostly farming of some sort, and were doing things they hadn't had time to do all week. Houses were cleaned in the morning, and if it was the first Saturday of the month, feather beds were placed in the sun to air out, awaiting fresh clean sheets upon their return. Front yards were swept—there wasn't much yard grass to speak of—as well as porches. Mamas made sure the family's Sunday-go-to-meeting clothes were clean and laid out for the next morning. By nightfall, the weekly tub baths began. Yes, like Saturday, autumn was a time of transition, a season of celebration and preparation.

The landscape finally began to change. Though she loved the natural beauty of the countryside, Hannah always felt a surge of excitement in her bones when the tall brick buildings of Kinston began to appear. The old plank bridge over the Neuse River creaked and groaned as Corbett's mare pulled her heavy burden into town. But it was when Corbett tugged on the left rein and yelled, "Haw!" that Hannah's eyes grew wide in awe. Queen Street was literally humming with the sounds of crowds of bustling Kinstonians rushing about their daily business. Rows of stores ran down both sides of the wide dirt street, anything from dry goods to Standard Drugs to specialty shops like milliners and clothing stores.

Hannah loved the scene her eyes beheld when the mare started clopping down the mile-long main street. Where the stores slacked off, giant oaks took their place, their wide branches forming a shady canopy across the road. Behind the oaks stood stately brick homes and lovely Victorians, usually white but sometimes painted in various pastel colors like mauve, butter yellow and sage green. To a girl born and raised in a small unpainted clapboard house in the backwoods of Duplin, Queen Street was a fairyland.

When the mare pulled the buggy up to the hitching post in front of Hannah's destination, she got the surprise of her life. There was Elbert Waller, leaning on the gaslight post a few yards from the lovely Victorian house where she was to live for the next three weeks. Thank the Good Lord he didn't move from his spot, just nodded her way and smiled. Mr. Corbett didn't know a thing about Mr. Waller, and Hannah wasn't about to embarrass herself by introducing them today.

Finally, after helping Hannah down from the buggy seat and carrying her carpet bag to the porch, Corbett bid her good day and drove off towards the south end of Queen Street and the tobacco warehouses. Again thanking the Good Lord that no one in the house had noted her arrival as yet, Hannah walked quickly over to where Elbert was still leaning against the lamp post.

"Good afternoon, Mr. Waller," she said.

"Have you already forgot my name, Miss Gresham?" He was a sad looking man. His black hair and eyebrows looked even darker than she remembered.

"Of course not, Elbert." This time Hannah's light blue eyes smiled, and he knew she was happy to see him.

"Will you get Sundays off this time?"

"I don't know yet, but I'm sure Doctor Parrott will come by often, and I can send word by him."

"That'd be good."

Elbert just stood there twisting the hat in his hand, knowing he needed to leave but wishing he didn't. He looked kind of like a sick puppy.

"I'd better go in now. They're expectin' me." Hannah turned to go.

"Yeah, I guess so. Well, don't forget to send word."

"I won't. I hope to see you soon, Mr. Waller...Elbert."

The smile on Hannah's face was surely enough encouragement to last him a week.

For the first time since their rather unusual courtship began, Elbert and Hannah's circumstances worked together for good. Thankfully, she was allowed Sundays off. And due to the results of Doctor Parrott's matchmaking scheme from the beginning, Hannah rode to the farm with the good doctor on Saturday evenings and spent Sundays with the Parrott and Waller families. During those weeks in Kinston, which turned out to be six instead of three, Hannah grew to feel great affection for Elbert's family, particularly his older brother, John, and his wife and children. Before long, she was as at ease in the Waller household as the Parrott's. More so, it seemed to her now.

Not since the days when she and all of her sisters were living at home did Hannah have so much fun. It seemed that all the Wallers were a bit late in marrying, so there was still a bunch of children at home plus growing numbers of grandchildren scattered about. Falling Creek ran through the farm, and nearly every Sunday after church, Elbert's mama—coincidentally, her name was Hannah— packed a large basket full of the fried chicken, cucumber pickles and biscuits she had prepared on Saturday. And everybody ambled off to the creek for a picnic.

Most of the time, Elbert left Hannah on the creek bank with his mother and sisters while he joined his brothers and the children in the cooling water. Watching the antics of the children—which Elbert and his brothers perpetrated—the proper young woman often found herself bent in half, giggling like the little girl she once was. Elbert glanced at her out of the corner of his eye, happily surprised at the side of Hannah he had never seen.

By the end of each September Sunday afternoon, she'd see Elbert ambling up the bank, coming toward her with a crooked smile on his face. The good thing was, nobody teased or taunted them. For some reason, they all just took Hannah's presence for granted like she was Elbert's twin or something. She loved it, and she loved this family. Hopefully, she would soon be a legal member.

Her old straw hat in one hand and a small sack of peppermint sticks in the other, Celie Thomas quickly climbed down the steps of Nate's store. Weary in soul but not body, she hurried across the deeply rutted road toward Doctor Kennedy's, stepping carefully over the piles of horse dung. Someone yelled, "Howdy, Miss Celie!" but she didn't hear it. Celie was a woman on a mission.

"Kate!" she shouted at the closed door.

"Come on in," Kate yelled back. She was changing the baby's diaper.

"Talk quieter, Celie. The doctor likes peace and quiet when patients are here." She clipped the final pin and set the baby on the floor with a few tin pans to play with.

Celie wondered about the peace and quiet. "Where is he?" she whispered loudly.

"In with the doctor," replied Kate. "I was so scared they'd be gone before you got here."

Kate's determined guest paced the floor, fidgeting with the bag in her hands.

"Oh, sit down, Celie." Kate's tone was filled with impatience. "All that moving around won't do any good. He'll be out when the doctor's finished with him and not a minute before."

"Alright."

Celie took a seat on the edge of Kate's new davenport as her thoughts returned to her plan. Her facial features contorted into frown after frown, easily matching Kate's any day.

Celie paused her thoughts long enough to ask, "So, who did you say brought him here?"

"His older sister, Martha. Of course, she's sixteen but doesn't look old enough to take care of herself, much less Johnny and the younger ones." Kate sighed and added, "But, she does."

"Well, I'm set on bringin' the boy home with me. Corbett will just have himself another young'un to raise. We've got Hepsy to help and Millie, too."

Kate was sprinkling the morning's washing and then folding it up tight to be ironed later. "What if he don't want to go home with you? That boy wouldn't know you and Corbett from Adam and Eve; you know that."

"I sure do know that, Kate Grissom. I'm not stupid. But why would he want to stay with that man? To be sure he'd rather be anywhere but with his pa."

"Well, I don't know, but I do know that children are funny. They want to be with their mamas and papas no matter what. Remember those young'uns of Theo Brinson back in his drinking days? He could be stone drunk, and they'd be wallowing all over him like he was the sweetest man in the world."

"I remember, Kate, but you'll have to admit that Theophilus was right sweet, even when he was drunk. He was never mean like Ike Hatcher."

"Hm, I guess you're right about that. Ike Hatcher's a mean man." Kate suddenly got so mad she shook the jar of water so hard it wet the floor.

Celie was in the same shape. "All I can say is, I wish somebody could prove Ike Hatcher hurt that boy and that deputy none of us can stand the sight of would catch him and hang him as dead as those boys who killed old James."

"That's what I'd call justice," agreed Kate.

All of a sudden, the door to Doctor Kennedy's office opened and out came a sad-looking young girl, obviously dressed in hand-me-down clothes too big for her thin body. She was holding the hand of little Johnny Hatcher. The boy had now reached nine years and was feeling much too old to hold anybody's hand. He had been old for a long, long time.

Being too kind to hurt his sister's feelings by jerking his hand away, Johnny obediently held on and thought how one day he'd take care of her. Martha had been good to him when they had the good fortune to live in the same house. When Ike had dragged his children from Kinston to Wilmington to work at the docks and in the cotton mills, Johnny had thought they'd be a family then, for sure. Maybe in a new place, his papa would change. But it was not to be.

Thankfully, Ike had given Martha and Johnny to the same farmer, Silas Sloan, who needed help barnin' tobacco and getting it tied and off to market. The children had lived with the Sloans all summer and would have actually felt at home by now if they hadn't been so anxious their pa would come back any minute. Early that morning, when Silas and his wife were sure Ike Hatcher was gone for good, he had showed up at the front door drunk as a skunk, demanding his children.

Silas told Doctor Kennedy that he and his wife knew something would happen to that boy when they left the house. When questioned as to how they knew something like that, Silas replied, "Because Hatcher was already mad at somethin' the boy said before they left."

"What was that?" The doctor was calm and eager to get back to the boy.

"Oh, the little fellow just asked his papa if they could stay with us for the winter, that's all. Me 'n my old lady talked to 'em about it the night before Hatcher showed up. We took a likin' to those young'uns. They're hard workin', too. Got my 'baccer in a week early this year."

"Anyway," he continued, "it made Ike madder 'n fire." Silas shook his head back and forth. "Now ain't that somethin', Doc? He don't want those young'uns, not one of 'em, but he thinks they ought to want to stay with the likes of him! Now, ain't that crazy?"

The doctor was looking uncharacteristically angry by now. "So, do you know how Johnny's arm was broken?"

"No, I don't. Except for Johnny and Ike, the only one who knows is Martha, the girl, and believe you me, she's not tellin'. Too scared."

Kate only knew all this because she listened at the door while the man told the doctor, and Celie only knew because Kate quickly sent a note over to her by Evan Thomas who was on his way to pick up his mama at Nate's store.

"Now, hurry on over there, Evan! It's an emergency!" Kate had yelled at Celie's unsuspecting son.

Celie could tell the Hatcher boy vaguely recognized her from church when he was staying with Corbett's brother, Pete Thomas. But like Kate said, he didn't know her from Adam, so he just turned toward the door to go, his arm wrapped stiff in a white bandage. The boy was in pain; that was obvious from his glassy blue eyes and the red blotches on his face.

Slowly, while Doctor Kennedy was giving Martha instructions on how to care for Johnny, Celie got up and walked over to the boy.

"Johnny," she said, "you probably don't remember me, but me and my husband saw you in church a few years ago."

The boy nodded. His recently cut and washed blonde hair made his blue eyes bluer. The boy looked cleaner than she had ever seen him, too. Perhaps Silas Sloan and his wife did care for the children after all.

"I was in Nate Gresham's store today, and for some reason, I decided to buy some candy. Would you like some?"

Johnny stared up at her like she had lost her mind. "Candy?" he replied.

"Uh, huh. I'd like you and your sister to have a piece."

Martha looked at Celie suspiciously. "Papa says we're never to take anything from strangers."

Oh, dang your papa! thought Celie. Kate looked as if she might spit nails.

"I understand that, child, and I always told my children the very same thing. But we're in the doctor's house, and I'm sure he and his wife here will assure you it's safe to take candy from me. We're good friends."

Johnny could smell the aroma of peppermint seeping out of the sack. Martha could, too, but Celie was holding it closer to Johnny's nose. About that time, the doctor came out of the room and saw what was going on.

"Mrs. Thomas is a friend of ours, children. I assure you that anything she offers you is safe to eat." He smiled and patted Johnny's shoulder.

Each child stuck out a hand, clean for a change. Just before Johnny crammed the end of the peppermint stick in his mouth, Martha poked him in the back. He knew what she meant.

"Thank you, ma'm," he said, almost in a whisper.

Celie smiled, her tough exterior melting at the sight of a tiny smile in the blue eyes well framed by the blondest hair she'd ever seen. *Why, the child is handsome*, thought Celie. His face was kind but sad, rather like Laney's since her loss.

Corbett's wife stared at the boy's unusual face, wondering what to do next. Thankfully, Kate cut in.

"Would y'all like some milk to go with that candy, children?" Not waiting for an answer, she picked up the baby and hurried off to the kitchen. "Sit down, you hear? I'll be right back."

Turning back to his office, the doctor said, "These ladies will take good care of you. Silas said he'd come back to check on you in a little while. You're to wait here until then."

One look into Martha's eyes, and Doctor Kennedy understood what she didn't say. "Nobody knows where your papa went, child. I'm sure he doesn't know you're here with us." He patted her hand which was still holding on to Johnny and walked back into his office.

"Now, children," said Celie. "Why don't we go sit down at Kate's table and wait for the milk? I'll tell you about our new foal while we wait."

Before Celie said "wait," Kate was back with two glasses of milk and a plate of cookies.

"We're going to make these children sick, Kate Grissom," Celie exclaimed with a scowl.

For some reason, that broke the ice. Martha's lips twitched, longing to smile but not sure it would be polite. Johnny, however, was too young to think about propriety. He laughed and giggled and sucked the peppermint stick at the same time, creating red syrup that dripped slowly down his chin.

Celie was stunned. All that work trying to get the children to just relax a little, and here they were laughing at something she hadn't thought a bit funny. *Do tell*, she thought.

Kate was just as surprised, but it didn't take her as long to get over it. Joining in the laughter, she teased, "Want to get sick, children? Have a cookie!"

"Uh, huh," replied Johnny, laughing so much Celie was afraid he'd get choked on the candy.

Martha joined in then. Celie noticed that the girl had the strangest smile. It might have been called a serious smile if there was such a thing. From then on, every time Johnny's sister smiled, it was as if

289

she was still thinking about a serious decision she had to make. *But she did smile,* thought Celie, *and that was a mighty big step.*

After a while, Kate went to put the babies down for a nap, and Celie walked back into the sitting room with the Hatcher children. "Why don't we go sit on the porch? Y'all can sit in the swing, and I'll sit in a rocking chair."

Both children's eyes lit up. Martha had politely finished her candy cane and licked her fingers when Celie wasn't looking. However, Johnny clutched what was left of his melting candy in his hand like it was gold. Unknown to the other, Martha and Celie were both aching to wash Johnny's sticky little hands. Both held back but for different reasons. Martha didn't know how to breach the subject considering she had no wash cloth, and Celie was afraid to take the candy from the child. He looked as if he'd never let go.

And so, they sat on the porch, the children swinging delightedly and Celie rocking. Every now and then Johnny and his sister would look at one another and start laughing. Celie Thomas wondered how often they laughed.

At the same time Kate came out the screened door, Silas Sloan pulled up in a wagon filled with sacks of corn meal freshly ground at the mill. Although unsure of his reasons for returning, the children were glad to see Silas. He and his barren wife had been good to them. The children, however, knew their papa better than Silas and were not a bit surprised when Ike came to take them back. Now, they didn't know what was going on. No matter where they went, no matter who took them in, good or bad, papa would be back to get them, and life would go on the same forever.

They greeted Silas with half smiles, and he did the same, not wanting to get their hopes up. Kate stuck her head in the open window and said, "Doctor, you said to call you when Silas came back." Turning around, she said, "Have a seat, Silas."

In a moment, the doctor walked out on the porch and greeted Silas with a handshake. "Why don't you all come on in the house," he said. "I'm sure the children will be fine here on the porch."

Martha and Johnny nodded in agreement. Their stomachs were not growling—actually, they felt a little sick like the old woman had warned—and nobody was beating or kicking them around. They were even clean and dressed in clothes that had no holes to speak of. They had no complaints at all other than the pain in Johnny's arm. Sadly, he had known worse pain in his short life. He certainly wouldn't allow himself to complain about this little thing.

After a lot of heated discussion in the sitting room—the heat coming from Kate and Celie—the conversation had come to a standstill. Having dealt with more of this type of person than anyone else, Doctor Kennedy assured the other three that there was no way short of shooting Ike Hatcher that anyone could take those children away from the drunken tyrant.

"Well, I'm all for shootin' him," said Kate, banging her fist on her knee.

"I vote with Kate," added Celie.

"That's not funny, Kate," said the doctor.

"I didn't mean to be funny," said Kate, "I'm as serious as can be."

"Me, too," said Celie. She looked a lot like she did the day she took the hatchet out to the woodpile.

"Well, civilized people don't go around shooting folks." The doctor shook his head and sighed. "I don't know that there is anything we can do, Silas. You can take them home with you, but beware that one of these days Ike will be back banging on your door."

Before Silas could reply, Celie jumped in. "I want him, Doctor."

"Celie! I had no idea you and Corbett wanted to adopt a child." The doctor was obviously surprised.

"*We* don't want to do anything. *I* want to, and I don't want to adopt any child. I want *that* boy out there. If his sister goes with him, I'll take her, too."

"But what if Corbett doesn't agree?" The doctor was obviously concerned about his friend. Corbett and Celie were well over sixty now. This was no time to start over with a young boy.

"He'll get over it," snipped Celie.

"Missus Thomas," said Silas, "I realize you have feelin's for this boy, and I know you'd take good care of him, but you and Mr. Corbett are getting' on in years and…."

Celie looked like she was spitting now. "I am *not* old, Mr. Sloan, and I'd appreciate it if you didn't refer to me as such."

The doctor looked over at Kate for help. For once, he got it. "Celie, calm down and listen to what Silas is saying. The children have been stayin' with him and his wife all summer. They like it there. And the Sloans like them. They're good people. I've heard the doctor say so many times."

Doctor Kennedy smiled in wonderment. This had turned out to be the most rewarding conversation with Kate in five years of marriage.

In reply, Celie didn't utter a word. She just placed her hand over her eyes as if shutting out the sun, sighing deeply.

"Celie," said Doctor Kennedy, "I know you want the boy, but most of all you want him to be cared for the best way possible. Isn't that true?"

She nodded her head, a rare tear trickling down her cheek.

Kate looked at the doctor and slowly shook her head back and forth. If she knew Celie Thomas as well as she thought she did, it was time for everyone to hush up. As Jeb Gresham often commented, "'Nuf said."

And so Martha and Johnny went back to the Sloan farm south of Chinquapin and happily stayed with Silas and his good wife two months and three days. Just before the children were to experience a real Christmas with a real family, Ike Hatcher appeared on the Sloans's doorsteps and took Martha and Johnny away. Silas and his wife stood on the porch and stared after Ike's wagon for a long, long time.

At Celie and Kate's request, Doctor Kennedy looked for them when he took a barge from Hallsville down to Wilmington for a medical meeting in January. He found them, but Ike wouldn't let him in the frigid house. He said his children were none of the doctor's business and ordered him to get out of there before he got his gun.

Two years later, the doctor returned from another medical meeting in Wilmington with the news that Ike Hatcher was dead of unknown causes. By that time, little Johnny was eleven years old and Martha was sixteen. Their older brothers and sister had escaped Ike's clutches years ago, but Johnny and Martha vowed in their hearts to take care of Maggie, Amon and Jenny for the rest of their lives. And they did.

Chapter Twenty-seven

Mid October, 1905—Kate and Jessie, both with a baby on each hip and Kate's third hanging on her skirt tail, were standing on the porch of Nate's store chatting with Laney who had finally gained some weight and looked a little more like her old self. When a buggy rolled through the crossroad and came to a stop not three yards away, they all turned to take a look. Instantly, three voices went silent, and three sets of female eyes turned to see who was getting out of the unfamiliar buggy. Strangers were a curiosity, few and far between. However, to the young Gresham women's surprise, the woman who alighted from the black buggy with the help of the now recognizable man with jet black hair was certainly not a stranger.

"Hannah!" yelled Jessie. "It's Cousin Hannah!" She ran down the steps, fat babies bouncing on her thin hips.

Laney and Kate followed more slowly, but smiling just as big a welcome as Jessie. No matter how big she smiled, Laney couldn't hide the sorrow in her eyes, especially not from Hannah. So both Laney and Hannah did what southern women do, they avoided one another's eyes.

Hannah turned around just in time to be swept into Jessie's outstretched arms, babies and all. Reserved as always, she blushed deeply, but it was obvious she was pleased to receive the warm welcome. Disentangling herself from Jessie's noose, she took the smallest child in her arms and laughed aloud…well, loud for her. It was probably more of a chuckle.

"Jessie Grissom, how come you went and had another baby without my help?" The baby snuggled up to her as if he had been held in her arms every day of his life.

Jessie began chattering a mile a minute, and Laney and Kate joined in until, all of a sudden, they all remembered the young man who had helped Cousin Hannah out of the buggy. Jessie almost tripped over her own feet and two toddlers as she whirled around to look at him. Elbert Waller was standing about a yard behind Hannah looking about as uncomfortable as a worm in a hen house. He stood first on one foot and then the other, nervously fumbling the hat in his hands. His straight dark hair flopped down over one eye.

"Oh…howdy do, Mr. Waller," said Kate, not too friendly-like.

Jessie grinned from ear to ear, reaching out her free hand to grab one of his, embarrassing him to no end. "Welcome, Elbert!" she said. "Glad you brought Cousin Hannah home to us again. She's been gone six weeks!"

Laney smiled at the man she had only heard about from Jessie and Kate. She agreed. It was nice of him to bring Hannah home.

He hinted at a smile and nodded back.

Hannah seemed not to notice the communication at all. She was focusing her attention on the five Gresham children, each of whom she had helped bring into the world except the one she held comfortably in her arms.

"Would you like to come in and have something to eat and drink before you head back to Kinston, Mr. Waller?" asked Laney. "I made some teacakes just this mornin' and we got fresh milk to go with 'em. Might even have some biscuit puddin' left from dinner."

She didn't wait for Elbert's reply but turned to Hannah and took hold of her hand. "You, too, Hannah. Come on in while you wait for Jeb. We've missed you something terrible." Her eyes revealed more than she said.

Laney reached for the door handle and turned back to ask, "When's your papa comin' to get you?"

Hannah looked up as calm as a cucumber and replied, "Papa's not coming this time. Mr. Waller will be drivin' me out to the farm." She nuzzled the baby again, never once looking at Laney or anybody else.

"Well, then…come on in, Mr. Waller," said Laney. She glanced back at Jessie and Kate whose eyes had suddenly changed shapes. Jessie's were round as the moon while Kate's were reduced to small squints in the frown she wore. "Y'all come on in and have teacakes with us. I'm sure Hannah would like that."

Laney didn't seem to notice that it was mighty strange for Elbert to take Hannah all the way out to the farm, at least five miles from Beulah in the opposite direction from Kinston, when the normal thing was for Jeb to meet them in town to fetch his daughter. But Jessie definitely noticed and so did Kate. The latter cousin was studying Hannah soberly while her sister's green eyes were darting back and forth from the miserable young man to Hannah's unreadable countenance.

Jessie's curiosity was about to get the best of her when Hannah said, "I'd sure like some teacakes, Laney, and more 'n that I'd like to visit with y'all a spell; but we really don't have time. Mama and Papa expect me home before dark. We would have just kept on going, but I saw the three of you out here on the porch and asked Mr. Waller if he would mind stopping so I could say hello. After I found out I'd be stayin' in Kinston three extra weeks, I missed you all so much I nearly cried."

The unusual expression of emotion melted Hannah's cousins' hearts, and once again, they all started chattering about how much they had missed her, too. As she turned back towards the buggy, Elbert leading the way, Kate said, "Now, you come on back into town as soon as you've visited with your ma and pa a spell. You can stay at my house a few days like you used to. The doctor'll be glad to see you."

Jessie was nodding and smiling her agreement as Laney joined in, "Don't forget our house. Lizzy'll be wantin' to see her Hannah."

"Where is that sweet baby?" asked Hannah, laying her hand on Elbert Waller's arm for support as she climbed up to the running board of the buggy.

"Oh, she rode out with her daddy to take Papa some supplies. He's been feeling mighty poorly lately." Laney looked grieved at the hint of facing another loss, but the peace she had first felt at the baptism still smiled in her eyes, no matter what.

"Well, you tell her that I'll be back in town soon, and I'll come straight to Lizzy Grissom's house." By then, Hannah was seated in the buggy, peeking out around the covering.

Elbert quickly pulled his lanky frame up and took his seat. Lightly flipping the reins, he guided the mare into a u-turn and then started off down the road towards Hallsville, his dark eyebrows hiding the relief in his deep-set eyes.

"Bye now!" Hannah smiled as she waved.

Laney and Kate and Jessie waved back, each smiling and shouting various versions of, "Come back soon, you hear?"

All of a sudden, Jessie couldn't stand it any longer. She quickly devised a way to find out something…anything! "Hannah! Mr. Waller can stay at my house. Clancy and I would be glad to have him!"

Elbert continued to look straight ahead, but Hannah turned slightly and replied—rather casually, they all remembered later, "Thank you kindly, Jessie, but there's no need. Mr. Waller and I are goin' to be married tomorrow."

And then Elbert flipped the reins once again, and the mare trotted off down the road.

Three young Gresham women came close to a heart attack in Beulah Land that day. It took quite awhile to recuperate.

꘏

Sarah Jane was sitting on the front porch in her favorite rocking chair when Elbert drove the tired mare up the path to the house. Jeb was perched on the top porch step, elbows resting on his knees as he whittled a toy dog for Nell's little boy's birthday. Neither of them had spoken a word for nearly thirty minutes. It seemed more like hours. Sarah Jane alternated soft sighs with the squeaking of the rocker while Jeb nearly whittled that dog down to near nothing. With no other sounds to compete, the crickets' chirping seemed to grow louder and louder. Once in a while, a chicken wandered by clucking to itself, or one of Sarah Jane's mallards quacked, but all in all the air waves were in cricket control.

Nobody moved, not even when the horse and buggy stopped within a few yards of the porch where they were waiting. Finally, when Elbert climbed down and nodded a somber greeting to his not-so-future in-laws, Sarah Jane got up, stiff as a board from sitting so long, and slowly limped over to grab the porch post. She naturally figured Jeb would get up to greet Hannah and her young man, but he didn't. He just sat there staring at the partially formed dog, whittling away. Sarah Jane gently tapped the toe of her right shoe into his behind and whispered loudly, "Get up, old man!"

He turned his head and gave her a look she was glad he hadn't thrown her way before company arrived, and then he pushed his shoulders up to a stubborn position and went back to whittling. By that time, Elbert Waller had helped Hannah down and was escorting her—without touching, of course—around the mare towards her waiting parents.

Now, one might remember that even though she was a midwife at an early age, Hannah was peculiarly naïve and terribly shy when it came to the subject of getting married and conceiving babies and all that. Therefore, it was about the hardest thing she ever had to do in her life to walk around that sweaty old mare and face her mama and papa that evening in mid October of 1905. She was glad it was almost dark so they couldn't see the color of her face. That didn't matter because Sarah Jane knew her daughter like a book and would have been able to sense her anxiety and embarrassment even if she were blind as a bat. As for Jeb, well, his melancholy state was naturally due to losing one more child—a mighty dependable one at that—to the inevitable state of matrimony. Furthermore, he had begun to feel mighty old this past year. And on top of that, the word, "cranky," wasn't too far from a good description of his temperament since Sarah Jane read him Hannah's letter. Unlike his wife, there were no birds and bees buzzing around in his mind, only nostalgic memories of five little girls with happy faces following their papa around the farm like he was the greatest person on earth.

And Elbert? Well, his feelings went from miserable to happy, back and forth. In a sense, he was worse off than Hannah, but his reaction took the form of a total refusal to look at anybody...Hannah included.

Subsequently, the bride and groom were mighty relieved when Sarah Jane sucked in a deep breath and forced a big smile on her face that beamed out to them like the electric light they had yet to see. She brushed past Jeb and walked out to meet a blushing daughter and her husband-to-be, arms outstretched and joints aching. Wordless, Hannah fell into her mother's open arms.

Finally, Jeb Gresham laid the knife and little wooden dog on the porch and stood up to greet the shy couple. *Might as well get it over with,* he thought. Shaking Elbert's hand—the boy never did look him in the face—Jeb couldn't think of a word to say, so he just kept shaking Elbert's hand and nodding. Gratefully, Elbert nodded back. The communication or lack thereof, seemed to be sufficient for both.

"How you doin', Pa?" asked Hannah as she reluctantly disentangled herself from her mother's arms.

"Doin' fine, just fine, child," replied Jeb with a slight smile in his weary eyes.

And that was the end of it. In those two short and seemingly irrelevant sentences, father and daughter spoke volumes to one another. The daughter really said, "Papa, you've been a good pa. You've taken care of me all these years, and now I ask you to bless my marriage to this young man I'm bringing home this evening. I know you will, and I thank you for it." And the father really said, "I love you, Hannah, and I'm proud you're my daughter. I'm mighty pleased to bless you and your young man."

Sarah Jane just stood there with tears in her eyes, listening to the words nobody said.

Sarah Jane and Jeb had promised Hannah they wouldn't tell the other girls she was getting married until the next morning. She didn't want a big to-do, and she particularly could not abide all the teasing her sisters would surely torture her with from the time she arrived at the farm until the following afternoon when the preacher performed the ceremony. It would make everything easier to keep quiet as long as possible. Hannah's only request was to be married in the little Baptist church she had loved so dearly since childhood. Reverend Aldridge and Lula Belle had promised Sarah Jane to meet the family there at two o'clock the following afternoon.

Jeb left Saturday around midmorning to surprise Nell with the news and bring her and the children back to the farm. By that time, however, Nell knew all about it because when Elbert and Hannah drove away from Nate's store the previous day, Jessie had thrust her little ones into Kate's arms and yelled, "I'm goin' to tell Nell! She'll probably faint."

Frannie was just down the road a bit visiting Cousin Bessie Bishop, so Sarah Jane sent Frank to get her while Liza stared at Hannah like she was the weirdest person she had ever met. For once, the boldest and brashest sister was at a loss for words.

Hannah was walking around like nothing unusual was going on at all, helping her mother with small chores in the house throughout the morning. Sarah Jane was as sober and quiet as her daughter so that by the time Liza figured her pa should be back with Nell, and Frank with Frannie, she was just about to go berserk.

"Hannah, shouldn't you be gettin' ready? Your hair looks terrible! What are you going to wear?" Liza looked as if the world was coming to an end.

"There's nothing much to do. I'm going to wear the dress Mama made for me when I left for Kinston."

Liza's eyes nearly popped out of her head. She plopped both hands on her hips and frowned. "But, it's drably gray! You can't wear a dull gray dress for your wedding!"

"It'll be just fine." Nothing seemed to shake Hannah's calm, and evidently, Sarah Jane was taking her cues from Hannah. According to Liza's report to Nell and Frannie later that afternoon, you'd have thought it was just any old day in the Gresham household. The younger girls were mortified, but Nell quietly reminded them that their sister's wedding day was exactly what Hannah wanted—no fuss, no big to-do and, most assuredly, no spotlight on the bride.

And that's just what it was to begin with—a nice, pleasant Saturday just like any other sunny October day on the farm. Simple chores were taken care of that morning so that by the time the sisters arrived just after noon, the entire household acted like nothing was going on other than a nice, Saturday afternoon visit with the preacher and his wife. Lula Belle had insisted on preparing a wedding supper for the family at her house across the road from the church so, as Hannah said, there was little to do.

Reverend Aldridge rode out to the farm just before noon and quietly took Elbert and Hannah aside to speak with them for a few minutes. Nell and Frannie dressed in their Sunday best and were working on Nell's boys while Jeb sat on the front porch whittling. Frank took care of preparing the horse and buggy and hitching the mule up to the wagon. Clyde Thomas sent his regrets saying he had work to do. If the truth be told, he didn't enjoy his own wedding, and there was no reason to think Hannah's would be any better.

After the reverend was satisfied Elbert and Hannah knew what they were doing, he walked out the door with a tip of his hat and said, "See you at the church house, Jeb."

Everybody loaded up in the family buggy, Elbert's buggy and the old wagon which had to be pulled by Nellie, the mule, who could never be trusted to get anywhere on time. That's why Hannah rode in the buggy with her pa and Elbert rode in Doctor Parrott's loaned buggy with Sarah Jane.

Just as the two buggies pulled into the sandy church yard—Nellie was a few minutes late—Lula Belle stuck her head out the door and yelled, "Y'all come on, now. Everything's ready."

The mule was just tugging the wagon through the deep sand beside the graveyard when Liza jumped down. She stumbled a bit but didn't fall. Experience had served her well. Holding her skirt up with one hand and a wreath of tiny yellow flowers from the creek bank in the other, she ran over to the church steps.

"I couldn't bear for Hannah not to have something special for her wedding," she said to Lula Belle with tears in her eyes.

The preacher's wife smiled and said, "It's beautiful, Liza. I'm sure your sister will be pleased with your gift, but even more with your thoughtfulness."

Liza wasn't used to that kind of intimate talk, so she hurried on by Lula Belle blushing terribly. But in her heart she rejoiced that someone thought she had done something good for a change. And Lula Belle was right. Waiting for Elbert on the church steps, Hannah accepted her unruly sister's gift and kindly allowed Liza to place it neatly atop her thin hair. She even laughed a little when Liza stood back and said, "You look almost pretty, Hannah!"

And so the bride's family went in to take their seats—everyone but Susie, that is. She lived nearly thirty miles away now on a farm near Warsaw, and there was just no way to get her there in time. The Gresham girl everyone privately predicted would be an old maid nurse walked into the little Hallsville Baptist church on the arm of Mr. Elbert Waller whom nobody knew a bit more than Adam.

However, the reserved young woman who wanted a private ceremony was in for a surprise. Only slightly touching Elbert's arm, Hannah walked the first few steps into the sanctuary looking down at the pine floor. When she lifted her head, she didn't know whether to laugh or cry. The first few pews were filled with her family and close friends. Behind Jeb and Sarah Jane sat Nell and her boys, Liza, Frank and their two, plus Frannie and Ira Hines.

Across the aisle sat Doctor Kennedy with a smile on his face that said, "I'm happy for you, Hannah." Next to him sat Kate, resigned but unsmiling, and beside her sat Jessie—grinning to beat the band—plus Clancy and their little ones. Margaret Gresham was there with two of her boys. Cousins Bessie and Bertha Bishop were there as well as other cousins in the Gresham clan. Hannah thought she had never seen such a beautiful bunch of people.

Finally, her eyes lit on Nate and Laney Gresham. Lizzy was standing backwards in the pew, smiling and giggling and sometimes clapping her hands in glee. That's when Hannah almost shocked everybody even more and burst into tears. The little family should have consisted of five members, but the two youngest were conspicuously missing. Hannah knew the pain was as fresh as it was six months ago, and it overwhelmed her to think that Nate and Laney had laid their grief aside to come to her wedding. On top of that, it was Saturday, the busiest day of the week at the store.

Smiling through her tears, Hannah's eyes said, *Thank you.*

The service was very simple and thankfully, very short, according to Jeb who was a lot more fidgety than he had expected to be. When Reverend Aldridge asked Elbert if he promised to be faithful to Hannah all the days of his life and to honor her and love her as

Christ loved the church, the dark-eyed, black-haired young man just nodded his head, his usual affirmative response to most any question. But it was enough for his practical bride, and noting that she seemed to accept it, the preacher went on to ask if she would do the same. Very quietly and calmly, Hannah replied simply, "I do."

That was it. And true to character, before the tearful sisters and cousins could move towards the bride and groom with their hugs and good wishes, Hannah turned around and said, "Miss Lula Belle, I'll be glad to help you in the kitchen."

Everyone laughed, even Jeb and Elbert. Margaret Gresham's eyes bulged at the thought, and Liza said, "Oh, Hannah, you can't cook your own wedding supper!"

Jessie whispered to Kate, "It'd be just like her to sneak off to the kitchen. But we'll not let her, will we, sister?"

"No, we won't," replied Kate, still concerned about Mr. Waller's character. Jessie told Liza later that Elbert was bound to have a headache where Kate's eyes bored into his skull.

Elbert stuck his hands in his pockets and bashfully eased out of the crowd onto the front steps with Jeb and Frank following close behind. As the three men stood on the porch taking deep breaths of the crisp autumn air, Elbert finally spoke for the first time that day.

"Heard you got a new hound dog."

"Yep," said Jeb, each hand gripping an overall strap. "Want to look him over when we get back to the house?"

Elbert nodded.

Jeb crammed a wad of chewing tobacco in his jaw. "Come on," he mumbled, "let's walk through Armstrong's yard and see how high the river is." Turning to Frank, he added, "You comin'?"

Frank said, "Uh, huh."

And so the old farmer and his two sons-in-law ambled off through the woods to the river while the women helped Lula Belle bring the wedding supper from her house to the chicken wire tables in the church yard. Reverend Aldridge, who had no idea how to slow cook anything, had hired one of William Hall's boys to prepare the fatted pig early that morning. Everything was ready, and the enticing aroma wafted through the little hamlet like the sound of the Pied Piper's flute.

Sarah Jane was pleased when Lula Belle gave her something to do. There was nothing more uncomfortable for a country woman than waiting for dinner to be set on the table without helping do it. Pushing up her sleeves, she began to arrange the various dishes on the wire table.

"Did you bake all these cakes?" she asked Lula Belle.

"Oh, no. All the guests brought something." She put her finger to her mouth, wondering what she had forgotten.

"How'd everybody know to come, Lula Belle?" It was a question Hannah wanted to ask but hadn't had the chance.

"Actually, it was Hannah herself who told Jessie and Kate, Sarah Jane. I ran into Kate at Nate's store about fifteen minutes after Hannah and Elbert left yesterday. Just as Kate and Laney were telling me about the bride and groom stopping by, Jessie came hurrying back from telling Nell about the wedding. That's when we all had the same idea.

"Laney was the one who said, 'Hannah should have a nice wedding, seein' as how she's waited so long and all.'

"I said, 'Yes, she should. She's waited a long time for this day.'

"As I recall, Kate stood there thinking while Jessie popped up and said, 'I know! Let's invite all the folks she's closest to, and she'll have a big, happy wedding. You know they'll all come, even those who're betting she'll never get married.'

"'Why, that's a fine idea, Jessie,' I said. 'We're cooking a pig so we'll have plenty of food.'

"Kate joined in then. 'Why don't we tell all the women to bring something? Then you won't have to cook so much, Lula Belle.'

"Anyway, by the time I left a few minutes later, we had the entire wedding and supper planned, and Jessie was off to spread the word." Lula Belle sighed in satisfaction and started off to check on the pig.

"Lula Belle?" said Sarah Jane.

"Yes?"

"It's mighty nice of you to do this. Hannah will have something to remember always."

Lula Belle smiled. "You would have done it for my Bonnie, Sarah Jane."

Jonas Aldridge had been standing in the doorway of the church watching the three men in Jeb's family communicate in the only way they knew how. Now he observed Sarah Jane working like a servant at her own daughter's wedding. He had long ago decided these country folks were a lot smarter and wiser than he had once believed.

Acceptance, he mused. *That says it all. These people accept life as it comes and never seem to question it. Whether joy or sorrow, suffering or celebration, they live their lives simply and usually without complaint.*

A slight smile spread over the reverend's face as he pulled a pipe out of his coat pocket and placed it in his mouth. And then he chuckled, realizing he was unconsciously nodding his head…just like Elbert Waller.

After supper was over and good-byes were said, Clyde Thomas gathered up Nell and the children and offered Frannie a ride back to Cousin Bessie's where she planned to spend the night. By the way, Clyde came to the wedding when he heard there was going to be a pig picking.

"No sense in missin' a good meal, Nell," he said to his wife.

Elbert and Hannah rode back to the farm alone, due only to Liza's manipulation. They said very few words on the way, but he did lay his right hand on her left one, and she left it there. It was strange being married. Hannah had no idea how it was supposed to feel, but "strange" certainly wasn't what she had expected. She thought of things that had escaped her before—things like making decisions and whether Elbert would mind if she continued nursing. What if Dr. Kennedy sent for her in the middle of the night? Would Elbert get up—like her pa had so often—and take her to Beulah or wherever the doctor's patient was giving birth? It was a lot to think about.

Elbert squeezed her hand. She looked over at him and smiled. *It'll be alright*, she thought.

"It was a mighty fine weddin'," said Elbert.

"Yes, it was…mighty fine."

They smiled at one another. Elbert looked back at the road ahead, but he didn't move his hand. He just squeezed hers tighter.

Sarah Jane pulled off her apron and hung it on the nail by the kitchen door. Jeb was stretching and yawning when his wife caught his eye and motioned for him to get on to bed. He didn't need much persuasion.

The problem was Liza. Frank was feeling about like Jeb, tired and sleepy, but his nosey wife was wondering where in the world Hannah and her new husband were going to bed down for their wedding night. She and Frank and their two little ones now occupied the back bedroom the sisters had shared for so many years. As Liza watched, her eyes darting from Hannah to Elbert and all about the sitting room, her mama and papa ambled off to their own bedroom, the one she thought should have been offered to the newlyweds. She had no idea that Sarah Jane had done just that earlier in the day while struggling to speak with her second oldest daughter concerning her wedding night.

One would have thought the mother of five daughters would have been proficient in premarital counseling after marrying off four of those daughters, but it seemed to be getting harder every time. With Nell, it had been nearly impossible, although her oldest daughter had tried to make it easier for her mother as well as herself by quietly responding, "It's alright, Mama. I've resigned myself."

The baby, Susie, had turned out to be the most indifferent of the bunch. Somehow, Sarah Jane never managed to broach the subject with her. It just didn't seem fitting somehow. But long before Susie tied the knot came Liza's wedding day. To her mother's dismay, Liza wasn't the least bit fearful or intimidated by thoughts of the marriage bed. Sarah Jane had quickly gotten the feeling her third daughter could have taught her a thing or two, so she just politely excused herself from the discussion and sneaked out of the room. She didn't expect the talk with comical Frannie to be any better. In fact, she had decided then and there to pretend to forget it. Frannie would probably be relieved.

But Hannah was another story. Somehow—perhaps because Hannah was more like herself—Sarah Jane knew her in a different way than either of her other daughters, and she had long been worried about her naiveté. Sometimes, Sarah Jane wondered if Hannah believed all you had to do was get married to have a baby.

Nevertheless, amid all her concerns, she knew her extremely short talk with Hannah late last night had been a dismal failure. About two minutes into the embarrassing discussion, the girl had quietly risen from her chair and said, "Don't worry, Mama. I'm sure that I'll be marrying a gentleman tomorrow." And then she smiled kindly at her mother and left the room.

For a long time, Sarah Jane sat there in the rocker by the fading embers, staring blankly into the hot ashes. And then, just as her grandmother's old mantle clock struck nine, jolting her back to reality, her mother's heart cried aloud, "Oh, God, help her!"

And He must have done just that because the following year Hannah gave birth to a tiny baby girl. Her joy was indescribable. It was six years later before she presented her husband with a bouncing baby boy. And that was it. In an era when women produced one baby after another from the time they married until they were over forty, Hannah only had two.

Her husband was a gentleman, you see.

Printed in the United States
131873LV00003B/3/P